Readers love the
Sinners Series by RHYS FORD

Sinner's Gin

"This is a sexy, fast-paced, hurt/comfort, murder mystery
with… scorching hot sexy times!"
—Gay Book Reviews

Whiskey and Wry

"It's one thing to write a great book. It's a whole other level of talent to write song lyrics, too, and Rhys delivers."
—Happy Ever After, *USA Today*

Tequila Mockingbird

"The author has done it again with a complex intriguing
story line that explodes from the beginning and never
slows down…"
—Guilty Indulgence Romance Reviews

Readers love the Sinners Series by RHYS FORD

Sloe Ride

"*Sloe Ride* is rife with mystery and intrigue. If you're looking for unconventional characters and action, Rhys Ford's books would be a perfect match for you."

—Fresh Fiction

Absinthe of Malice

"It made me laugh, it made me angry, it made me irritated and at times, I was gutted. But in the end... it made me smile and be grateful I got to go on this journey with the guys."

—The Novel Approach

Sin and Tonic

"Rhys Ford has with mere words created a magical, at times rambunctious, blue bleeding family that loves deeply and fully."

—Love Bytes

By Rhys Ford

SINNERS SERIES
Sinner's Gin
Whiskey and Wry
The Devil's Brew
Tequila Mockingbird
Sloe Ride
Absinthe of Malice
Sin and Tonic

HALF MOON BAY
Fish Stick Fridays
Hanging the Stars
Tutus and Tinsel

RAMEN ASSASSIN
Ramen Assassin

HELLSINGER
Fish and Ghosts
Duck Duck Ghost

415 INK
Rebel
Savior
Hellion

WAYWARD WOLVES
Once Upon a Wolf

KAI GRACEN
Black Dog Blues
Mad Lizard Mambo
Jacked Cat Jive

**MURDER AND
MAYHEM**
Murder and Mayhem
Tramps and Thieves
Cops and Comix

There's This Guy
Dim Sum Asylum
Ink and Shadows
Clockwork Tangerine
Creature Feature 2 *with
Poppy Dennison*

**COLE MCGINNIS
MYSTERIES**
Dirty Kiss
Dirty Secret
Dirty Laundry
Dirty Deeds
Down and Dirty
Dirty Heart
Dirty Bites

Published by DREAMSPINNER PRESS
www.dreamspinnerpress.com

RHYS FORD
SLOE
RIDE

Published by
DREAMSPINNER PRESS

5032 Capital Circle SW, Suite 2, PMB# 279,
Tallahassee, FL 32305-7886 USA
www.dreamspinnerpress.com

This is a work of fiction. Names, characters, places, and incidents either are the product of author imagination or are used fictitiously, and any resemblance to actual persons, living or dead, business establishments, events, or locales is entirely coincidental.

Sloe Ride
© 2015, 2019 Rhys Ford

Cover Art
© 2018, 2019 Reece Notley
reece@vitaenoir.com
Cover content is for illustrative purposes only and any person depicted on the cover is a model.

Digital ISBN: 978-1-63476-528-2
Mass Market Paperback ISBN: 978-1-64108-195-5
Trade Paperback ISBN: 978-1-63476-527-5
Library of Congress Control Number: 2015945178
Mass Market Paperback published October 2019
v. 1.0

Printed in the United States of America
∞
This paper meets the requirements of
ANSI/NISO Z39.48-1992 (Permanence of Paper).

This book is dedicated to the following authors who have put up with so much of my crap and still let me harangue them: Mercy Celeste, Jordan Castillo Price, Jordan L. Hawk, and of course, Mary Calmes.

And a special shout-out to Trish, who is greater than the sum of her parts.

ACKNOWLEDGMENTS

As ALWAYS to the Five! Jenn, Tamm, Lea, and Penny. May the road rise up to meet your feet—although knowing us, it's 'cause we tripped over the dog and went ass over teakettle to land in the hedge. Kisses and hugs to my sisters: Lisa, Ree, and Ren.

I am forever grateful to Elizabeth North and everyone at Dreamspinner. They polish the apple to a gleam. And a special love, adoration, and affection to Grace and the editing team who slogs through my words. A special thank you to lyric, who is beyond delightful and everyone else who has lent a hand with this novel.

I would also like to send a bit of love to everyone who has been told they are wired wrong, off-in-the-head, off-in-the-clouds, or any of those other labels people like to hang on us. Being in the "spectrum" means we're sitting in the middle of the rainbow looking out. No one can see the colors we do nor hear the songs of the clouds as they pass. So the world for us is a little different, and sometimes it's a bitch to cope, but please remember to stop and breathe. It's important for us to be here. Who else is going to share those songs and colors but us?

PROLOGUE

Got shadows on my ass
Time's not on my side
Life came to give me a kiss
Then Death took me for a ride
—Riding A Pale Horse

A Couple of Years Ago

RAFE ANDRADE couldn't shake off the black tendrils wrapped around the base of his brain. Whatever he'd taken the night before lingered, dragging him down, and there were stretches along his back and legs where he couldn't seem to get warm. His bones ached from the cold, a brutal, icy seep into his marrow. Rafe didn't think he would survive if he didn't stop it soon. Moving didn't seem to help, or at least not when he tried to shift about. For some reason he couldn't get his arms and legs to work properly, and his balls were pulled up someplace beneath his destroyed liver. After a moment or two of flailing about, Rafe realized he was trapped, contained in a small, hard box he was painfully banging his elbows and shins against whenever he moved.

"Oh God." Panic and fear set in when he opened his eyes and found nothing around him but a darkness his vision couldn't penetrate. "They buried me. Oh God, they thought I was dead and buried me. God, *no.*"

He fought against the box's solid, icy sides, his elbows and heels shocked with pain with each glancing blow. The air in his chest grew hot, and his lungs folded in, tightening until Rafe couldn't draw in another breath.

"Think, dude. I'm naked. Who the fuck buries someone naked? Up. Push. Up." His feeble brain sparked a thought from its murky drowning. Shoving his hands up against the top of the box, Rafe felt... nothing. His arms shot straight up into the air, momentum carrying him off the cold bottom an inch before gravity slammed him back down.

"What the fuck?" The box wasn't covered. "Where the hell am I?"

Rafe slowly sat up, ducking his head in case he hit a top as solid as the walls, but once he got upright, he found he could grasp the thick sides. Moving was still a problem, and his foot struck something solid at the bottom of the box. Feeling around the space's slightly rounded sides, he found a spigot sticking out of the short wall by his foot, its metal surface as frigid as the slick walls around him.

"I'm in a goddamned bathtub." His relief nearly made him sick. Sucking in heaving breaths, Rafe tried to figure out exactly where he was. There wasn't a whisper of memory in his confused mind. Nothing to pinpoint where he'd been before the tub's high walls held him in. The air was warmer once he'd sat up, although his ass was still freezing, and Rafe blinked, waiting for his eyes to adjust.

Nothing. Not even a sliver of light coming from under a door.

"Okay, Andrade. You can do this." He carefully tried to stand up, but his legs didn't seem to be connected to whatever part of his brain he normally used to move him around. It took what felt like forever before he could hook a leg over the side of the tub and then another long hour or so before he felt the floor with his toes. Stepping carefully, he lowered his foot to the solid tiled surface, then gripped the tub tightly until he could get his other leg similarly untangled.

Being upright was a significant challenge. The dark didn't help. Rafe couldn't tell which way was up or even how large the room was. As odd as his blackened prison was, his body seemed to be in a very familiar state.

He ached from sex, and a sour rankness poured off his body, a combination of drugs, vomit, and come filming over swathes of his skin. Rafe wasn't exactly sure if he was on the upswing of drunk and stoned or coming down. It was too soon to tell. He'd have to give it a few minutes to see if he got happier or sadder with healthy doses of belligerence and anger if whatever he took hit those spots in his brain. Thinking hurt. His skull felt boiled solid by his muddled thoughts, and as he stumbled forward, looking for a wall or a doorknob, Rafe heard his subconscious whisper for him to crawl back into the tub and wait for death to take him.

It would be easier than actually killing himself. And sure as hell less painful than how he'd been at it before.

"Fuck the pity party, Andrade," he grumbled aloud. "Just find the fucking door."

The knob seemed to appear beneath his grasping fingers, and he lunged for it, using one hand to slap at the wall nearby. Feeling up around the frame, Rafe found a switch, then flicked it up, hoping to finally see what he was doing.

A simple click, and suddenly he was blinded by floodlights bouncing off white marble. A turn of the knob and he was free, blindly stumbling into a bedroom he didn't remember but knew its stench. It was intimate and cloying, just like the odor bleeding out of his pores. There was a pounding coming from somewhere, but Rafe couldn't figure out if it was his head or the anxious tap of his heart in his chest.

"Hotel." He carefully looked around. Double doors, one hanging off its hinges, led to a living room off the bedroom. "And I've trashed it. That's par for the course. But where the fuck is the hotel?"

The king-size bed was a mess, and something'd leaked on the floor near an overturned nightstand. It was standard high-star hotel fare, slithery duvet crumpled up and probably full of dried come. Somehow either he or someone else got all the artwork off the walls and thrown into a pile of torn canvas and frames in a corner of the room. Burn marks on the wood pieces were a hint at an attempted bonfire. The water-soaked carpet and an empty ice bucket set on top of the pile spoke of at least a panicked success.

Oddly enough, the bedroom was empty. Rafe's bedroom was never empty. Hell, even if he had to sneak a piece of ass around Jack once in a while, his bed was always filled.

"Okay, so somewhere, I probably lost a boy." He rubbed at his face, shivering in the air-conditioned room. "God, I could use a good fuck. Better than coffee."

His balls were still AWOL, and his dick was limp between his legs. He was thinking about sex, and nothing. Not even a stirring want churning up in his belly. Common enough. The drugs were taking their toll, and for the umpteenth time in his life, Rafe promised himself he'd cut back. A few little blue pills took care of any nonsense his body decided to toss back at him, but au natural was definitely a better way to go. Looking down at his cock, Rafe suddenly realized the chafing on his skin had less to do with fucking himself senseless and more about the condom rolled down his shaft.

"Jesus Christ." The sheath was hard to get off, and he tugged at it, snapping it clean off, then tossing it into the failed bonfire. Rubbing at his temple, the pounding continued, a muted thump-thump echoing across his skull. "Okay, forget the guy. Where the fuck am I? I don't even know what city I'm in."

Panic was starting to set in. He felt like he'd missed something—a birthday or even maybe a show. It wouldn't have been the first time he'd slept through a gig, but Jack'd been harsh on his ass the last time he skipped out. The band wasn't going to take much more of his shit, but for the life of him, Rafe couldn't recall if they were on tour or if he'd just gone someplace all by himself and got stinking-ass wasted.

"No, not on tour. Come on, where's your stuff, Andrade? There'd be a bass in here if—"

He found the guy he'd been looking for in the living room.

Unfortunately for both of them, he was as cold and lifeless as Rafe's cock. A pretty blond, barely old enough to know better than to let a rock star lure him up to a hotel room, or maybe he hadn't cared. Either way, it was a decision he'd never live to regret. His lifeless brown eyes stared up accusingly at Rafe, a froth of vomit speckled with something black drying over his parted lips and long throat. Sprawled out naked on the floor, his fingers were covered in dried blood, the carpet near his thighs streaked a dark brown where he'd clawed at the pile. Shock closed Rafe's throat, and suddenly the pounding grew louder, shattering the silence.

Then the door flew open, and Rafe's world broke apart.

"Police! Hands up! Clear the room!" There were a ton of cops, too many to count. Hell, too many for Rafe to even see. It was a tidal wave of uniforms, some blue cotton while others wore the red-gray livery of a Los Angeles hotel he'd stayed in before.

And in the middle of it—Jack *fucking* Collins, lead guitarist and Rafe's mostly-on-sometimes-off lover, staring him straight in the face. Jack's handsome face was curdled with rage, and the white light coming from the hotel corridor formed a corona around his broad shoulders, gilding his sun-streaked hair.

"Fucking Christ, Rafe. What the *hell* did you do?" Jack accused, a hot spit of words and anger pouring from his lanky body. "You're out of the band. Missing last night? Too fucking much, but—*this*? I just—God, Rafe. What the *hell*?"

Naked, cold, and hungover, Rafe did the only thing any rational bass player would do when standing over a stiff corpse and being surrounded by cops. He leaned over and vomited all over the dead guy's body.

Nine Months Later

REHAB TOOK everything out of him. More than two hundred days of white walls, porridge, and singing "Kumbaya My Lord," and Rafe'd been about to kill himself just to get free. Sobriety sucked, and even worse, he'd spent his birthday craving a blow job and some coke. What he'd gotten was a cupcake and a call from his mother.

He'd clung to her voice. In an instant he'd become a little boy again, curled up around a plastic headset and crying, deep, jagged sobs violent enough to tear him apart. They'd been the longest five minutes of his life, too short for his brain to grasp and too long for his soul to take.

It would be the last time they spoke for months.

Thank God for Brigid and Donal, or he'd have gone mad.

Rafe's skin didn't stop itching until three months into his sentence. As court orders went, he'd gotten off easy. Locked up in rehab on a suspended sentence was nothing compared to jail time, and despite a grumpy judge's opinion of Rafe failing the course, he'd done pretty good. Despite what everyone'd thought of him, when he sobered up later that fateful evening, the horror of what happened in his hotel room haunted him.

He also couldn't seem to get his feet clean of the dead blond's—of Mark's vomit.

Now he was slinking home, worn through and torn apart by his own demons. Despite the cleaning service his former manager set up, his Nob Hill penthouse smelled stale and dead. The doorman'd been friendly enough. Once Rafe established he actually belonged in the building and once security reassured themselves of his ownership, the property manager scurried out from his office and handed Rafe his new keys.

"There were some issues, Mr. Andrade," the beak-nosed man simpered. "Some very hateful things painted on the side of the building, but it was taken care of. Have no worries. We rekeyed the penthouse as a precaution."

There was no good-to-have-you-back nonsense from the sour-faced man. Rafe knew if he hadn't actually bought the penthouse outright, there'd have been a fight to get him out. No matter what anyone said, life was always just like high school. Fuck up royally and people were more than happy to rip his ass to shreds and hand it back to him piece by piece.

This time he didn't blame them.

Set on one of San Francisco's steep hills, the building had gorgeous views of the city and bay. When he'd first seen the penthouse, Rafe knew he had to have it. It was the furthest thing from the shithole he'd grown up in, a symbol of how far he'd climbed from being a charity case begging for scraps of education and food. He'd always wanted more—wanted what his friends Connor and Sionn had, longed for a time when he didn't have to look at price tags and juggle food against electricity or snatch cigarettes off the back of a truck to sell in a Chinatown alleyway for a bit of extra money.

The water glittered off in the distance, and the city's spires below hadn't quite shaken off their foggy veil. On a clear day he could see Finnegan's, where he'd washed dishes for Sionn's grandmother, wanting to be too proud to take the day's leftover food home, but he hadn't been stupid. He'd taken everything anyone offered and sometimes without permission. He'd sucked out what he could from the private school education his mother'd gotten him and charmed his way out of shit he'd fallen into.

Oddly enough, the penthouse and its million-dollar view meant nothing now. He owned it. He owned a lot of things. Stashing money and hiring people to keep every damned cent he made was the best piece of advice he'd gotten from Donal Morgan. It was a pity that was the only advice he'd listened to.

Despite the months he'd spent in Malibu soaking up sobriety, his place looked almost exactly the same as when he'd left it. Rich, warm, buttery walls and comfortable furniture with a few dashes of art the decorator tossed in warmed the empty apartment. A sparkling kitchen armed with gadgets he had no idea how to use and bedrooms with beds soft enough to sink into lay off the main entrance. He'd paid for a room to be soundproofed and set up amps and a soundboard, intending to blow out his own ears while staying up all hours of the night with Jack.

That bit of life never happened, and Rafe wondered if it ever would have to begin with.

To the left of the front door, unread books lined a bank of cases, and the view from the midcentury modern living room was heart-stopping, the Golden

Gate Bridge poking up through the far-off mist. His favorite part of the place was the guitars hanging from a long wall separating the rest of the house from the long living space, bright spots of color splashed up against white paint and what he'd used to pull himself up out of perdition.

Some of which were now gone, taken by the man he'd built his escape on.

There hadn't been love. Not the love he felt for Quinn Morgan—the love he'd tucked away deep inside of himself so it wouldn't hurt—but a casual affection, a kindred musical spirit he'd not found in his other relationships.

Fuck, Jack dumping him out of his life *really* hurt.

The gaps in the guitars hurt the most, and Rafe stumbled to sit down on something before he fell to his knees and cried. Of all the things Rafe'd fucked up in his life, losing Jack Collins's friendship left the biggest hole. It was more than hurt, he realized, staring at the white spaces where Jack'd once hung some of his favorite instruments. It was losing parts of his life Rafe knew he'd never get back. The band was gone. Jack was gone. There was no one he hadn't fucked over, including the person he'd thought he'd always have, his own mother. As empty as he felt inside, Rafe knew he'd run out of excuses. Reality came back and bit him hard because he'd been the one to set it all on fire and laughed when it burned to a crisp.

A note was tucked into one of the wall mounts, and Rafe debated leaving it there for the housekeeper to clean up. His resolve lasted about a minute before he snatched it out of its perch. He wanted a drink, something to steady his nerves, but the stint in rehab left him with a sour taste for numbing his brain when things got rough. While anything chemical was now off-limits, alcohol hadn't been his problem—wasn't his problem, Rafe corrected himself.

"Shit's not going to go away just because you want it to. Always going to be there." He sat down on a fluffy armchair he didn't remember owning. The whole place looked odd, unfamiliar in so many ways, leaving him to wonder if the guitars weren't the only thing Jack took with him.

From the look of the handwriting on the folded paper, Jack at least left him a Dear John letter.

"More like a fuck off and die," Rafe muttered, opening the note.

It was everything he'd imagined. Clear and strong in black ink, Jack left Rafe with no delusions he'd ever be welcomed back into Jack's band or life. There'd been too many times, too many disappointments, and one too many deaths for Jack Collins's liking, and Rafe Andrade could go twist in the wind for all he cared.

They'd not been in love. They'd fought as much as they'd fucked, bound by rhythms, words, and a shared hardscrabble past. Rafe wasn't a fool to think Jack cared for him more than he liked a good piece of steak or a fine bottle of tequila, but they'd been friends. Hell, they'd gone through so much together. Rafe'd created the band with Jack, and despite it all—or maybe because of it all—he hadn't fought Jack when he'd been pushed out. It was all over between them except for the legal wrangling as lawyers and record companies untangled Rafe's half ownership of a band he'd help put on the map.

"I should fuck them all up and refuse to sell." Even as the spite gushed from the sourness in his belly, Rafe knew he wouldn't do it. He owed Jack. With as much shit as they'd been through at the start, it'd been Jack who'd held it all together once Rafe began to destroy it all in the end. "Hell, Jack. I wish you'd just let me say I'm sorry. Would you fucking at least give me that much?"

He'd fallen so damned far, crashing down on sharp rocks and tearing out the wings he'd built for himself to get away from who he'd been. And now Rafe was back where he started. Alone, unwanted, and most of all, scared down deep into his soul.

"Damn it, Andrade." Rafe swallowed around the pain hitching up through his throat. "Should have just done the shitty world a favor and taken one last handful of fucking pills. 'Cause after all of this crap, no one's going to fucking want you around."

CHAPTER ONE

Late at night, Miki and Kane's bedroom

Kane: Mick, you're a good judge of character. Do you think there's something wrong with Quinn?

Miki, turning over under the covers to face Kane: I think there's something wrong with you for even asking that. When are you going to let go of the Quinn you've got in your head and see the one that's in your heart?

K: Way to kick a man in the balls there, love.

M: Hey, if ever you develop that kind of kink, you just let me know. There are times I really want to kick you in the balls.

"PROFESSOR MORGAN!" A shout across the campus parking structure brought Quinn to a stuttering halt. "Excuse me! Professor!"

Despite the college's nest up against the hills, the cold wind coming up off the Bay snarled and bit at his face, playing with the soft black scarf he'd wrapped around his neck, and Quinn shivered, zipping his bomber jacket up to his chest. Next to him, Graham Merris, one of his older colleagues at the school's history department, flared his nostrils, a sneer working up from his tight lips to his narrowed black eyes.

"It is *Doctor* Morgan," Graham sniffed when a ponytailed young woman caught up with them. "He has earned the right to that title—"

"It's okay, Graham," Quinn murmured, shoving his hands back into his jacket's warm pockets. Smiling at the young woman, he tried to remember where he'd seen her before. "Quinn's fine too. Can I help you?"

She exhaled, straining her thin T-shirt with the press of her large breasts and steaming up the air in front of her flushed face. Goose bumps carpeted her bare arms, undulating waves of prickled skin and raised hair. A slight dip in her skin, some remnant of a childhood injury, changed the flow of the wind, fluttering the hair along its ridge. She shifted and the process began again, a full ripple of flowing hair, then a skittering, defiant broken line cutting the dynamics of the chilled wind.

A silence settled over the space, and in the pregnant nothingness, Quinn suddenly realized she'd been speaking to him.

"I'm sorry. Distracted." It was a common apology, one he rattled off without even thinking about it. It was such a familiar phrase. His family'd grown used to repeating things twice, sometimes even when he'd been paying attention. He had no idea what she'd said or who she even was. "Can you say that again?"

"I was asking about our final papers. If I could have a couple of days extension? I was sick and—"

That was where he'd seen her. She was in one of his classes. A back-of-the-room sitter who spent a lot of time slipping in and out of the last row of seats instead of taking notes. He couldn't remember her name or even her grades, but from the warning tickle in his brain, they weren't very good. He blinked, catching the tail end of her reasoning for the extension—something about a cat throwing up everywhere.

Since he had a cat, he understood the severe consequences of too much rich tuna and a sip of milk. He just wasn't sure what cat hork had to do with needing more time on a paper.

"The paper isn't due until a week from now." Quinn counted off the days in his head, making sure he had the right timeline. "It's only five thousand words—"

"Yeah, I kind of lost my research notes. That's what I was telling you." More wiggling, and she pressed in closer, leeching some of his warmth. Her nipples were poking up tiny points in her T-shirt, and if he looked hard enough, he could make out thin blue lines of chapped skin around the edges of her gloss-covered lips.

"Do you have a jacket? I don't know if I have something in the car." His Audi was new, too new for him to have anything other than a spare tire and an emergency kit in the trunk. "Graham, do you keep anything in your car? A throw or towel? Oh, I might have one of those fleece throws. My mother's always—"

"Doctor Morgan, I just need more time." His student rubbed her arms briskly. "I don't need a jacket. I've got one with my stuff. About the paper? Can I have another week?"

"Then why aren't you wearing—?" Quinn caught Graham's eye roll. "Um, I can probably give you another week, but that'll dock your grade down a half step. You'll have to write a really good paper on...." Hell, he didn't even know what topic she'd chosen. "You're Industrial Revolution?"

"And its Artistic Influences." Her teeth chattered through her smile. "A week's great. Thanks. And oh, I love your accent."

She was gone before he could catch her name, and Quinn sighed, resigned to writing himself a text to remind him about the conversation. He'd tapped in a few letters on his tablet when Graham cleared his throat. Looking up, he was surprised to find the older man's curled lip directed at him.

"You're too nice to them. They have to learn there are no second chances in life," the professor droned.

His speech was a flat line, hardly wavering with any emotion, and Quinn fought to parse out if the scold was a gentle reproach or condemnation. Luckily for him, Graham's face changed, softening back into its normal stiff features.

"Really, Morgan. A deadline is a deadline. They have to keep to it. You shouldn't give out special compensations just because a girl is pretty and doesn't wear a bra when she asks you for more time."

"A bra? The bra's the least of it. She should have worn a *jacket*. It's cold enough to lose body parts out here," he snorted, finishing up his notes. "I didn't really give her an extension. Any student can turn a paper in a week late and take the dock. They've just got to tell me. She probably forgot."

"I...." Graham sighed. "Are you heading straight home? Or do you have time for a pint? The Goose and Pig is having a reading in an hour. If you're free."

"Damn, I would, but I have a family thing." His mind chased down where he needed to be, lost in what was waiting for him across the bridge. If he was lucky, traffic on the 80 and across the Oakland Bridge would be light. A second later he remembered he needed to respond better, slap on a smear of normal to the flat answer he'd given Graham. "Brother's boyfriend is reopening his coffee shop. It's an all-Morgans-on-deck thing. Next time?"

"Definitely family first." Graham's nose twitched, a flare of nostrils at odds with the tiny smile on his thin lips. "I'll see you on Monday if you come in. Remind me to give you that book if I forget. It's in my office."

Quinn was halfway across the quad before it dawned on him to ask Graham to join him. Looking back over his shoulder, he muttered a quick curse when he saw the other professor was nowhere to be found.

"Fuck. Invite. People want to be invited. Shit." A bit of shame rolled over him, a guilt born of knowing he'd fucked up. It burned a hot roll of sand over his thoughts, prickling at his mind. "Hell. Fuck."

Envy was a silly thing, but he had it in spades. Con and Kane socialized like it was as easy as breathing, and Quinn loathed the awkward starts and fits he

had when interacting with people. Every conversation
was a minefield, filled with nuances and trip wires he
couldn't see and quicksand deep enough to suck him
straight down and drown him in situations he didn't
understand.

"No, that's not right," he muttered to himself as
he approached his car. "Quicksand doesn't suck people down. Not usually. It'd have to be pretty deep.
And depends on where it is. Sand-to-water ratio—and
how the hell did I get to that? God, how many times
has Da said, 'Pull your brain up, Quinn boy'? Fecking
hell, but ah, here you are. How are you, love?"

He'd found the love of his life—or at least bought
it. Gleaming black and low, the R8 was a stupid ex-
pense in the scheme of things, an impractical sports
car with sleek lines and a wicked smile, and Quinn'd
wanted it as soon as he'd seen it. He had no regrets.
The money was there to be used, and even as his siblings gave him a lot of crap for buying what was basi-
cally an engine and two seats, he stood by his choice.
Unlike his brothers and one sister, he didn't need a vehicle sturdy enough to be used as a tank in case police
action was needed. What *he* needed was something
comfortable, fast, and aggressive to make the drive
from his townhouse in the city to his alma mater and
back. If he'd been smart, he would have parked the
Audi out in the sun instead of in the structure, but a
quick flick of the heater and Quinn was on his way to
being warmed up.

If only the hot air could reach the cold kernel
of fear lodged in his belly, because no matter how
comfortable a drive it was going to be to Marshall's
Amp, he was going there not only to celebrate Forest's

reopening of his inherited coffee shop but also to face the biggest mistake Quinn'd ever made in his life.

Rafe Andrade.

God, he was going to have to face Rafe Andrade.

QUINN MADE it off the bridge in record time. Normally he would have taken his time driving past the hulking structures, their metal forms an inspiration for AT-ATs everywhere. He liked driving through to the city, and the Audi was like handling hot butter on a sharp knife. Coming off the 80, the Audi hugged the road, and Quinn let it drift up into the oncoming curve, taking the swell a bit high. Steering the car down was easy, its engine growling and responsive when he pulled it back into the loop. The Audi responded.

Unfortunately, the large white panel truck behind him didn't.

The first tap was a nudge, a quick kiss against Quinn's new bumper, and he swore, pissed at the grill staring back at him in his rearview mirror. A hasty swerve to the next lane did him no favors. The truck echoed his slide, tapping him again, a harder push strong enough to stroke Quinn's tires on the slick blacktop. With his window down an inch, the truck's engine screamed and protested its existence, a dangerous *tok-tok* sound of a broken rod coming from its front end.

He couldn't see into the cab, not with the differences of heights between the Audi and the truck, but Quinn knew he had one advantage. There was no way the truck would be able to keep up with him.

The road stretched out before them, and he knew it well. There wouldn't be much time for him to maneuver freely. A mess of construction and signals was coming up fast. For the life of him, he couldn't remember even passing a panel truck on the way over the bridge, much less cutting one off, but road rage was the only reason he could think someone would lose their shit enough to bump him more than once.

He instinctively slowed down coming out of the last curve before the final straight shot into the city streets. Habits born of daily commutes guided his brain, and Quinn shook them off, focusing on putting enough room between him and the insane driver behind him so he could slip away into San Francisco's tangle of streets. A few hundred yards ahead, a warning light flashed yellow to caution drivers of a road split leading either to Fremont or Folsom, and Quinn tapped at the brakes to slow down, needing the car at a slower speed to make the turn.

The truck's driver had a different approach. Instead of putting on his brakes, he used the back of Quinn's R8 to slow himself down, slamming hard into the Audi's rear and jerking it forward.

"Shite and hell, what is his problem?" Quinn spat a bit of blood out of his window, licking at his torn cheek, where he'd sunk his teeth into the meat. "Fine. Let's lose this bastard, then."

The split screamed past him, and Quinn pushed the Audi over to the farthest lane. A construction crew had the break tied up with equipment and men in orange vests, and Quinn debated his options as the truck sped up once again, filling his rearview mirror. Fremont did a quick cut to the left, and Quinn took it hot, counting on the Audi's low profile to tighten down on the road. He caught a flash of white as the truck lurched to follow, its unwieldy boxy shape unable to maneuver the tight turn. Its tires lifted and it swayed, threatening to fall side-down into the next lane, and Quinn's heart stuttered, more worried for the tiny Camry next to the out-of-control truck than he was for himself.

At the last second, the truck righted itself, slamming back down on its tires, bouncing once before catching momentum, then gunning forward.

Straight for Quinn.

He hit the gas, pushing the Audi through half a block lined with concrete and glass. The Howard Street intersection turned green, and the road was clear in front of him. Flying past a tavern on the corner, the Audi hummed over the damp street. A quick look back told Quinn the truck wasn't far behind. A delivery truck coming out of an alley cut in front of the Audi, and Quinn pulled the car over, narrowly missing a bicyclist straying out of the bike lane and into the street. Forced to slow down, Quinn cursed under his breath when the alley he'd planned on ducking down was blocked off by a cluster of women stopping to chat in the middle of the walk.

"Okay, shit. What the hell is going on?" It was bad enough he was talking to himself, but it was worse knowing the answers he needed could be handed to him by whomever was driving the truck. The same truck who'd caught up with him once again, clipping the right side of the Audi's bumper. The scrape of paint and metal wasn't a pleasant sound, but Quinn was more concerned about keeping the car going straight.

The car's tires fought to catch at the road, but the truck's hit was enough to push Quinn to the side. A couple of cement trucks momentarily filled Quinn's peripheral vision, and he fought down the panic clamping his jaw. Breathing in deeply, he shoved aside all the noise and scary shit his mind was coming up with and focused on the car instead. Yanking the wheel would only spin him about, slamming the low Audi under the bulbous mixer, shearing off the car's roof. Pushing into the spin, Quinn counted off a few seconds, then eased into the gas, forcing the Audi back into the lane by holding its weight firm with a punishing grasp of the steering wheel. His shoulder ached from maneuvering the car out of its turn, but the Audi snapped forward, taking the pressure off his arm.

Rain splattered the Audi's windshield, a sudden burst of drops barely thick enough to turn on the wipers, but Quinn kept his window cracked, counting on the street rattle to clue him in on the truck's noisy progress. The street tightened, dropping a lane as another construction project swallowed up one from the right. A dip in the road lifted the Audi up off the asphalt for a moment. Then it landed softly. The truck didn't fare as well.

Quinn didn't have to watch to know the heavy vehicle hit hard. The crunch of the truck's undercarriage hitting the street was loud enough to rattle his teeth. Then a booming noise shook the air, bouncing back and forth between the tightly packed buildings until Quinn's ears buzzed with the sound.

He risked a quick look, trying to weave around a bus pulling over to a stop. Behind him, the truck continued to wobble forward, sparks flying up from its front wheel well as pieces of torn tire flopped about an exposed rim. The Audi's rear seemed to be holding up well. A far sight better than the truck's front end.

Quinn heard sirens cutting through the traffic noise, but any thought of stopping flew out the Audi's open window when the truck lurched forward, hemming him in. He dove to the side, sliding the Audi out of the truck's next jerking lunge. Off-balance and uneven, the truck's popped tire hit a swell in the blacktop and tilted it toward Quinn's lane.

Its tall sides drew up against the R8, casting a long shadow over the windshield and blocking off the scant light filtering down between Fremont's packed buildings. He wasn't going to make it to the next intersection without another hit, possibly one hard enough to cripple the Audi, and even if he was able to avoid the truck, the street took a hard right after Market, dangerously thickening the traffic.

The light turned red on Mission, and the world went dark. Quinn glanced up to see the truck's weight give in to gravity, tipping over, its beaten white steel sides looming over him. Slamming on his brakes, he locked the Audi up, pulling it sideways and out from under the toppling truck's way.

Smoke poured out from the Audi's tires, choking Quinn. Its acrid sting brought water to his eyes, and he tried to blink it away, but nothing helped. He felt the truck hit the street, a shock wave of screaming metal slamming hard into the blacktop, and then a barrage of sirens overwhelmed him. Sitting sideways in the middle of the road, the Audi continued to idle, battered to hell but apparently ready for another round. Someone shouted nearby, and as the smoke cleared, Quinn saw the Muni bus he'd passed heading straight for him, its front rack bristling with bicycles. He caught a momentary flash of the bus driver's horrified face, then heard screeching brakes as he tightened into a ball to brace for impact.

A second later, the only thing Quinn heard was his panicked breathing and the rapid trot of his heart racing hard enough to clear a tall fence if it had to. The world was lost under the whooshing sound of his blood pounding in his ears, and Quinn blinked, his lashes catching on his jacket's soft leather.

"Hey, you okay?" The voice could have come from God for all he knew, but Quinn seriously doubted God sounded like a stoner from Haight. He peeled his arm out from around his face, then peered out the Audi's window, straight into the business end of the Muni bus, the nut on a bike tire only a few inches away from the car's tinted glass. Slowly turning his head to the right, he found the source of the worried voice, a long-haired man dressed in a food-stained chef's coat, his fingers clenched around a partially chopped handful of kale.

"Yeah, I'm fine," Quinn stuttered, snagging his teeth on his tongue. "Fecking hell and shite."

The sirens were a waterfall of noise pouring down over his head. Then as quickly as they'd swelled up from the street noise, they fell silent. The chatter of voices around the Audi and the bus faded, quieted by authoritarian growls ordering everyone to back away from the street. The chef disappeared, replaced by a craggy-faced veteran in patrol blues.

"You okay, sir?" The scowl on the cop's face was epic but tempered by concern in his warm brown eyes. "Can you move? Do you need medical assistance?"

"No, I'm… good. That truck…." He tried to see past the cop toward the truck lying side down in the middle of the street, but all Quinn could make out was one of the back tires. "He just wouldn't stop… hell."

His nerves finally snapped, crawling out from under the odd calm he'd felt when he realized the bus had nearly killed him. He shook as he grabbed what he needed out of the car's console, and Quinn's skin tingled with shock as he slung his messenger bag over his neck and popped open the far-side door. Crawling over the passenger seat was tricky, but Quinn didn't trust himself to stay in the car much longer. The cop grabbed at him once he cleared the open door, stopping Quinn from falling flat on his face next to the Audi's beaten side.

"Let me get your license and registration—shit, thanks," the cop said as Quinn handed them over without a word. "Wait here. The medics really should look you over, kid."

"Fuck. My poor baby," Quinn sighed heavily. The Audi's glossy black coat was crackled and peeled up in spots. One of the truck's strikes drove a piece of the rear bumper into one of the back wells, but its tire remained untouched. Running his hand over the car's back window, Quinn's heart seized up at the extent of the damage done by the truck.

"Driver's gone from the truck. Witnesses say he climbed out and booked down the alley as soon as the R8 went sideways." Another cop, younger and muscled enough to strain the seams of his uniform, glanced at Quinn. "Sorry about your ride, man. It's a sweet car."

"Insurance. I've got… hell." His knees gave out, and Quinn grabbed at the R8 for support. The older cop grabbed his arm, steadying him.

"You okay?" he rumbled, checking Quinn's license. "Morgan? Huh. Any relation to Donal Morgan? You kind of look like one of his kids."

"Yeah, he's... my da," Quinn muttered softly. "Shit, Mum's going to lose her shit."

The older cop quirked a grin. "Kid, you could have gotten killed here. I think she'll be happy you walked out of that."

"Yeah, for about five seconds." Quinn blinked at the man, shaking his head. "Then she'll be having my head for being late."

CHAPTER TWO

One moon, a thousand stars
Come crack the sky open for me
And point me towards Mars
Leaving you a bit of my soul
Hold on to it tight
'Cause nothing's forever, baby,
Not even tonight.
—One Thousand Stars

MARSHALL'S AMP was right where Rafe'd left it, sharing a wall with the Sound recording studio on the corner of bad memories and regret. He'd missed his first gig as Rising Black's bassist because he'd gotten into a fight with Mario, one of the studio musicians, a slimy asshole with light fingers and a drug habit, Rafe'd been amazed he could find his own nose to shove coke into.

He'd also been sorry to hear about Frank's death, even sorrier to find out Connor Morgan'd hooked up with the blond kid who'd drummed there.

"Not sorry," Rafe corrected as he got out of his Chevelle. "Surprised. Fucking surprised. Didn't know Connie even *liked* dick. Shit, I'd have tapped that back in high school if I'd thought it was open season."

That was a lie. Connor Morgan was so far above his reach in high school, Rafe might as well have wanted to have a threesome with Pussy Galore and Godzilla. His running alongside the Morgan boys and their cousin, Sionn, was as close to cool as he was going to get in those days, and even then he'd been the one to steer the four of them right to the edge of gone-too-far.

It was usually Connor who'd dragged them right back.

The neighborhood had changed since he'd seen it last. Trendy-looking townhouses lined the street opposite the Sound's parking lot, petunias and pansies fighting for space in narrow window boxes hooked over wrought-iron balcony railings. There were a few nods to San Francisco's pre-earthquake architecture, bits of concrete embellishments meant to age the structure, but its youth peeked out in its fake-tree cell tower poking up out of a stand of pines. The restaurant's back door on the other end of the parking lot was as grubby and oily as Rafe remembered, and a line of old dumpsters still leaned up against the coffeehouse's back wall, their lids splattered with seagull shit and food specks. A new coat of paint and a power wash did wonders for the brick building, and at some point a sturdy gridded metal-and-wood staircase replaced the rickety wood steps leading up to the crappy studio apartment over the Sound.

What was missing from the picture was Frank's old RV, with its concrete blocks and plywood porch and the umbrella, table, and seats he'd liberated from a burrito shop's trash pile.

The parking lot seemed odd, echoingly still in Rafe's mind. He couldn't remember a time when the Sound's parking lot hadn't smelled like patchouli and sweet Thai smoke, and the sleek, polished deep black was at odds with the faded gray memory of patchy asphalt and crooked lines Frank'd painted for parking spaces around his Winnebago palace.

It was funny what an empty space on a parking lot could do to a person's insides.

The inside of Marshall's Amp was like stepping into a blue police box and coming out in another era. Or a movie set in the '60s. White tile gleamed, throwing moonlight reflections up of the squishy spaceship chairs and sweeps of tables. If there was music playing, Rafe couldn't hear it, but he caught snatches of guitar threading through the murmuring crowd noise. The splashes of color around the coffee shop were nearly as loud as the cop chatter filling it, and the smell of brewing roasts and sweet pastries made Rafe's mouth water.

"Shit, there's a lot of cops." And only a few of them were Morgans.

He'd been about to search for Connor or Sionn in the sea of Irish and badges when a frill of eye-bleeding red hair appeared at someone's shoulder, and Rafe stopped dead in his tracks. The exit was cut off from him. He'd gone too far into the shop and was too tangled in its crowd to beat a hasty retreat. Another flash of crimson, and Rafe's belly turned to ice, melting slightly when he spotted the face beneath the hair.

"Fuck, thank God. That's Kiki." He exhaled hard, turning back around to grab some coffee, and smacked right into the stuff of nightmares—Brigid Finnegan Morgan.

Brigid *fucking* Finnegan Morgan. Bane of his existence and his de facto second mother.

To the casual observer, Brigid Morgan would appear to be a gloriously adult version of a Disney princess, sans bow and an enormous horse named Angus. Tall heels the height of a cat brought Brigid up to Rafe's collarbone, and her gamine face was brightened by a brilliant, broad smile. A classic porcelain-skinned Irish beauty, Brigid Morgan looked as if she'd pour sweetness, light, and sugar into the life of someone she loved.

Fortunately, Rafe knew better, and he certainly wasn't fooled by the cupcake-offering hellion standing right under his nose.

"Well, then, it appears the rumors of yer demise were greatly exaggerated there, Rafey boy," Brigid purred, holding out a tall cup of coffee and a devil's food cupcake. She was playing up her Irish, probably intent on luring him into a false complacency. "Obviously yer weak from not eating or summat, because if ye'd been well, ye'd have been at the Sunday table like the rest of the miscreants I have there."

"Hello, Bridge." He took the coffee and cupcake, then bent over. Kissing her cheek was safe, or so he thought right before she grabbed a hold of his right ear. Pinching and pulling at his lobe, Brigid drew Rafe down until they were nose-to-nose. "Ouch... *ouch.*

Okay, let go. *Leggo!* What? Shit, it's just dinner. I'm not even one of your kids—"

"I've been worried about ye, ye fecking fool."

If anything, it felt like Brigid grew lobster claws on her hands and was about to give Rafe another piercing to go with the daith he already had in that ear.

"Did ye cook that brain of yers so much ye forgot the house number?"

"Leave the boy alone, love."

Donal eased Brigid's fingers from Rafe's ear. Rafe refused to rub at it, even though it tingled as the feeling rushed back into the side of his head, but his pride could only carry him so far, and he stumbled forward when Donal slapped him across the back.

"It's good to see ye here, Rafe. But the bride's right. Yer missed up at the house."

"I figured you didn't want to start counting the silverware again." Teasing usually dulled the ache under his breastbone, but this time it did nothing to lessen the burn across his chest. "Honestly, didn't know if I was…. It's been rough. Lots of doors slamming in my face."

"Don't give me that shite, brat. I know where ye live," Brigid shot back. "Don't think I won't be coming to dig you out of your rock like the stubborn barnacle that you are. I'll be having shellfish for dinner this week, and ye'll be served right up on that plate alongside of it."

"Secured building, Brigid." He smiled back, matching her tooth for tooth. "Doormen and everything. You won't be able to get to me."

She snorted and poked his chest. "I either see ye this Sunday, or I'll be sending the cavalry out for ye. I'm going to find Kiki. Later with yer nonsense."

Donal watched his wife trot off, then drew Rafe into a steely one-armed hug. Leaning over, the older Irish man whispered, "I've got a badge, ye silly git. There's not anywhere ye can hide in this city that I can't find ye. So ye get yer ass to the house this Sunday and make that woman happy, or ye'll be seeing the kind of hell and holy fire I can bring down on ye with just a knock on yer door. Understand me, son?"

"Got it." Rafe nodded curtly. "Sunday. Six."

"Make it four thirty. It'll give her time to coo over ye, and we'll be having dinner on time, then." Donal gave him a quick squeeze, then let Rafe go. "It's good to see ye, boyo. We'll be seeing more of ye now, understand?"

"Yeah, I got it." Rafe sucked at the coffee drops he'd gotten on his hand when Donal nearly folded him in half, then muttered at Donal's retreating back. He put the cup and treat down on a tiny speck of a table, then wrung his hand dry with a napkin. "*Sir*."

"Ah, and you know how he hates that word. Might as well be telling my uncle to fuck off and die," Sionn Murphy growled, pulling Rafe into a tight hug. "God, it is good to see you, Andrade."

"Sionn." Rafe returned the hug, and their embrace grew as painful as the burn in Rafe's chest when he'd seen the Morgans. "Dude, can't breathe. I just fucking saw you yesterday. You act like I'm dead."

"Just glad you came. And good, now that the aunt's done torn a piece of your sorry hide off your ass, I can introduce you to the guys without having to look over my shoulder for Boadicea."

"Your aunt know you call her that?" Whoever or whatever Boadi-something was, Rafe was pretty sure it wasn't flattering Brigid in any way she'd like. "Sounds… naughty."

"Please. She'd preen and slap my arm," Sionn shot back. "Come on. I want you to meet Damie finally."

He pulled back, sneakers squeaking on the floor. "Dude, I don't know. I'm not exactly welcome in a lot of places. They might—"

"D came back from the dead, and Miki had a murder victim tossed into his car," Sionn reminded him gruffly. "If anyone can talk to you about living in a shitstorm, it's these guys. Besides, you've got a choice. Musicians or cops?"

"Musicians it is." He followed Sionn over to where the remaining members of Sinner's Gin stood talking with a tall blond he recognized as Frank's kid. "Jesus, is that Forest?"

"One and the same," his best friend muttered. "And put your eyes back into your head, or Connor'll pull them out for you. You know Con. The word 'possessive' was invented for him."

"It's just so… fucking weird. I should have been around more, I guess. And Con's more than possessive, he's insane." Rafe could still feel the steely clamp of Connor's fingers on the back of his neck when he'd been warned off a fourteen-year-old Quinn.

"Yeah, you should have been around more," Sionn agreed. "But here you are, so let's go, then."

"Okay, for those who are about to something or other, we salute you."

He'd met the Sinner's guys before, and still it shocked him to discover how tall Miki St. John was. And how growly. He'd seen feral cats taking down a seagull that were more approachable than the Sinner's singer, but his quirk of a smile when Rafe held his hand out was heartening. A few tidbits of *hello*s and *yeah-I-remember-you*s, and Rafe felt the pressure along his spine ease.

The conversation turned to the Sound, and Rafe grimaced at Forest. "Sorry about your dad, man. Frank was a good guy."

"For a stoner." Forest's eyes softened at the mention of the irascible hippie who'd mostly raised him. "But yeah, he was a good dad. Miss the shit out of him. More than I thought I would, but Connor's offered to share Donal and Brigid, so I kind of got them now too."

"Brigid is kind of like Russia. She kind of gets you, not the other way around," Miki muttered only low enough for them to hear. "With teeth. Big, scary, kissy-faced teeth."

"Hey, best mom I've ever had." Forest toasted the firebrand matriarch with his coffee cup. "'Course, I've only had her officially for about half an hour or so."

"Yeah, you keep thinking that, Ackerman," Damie scoffed. "She had your ass in her sights as soon as she found out you existed. Only reason I'm safe is 'cause I'm with Sionn. Default to nephew status rocks."

They found a lot to talk about: shitty road tours, crappy hotels, and the types of music that made their hearts sing. No one tossed out Rafe's fall from grace, but as the conversation drifted over to Damie's need to go back into a studio, Rafe felt the walls closing in on them.

"So, you're getting a band together?" It was a small toe poke into the water, but the ripple it created was huge. Rafe tried not to let the flare of excitement in his belly get further than an ember, but he almost felt his cock harden at the thought of hitting a stage to drive a beat down into an audience. "Like kicking around together or actually going on the road?"

"Haven't gotten that far." Forest shrugged. "But I'm not saying no to a couple of road things."

"Still need a name," Miki tossed back. "And a bassist. Gotta be someone I can stand, because I get sick of looking at Damie jumping around in front of me. Need someone sane with me during the damned hour-long guitar wanks he has."

"Leads do like their wanks," Rafe agreed softly, grinning back at Damien's smirk. "So, you all are really going to make that leap?"

"Yeah, just don't say shit to anyone about it." Damien dropped his voice down. "Nothing's engraved in stone—well, we've been kicking it around for a month, and I've still got to convince Sinjun that he wants to sleep on hotel mattresses again. Such a fucking princess."

"I don't give a shit where I sleep." The singer made a face. "You're the one with the five-million-thread-count sheets."

Damie lightly pushed his best friend. "Hey, you go live in Arkham for a bit, and you tell me how you like scratchy sheets."

The conversation with the three musicians felt... *normal*, as if he hadn't fucked up his life so badly Satan didn't want him around. He wasn't used to it. Even in the milquetoast, sing-around-the-campfire lovefest of a rehab, he'd caught censure from the other so-called celebrities and spoiled children.

"Shit, burn down one hotel room," Rafe muttered to himself. "No one got hurt, and I put it out."

Yeah, it'd been more than the fire. The dead body in his hotel room had a lot to do with it. Mark, Rafe corrected. Not *dead body*. Guy had a name. He deserved to have a name after everything was all said and done. He hadn't killed Mark. Not like a knife to the heart or a bullet to the brain kind of murder, but Rafe'd been the one to lure the man upstairs with a promise of a good time.

He just hadn't planned for it to be Mark's *last* good time.

Rehab hadn't been easy. He'd fought it viciously at first. Then when the place began to lock down around him so tight he couldn't move, Rafe went subversive. There'd been a lot of denial. Even as he sat in the middle of a group of addicts with everyone singing their tales of woe, Rafe refused to believe he was one of the fallen. He'd made a mistake. Everyone did. He'd just be more careful next time: do less, drink more water, pay more attention. What happened in Los Angeles was a fluke, and Mark's death, while unfortunate, couldn't be laid down at Rafe's door.

Disgusted, he'd broken his sobriety pact in small transgressions, tiny bits of pot or X picked up from other patients. Then a blowup at group drove him over the wall, and he'd said fuck it. He was going to spend an evening as numbed up as he could, just to take the edge off his brain. A few bribes here and there scored Rafe a large bottle of vodka and prescription weight-loss pills, and he'd been determined to pump it all into himself until he saw flying kittens.

That got him a weekend in the hospital and an extra fourteen days tacked onto his sentence.

He'd woken up breathing in his own vomit, face-down on the cold, hard floor and choking. His lungs weren't functioning, too wet from the fluids he'd aspirated, and Rafe found himself staring straight into Death's face.

And he didn't like what he'd seen.

The Sinners guys had been kind, but Rafe'd noticed the slight hesitation in Damien's eyes before they shook hands. When even a guy who'd been *dead* knows about someone's burned bridges, there wasn't much else Rafe could say. He'd wasted his life. To be fair, *wasted* was an understatement. *Decimated* came closer, leaving *destroyed* a distant second. He'd gathered it up like he'd done to the artwork in the hotel room and set it on fire. Unlike the impromptu bonfire, he'd burned his life until there was nothing left of it but ashes and the stink of regret.

Something in the crowd shifted, and the world went still, leaving Rafe with only the beat of his heart in his ears and the sudden awareness that Quinn Morgan had walked into the coffee shop. Even through a sea of cops and musicians, Rafe knew Connor's younger brother had come through the door.

But then, he'd always had a thing for the Morgans' changeling.

Then, much like his mother'd done an hour before, Quinn Morgan slipped out of thin air and appeared a few feet away, looking right at him.

And it was all Rafe could do not to whisper *fucking hell* at the sight of Connor's baby brother all grown up and sexy.

Quinn was definitely a Morgan, a leaner version of the standard-issue, carved-from-granite Morgan, but still as molten sensual as a shot of whiskey in hot drinking chocolate on a cold night. More poet than justiciar, the third Morgan boy carried himself looser than the others, sliding gracefully through the crowd instead of shouldering past anyone standing in his way. He was tall, a little bit taller since the last time Rafe'd seen him, or maybe just taller because there was no shoving Quinn back into the little-boy box Rafe'd placed him in years ago. There was no denying it anymore. Quinn Morgan had definitely hit manhood and made it his bitch.

His black hair was longer than his brothers', evidence of his life outside law enforcement. It fell down to nearly his shoulders, tousled carelessly away from his handsome face. The deep green of Quinn's gaze was still a sharp flash of lush forests, but Rafe knew he'd see little specks of gold dappling Quinn's irises when he got close. His mouth was full, kissable, and Rafe swallowed, remembering the taste of Quinn's lips the *one* time he'd risked life and limb to sample a bit of forbidden fruit.

A single birthday kiss—one given to an innocent eighteen-year-old boy who celebrated adulthood and master degrees all in one fell swoop.

It had been like sucking on lightning, burning away Rafe's reluctance in agreeing to give Quinn the one thing he'd asked for—a single birthday kiss in the shadowy darkness of his parents' backyard before Rafe went back to live out his life as a rock star.

His heart seized up when Quinn gave him a short nod and began to head straight for him. *Fucking hell, now what are you going to do, Andrade?*

Rafe excused himself from the conversation, giving Damien a quick, distracted grin when the guitarist said they'd hook up soon. He didn't have time to think about promises and music. Not when Quinn was closing in on him.

"Excuse me," Quinn murmured to a short woman with pigtails sticking out from either side of her head. His Irish accent was a softer roll than his father's, more than a hint of green and peat hidden in its silky depths. Quinn got in close, their shoulders brushing as he jockeyed for space. "Hey. Just the guy I'm looking for."

"Yeah?" He played it cool. If there was one thing Rafe knew, it was how to be cool in the face of a firing squad, and Quinn Morgan was definitely a loaded gun waiting to go off—and usually at the wrong moment. "Whatcha need?"

"I needed to ask you a question." Quinn blinked, his lashes sweeping shadows down over his cheeks. "I kind of need to lose my virginity. And I was wondering if you could help me out."

If the earth could have opened up beneath his feet and swallowed him whole, Rafe would have been okay with that. Or even if a dragon imprisoned in the depths of the Bay somehow broke loose and rampaged through San Francisco, looking for a single bite of Portuguese meat to satiate its appetite, Rafe would have volunteered—willingly—and asked his draconian executioner if there were any particular condiments he preferred Rafe baste himself in.

"Wait." The still-functioning bit of Rafe's brain seized on the *one* piece of information he didn't need to have in his life. He reached for something to hold on to, snagging an old familiar teasing from their younger days, and Rafe snapped back. "You're joking, right? This is a joke. Hard to tell with you sometimes, Q."

If there was anything Rafe'd learned in the short time he'd spent sober, it was that the universe had a really fucked-up sense of humor. In the scheme of things, he could have been saying something much more inflammatory just as the conversation din in the coffeehouse dropped, and his voice carried across the now relatively silent floor.

"Seriously, Q? A virgin?"

He'd been onstage in front of amps powerful enough to blow his hair back, and when a night was done, there was a silence throbbing in his eardrums that he could only call deafening. It was a whisper compared to the echoing stillness around him, and Rafe realized he'd caught the attention of every Morgan, Finnegan, and Murphy in the shop.

"Yeah, it was a joke. Just… something silly."

As if they weren't standing in a pool of quiet so deep Rafe could hear the demons beneath his feet cackling in hell at his discomfort, Quinn's full mouth quirked with rueful remorse.

"God, I was just trying to tease. This is why teasing never works for me. It always ends up going really stupid."

"Teasing's never been your thing, Q." Rafe pulled up short as a flush pinked Quinn's cheeks. "It's kind of like getting into a fight. You… you've always been the go-in-to-end-it kind of guy when usually the punching's kind of what you need. How're you doing, kid?"

It was safer to call him *kid*, so much safer for Rafe's brain to handle, but something in the way he said it must have rubbed Quinn wrong because he bristled, tightening his shoulders. Rafe couldn't count the number of times he'd shoved Quinn back, needing a bit of space from his best friend's all-too-delectable younger brother. Kid, that kept Quinn back, back into the toy box and Little League games neither one of them excelled at.

"I'm okay, just… not a kid, Rafe. Not for a long time. Hey, it was good to see you. I just wanted to come by and say hi. Mum's right. You need to come up to the house more. They… we… miss you." Quinn's throat bobbled as he swallowed, and in true Q fashion, his eyes slid from Rafe's face to scan the crowd. "Really. Come by."

As quick as he'd appeared, Quinn melted away, a mist of Irish sinew and bone swallowed up by the crowd. Wall-to-wall cops and Morgans, and for the life of him, Rafe couldn't find the one he wanted. He couldn't really afford to look at what he wanted to do—not with Quinn.

"Jesus fucking Christ, stick your foot in your mouth, Andrade. What an asshole." Rafe scrubbed at his face, exasperated at the emotions rising up from the dark, cold place he'd shoved them into a long time ago. "And I'm still jonesing for Quinn. Great. Just. Fucking. Great."

He shouldn't have hurt Quinn. Shouldn't have thrown up the walls he always put up whenever Q came near. Despite the effort Rafe'd put into distancing them, he'd given in a few times too many. A kiss under moonlight, a brief slide of his hand down the length of Quinn's back, as if daring himself to take more, and even the times they'd shared a beer bottle, their mouths touching and sharing a slip of glass between them. They'd danced around each other. Rafe knew it even if Quinn hadn't. Either way, he brought a bit of pain to those deep emerald eyes, and Rafe hated himself for doing it.

"Well, screw it." He retrieved his now cold coffee and drained it. "I pissed him off. Time to man up and chew down some crow."

CHAPTER THREE

Living room session
Damie: We need more songs about love.
Miki: We'd need to know more about love to write about love. Pain I know. Love's kind of iffy.
D: What do you mean we don't know love? You've got Kane! I've got Sionn! We so know love.
M: Because I'm not ready to share Kane with anyone else. With any stranger. He's mine. That's mine. I've not had enough mine in my life yet. When I do, I'll start writing fucking love songs.

QUINN RAN.

He wasn't going to sugarcoat it. The truth was, he'd taken one look at the passionate emotion flaring in Rafe's liquid-brown eyes, turning golden treacle to burned caramel, and ran.

Quinn could have called it a strategic retreat, but he was going to call it what it was—pure tongue-swelling, awkward fucking up, and he was running from it. The moment he'd seen Rafe, Quinn thought he could for once in his life pull off the easy banter he'd grown up around. The *one* time he needed to just be *normal*, and he couldn't do it.

The stupid bravado he'd somehow scraped up from the tiny bit of Irish snarl he'd inherited from his parents whispered away when Rafe's hot gaze seared into him, a swirl of misty smoke caught in the wind of Rafe's flaring challenge. In that second Quinn was back in high school, standing on the edges of his brothers' circle, listening to Rafe's burled rasp turn deep as they bantered about sex and trouble.

He'd so wanted to be a part of that—longed to reach out, touch the sunburst heat of Rafe's body and feel the strength in his crush's lean hips and powerful arms. Instead he'd run then too.

Back then he'd been a thirteen-year-old awkwardly hanging out with his older brothers, hoping their coolness would rub off on him. It was funny how even a decade or so later, he was pretty much still hoping that would happen—but it never did.

"Seriously. Stupid. Degrees out the ass, and you can't even talk to someone you've known for years?" Quinn grumbled, trying to ease his way past the people gathered in front of the shop. "It's not hard. You do it with other people, right? Shit, why the hell can't you do it with Rafe? He's just another guy. Just another *damned* guy."

A cool bath of fresh air splashed a bit of the heat in Quinn's face, and he hurried over to the rental he'd gotten from the Audi dealer. There were footsteps behind him, a heavy tread he chose to ignore, because if he turned around and found Rafe there, he'd... probably sink down into the ground.

He turned anyway. Not Rafe. Hipsters. Hairy-faced, boot-wearing young men who wouldn't be out of place in one of Quinn's classes and definitely heading to Forest's coffee shop. Quinn couldn't decide if he was disappointed or relieved it wasn't Rafe.

Until he turned back around and found himself nose-to-nose with the man he'd just fled. Seeing Rafe again was like being punched in the nuts by one of his younger sisters, not as powerful but angled in such a way he ached in places not even touched.

With his sun-streaked golden-brown hair, a body hard enough Michelangelo would long for a block of marble, and a mouth Quinn still tasted in his dreams, Rafe looked like the rock star he'd been. Or still was. Quinn wasn't sure where Rafe stood with his career or his music. Or if it even mattered anymore.

No, the music would always matter. Regardless of what the world did to him, Rafe would always submerge himself in his music. It was one of the few constants of Quinn's horrible teenage years, discovering a lanky Rafe sprawled out on one of the beds in the attic room, cradling a bass to his body, and working through deep threads of rolling grumbles.

Rafe *fucking* Andrade.

Quinn hated how Rafe made him feel. Or loved it. He wasn't sure about that either.

"Hey, hold up there, Q."

Rafe's fingers were a hot sear through his shirt-sleeve where he grabbed at Quinn.

"And come on, dude. When have I ever been the one you've run from?"

"Nearly every single fucking time," Quinn muttered under his breath. A part of him wanted to shake Rafe off and push him back inside where he belonged, with all the people who didn't stumble over their own brains to make conversation. "It's okay. I'm not—"

"You're not what, dude?" His fingers gentled, but they stayed wrapped around Quinn's upper arm. "I think I ran over one of the kitchen guys to make it out the back door before you took off. I'm sorry. I fucked up. I always seem to say the wrong damned thing and—"

"So not you. Mum says you out-Irish the Irish."

"Your mom's pretty easy to con shit out of," Rafe shot back, giving Quinn his mad-pirate grin when Quinn yanked his arm away. "Sure, deny it, but she's like Wendy with the Lost Boys. Or Little Bunny Foo Foo—and we're the field mice. Come on, dude. It's me. Rafe, longtime friend and even longer time fuck-up." Rafe's expression sobered, the cavalier light in his eyes replaced by something more serious, more soulful. "I'm sorry, Q. I didn't mean to make you feel like shit back there. Really."

"And here I thought I was the one who fucked up." The wind kicked up, brushing an icy chill into Quinn's skin. "What I said in there? *Really* stupid."

"So the virgin thing isn't for real?" Rafe made a show of eyeballing Quinn's body. "Because I didn't think all the guys in this damned city were blind."

Quinn shoved Rafe away, giving himself a bit of space to breathe. "Shut up, Rafe."

"Look, it's fucking freezing. How about if we go grab a cup of coffee and catch up?"

"We just left a coffee shop."

"How about one with less cops? And maybe more food." Rafe patted his flat belly. "I could eat."

"You always could eat." Quinn snorted. "You went away, and Mum couldn't figure out why she had so many leftovers."

"That's a fucking lie. I've seen Kiki chow down." Rafe bobbed his head toward the parking lot. "Come on. Let's get out of the wind and someplace warm. Probably need to take both cars. Your family's crawling with cops. They'll notice if one of us left our car here, and then they'd be all in our shit."

"Yeah, probably not. About the noticing. Mine kind of got in a wreck, so I have a loaner." Quinn shook his head, stalling Rafe's questioning look. "Follow me. I know where to take you."

Rafe grinned wickedly. "Q, you have no idea how long I've waited to hear you say that."

"WHYBORNE'S COFFEE House?" An elegant gold script on the storefront's frosted window was the only hint Rafe had of what lay beyond the Nob Hill shop's heavy wooden door. "How long has this been here?"

"A few years now. One of the professors I'm friends with owns it. Well, he and his husband own it, but someone manages it for them. They live upstairs." Quinn opened the street-facing door and waved Rafe in. "I almost bought one of the apartments in the building, but then the house came up, and well, I really liked it."

Built a decade after the great earthquake, the multistory building's street level discreetly offered not only a coffee shop but a bento deli and a dance studio for the uninitiated. Rafe grinned at the flock of tiny purple-haired elderly women pouring past them, their chattering punctuated with admiration for their salsa instructor's ass and one woman's chocolate Thai plant she'd been cultivating for the past month. One of the city's trolleys clanged by, swaying as it chugged up to the hill's crest. Rafe spotted his own apartment building among the spires rising above them, then had to duck out of the way as a young woman with bouncy blonde pigtails careened past him on an old red bicycle. She tossed off a few rings from the bell on her handlebar as a thank-you, speeding off toward Japantown.

"Coming in?" Quinn's throaty Irish purr drew Rafe back. "Or do you want to keep sightseeing?"

"You never were the impatient one, Q," he tossed back to the Irish man waiting by the door.

"I'm standing on a corner where the winds cut up from the Bay and wearing too thin of a shirt. I'm going to be impatient."

Rafe glanced at the prick of nipples under Quinn's shirt, letting his gaze slip over Quinn's chest and shoulders.

"Where's your jacket, Q?"

"I forgot my jacket in the car. Had other things on my mind." He rattled the open door. "I'm going in without you. Save yourself. Don't let Gojira get you."

It was a silly thing, a simple toss-off comment from their younger years Rafe'd nearly forgotten about. Shaking his head, he followed Quinn in, still marveling at how tall Connor's baby brother had gotten over the years.

Outside the place hid itself like a speakeasy. Inside it was like stepping into an old British gentlemen's club, complete with cherrywood wainscoting, antique furniture, and a large expanse of a bar dedicated to brewing teas and rich-bodied coffees. Small intimate alcoves were set up along the walls, cordoned off by old Asian screens or half walls of wood and frosted glass. Behind the bar a bald, nearly cadaverous man with a curled-up mustache the color of bright pennies steamed milk, and he looked up to nod at Quinn as they passed.

"Two of the same, Professor Morgan?" A young woman in a black shirtwaist dress fell into step between them, and Rafe found himself frowning at the pretty, flirtatious smile she gave Quinn.

"Are lattes okay, Rafe?" Quinn got tangled in the young girl's path when he turned back. He stumbled, sidestepping her again as she moved into his way. "Damn. Pardon me."

"I'm sorry, is *he* with you?"

Rafe caught the slight assessing look the elf-in-faced brunette shot his way. He also saw Quinn stiffen slightly when her hand drifted across the small of Quinn's back.

"Yeah, sugar. He's with me." Rafe glided up into Quinn's space, neatly paring her off him. "We order off the menu here or up at the bar? I'd like something besides sugar and cop in my stomach right now."

"Menus are on the tables. We'll be at the back, Jeanine," Quinn called out as Rafe shuffled behind him toward a corner of the wedge-shaped shop. "By the bookcases."

Rafe could see why Quinn chose the spot he had. Chances were it was a favorite, familiar niche in Q's life, a square carved out by a pair of heavy shelves and up against one of the half-curtained windows looking out into the street. A couple of wingback chairs, worn sage velvet and nearly black wood, sat abreast of a round tea table in the same dark wood—a matched set from someone's purloined estate, Rafe guessed. With the shelves on either side of them, it was a cozy nook, large enough to move about in yet intimate and warm for conversation.

Or in Quinn's case, a space to breathe and get away from the noisy rush of people around him.

It hadn't been that long since Rafe'd been with the green-eyed apple of Donal's eye. He'd not forgotten the nearly panicky need Quinn had at times to get away—to not be touched—to seek out some quiet from the simmering bustle of his family and the rest of the world.

Or at least that's what Rafe was sure pissed him off about the brunette nearly putting her hand on Quinn's ass.

"Nice place." Rafe slid into the chair, keeping an eye on the ever-helpful Jeanine as she bustled about gathering their coffees. "One of the guys you work with owns it, you said?"

"He's a professor. Really brilliant. A linguist—a damned good one. Speaks thirteen languages. Reads more. His husband's an investigator. I like them." Quinn passed over a sheet of paper with the coffee shop's food selections. "They're in Egypt right now."

"What're they doing there?"

"Chasing mummies. Or being chased by mummies. One of the two." Quinn's eyes sparkled when

Rafe looked up at him. "The pastrami's good, but avoid the vegan grilled cheese."

"I barely like vegetables there, Q. I'm not going to eat cheese made out of them." Rafe could almost taste the foul on his tongue. "Pass."

"They're not made from vegetables. And I've had some really good ones, but those are made out of tree nut milk. I think they're using something cheddar-like for the grilled cheese—"

"What the fucking hell is a tree nut? Like almonds? Why not just tell you it's almonds?" He cut Quinn off, mostly to see the light hit Quinn's face as he geared up to answer. Rafe didn't realize how much he missed hearing Quinn *talk*. How he got lost in the labyrinth of his brain, pulling out pieces of floss and brightly hued scraps of information Rafe adored listening to.

Mostly, he missed the soft smile Quinn got when he began to share the brilliant slivers of things he'd gathered along the way. It was one of the reasons his family called him *breac*—magpie—and Rafe adored making Quinn smile.

Teasing slightly, Rafe continued, "And how do you milk them? They come with little teats like cows?"

With that, Quinn was off and running.

GOD, HE'D forgotten how much he loved sitting around listening to Quinn babble. There was a song to Quinn's mind, a diving, swooping, gleeful dance with somber passages as the conversation grew dearthen, taking off again on a gallivant when something intriguing came up. He'd taken the plates from the waitress when she came by, sliding Quinn's around so his fries were near his left hand and a napkin right above that. Everything came back to him easily. The caring of Quinn—taking the small steps in easing some of the roughness around them before the burrs caught on Quinn's velvety soul.

Rafe'd missed that. Missed *him*. Something about Quinn Morgan soothed even as it ruffled other parts of Rafe's mind... of Rafe's body and soul.

He'd hesitated before trying to steal a piece of swiss cheese from Quinn's sandwich, not knowing if he still had that right—that permission—to intrude on Q's world. This Quinn was older, yes—a little bit looser—but the rules governing Quinn's delicate balance remained the same. Ask. Don't push. And let him fly.

There was nothing more glorious than to see Quinn Morgan flying in the spectral rainbow of the world he'd plunged into.

Little bits of things suddenly became enormously important. The pop of a mustard seed on Rafe's tongue held a tart wonder he'd not have stopped to see if Quinn hadn't pointed it out to him. They'd spent at least five minutes dissecting the different flavors in the shop's homemade bread-and-butter pickles, chortling when Rafe dared Quinn to taste the pickling juice, then finding himself intrigued at the flavor of it on a piece of sourdough from his pastrami sandwich.

Then Quinn was off again. Running along the weaving paths of his mind, dragging Rafe along for the ride.

They eventually found music, a commonality they'd shared from the very beginning. Of everyone Rafe'd ever met, it'd been Quinn who'd gotten his love for the deep, rolling thread beneath the music, the river feeding the land a song was built on. Before he knew it, they were scooted up together, debating a sweet from the menu, and the sky outside was pitch black through the frosted panes.

And discovered he'd placed his hand across Quinn's, stroking at Q's long fingers with his own rough touch.

"Do you have school tomorrow?" Rafe didn't want to stop touching Quinn. Especially not when Quinn turned his hand over and rubbed his fingertips across Rafe's palm. "Shit, all these years of trying to get out of school, and you go and jump right back in with both feet."

"I have a few student meetings tomorrow, and *you* hated school because they made you do homework," Quinn pointed out. "Which you tried to shove off on me."

"Hey, you *liked* it. 'Sides, what was smarter? Doing it myself or bribing a resident genius to give me a hand?"

"Once. I helped you once." Quinn held up a single finger—and not with the hand Rafe was playing with. "And that's because I felt sorry for you. Learned our lesson, didn't we?"

"Yeah. When writing a paper for an idiot, write *like* an idiot." Rafe snorted, recalling the thunderous roll of Donal's voice when the school's dean dragged them all in for punishment. "Your dad went to the mat for me there. I thought I was out for sure. One too many fuckups."

"And all because you *had* to see if that band would let you play with them." Quinn leaned against the chair's arm, his shoulder nearly brushing Rafe's. "I was scared Da was going to skin us alive."

"Yeah, the *one* time I wished your mom showed up." Rafe chuckled. "But she didn't. Neither did mine, though, so there's that."

"She worked," Quinn pointed out softly.

It was a long-standing truth. Rafe lived in the Morgans' back pocket, and his mother worked to keep him there.

"It's hard if there's only one parent. She spent a hell of a lot of time working."

"Not anymore." Rafe reached for his second latte, then saluted his absent mother. "I'm glad she's... not here, you know? That sounds fucked-up, but it's rough between us right now. And that's not on her. I mean, she did her best. Me, not so much. But at least she's taken care of. No more working for her. Not ever again."

"You doing okay?"

And now, Rafe thought, came the dramatic portion of the evening.

"Seriously, Q, don't I look okay?" Rolling his shoulders back, Rafe tangled his fingers into Quinn's, tightening his hold. Lying was easy. Or it should have been, but his tongue stumbled over the words he was forcing over them. "All the rock-star money, none of the responsibilities."

It was Quinn's soul-piercing look into his eyes that undid Rafe, and he swallowed hard, forcing himself to look away before he fell into the despair he saw mirrored back at him. Folding his hands around Rafe's, Quinn angled his head down until he was in Rafe's field of vision.

"This is *me*, Andrade," Quinn reminded him. "I *know* you. Don't give me the crap you give everyone else. After all these years, don't I deserve the truth?"

"Truth is, Q—" Rafe inhaled sharply, tasting the coffee, sugar, and the man next to him in the warm air swirling around them. "I don't know. I don't know what the fuck I'm doing with myself, and if I don't find something soon, I know I'm going to be crawling right back into the bad habits that got me kicked out of my own band.

"I haven't done drugs in fucking forever, and I don't miss them. That's the sad part, right? I should miss them more. Instead I miss what I screwed up, because shit, I had *everything*, Q. Fucking everything. And I didn't just let it go. I set it on fire and watched the whole thing burn. And for what? I still don't know why."

"Maybe you're missing something inside of you? Maybe you walked too far away from the music?" The whiskey was back in Quinn's voice, a thick Irish malt heady enough for Rafe to get drunk off from a single sip. "Maybe if you can find that again. I remember how much you used to love playing. All the time your fingers were going, even when you didn't have an instrument. Where did *that* go?"

"Maybe that guy Mark wasn't the only thing that died that night." Rafe tried to laugh off the welling thickness in his throat, but it soon became too difficult to breathe. His eyes were losing focus, drowning beneath a wash of stinging emotion he couldn't control. "I don't know, magpie. I just feel like I'm dead inside, and nothing—*nothing*—I do can bring me back. And I'm so fucking alone. So damned fucking dead and alone."

"Hey." Quinn's breath was warm on Rafe's cheek, his mouth a few butterfly wings away from brushing Rafe's skin and frosting it with heat. "You're not alone. Never alone. I'm here. Anytime. You know that, right?"

"Maybe I just forgot." Quinn was close, too close for Rafe's comfort or perhaps not close enough for Rafe's liking. Leaning forward would shatter Rafe's world, confusing his already jumbled mess of a life, but in that moment when Quinn was so close Rafe could dab his tongue out and lick the curve of Quinn's upper lip, finding out if his rainbow-chattering magpie tasted as sweet as he had before was all Rafe could think about.

"Last call!" The barista's booming voice was a clumsy elephant dancing across their toes, and Quinn jerked back, startled by the echoing refrain bouncing about the coffee shop walls. "Closing in fifteen! Take something to go!"

"Well, shit, Q. Looks like we closed the place down." Rafe leaned back, reluctantly letting Quinn's fingers go. "Not as good as shutting a bar down, but hey, I take my kicks where I can get them. Look, Q, I've got to—"

"You're going to say you've got to go when you and I both know you're only saying that to avoid the emotions of this… between us. Our friendship. Our… brotherhood."

"Trust me, Q. The last thing I think of when I look at you is being a brother." The expression on Quinn's face was priceless, and if it hadn't been so late… if he didn't hurt so deep inside, he'd have loved to kiss Quinn full on the mouth to watch it bloom. "Thanks for listening, kid—"

"Not a kid," Quinn cut him off, shaking his head. "Stop trying to make me small, Andrade. That's not going to work."

It wouldn't. Rafe knew that. He did it because it helped him deal with how Quinn looked, the want of Quinn's taste on his mouth, and for all the missteps and fumbling emotions between them.

"No, not a kid," he agreed softly, then winked. "But wait, the virgin thing. Real or no?"

"Sadly, real." Quinn pulled a face and got up out of the chair. "Well, depending on how you define sex. I don't... date well, and my last boyfriend... had some problems with body fluids. So we never really... got too far."

"Oh, babe. See, that's a crying shame," Rafe whispered, leaning over to brush his lips against Quinn's earlobe. "We'll have to see what we can do about that. Because if done right, bodily fluids are sometimes the best damned part about the whole fucking business."

CHAPTER FOUR

On the warehouse rooftop, looking out over the Bay

Quinn: *You ever wonder at what point someone thinks they can murder someone. I mean, where is that point? How do you get there? To that point?*

Miki: *That's fucking easy. It's 'cause some people are assholes, and instead of seeing a person... instead of seeing a soul, they look at a guy or chick and say: that over there, that's just meat. That's all that person is to the asshole. Just another piece of meat.*

Damie: *And this kind of shit is why no one will come up here and hang with the two of you.*

"HEY, HOW are the kiddies?" Rafe would have swallowed his tongue had he known *that* was going to come out of his mouth. Any bit of swag and polish he had seemed to go out the window where Quinn was concerned. He tried to recover, fumbling about until he just gave up and shot Quinn a shit-eating grin.

"They're old enough to vote. Hardly kids."

"Don't give me that look. Fuck it, they're kids. I'm an old man, or at least in musician years."

"Is that seven for any one, like a dog? Or is it more?" Quinn cocked his head, an oh-so-familiar gesture guaranteed to tug at Rafe's heart. "What is the ratio for one rock star year to mere mortal?"

"I think it depends on the fame. And the fuckery they've done," Rafe replied, leaning on his broom. "Wasn't famous or fucked-up enough for the 27 Club, but I sure as shit gave it my best to get in."

Quinn made a face. "Yeah, that's one membership I'm glad you passed on, Andrade."

FINNEGAN'S WAS open for late breakfast, a smattering of baking-soda biscuits, eggs, and rashers. Leigh'd put up a fight with Sionn, insisting on catching at least some of the morning tourist traffic by pointing out it cost them little to nothing to open, and staffing would be to a minimum, especially if they kept the food to something people could grab before hitting the pier. Unfortunately for Leigh, she was often busier than expected and had no shame in calling in a favor or five to boost her morning staff in a pinch.

Rafe was subsequently amazed at how many favors he seemed to owe Finnegan's and how they never seemed to go down in number.

Sweeping the outside café area for opening was an easy job. He'd been conned into doing that by a pouty Leigh. Still, sweeping was a far better job than the one Sionn had inside, which seemed to be mostly picking shells out of the eggs he'd been assigned to crack open for scrambles. Half-energized and a bit sore from their morning run, Rafe enjoyed the brisk wind coming off the Bay and the hot Irish spitting out from the open pub doors.

Seagulls outnumbered the tourists. It was too early but for the most stalwart of vacationers, but the local crowd was already shuffling from their homes and onto BART or the ferries. It was quiet enough to hear the sea lions barking from their docks, sleek-bodied squatters ready for a long day's bake once the sun broke through the morning fog.

It was a normal, simple day. Much like every other normal day Rafe and Sionn did their run from Finnegan's and up past to Ghirardelli's. With one exception.

Most mornings didn't have a long-legged, angelic-faced, green-eyed Irish man showing up in a pair of worn jeans and an easy smile, but if Rafe had a choice, he'd opt for a Quinn Morgan appearance any day.

"Let me guess. You came down here for the greasy ham and flapjack special? Although from what I hear going on in there, you might want to stick with cold cereal." Rafe looked back behind him. Leigh joined Sionn's battle with some piece of equipment, cajoling him to move it a bit to the right and it would slide right in. He'd have made a dirty joke if he didn't think either or both of them would stomp outside and shove the broomstick up his ass. "Then again, you'd be safer with the coffee. At least it's decent."

"I called Sionn to ask him something about brewing so we could talk about me investing in his mad schemes, but it sounds like he's busy." Quinn shoved his hands into his pockets, his forearms powerful with lean muscle. "He told me you were down here. Mind if I hang out with you for a bit? But if you're busy…."

"I'm never too busy for you, Q. It's not like they can fire me. I'm a volunteer. Actually, an indentured servant paying off a lifetime of bar tabs and imagined slights. Hang on a second. I'll sneak in and get us a couple of coffees." Rafe handed Quinn the broom, then slithered his way into the pub. It took him a few minutes, most of them spent picking up sugar packets he'd spilled onto the floor, but he made it back outside with no one noticing.

Quinn was still there, sitting in one of the café chairs, legs stretched out and keen, sharp eyes drinking in the crowd scurrying by.

They sat silent for a few minutes. An occasional murmur of curiosity came from Quinn when someone dressed in too much of a contrast for his sensibilities strolled by. Rafe had to agree with him on most judgments, but he argued vehemently for the woman in the giraffe-print T-shirt and red pants, pointing out the spikes on her shiny black leather heels.

"You have to give points for a woman with style, Q. She's rocking that." Rafe nodded in her wake. "Shoulders back, head high. Chick's got balls."

"Her shirt has tassels on the hem. It would be okay without the tassels. Small little tassels." Quinn wiggled his fingers at Rafe. "Why? Why would you put tassels on a shirt like that?"

"Rocking the tassels, Q. No hating the fringe."

"Makes her look like a lamp. A cheap lamp. In a hotel where merrow come up out of the toilets." Quinn wrinkled his nose as Rafe's laughter carried across the courtyard in front of Finnegan's. "It does."

"Maybe her shirt's reincarnated. Its past life was a whorehouse pillow." His cheeks were beginning to hurt, especially when a bit of coffee went down wrong and Quinn began pounding on his back to help him stop coughing. Waving Quinn off, Rafe caught his breath. "Sorry, bad image of you handing out red cards for fashion violations."

"I don't know shite about fashion," he shot back. "It's the colors. Look at the colors she's wearing. It's like they can't see the difference between khaki and olive green. Why would you go out wearing an indigo shirt and olive-green pants? What kind of monster does that to the world?"

They talked more after that. Stupid things they'd done and probably would do again. Quinn mourned the loss of his Audi, wishing he'd had the chance to take Rafe out in it at least once before he'd nearly rolled it. After extracting a promise of a ride after the car was repaired, Rafe leaned back and sighed contentedly.

"This is really nice, Q. No worries. No fuss."

"What is nice? What fuss?"

"This. You and me. Why didn't we do you and me more often? I really could have used this. Still can use more of this in my life."

"Because you were off being a rock god, and I was still some clueless nerd with my face pressed to a computer screen?"

"Stupid of me. You know that, right?" Rafe glanced over at Quinn, who studiously avoided making eye contact. "I'm serious, Q. You're one of the best fucking things—people—I've got in my life, and I didn't make time for you. Time I should have. You're like a touchstone for me. And I feel like I buried you in my pocket when I should have held you in my hand."

Quinn frowned, his eyebrows knitted over his strong nose. "I'm a flat piece of slate you use to test metals on?"

"Wait. What?" He sat up a little bit, leaning an elbow on the table. Quinn was off again, veering into the stratosphere while the rest of the world looked up, earthbound and confused. Or at least Rafe was confused. Patient and waiting but still a bit confused. "Explain it to me."

"A touchstone. People used to smear golds—types of golds—on a certain type of stone, like slate, then compare it to known samples. It's how they tested for purity." Quinn sipped at his cup. "Or do you mean metaphorically? Like a point of reference."

"Um, no. Not the rock one. The other one. The metaphorical one. The one where you bring balance. And sanity. God knows I need some fucking sanity." Rafe slouched back down in his chair, chuckling to himself. "Nicely done, by the way. Good ducking a compliment there, magpie."

They watched a flock of like-shirted Asian tourists waddle after a woman holding a red flag above her head, a stream of quicksilver Japanese and Cantonese. Rafe coughed again, mostly to clear his throat, but Quinn glanced over, worry on his face.

"Are you okay?" He leaned over, nudging Rafe's sneaker with his foot.

"Better now you're here." It wasn't hard to admit that to Quinn. Something inside him lightened when Quinn was near. He'd never noticed it before. Not until his life'd hung too heavy on him, and Rafe felt like he was one step away from flinging himself off the Bay Bridge with a necklace of albatrosses slung around his throat. "Missed you, Q. Never knew how fucking much until right now. But I did. I do."

"Missed you too, Rafe."

Quinn's fingers brushed over his, and Rafe grabbed them, holding them tightly.

"I'd be stupid to let you go again." He squeezed lightly, caught in Quinn's deep emerald gaze.

"You won't." Quinn smiled. "Let go, I mean. 'Cause I love you and everything, but sometimes, Andrade, you do stupid *really* well."

QUINN COULD have done without the flat tire.

After sitting through a two-hour play about cubist painters falling in love during their exploration of the color red, a flat tire wasn't how he wanted to finish up the afternoon. But the universe had other plans, and they apparently included Quinn digging out the spare from the loaner's trunk and swapping out a tire nearly as terminally depressing as the avant-garde performance he'd just endured.

The art-house theater still retained a lingering aroma of its time as a meatpacking warehouse and, from what Quinn could tell, was just as cold. Nearly two hundred people packed into a corner of the squat brick building barely dented the frigidity of the theater's interior, and he'd been thankful for the black peacoat he brought in with him.

The five-minute intermission brought a quickly dashed hope of scoring a cup of hot coffee. Instead the director'd insisted on carrying on his vision of frigidity in love by serving frozen unsweetened strawberry Kool-Aid, made even more bitter by the reality of having to watch the second half of the play only because he'd promised a former colleague he'd attend.

Since Graham'd made that exact same promise to the director, Quinn suspected the rest of the audience were riveted to their seats out of guilt and frostbite more than a vested interest in Isabelle's expansion into chartreuse and her growing love-hate for banana-adoring Beauregard.

"We can wait inside until the car service comes," Graham suggested. The thin man shivered beside Quinn, pressing in close to keep warm. "That tire is as flat as the play's dialogue. God, what rubbish that all was. I am so sorry I dragged you to it. I'm sorry I dragged *me* to it."

Quinn tried not to mind the touch of Graham's arm on his side, but it was difficult. As familiar as he was with the other professor, Quinn's skin ruffled under his shirt at the brush of Graham's body on his. A far different reaction from his casual stroking of Rafe's fingers a few nights before.

"It's a pity your friend couldn't make it."

"Don't think the director would have thought so. He'd have stayed because I wouldn't leave and made comments the whole time. He was smart enough to weasel out of it." He paused in his contemplation of the tire. "We've got to learn to weasel better."

Calling a tow truck to change the tire would mean standing around for an hour, and Quinn was tired. He'd put in a long day of counseling students on their papers, with a sidetrack of one male student nearly crying in his lap about a dead goldfish. The papers he dealt with easily, working through the topics until he was certain the students knew what they were doing. The goldfish-mourning basketball player was subsequently passed along to a grief counselor at the student center with a hearty wish he'd feel better.

It took Quinn about five minutes before he realized he'd probably sounded as if he wished the goldfish would somehow get better instead of the student. Thoughts of a yellow-and-white zombie fish lurking in the halls of a coed dorm kept him amused during Beauregard's long discourse on the perils of a rotten pear in his still life.

"Here, put this on and stay warm. I'll change the tire." Quinn shrugged his peacoat off, handing it over to Graham once he got his arms loose.

The brisk afternoon air cut through his T-shirt, although his jeans seemed sturdy enough to hold the chill back. Once the doors had opened, signaling the audience's release, the theater vomited out people as if it'd eaten too much cake. No one appeared willing to linger, and the theater's small parking lot was practically empty save for Quinn's borrowed sedan and a VW van he suspected the director lived in, based on the piles of fast-food wrappers on the front seat.

Graham's spine went rigid, and he clasped Quinn's coat to his chest. "I can't... I mean, we can call someone. No need for you to catch a cold. Well, to catch a—"

"It's just a tire, Graham." Quinn patted his shoulder, then headed to the trunk. "Easy enough to do. I'd tell you to go inside and wait, but you'll freeze to death in there, even with the coat. Trust me. Five minutes into changing a tire and I'll be plenty warm enough."

Thankfully, the loaner's spare tire was a standard size and not a rubber donut he'd have to exchange at the dealership. Graham made noises about helping, but Quinn waved him off, hefting the jack out of its hole beneath the trunk hatch.

"How about if you see if you can find us some hot coffee?" Quinn peered down the street. "Actually, if there's someplace open, stay there and get out of the wind. I can call you when I'm done."

"Are you sure?" Graham swaddled himself in Quinn's coat, pulling its soft wool lapels up to his sharp chin. "It seems rude to… desert you. Suppose someone comes by and—"

"Attacks me?" Quinn held up the jack's tire iron. "I'm armed and dangerous. Besides, it's in the middle of the afternoon. If anyone starts anything, I'll just start quoting the second act until their head goes full watermelon. It'll be fine. Promise."

The five minutes stretched into ten as the car refused to give up its hard-won flat. Deep breathing helped, as did swearing. He'd gone through all the Latin he knew when the final lug nut gave in, and Quinn spun the tire off to the side, resisting the urge to fling it against the far wall to teach it a lesson. With the spare in place, he'd just put the flat in the trunk and was about to lower the car to the ground when a siren jolted him out of his focus.

"What the hell?" A black SUV with darkened windows pulled up beside him, and Quinn groaned, wondering what he'd done to bring down the wrath of gods on his head that afternoon. "Of course. Why not."

The SUV's lights flashed twice; then the car engine cut off. A few seconds later, the driver's door opened, and a broad-shouldered, hard-jawed cop got out, the afternoon sun glinting on the metal star fixed to his dark uniform jacket. From the look on the man's face, Quinn was in for a reckoning—but for the life of him, he couldn't figure out exactly what he'd done wrong.

Until he caught the captain eyeing the sedan perched on its jack, trunk open and disabled tire displayed for all to see.

"*Quinn.*" The man's rolling Irish and deep golden voice seemed as cold as the air Quinn sucked into his lungs. "Imagine. I'd thought I'd seen ye but then said to meself, no, that's not m'boy's speedster. It couldn't be me son, but then I remembered something—a conversation I'd just had with Mullens up at Southern. Something about a truck and a tin can about wide enough only to hold a sardine."

"Hello, Da." Sidestepping Donal Morgan's ire wasn't something easily done. It was best to accept the inevitable and show remorse, but Donal's eyes narrowed, and he drew up closer, his long legs shortening the distance between them. Donal was nearly against Quinn's chest when he stopped short, studying his son intently.

"I was actually going to be hunting ye down later, but here ye were, right on my way home." His father chewed through the bite in the air, spitting it back out hot and worried. "Want to be telling me anything about the other night? Say, perhaps why ye nearly got killed and didn't tell me or yer mum?"

"Da, I'm fine." He switched to Gaelic, mindful of the people walking by. The sidewalk suddenly appeared to be teeming with people, many throwing curious glances at the mountain of a cop standing ready to dress Quinn down. "Can we do this later? I've got to finish this up and then take Graham home. We were just at this... thing and—"

"We cannot be doing this later, Quinn." Donal's paternal concern battled the raging thread in his voice. Long inured to the duality of his father's gut instincts and parenting, Quinn waited Donal out, wondering which side would win out—the protective anger or the comforting coddle. "*Now*."

"Da, I don't want to talk about what—" He waved toward the building, the borrowed car's fobs clicking together. "Wait, on your way home? This isn't near home."

"I went down to Southern to talk to an old friend, and then one of the lieutenants comes up to ask me about how ye were doing. As if I knew someone tried to fold ye in an accordion." Donal cut him off quickly. "When were ye thinking of telling me about that, son? Instead I have to hear about it from another cop? Oh, and because ye'd left yer phone in what remains of that deathtrap ye drive."

"Shit, that's my school phone. I forgot all about it. No wonder people kept saying they couldn't reach me." He felt at his pockets. "I had it charging. Does he still have it? I don't know if it even works—"

"Forget the fucking phone, *breac*. I've got it with me in the car," his father growled, looming over him despite their similar heights. "Are ye fine? Or did ye hit that already cracked head of yers, and ah'll be needing to take you down to the hospital to sew yer brains to the inside of yer skull so they stay there?"

"Oh." He'd forgotten about the car. "*That*."

"*That*." Donal poked at Quinn's chest, a light tap over his heart. "Instead ye show up late at the coffee shop with an apology, as if you'd slept in or summat, then slink around yer brothers before chatting up Rafe, as if ye hadn't kissed Death's ass on the way over there."

"I'm sorry." Quinn kept his shoulders down, not wanting to add to the apology with a quick shrug. It was a surefire way to incite his mother, and his father wasn't one for the gesture when contriteness was required. "I wasn't thinking. It wasn't… important?"

Yeah, that last word was a bad choice, judging by the storm kicked up in his father's already thunderous gaze, and Quinn bared his teeth in a hearty smile. Instead of the rain and hellfire he'd been expecting, Donal sighed and drew him into a tight embrace.

"I worry fer ye, *breac*."

His father smelled good, a blend of coffee, cinnamon, and dad.

"Yer always off with yer head in the clouds for all of yer smarts. I worry more fer ye in yer tweed jackets and chalkboards than I do fer yer brothers going through doors with bullets coming at them."

"I'm *fine*, Da." He hugged his father back, then pulled loose. "Really, I'm good. It was just something stupid, and I was focused on getting there to support Forest. That's all."

"That's all," Donal parroted back, clapping Quinn's shoulders, then stepping back. "Take yer friend on. Then ye call me when ye get home. I want to know yer safe."

Quinn started to nod, then stopped short. "Are you going to be asking Kane to call you when he gets home? Maybe Connor too?"

"That's different—"

"How?" He shoved his way into his father's line of sight, forcing Donal to face him. "How is that different, Da?"

"Because no one tried to kill Con or Kane with a truck the other day, and now ye're standing here fixing a slashed tire. I'll come by and dust it for prints, see if anything pulls off of it. One thing could be nothing, but twice ill in a week means there's a pattern, or at least the start of one." Donal's knuckles swept a soft caress over Quinn's cheek, a familiar gesture from Quinn's childhood. "So, ye call me when ye get home. Or I'll be knowing the reason you haven't."

TRAFFIC THROUGH the city was tight, too tight for Quinn's liking. A delivery truck pulled up next to him at a stoplight about a block away from his Bay Street home, and he couldn't repress the crawling shudder in his spine. He took the corner a bit faster than he'd have liked, skidding the borrowed Audi across the wet street.

"Yeah, kill yourself and watch Da go through the roof." He steadied the car out, slowing down as he reached his street. "Finally, home."

It was a hell of a commute to and from the university, then the theater. Anywhere across the bridge usually meant an hour or more during the best of days, but Quinn wouldn't have traded his row-house-style home for anything. The street was a private nook of old buildings and tucked-in courtyards. Built tightly against each other, a nest of townhomes wrapped around the outside of a communal courtyard, and he'd fallen in love with its quirky three-storied structure, the garden patio built on top of his garage, and its rooftop terrace. Perched on a crest, the terrace gave him a clear view over long stretches of warehouses, down to the piers, and across to Alcatraz.

On a clear day, the sound of a nearby school carried children's voices across the way, and at night the heavy fog rolling off the water bounced up the sounds of the pier—a jangle of nightclubs, ship bells, and muddled-together music.

There was also the bonus of living someplace with little to no guest parking—a necessity when needing to circumvent a descending horde of Morgans.

The place had been a bit of hard work, not as intense as Connor's old Victorian but close enough for Quinn to gain a hatred of smelling varnish. Unlike Connor, his forays into renovation began and ended at stripping floors and repainting rooms once a team of contractors broke down walls and rewired everything. Six months after purchasing the place, he'd moved in and settled in for a long life.

"Shit, garage remote's still in the kitchen where you left it, you daft ass. Screw it. Car can sit in the drive for a bit." Leaving the replacement Audi in front of his garage, he headed around the corner to the cluster of mailboxes he shared with the other row houses.

And was faced with a very familiar dilemma, knowing he'd met the woman standing in front of the mailboxes, but for the life of him, he couldn't remember her name.

She smiled when he drew near, holding up a stack of envelopes for him to see. There were a jumble of names on them, including his own, and none of it a helpful clue to the identity of the woman who'd just moved into the place with her white Maltese named Max. She was tall, her green eyes even with his own, and her short dark hair fluttered across her cheekbones when she kicked up a slight wind fanning the envelopes.

"I didn't know you were a doctor," she sang out to him. "What kind?"

"Kind of doctor?" He blinked, trying to remember if he'd introduced himself to her that way. It wasn't something he did, not usually. Not ever. He hated the pretentiousness of it, hanging sheepskins on his shoulder as if he were some conquering hero returning from a long journey filled with Cyclops, Minotaur, and sirens. "Um, the usual kind—okay, not like the body kind, but... I did a dual first field, British and East Asia.... Japan, not China. But what—?"

"I've got your mail. Well, I think I've got everyone's mail."

Her smile was blinding, sucking in all the ambient light coming through the trees and throwing it back into his face.

"Seems like the mailman decided he'd had enough of our crap and shoved all of the mail into my box. I was going to pick out the good ones and toss the junk mail, but I think that's a federal offense or something. Makes you wonder what he'd do if he had to actually walk the street and deliver it to our houses."

"Er... what?" Her name still eluded him, but if Quinn remembered correctly, Max'd needed to get booster shot, and he wondered if he should ask her about it. "I'm sorry. What's a federal offense?"

"Tossing out someone's mail. Is it really a federal offense? I mean, do you really want to read—" She studied a catalog cover. "—the *Fantasy Swords of Ireland and Beyond*?"

"Um, yes. Please." He took the booklet out of her fingers, then tucked it under his arm. "And I think it is—a federal offense. They've found over 2500 pounds of mail—well, a postman didn't deliver. I believe the paper said it was a federal offense."

"So's dumping everyone's mail into my lock box and walking away, but what can you do, you know? Want to help me sort through this stuff?" She rattled a packet of fabric softener samples. "I can make it worth your while. Nice smelly clothes! Free with every ten pieces of crap sorted."

"I'm good on the clothes." Quinn edged back when she flapped them again. "But I'll help. Thing is, what do we do with them afterwards?"

It took them a good ten minutes of crouching over a plastic bin to get everything squared away. For some reason the piles kept intermingling, and no matter what Quinn did to keep them straight, his mail migrated over to the unsorted pile. After a rousing argument on why sword magazines were not junk mail, Quinn dusted himself off, then stood up.

"Thanks for helping." She beamed up at him, her eyes bright from their laughing. "Although I feel kind of dirty knowing Mr. Kwan subscribes to women's underwear magazines."

"No judging. For all we know, he finds them very comfortable." Quinn nodded solemnly.

"Oh, trust me, coming from a woman, anything you find inside of that kind of magazine goes from zero to itch a minute after you put it on." Cocking her head, she glanced behind her toward the street. "Want to go door-to-door with—"

Quinn never got to answer. A second later the sky was lit on fire, and the heat of it rushed over them. An echoing boom sent them both to their knees, a shock wave of sound and force strong enough to scatter the envelopes she had in her hand. Smoke and flames shot up into the air, its source hidden by a copse of trees on the corner.

Splinters flew into them, stinging his face and arms. Quinn grabbed at the woman—Raia, his brain'd finally kicked in—and pulled her under him, sheltering her from the debris being ripped up by the explosion, then rained down upon their heads.

He buried his face between her shoulder blades, protecting his eyes from the shrill storm of wood and metal flying into him. Quinn felt Raia's screams reverberate through her slender body as he covered her back and head, the sound of her terror lost in the booming echoes around them. Quinn's hearing shut down, overwhelmed by the deep, rolling bass. Then the world shifted, sharper-edged and piercing through the numbness, until he was drowning in the woman's terrified screams.

"It's okay. You're okay," Quinn reassured her, stroking at her short hair as he dared to look up. "It's over now. You're safe."

"Max!"

Raia struggled to get out from under him, but Quinn held her down.

"I have to get Max!"

"Hold on. Wait and see if it's over," he murmured, fishing out his phone. All Quinn could hear was the crackling of flames, and he eased off Raia to help her to her feet. "Call 911 and tell them there was an explosion. I need you to stay calm. You're not going to help Max if you're panicking. Let me go see what happened, and if Max is in danger, we'll get him out, okay?"

He didn't wait for Raia to answer him. Instead Quinn took the corner at a hard run, only to skid to a stop a hundred feet later. From what he could see, the houses were still standing firm, although many, including his own, now sported broken windows and torn-off siding. The landscaping beside his driveway was in flames, so brightly engulfed he wondered if he'd hear the voice of God speaking from it.

Car alarms screamed violently, and Quinn saw more than a few people stumble out of their damaged houses to find out what had torn apart their neighborhood. He couldn't remember which house was Raia's, but he knew one thing for certain. He was going to have a hard time explaining to the Audi dealership about how their sedan ended up as a smoldering crater in the middle of his driveway.

"Well, shite." He stared at the flaming chunk of metal he'd driven just half an hour ago, exhausted just looking at the mess he'd somehow brought to the neighborhood. "I fucking hate it when Da's right."

CHAPTER FIVE

Warehouse garage

*Kane, joining Miki in the garage: Hey,
    the GTO is here. It's all ready to go
    then?*

*Miki: Yeah, that's what the auto guys
    said. They just unloaded the flat-
    bed and left it here. Made me sign a
    few papers, tossed me the keys, and
    headed out.*

*K: So, you want to take it for a short
    road trip? Maybe across the Bay?*

M: Nope.

K: Why not?

*M: Haven't checked the trunk. Could be
    a dead body in there.*

*K: Why would there be a dead body in
    the trunk, Mick?*

> M: *'Cause the way our lives go, I'd be*
> *surprised if there wasn't. Here's*
> *the keys. You go fucking check,*
> *then let me know if we need to call*
> *the morgue. I've got Horan on*
> *speed-dial.*

THE DEEP thrum of his bass curled down into Rafe's belly, stroking at his core, then plunging him back into the earthy roll of pleasure he found licking his fingers across its strings. A whine and hiss of an old tube amp kept him company, the tall beaten-up box bearing the marks of being dragged around in the back of a van. Water rings stained its top, the paper softened from countless beer bottles, then dried by the heat of too-bright stage lights. Its crackling subsided once Rafe got settled in, and its hum hit the back of Rafe's teeth as soon as he touched his fingertips to the strings.

And once Rafe got settled in, he never wanted to stop.

Seeing the Sound again brought back memories, fond ones of long nights spent with Jack and the rotating drummers and guitar players who'd eventually faded into the background. Half of their first album'd been cobbled together in the Sound's back studio, the space then barely large enough to hold a full set of drums, much less an entire band. Renovations brought more room to play, but the old studio walls still held their magic, bouncing his playing back onto him in dark rainbows of gritty sound.

Rafe didn't even mind he was playing alone—or so he kept telling himself.

A rap on the glass behind him brought him up short, and he frowned, checking the clock on the wall. Turning around to shout he had two more hours of time, Rafe caught sight of Connor Morgan scratching at the pane separating the sound booth from the mixing room. Flipping Con off made them both grin, and Rafe broke out into a full laugh when his friend drew out his badge and plastered it up against the glass for Rafe to see.

"Open the fucking door, Andrade," Connor mouthed from behind the windowpane. "Now."

"It's unlocked, asshole," Rafe mouthed back. The door opened, and Connor swaggered in, filling up the space the rest of Rafe's old band might have taken. "Jesus, you're fucking huge. What's Brigid feeding you these days? She just tossing a whole bison at you, and you pick it clean like a piranha?"

"Always count on you to be the smartass, eh? You forget. I moved out a while back. Now I have to hunt my own bison."

Con didn't wait for Rafe to take the bass off from around his neck and pulled him into a tight hug. Feedback screamed through the amp, thumping and screeching across the walls until Rafe could yank the cord that connected it to the bass.

Rubbing at his ears, Connor shouted, "Fuck, that's loud."

"You never learn, Morgan." He pulled loose of Connor's hug, undoing the strap from his bass. Setting it gently on the floor, Rafe shook his head. "Never, *ever* fucking learn. You'd think now you're fucking a drummer—"

"Correct me if I'm wrong, but drummers don't get wired up and tangled into those kinds of things, right?" Connor nudged the cords wrapped around Rafe's feet. "And what's this mess? Can't afford anything new, Rafie?"

"Sometimes old is best, Connie."

He yelped when Connor punched him lightly in the arm, and Rafe staggered back from the blow, counting on Con's overpreened conscience to play on his guilt. It worked. Connor reached out to steady Rafe, and Rafe dug his fingers into Con's left armpit, hitting the man's ticklish spot.

"Fucking git!" Connor spat.

"Yep, never, ever fucking learn." Rafe chuckled as he began to wrap the cords up from the floor. "Stalking me?"

"Saw the Chevelle outside when I dropped Forest off to talk to Jules. Figured you'd be in here instead of sucking down coffee."

"Hell, no more fucking coffee for a bit. Swear to God, that's all people around here drink anymore." He made a face. "Surprised Finnegan's still in business."

"Yeah, as long as there are Irish around, there's a market for a well-poured Guinness and some chips." Connor looked around the room, empty except for Rafe, his bass, and the battered amp. "You about done here?"

"Paid for the whole afternoon." Rafe shrugged as he wrapped a soft tie around the amp cable to keep it from unraveling. "But not like I'm paying the bills here. What's up?"

"Thought maybe you'd like to go for one of those beers." Connor pulled himself up. "Beer's okay, right?"

"Yeah, alcohol's okay. It's the coke, pills, and pot that does me in." Rafe rapped his forehead with a finger. "Still, don't overindulge. That's kind of the rule about everything now, isn't it?"

"Maybe—yes," Connor agreed. "You can store your shite here in the office if you want, or we can run it home. I've got an in with the owner, you know? We can take the Hummer out for a run on the hills, then grab a brew. Unless you've got someplace you've got to be?"

"Like I said, Connie." He snorted derisively. "I'm not paying the bills here. Not anymore. Don't know if I ever will be again."

"HOW DID grabbing a beer become horchata and grease at Felix's chip shop?" Rafe grabbed the red baskets from Connor's hand before they bobbled loose. Setting them down on the table, he squished himself in against the picnic tabletop so Connor could get by. Catching a look of disapproval, he grinned up foolishly at the man straddling the bench seat next to him. "Not that I don't like a good cinnamon rice drink instead of a cold malty beverage. Wait, I *don't*."

"Hey, you said that smells really good, so I pulled over," Connor grumbled back. "You complaining *now*?"

"Not a whimper. Hey, Orange Bang! Much better than horchata. I approve." Rafe snagged the bucket of frothy orange drink Connor placed in front of him.

The fish-and-chip shop was exactly the same, slightly greasy, with loud paint and even louder pop music coming from an ancient wheezing jukebox. A string of rainbow streamers danced along the edge of the shop's takeout window, catching a light afternoon breeze. The street was packed, but they'd lucked out finding a spot to perch Connor's Hummer, and Rafe was thankful he'd dropped the Chevelle and equipment off at his place before venturing out. Connor's driving hadn't improved, but at least the Hummer gave Rafe a sense of invulnerability as they wove between San Francisco's crawling traffic like they were chasing golden rings through a spiked forest.

"Open some of the mayo packets for me," Con ordered. "Maybe one of the lemon juice things too."

"Always so fucking bossy." Rafe waited impatiently as Connor took his time blending mayonnaise and sriracha, then dipped a seasoned steak fry into the mix. "Damn, this stuff's good. One of the things I missed out on the road, you know? Well, that and carne asada. And dim sum. It also sucks when you really want shrimp-and-pineapple fried rice in the middle of Tennessee, because that shit ain't happening."

"What? You didn't have someone fly it in from Bangkok for you?" Connor sneered, slapping Rafe's hand as he made another dive for the spicy mayo. "Wait until I mix it all up, dickwad."

"Flying it in would have been too… I mean, I get arrogant, but that shit's crazy." He shrugged, sneaking his finger around the styrofoam bowl's rim. Sucking the mayo off, he mumbled around his finger, "One of the hotel's dishwashers was Thai. I bribed him fifty bucks to cook some for me. Best fucking food I had in my entire life."

"Really? I'll tell Mum that so she doesn't have to worry about feeding your sorry ass." He pushed the bowl out, centering it between them. "You're just eating rice from now on?"

"Could have been because I was stoned, but dude, it was awesome. Charred pineapple, a bit of curried rice, and the biggest damned shrimp I'd ever

seen—like baby lobsters or something—but so fucking good." Rafe sighed, thinking of the sloe-eyed,
pretty young man who'd served him up more than a
3:00 a.m. snack. "How sad is it that the best memory
I've got of that tour is a bowl of fried rice?"

"Pretty pathetic," Connor agreed through a
mouthful of potato. "Spent all of your life to get up on
stage, and now what? Don't have jack to show for it
but money in the bank and a scarred brain."

"Hey, don't spare my feelings or shit." Rafe nearly choked on a mouthful of his drink.

"You want a hug?" Con eyed him from across the
bench, then turned so his thighs were on either side
of the seat and he faced Rafe. "'Cause I'll give you
one, but doesn't mean it'll do you any good. Talk to
me about what you're doing now. And how come you
lit out of the grand opening without saying goodbye
to anyone?"

"Ah, yeah—Quinn and I went for some coffee after we left Forest's place."

"You were *at* a coffee shop."

"Yeah, funny how that kept coming up. I think
we just needed some space to breathe. You know how
he is."

"Yeah, Q-bert's not good with crowds sometimes." Connor stole a sip of Rafe's drink, making a
face at its taste. "God, that's shite."

"He hates that nickname, you know?" Rafe didn't
mind the drink theft, but Connor's casual shrug at
Quinn's dislike nettled his anger. "Dude, I'm serious.
He hates it. Stop it."

The steely look Rafe got was a long one, layered
with everything from mild disbelief to suspicion. Rafe
was about to ask Connor what his problem was when

his friend finally nodded. "Okay. I'll try not to call him that. Habit, you know?"

"If there's anyone who knows about habits, it's me," Rafe muttered, saluting Connor with his cup. "We've been talking. On the phone. Doing some things together. It's been nice. I forgot how fucking easy it is to be with him."

"You're one of the few to think so." Connor wiped his hands on a napkin. "So you and Quinn, then?"

"It's been talking and *coffee*, Con. Wasn't like I took him on a gondola ride or shared a meatball in a back alley. *Coffee*."

"He take you to that funky steampunk shop he likes? The one near your apartment?"

"Yeah…," Rafe drawled. "Why?"

"A little more than coffee, then. Maybe he doesn't know it yet, but it was. Remember high school? Remember he had a thing for you back then, before you left? Took a bit out of him when you left. Sionn too." Connor tore open another mayo packet and spit the edge out from between his teeth. "Quinn, I mean. Had the thing for you. Not Sionn."

"Didn't think you were talking about anyone else. If it were Sionn, that'd be…. God, no." His heart oddly skipped a beat, and Rafe leaned back from the table, taking a breath to cool himself down. "If I recall, you told me you'd break my head open if I ever came near any of your brothers. Or sisters for that matter, either. So if he had a thing, I didn't know."

"He was a kid—our magpie." More mayo filled the bowl; then Connor layered in more pepper sauce. "There was a lot of shit going on in his head. Things were pretty bad there for a bit."

"I remember," Rafe replied softly. "He says he's doing okay. What do you think?"

"Think so." Connor cocked his head as if assessing his brother's life. "I'd say yeah. Brighter. Happier. I think coming out to the family helped. Not like we didn't already know, but I think it needed saying for him. 'Course Ian went and fucked the whole thing up, but that's Ian for you. Reminds me of you. A lot."

"Thanks. Good to know I've got someone to step into my shoes once I'm gone." He sneered. "Any reason you're giving me shit about Quinn? Or are we going someplace with it?"

"I'm getting there. See, before—when we were in school—Quinn was too young, and well, Andrade, you were a piece of shit looking for a place to smear yourself against."

Connor fixed a hard look on Rafe, pointed enough to stab him to the seat he sat on.

"Good to know you think so highly of me." If anything, Connor's face was harder to read than ever before, and Rafe hated not knowing what was going on behind his friend's frosted blue gaze. "Warning me off your little brother? 'Cause we just talked—"

He wasn't going to mention the laughter or the soft caress of Quinn's long fingers against his palm. Rafe wasn't stupid. He wasn't going to say a damned thing about what he and Quinn shared while Connor held his cards close to his chest. Rafe didn't have to wait long.

A second later, Connor cleared his throat and said, "It's not about Quinn, Rafe. Here you are, back and a little damaged—"

"I've always been a little damaged, Connie," he snorted as he reached for another fry. "If you're trying to get around to threatening to break my legs 'cause I'm spending time with your baby brother—"

"See, I'm not... threatening." Connor shook Rafe's impending protest off by looping his hand around the back of Rafe's neck and squeezing. "I'm not promising anything either."

"No! Intimidation never crosses your mind. The Morgans are so easygoing. Always the peacekeepers." Rafe gave a halfhearted attempt to break away, but Connor held him firmly in place.

"Gonna say it one more time in case you weren't listening... this isn't about Quinn, Rafe. It's about you." Connor's expression softened. "I don't want you to feel like you've only got Q and Sionn because you feel like you're drowning. I don't know why you thought you couldn't come to me or Kane. The two of us gave you some room because we thought that's what you wanted. Then K said something the other night...."

"Said what?"

Another tug back, but this time Connor let go a little bit, enough to let the itch ease away from Rafe's skin.

"That you made shitty life choices and giving you space was probably the last thing in the world you needed." Con shrugged. "I figured Sionn, yeah, because you guys are tight, but Quinn and not me or K? Maybe you thought Quinn was safe. Because he *is* easygoing—"

"Dude, your brother's only easygoing for as long as you don't piss him off." Rafe laughed, pushing Connor gently away. "Yeah, he's the one you can push the most but definitely not the one I'd want to take to the edge. I've seen him lose it."

"Fair enough," Connor conceded. "I just wanted to give you fair warning Kane and I aren't going to sit back anymore. We're going to be in your face so much you're going to think you're a Siamese twin."

"And all of this because I left the coffee shop with Quinn?" Rafe made a face. "Want the truth?"

"Most of the time," Connor agreed. "Truth's sometimes a hard thing to come by with you, but that's just how you are."

"And you're one of my best fucking friends—"

"I say it because I love you, Rafe. Like a brother. Doesn't mean I don't know how you are."

"Truth is, I didn't know what the fuck I was do-ing. Meetings—fucking NA meetings and Sionn make up my entire life, so having coffee with Quinn is a damned treat. I didn't want you guys around because, let's face it, I've got shit all over my hands." This time Rafe was the one shaking Connor's protests off. "Hear me out. You guys are *cops*. Even Sionn in his own fucked-up superhero kind of way. I *killed* a guy, Con. I might not have taken a gun to his head, but I got him killed. How the hell was I supposed to look you guys in the eye when I couldn't even look at myself in the mirror?"

Felix's Fish and Chips probably wasn't the best place to have a breakdown, but in true Andrade fash-ion, Rafe's mind always chose the most public of places to crack. The buzz of voices around them faded to a slow hum, turning into a white noise below Con-nor's steady breaths.

"Today was the first day I felt like playing. Like really playing. I went out of my damned house and booked studio time because I need to move forward. Quinn kind of made me see that. I sat next to Q, and he babbled off into his own little Q world, and it was so damned nice. Like it was normal. Sweet. He made me feel good, Con. Better than I'd felt in a damned long time."

"That's good, then, summat," Connor said softly as he pulled Rafe into a rib-crushing hug. "Fucking good, then."

It was awkward. The angle between them made the embrace difficult, but Rafe wouldn't have changed a damned thing about it. Connor's enormous strength enveloped him in a familiar warmth, and he caught himself sniffling as he hugged back.

"Hey, get a room," a young man sniped as he strolled by, and Connor pulled himself back, nearly getting to his feet. The teenager backpedaled, throwing his hands up in surrender. "Joke, dude. Just a joke. Sheesh."

"Fucking beat it."

Rafe could feel Connor's growl across the bench.

"Settle down, Simba." Rafe laughed, patting his friend's stomach.

"Shit like that pisses me off," Con grumbled, but he sat, reaching for a piece of fish from the basket. "People should be able to fucking hug or love who they want without some asshole getting their nose into it."

"Even if it's me and Q?" Rafe teased, withholding the vinegar from Connor's grasping hand.

"Tell you what, Andrade—you hook up with my baby brother, and you're on your own with it. No interference from me," Connor promised. "Quinn's a big boy, but don't sow what you can't reap. You want to take on a Morgan? Make sure you've got the balls for it or don't come to the table."

"Not like he'd have me," he snorted, giving up the malt.

It was the scariest thing Rafe'd ever done—admitting he wanted Quinn Morgan in a way other than a quiet chat over steaming coffee or nudged up against him at Brigid's table. The want of Quinn hit Rafe hard in the chest, and he struggled to breathe, fighting to pull air into himself and listen to Connor go on about a relationship Rafe never thought he'd ever contemplate.

Having Quinn as a lover was never something within reach. Hell, he'd sooner thought to be a rock star than stealing more than a kiss from Connor's sweet-mouthed younger brother. But there he was, fingers sore from playing an old bass and sipping Orange Bang while *thinking* about Quinn's lanky body and pretty face.

"Oh, he'd probably have you. Maybe. You'll just have a fight bringing him in, 'cause he's clueless most of the time—" Connor's phone burbled with an alarming shriek, and he dropped his fish. The grin he'd had plastered on his face froze off, and Connor hastily wiped his free hand on his jeans as he answered the call.

"What's up?" Rafe leaned forward, drink and fries forgotten. "Con, what the fuck is going on?"

"Be right there, Da." Connor hung up, then tossed a handful of napkins at Rafe. "Here, let's clean this shit up. We've got to get going. Someone just tried to kill Quinn. And Da says it's not the first fucking time of it. Seems like I've got to go and rattle some sense into baby brother's brain before Da cracks his skull open."

"BOMB SQUAD'S taking their fucking time," Connor growled, pacing off the same ten feet he'd already stalked over at least twenty times before.

"I'm pretty sure the bomb part of the day is over." Quinn rested his elbows on the step behind the one he sat on. Raia's townhouse was three doors down from his and relatively undamaged. The same couldn't be said about his. "And it's only been ten minutes since they got here. Don't we want them to take their time looking for more explosives?"

"Sometimes, Q-bert, I could use less logic and more outrage from you," his older brother grumbled. "There's Da and Kane. Maybe they've got something useful to add."

"Not Q-bert, Con," Rafe muttered barely loud enough for Quinn to catch. "Dude. Come on. We talked about that shit."

"Give it up. They don't listen." Quinn eased his hands into his pockets. "Kinda used to it."

"Yeah, you don't like it. It should stop."

Rafe's fury at his hated nickname amused him, but he was more disturbed by the bassist's hand on his lower back. Rafe's fingers made small circles up his spine, and Quinn was finding it hard to think.

"What's that tapping sound?"

"Harley. My cat." He'd put Harley into the back of Kane's SUV, securing her large kennel cage with Velcro ties. From the occasional tiny taps of her paw against the tinted glass, he guessed she was amusing herself chasing the shadows from the streetlight nearby. "She's probably hunting something only she can see. She's kind of weird that way."

"Aren't you at least a little pissed off about this, Q?" Connor snarled. "A little bit?"

"What's outrage going to get me?" he asked Con, getting another irritated hiss out of his eldest brother. "No one was hurt, and once I got Raia's dog out from under her bed, she was okay."

"And the car, little brother?" Connor shot back.

"The car wasn't mine." He made a face, swallowing a gulp as Rafe's fingers made another circuit. "The insurance guy said they'd have another one out for me to use, probably tomorrow."

"You'll be lucky if they let you have a bicycle, Q," Kane said, strolling up to Connor's side. "There's hardly anything left of the last one they gave you."

"Not my fault." Standing was better. It not only eased the ache Quinn had growing in his back but also brought him shoulder to shoulder with his brothers. "Who goes home thinking his loaner car's going to be blown to smithereens? I'm a history professor, for fuck's sake."

"That's what has me worried there, *breac*."

His father joined them, wearing every inch of cop he had in him. The uniforms he'd been talking to scattered, and Quinn watched curiously as they headed to different houses on the street.

"Rafe, good to see you. Hope you came to help talk some sense into my fool son here. God knows the first on the scene tried and got nowhere."

"Didn't they have anything better to do? It was like a fucking flash mob. What do you suppose a group of cops are called?" Quinn turned to ask Rafe. "A group of owls is called a parliament. So what would a group of cops be called? Do you know?"

"Focus, Q," Connor interrupted.

"What's there to focus on? You three are going to stand around discussing what you think I should do, and I'm going to get slowly pissed off because none of you are going to listen to me." Looking around at his brothers and father, Quinn was slightly disgusted to see the lack of shame on their faces. "See, Rafe? Not a damned bit of respect. It's like I'm still three and licking electrical sockets."

"Yer not thinking straight, *a tríu*." His father spoke up. They ringed him, hedging Quinn in against the stairs. "Someone is trying to kill ye."

"Donal," Rafe spoke up. "Space, man. Give him some space."

It was odd having Rafe stand as a wall between him and his family. Odd but… nice.

Surprisingly, his brothers stepped back, but his father appeared reluctant to move. Donal frowned.

"This is serious. The truck and now this. What does he have to do to ye for ye to realize he means business?"

"I know he means business," Quinn replied softly. "Doesn't mean I'm going to let this asshole get to me. You're the cops. I'm not interfering, but I'm not going to just curl up into a ball and let him kick at me, Da."

He took a step forward, pushing his way into the space left between them. His father and brothers all reacted the same way, a tilt of their chins and a defiant challenge flaring in their hard gazes, but none of them stepped back. It was typical of the older Morgans and a position Quinn found himself in time and time again—crowded in and coddled.

Rafe's presence was new—a startling, confusingly happy new Quinn couldn't spare a moment to examine. Still, the quiver in his belly settled when Rafe's hand pressed flat up against his back again.

"Yer going to have to take a leave of absence," Donal declared. "Until we get this guy locked down."

"It's break right now. A week and change. I'm just doing papers and consults right now. After that I start classes again." He shook his head to stave off their protests, but the arguments came at him as hot and fast as the explosion he'd just gone through. "I can't let you all run my life. I love you, but I just can't. If I did, you'd have me bundled up and carted off to the attic to wait for my arsenic cookies."

"This isn't just your life that's been affected here, Quinn." Kane shot a cop look at their father, having a silent conversation between them in the split second between glances and Donal's nod. "You've got to know the family's going to be worried about you."

They had cop discussions all the time, a few grumbled words, a muttering, and plenty of mouth movement that ended up with Quinn somehow on the outside looking in on nearly every bad situation he was involved in.

"Can he go back into his house?" Rafe pulled in closer, and Quinn found himself leaning against him, grateful for the touch. "Or is it unsafe?"

"Guessing they won't let him back into the house. It's bad and needs some work. Foundation's cracked. The fire burned hot and fast." Kane nodded to the Audi's smoking remains. "What you heard go sky high was the metal fuel cans this asshole dumped by the car. One of them landed under the car, but the main problem was the guy broke off a gas line lever. Leak caught fire, and that's what blew the driveway."

"Probably ignited the gas tank too." Connor wrinkled his nose. "Not sure how that would work. You'd think it could take that kind of flame, but I've seen it happen."

Kane grunted back. "Burned pretty hot there for a bit. Could have found a seal—"

"Can we shut up about the fire and get back to me not being able to get back into my house?" Quinn grumbled. "What the hell am I supposed to do now?"

"Now, little brother—" Kane grinned wickedly. "—you move in with me where I can watch you."

HIS RINGING phone was a lifesaver. Or at least a chance to close the bedroom door behind him and hide. And if there was one thing Quinn wanted desperately, it was a chance to hide.

"Hey, Q." Rafe's silky voice tickled Quinn's ear. "How're you feeling? Doing okay? Been thinking about you."

Just those words, spoken in Rafe's soft husky rasp, and Quinn's world turned golden.

"Yeah, I'm… okay." He slid his slug of a cat toward the far side of the bed, then lay down. Stretched out over the duvet, Quinn sank his head into the pillows. "Kind of tired. It's been rough."

"Kane being an asshole rough or just everything all adding up together?"

That was the best part about Rafe for Quinn. The easygoing acceptance of Quinn's sometimes too-tight skin. Not everyone understood how Quinn felt full, past emotionally and into a physical tautness when too much too soon happened around him. Even heading up to his room for a space to breathe in was met with questions, well-meaning ones, but an assault on Quinn's senses just the same.

He'd been coaxed and prodded to stay down-stairs, to interact with everyone else when the last thing Quinn wanted or needed was to breathe air warmed by someone else's lungs. Rafe got that. Rafe understood that.

Which was probably why Quinn was relieved to hear Rafe's voice in the middle of his overstimulated breaking point instead of one of his siblings'.

"Talk to me, magpie. What's going on in that busy head of yours? You're awfully quiet." Rafe cleared his throat. "Unless you want some down time. No worries on that. I can hang—"

"No, no. *You* I want to talk to." He snuggled down into the bed, getting comfortable. "I'm just trying to get... trying to get things to fit around me."

The pillows were unfamiliar. Not bad, just unfa-miliar. Donal'd been firm about him not taking any-thing out of his house but some clothes and the cat, but Quinn wished he'd thought to grab his bed pil-lows. It would make sleeping that much easier. Harley appeared to not be bothered as she stamped out a hol-low in one, then curled her slinky body into it.

"I can hear you nesting," Rafe teased. "Comfortable?"

"Now." Quinn sighed, toeing off his shoes. "Okay. Really now."

"Tell me how you're doing. Gotta be shitty pick-ing up pieces of your life and going over to Kane's."

"Miki's. And Kane's. And Sionn's. And Damie's." He knew he sounded irritated, but Quinn'd gone past caring. "Shit, even the dog's got an opinion. Harley's not too happy about Dude's existence. If there was a volcano nearby, there'd be a virgin canine sacrifice."

"I think I can safely say that dog's not a virgin. Sionn said he was packing up until a couple of months ago. Maybe six, tops." Quinn could *hear* Rafe's smirk. "Dude's partially Kane's dog too. Surprised the mutt isn't as bowlegged as his master."

"Kane's not that bad." It was a weak protest. Kane definitely *was* that bad, something Quinn learned after discovering the house had no-sex zones mapped out among its inhabitants.

"Q, somebody can get pregnant just by standing *between* Miki and Kane," Rafe teased. "Just don't sit on anything without a tarp on it."

"I thought that was only for murders."

"No. You don't *stand* on a tarp. Walk into an office, and there's a tarp. End game. Sit on a tarp in Kane's house, don't get pregnant," Rafe clarified. "But I can see how you'd get confused."

They went silly. They usually did. Talking with Rafe was like sliding into a sun-warmed freshwater pool, its soothing movements lapping over his body. Quinn felt his muscles unclench, his hips sink down and loosen. A few minutes passed, and he realized it didn't hurt anymore to breathe.

It *always* hurt to breathe.

There were prickles and stones, small hiccups in a road of conversation where he stubbed himself to a stupor, playing pinball among unseen walls or things he should have taken care for. Quinn couldn't begin to count the times when he said something and it poured out of him sideways, splashing acid instead of rose petals, burning the person's ear.

He had no fear of that with Rafe.

There was never, *ever* any fear with Rafe.

He must have said something to Quinn, something Quinn should have answered, because a tickling whistle sounded through the phone. Jerking his attention away from the soft lull of his mind, Quinn blurted out, "I'm not asleep."

"Didn't think you were, babe. I could hear you breathing. And thinking." A laugh, teasing to play, not to hurt, then Rafe rumbled, "Like the purr of my Chevelle. Listening to you think. I like watching you think too. Your eyes go all misty Irish green, like if I could fall into them, I'd find stone circles and rivers and daisy-covered hills."

"I like that," Quinn murmured back. "That I can just think with you. That I can talk to you."

"Always, magpie. Always."

Rafe was silent. Then Quinn heard him sigh, a heavy weight of air pushing out of Rafe's soul.

"I never meant to hurt you, Q. Back then. Well, now too, but really, back then."

There wasn't ever a time when Quinn couldn't turn around and find the specter of his youthful disillusionment haunting his every step. To have Rafe drag its corpse out, slathering it with an apology he didn't need to make, was not something Quinn ever wanted to face.

"What did Connor tell you? About what I said… then?"

"That you were hurting inside. And that you loved me." Another sigh, this time wistful. "You were distraught because I'd left. Because I didn't see you as someone worth loving. That I'd broke you somehow by leaving. But we'd never… you and I never once crossed that line. I couldn't back then, Q. Shit,

I barely had enough to offer myself, much less something you could hang onto. But you've got to know, I never thought you were shit. If I'd known—"

"You would have had to leave anyway, Rafe," he said gently. "I never told you I loved you, and what could you have done with it? Dated me? I was fifteen. And pretty fucked-up. I had some therapist telling me I liked being eccentric and weird... and just to cut it out, or that I'd grow out of it. There were five doctors playing a shell game with placebos and drugs, thinking they could just snap me out of a depression with a bit of sugar candy and shaming.

"I was too young, scared to be gay, and trying to carve off pieces of who I was just so I could fit into a box someone made for me." Quinn sighed, rubbing at his face. "It just got all too much. And I... missed you. I've got my family, yeah, but they didn't get it... most of them still don't get it, but you always did. You made me feel normal—*my* normal—and I just couldn't see past the darkness I was drowning in."

"I came back. To see you. To find you in that."

Rafe's voice broke, taking a piece of Quinn's heart with it.

"You're doing okay now, right?"

"Yeah, a lot better. Stronger. I know me now." Quinn caught himself before he confessed his soul still ached for Rafe to be near. "I'm okay."

"Just want you to know one thing, magpie."

"What's that, Andrade?" he asked, keeping his tone as light as he could.

"I'll always come and find you. I will always come see you. No matter what. No matter where," Rafe promised, his words thick with emotion.

"You're never going to be in that darkness again, magpie. Not as long as I'm around. I swear on everything I am... everything I have, I will *never* let you drown."

CHAPTER SIX

The road holds no life
Nothing to keep me warm
Hotel rooms bleached and fallow
Strings leaving my tips all torn
Just one more day without you
Another day gone in time
I'm another step away from you, baby
Please don't forget that you're mine
—Love Letter to the Lost

STEAM ROSE up from the blacktop beneath their feet as the morning air heated up Beach Street. The cool fog tightened its grip on the piers, refusing to loosen its murky gray embrace despite the sun's best efforts to pierce through the almost-drizzle Sionn and Rafe ran through. At 5:00 a.m. the docks were sparsely populated, but the sea birds were already out in force, pecking through the pockets of debris lying in the gutter, looking for a greasy undisturbed breakfast before the tourists descended, and battles would be fought over scraps of unattended food.

Sionn slowed as they hit the long stretch before Pier 39, and Rafe threw him a curious look, shortening his steps to keep in time with his best friend. Nodding at Finnegan's coming into view through the patchy fog, Sionn grunted between exhales, "Let's call it at five miles today. Didn't get much sleep."

"Getting old, Murphy," Rafe teased. "Sprint it the rest of the way and beat me. Then I'll call it good. Lose and we go another two."

It was a hard run, flat-out and full speed across cold, damp concrete, their feet kicking up sprays as they pounded through the walk's shallow puddles. Rafe liked the burn in his lungs as the rain finally hit the docks.

Rafe could barely hear the sea lions barking over his huffing breaths, and he'd lost Sionn somewhere behind him, but he couldn't risk a glance back. A few feet more, and he would have had it, but Sionn's powerful body lunged past his shoulder just as Rafe reached the pub's patio railing. His friend grabbed at Rafe's ponytail as he went by, jerking Rafe's head back with a quick, sharp tug.

"Fucker," Rafe gasped, pushing forward to catch up, but Sionn beat him to the door. Pushing his friend on the shoulder, he grumbled, "Cheating asshole."

"Winning's winning," Sionn shot back, laughing as he got out his keys.

Rafe collapsed into a chair on the pub's covered outside patio. He liked the pier best at the brush of dawn, when the only ones out were the hard core and the antisocial.

A woman setting up the sand-in-a-bottle shop hummed loud enough to startle the gulls angling for space near the pub's railing, their beady eyes sharp for a handout. A few feet away, a pear-shaped man dressed in pink sweats and neon-green sneakers stretched his legs, doing soft lunges to lengthen and warm his muscles. He caught Rafe staring his way, and his slight frown turned into a smile when Rafe threw him a thumbs-up and wished him a good run.

The pier was like a second home in a way. Rafe'd spent countless hours busing tables and slinging food out of Finnegan's kitchen before he'd made a living as a musician. It was too quiet, he realized, much too quiet without Gran around. He still felt odd sitting down at the pub, on edge and ready for the curled-over, cheroot-smoking old Irish woman to turn a corner to harass him into working the floor.

"Shit, fucking platinum records out my ass, and the old woman had me behind the counter pulling pints." He snorted, remembering the last time he'd seen her, a wrinkled despot with a wicked broom and an evil eye sharp enough to make a pope blush with guilt. "Gran. God help those fucking angels up there with you. You're probably chewing them new assholes 'cause they're singing near your cloud."

Sionn's voice carried through the partially open door as he spoke to his manager, his rolling Irish baritone smoothing the way to conning her into making them coffee. A few seconds later, Sionn emerged from the pub with a tray of shortbread, scones, and condiment cups filled with butter, then set it down on the table in front of Rafe.

"No stale bagels, then? What happened to a man's full breakfast? Damn, I was looking forward to the slight high all of those old poppy seeds would have given me." Rafe reached for one of the scones, juggling it when the soft cake burned his fingers. "Shit, that's hot."

"Leigh just made them, so yeah, they're hot. It's too early for the bacon and eggs." Sionn kicked at Rafe's foot as he sat down. "And none of that shite about poppy seeds from you. Those days are done and gone, boyo."

"Yep, only jalapeño cheese for me now. Not even sesame bagels, 'cause those are just gateway bagels to the hard-core stuff." Rafe snorted. "It was a joke, Murphy. Get a sense of humor."

"Joking right back, Andrade." Sionn poked Rafe's arm with a plastic knife. "And don't use all the butter. Coffee's coming in a bit. I got kicked out of my own pub. Did you hear that?"

"Your Irish is on thick this morning." He bit into a buttered scone and moaned at the melt of orange and cranberries on his tongue.

"I think it gets worse now that Quinn and Kane are both there. Wasn't so bad with just Kane, but Quinn, he breaks out in Gaelic when he's talking, and my brain just slides in right behind him. A week's gone now, and they're not any closer to finding out who set fire to Q's car." Sionn split his scone in two. "The brothers Morgan are about to rip each other's throats out, but no way the family's going to let Quinn head back to that house of his without them knowing he's safe."

"Thought the place was kind of fucked-up. The front wall took some major damage. Heard Connor say it's two steps away from being condemned." He fought Sionn for the orange marmalade, victoriously scooping some on a knife, then getting stabbed with Sionn's in return. "He could always go live up at the main house. You know Brigid would love to get her hands on him again."

"Yeah, that's not going to happen. Quinn needs his space. And, well, we're just *loud*. I can see him wincing. Con and Forest's place is a wreck. Can't see him going there. And no one will let him go to a hotel. Not safe enough. Not really. I'd offer one of my places, but we're back to the not secure enough. If I get killed in my sleep, you know Q's done it."

A clatter of coffee cups behind them warned Sionn to get out of Leigh's way as she came through the front doors.

"Like Q would kill you." Rafe snorted. "He'd skin you alive and experiment on you first."

Sionn snorted. "And then there's Damie giving Quinn the eye when he comes out of the shower wearing nothing but a towel. I know he's whistling at him to get a rise out of me, but really, Q's not one for teasing. You know how Quinn is. That, and his fuck-ugly cat and Dude do *not* get along."

The thought of Quinn naked and wet short-circuited Rafe's brain, and he mumbled something under his breath about Damie needing to keep his eyes to himself when Leigh nudged his shoulder in a silent hello.

Her hair amused Rafe to no end. A jumble of purple and blue curls poufed out from ponytails on either side of her head, and she snarled at Sionn when he tried to take the tray from her. Her jeans were dusted with a bit of flour on her thigh, and her worn Finnegan's Pub shirt definitely had seen better days, but her smile was bright when she spotted Rafe at the table.

"Sit your fucking ass down and pretend you own the place, Murphy." Leigh warned Sionn off. "Rafe, can't you take him someplace and drop him off a pier? He's underfoot."

"Sorry—best friend. Brother really," Rafe drawled. "Kind of the only family I've got now that my mom's gone and found God... again."

"Hey, the Morgans adore you, fuckwad." Sionn's protest was hot and fierce. "Dare you to say *that* in front of Brigid."

"The Morgans adore everyone. It's kind of what they do." He shrugged off the sentiment but gave Sionn's arm a hearty squeeze. "And don't get all mushy on me, Murphy. Your gushing back makes me speechless."

"Git," Sionn muttered at Rafe as Leigh left. "You know it's been the two of us since forever. Don't be making a thing of it now."

They'd met over fists and hard words, two ill-fitting pieces in a puzzle neither one of them were familiar with. Sionn had it easier being a Morgan cousin, and he'd already grown into his broad shoulders but hadn't quite mastered his gangly legs. Not knowing the Morgan connection, Rafe'd gotten into it with the Irish hazard, and they'd bonded over licking their wounds while waiting for the principal's decision on their punishment.

It'd been Sionn who'd been there for him when the need for drugs ripped through his blood, and he'd helped Sionn get stinking drunk over the deaths he'd seen. Damien'd come as a surprise, cutting through Sionn's affable but distant personality, and Rafe still reeled at the idea of his best friend being with Sinner's Gin's lead guitarist.

Their lives had definitely jumped down a rabbit hole and gone surreal.

"Not sleeping because you're doing too much fucking? Or does Damien snore?" Rafe cocked his head when Sionn yawned. "Wait, I just thought of something. When you two go at it... do you do it all polite and British? All... my God that's brilliant and oh, that's nice? And when you're all done, do you shake hands and say, 'Well, that was okay. Good job'?"

"For the last time, brilliant is best, okay and nice are good, and good is just... well, decent," Sionn growled over his coffee. "And no, not fucking. Mostly, the three of them—D, Miki, and Forest—muttering together and talking about bassists. They've been back and forth to the Sound at all hours of the night for auditions...."

Rafe's heart stopped. He could still hear it, but nothing in him moved. There was a gurgle in the back of his brain, just enough for him to know it was still working, but nothing else functioned. Instead he'd fixed on a single point in Sionn's rambling diatribe.

Damien was actually going through with it, and Sinner's Gin needed a bassist.

"What's going on in that rotten head of yours, Andrade?" Sionn eyed him suspiciously. "You look kind of sick to your stomach but happy at the same time."

"How long has Damien been looking for a bassist? I know he was talking about it, but St. John didn't sound like he was all that into going on the road." Rafe bit his lower lip. "Fuck, I'd kill to get in front of them."

His brain flirted with the idea of begging Sionn to speak to Damien, but his gut and heart iced over at the thought. It was too much to ask for. Especially of Sionn. Their friendship—their kinship—was too important, too precious for Rafe to risk muddying with favors and broken promises. But the lure of it—of begging for a chance to play again—burned through Rafe hotter than any drug hook he'd ever had.

Because if Rafe was going to be completely honest, he was addicted to music and the stage a hell of a lot more than any chemical he'd pumped into his system.

"No," Sionn muttered, shaking his head. "You don't want in on that, Rafe. It'd be crazy to."

"I haven't asked you for it." A rattle of chains against wood drew Rafe's attention, and he glanced over toward the square, where a coffee kiosk was beginning its morning setup. "I wouldn't put you between me and Damie. That's not like me. You know that."

"Yeah, but I also know you're itching to be back into it," Sionn pointed out. "Thing is, brother, you can't do that life anymore. Look what it did to you the last time. You've just come back from the edge of that hell. I don't want to—I can't risk losing you to it again."

"I can do this, Sionn. Fuck, I *have* to do this. Or at least try." It was hard to explain away the burn in his blood, especially to someone who'd never felt the itch to cut himself open and have music pour free from inside him. As much as he loved Sionn, it was something they'd never shared. Of course, it went both ways. *He'd* never understood Sionn's need to run into dangerous situations with all guns blazing. "I just need the chance. Shit, even if I don't make it in with them, just getting the chance would be great."

"I don't agree with you," his friend argued, his words nearly lost in a barrage of seagull cries as the birds descended on the scone he'd crumbled up and tossed onto the walk. "You get around those crowds, those people who'd want to take you for a ride with them, and then what? You're back to where you were before. Maybe even worse. I don't want the next call I get to be that you're the one lying dead on that carpet instead of that boy you were with."

"I need the music more than I need the drugs, Sionn," Rafe pleaded softly, wishing he could get Sionn to understand. "I am going crazy here, dude. No one will give me the fucking time of day because of how badly I fucked up. I get that. I do. But shit, you want to know what my day's like? I get up in the morning, have some coffee, and go on a run with you, or we hit the gym. And *that's* the highlight of my day. I love you, Sionn, but I can't have you be the best part of my life."

"Shit, you've got money coming out of your ears—"

"It's not about the money, Sionn. It's about the music. It's about the stage. It's about laying down a bass line and having other guys build on top of that. I *miss* being the foundation of a song. Of having licks and rolls layering on top of what I'm playing." His breath came hot out of his lungs as he spoke. "I'm not a songwriter. I can add in stuff or shift how something's written, but the crafting it all up, I can't do that. I'm not that kind of smart. Shit, I'm not any kind of smart. Playing's all I know. It's all I'm good at. And now, *right now*, it's all I'm *not* doing."

"Maybe you should go get laid, boyo." Sionn sighed heavily, refilling his cup from the carafe

Leigh'd given them. "Or maybe what you need, An-drade, is to fall in love."

"That's the *last* thing in the world I want, Mur-phy," Rafe snorted, but his heart flashed on Quinn. "I barely like *me* right now. You expect me to love someone else?"

"Tell you what, how about if you show up at one of the Sunday dinners? This coming one. We're go-ing to be there. Maybe that's a good time you can ap-proach my Damie." Sionn tapped his fingers against the rim of his mug. "I can't say he'll give you the time of day, but it's your best bet."

"That's a good idea. Right after Brigid's done squeezing the blood out of my bones." Rafe grimaced. "She gave me a lot of shit when I was in rehab. Wasn't sure what was worse, group therapy or her phone calls."

"At least you got calls," he pointed out. "That's not a bad thing."

"Damned shit more than I got from my own mom." His words came out bitter, harsher than he'd intended, but the sting of it all still hurt. They'd never been close. She worked, and well, he'd been an as-shole of a kid, but Rafe'd always thought she'd be there if shit ever got real. He already blamed himself for Mark's death. He hadn't really needed his own mother to call him a murderer.

"Thought things were better now."

"Better? Yeah, we talk. It's hard, but I'm trying." He shrugged. "I don't know if she's trying. I guess I'm still kind of pissed off that she wasn't... *there*. After-wards. I'm good enough to take a house and money from but not good enough to give the benefit of the doubt? That kind of shit stays with me."

"And Brigid caring about you makes it worse?" Sionn grunted at Rafe's nod. "Yeah, I can see that. Same thing with my da and them. There's that moment when you stop asking 'Why aren't I good enough?' and start asking 'Why aren't you better than you are?' Hardest thing in the world is finding out your parents are people."

"That, and they have sex," Rafe grumbled. "Brigid and Donal. That's something I never needed to walk in on. Okay, Murphy. I'll go to the Sunday thing. Just do me a favor."

"I'm already not speaking to Damie about you. Isn't that enough?"

"No. I want you to promise me that if it looks like Donal or Brigid have got me cornered, you'd come rescue me."

"Just like the old days, then?"

"Yeah." He grinned foolishly at Sionn. "Just like the old days."

"And the answer to that, boyo, is also no." Sionn patted Rafe's cheek. "It's time you grew up and fought your own battles on all fronts, Andrade. Just like the rest of us have."

"WHAT THE fuck is that?" Rafe recoiled at the wrinkled green ball sac of a squash in Quinn's hand. "Dude, put that down before it releases its tentacles and sucks the salt out of your body."

Rafe's aversion to all things vegetable was well known in the family, but Quinn liked poking at him for it all the same. "It's bitter melon. Supposed to be good for you."

"So's shoving coffee up your colon, but I don't do that either." Rafe bared his teeth and took a step back.

That gave Quinn pause. "Really? People really do that?"

"Yep. Big thing in Los Angeles. Those people"—he waved a bunch of leeks under Quinn's nose—"are fucking crazy."

Spread out over St. Patrick's parking lot, the farmers' market sat in the cathedral's shade, a weekly sprawl of tables and tents set up by local agriculturists, craftsmen, bakers, and the occasional pickle maker. An olive briner did a brisk business next to a woman who made artisan breads, his flavored oils and vinegars poured out into disposable paper cups to use as dip for the warm, crusty pieces she handed out for samples.

Children darted in between adults, eating their way through the afternoon and probably spoiling their evening meal, but harried parents seemed to care less about what they ate so long as they were still in sight. A woman with three identical toddlers battled with one flopped onto the asphalt, its high-pitched caterwauling growing louder and louder despite its mother's cajoling. A second later, another woman strode out from a fruit stand, scooped up the ill-behaved child without even stopping, then carried it off with a jaunty wave to her partner.

Quinn wasn't sure whose sigh of relief was larger—the mother's or Rafe's.

"Do you like kids?" he ventured.

"In theory? Yes. In practice, haven't had any," Rafe said with a shrug. "Do Ian and Ryan count?"

"Sort of." Quinn cocked his head, counting back the years. "You were around when Ryan was born, yes?"

"Yeah, Ian too."

He dodged a little girl with a triple-decker ice cream cone, lifting his arms up over his head when it appeared she was heading straight for him. The girl careened to the side, drawn off by a gentle tug on her shirt by a gray-haired older woman following her.

"Braeden? I don't think he was ever a kid. Your mom found him under a cabbage chewing up rocks and some shit like that. What about you? Kids?"

"To keep? Like a father? Or just in general?" A crackling fear iced down Quinn's spine at the thought of a child looking to him for guidance. "My gut just now said no. I will go with my instincts and say no. Connor and Forest. They're very paternal. They can have them."

"I can see Connor showing up for parents' assistance committees all SWATed up and wiping ketchup off of some petri-dished Morgan with big blue eyes and a black mop of hair." Rafe shook his head. "Those husbands aren't going to know what hit them when their wives go home and jump them. Probably think someone's serving raw oysters and rhino-horn truffles at the bake-sale meetings. So no little Quinns?"

"I'm gay," Quinn reminded him.

"Yeah, best part about you, Q." Rafe stalled a bit, patting Quinn's ass. "This too."

Quinn grabbed at Rafe's hand to push it away, but Rafe worked their fingers together. Quinn gave a gentle tug, a halfhearted attempt to get loose, but Rafe refused to let him go. Giving an exaggerated sigh of resignation, Quinn fell into step next to him, their clasped hands swinging slightly as they walked.

"You've got a cat, though, right? Cats are okay."

Rafe smiled at Quinn's mumbled, "Sometimes."

"How about dogs? I like dogs."

"Harder to take care of. You have to be there at certain times. Dogs need a schedule." A certain blond mutt stuck in Quinn's mind. "And some of them steal shit. I can't have any clothes out in the bedroom I'm in, or Dude'll take them."

"Just your stuff? Or does he do it to everyone?"

"Me. Damie. Kane. Not sure if it's because he likes us or if it's just because he hates people with black hair."

"Never thought about that. Good common denominator. I'd have gone for Morgan, but that would leave out Damie. Sionn's a Finnegan, via Murphy. My shit would be safe." Rafe ran his other hand through his sun-gilded hair. "Speaking of Sionn, talked to him today about Damie and Miki's band. He said they're looking for a bassist."

Quinn's stomach sank, but he soldiered on, barely missing a step. "Is that really what you want? To go on the road and all of that?"

"Playing, yes. Best thing about Damie and his crew? I don't think they'll be slogging on the road. Miki won't be able to survive that kind of long haul." There was something dark in Rafe's expression, a weight pulling down the brightness in his spirit. "Want the truth, Q?"

"Please." Quinn tightened his grip slightly, a gentle squeeze meant to comfort.

"I know I'd be safe with them, you know?"

They'd reached the end of one line, cooled under thick shade from a row of old tall trees growing along the edge of the lot. Rafe stopped, sliding his feet on either side of Quinn's so they stood facing one another, their chests brushing lightly.

What Rafe said next scared Quinn much more than the thought of parenting any child.

"I can't be near drugs, Q. Not even close." Rafe's gaze drifted off of Quinn's face, fixing on something off in the distance. "I crawl into that pill bottle one more time, I'm not going to make it out. I'll fucking die, Q. And I'll kill off any love I've got from someone else along the way."

"Rafe…. Raphael, you're not—"

"You didn't see me, Q. I couldn't let you see me. Not like that." Rafe's brown eyes swam with tears, glazing them with a sheen. "I burned every bridge I had. Hell, I'm surprised your mom and dad are still talking to me. God knows my mom's iffy sometimes. The shit I did. The crap I said to them. I can't do that again, Quinn. And I sure as shit don't ever want to do that to you."

"Is that why you told Mum I couldn't go see you down in Los Angeles?" He captured Rafe's chin in his free hand, keeping a tight hold on Rafe's hand with the other. "Because you think I couldn't stand to see you like that?"

"I couldn't… risk it. Not you, Q. Never you." Rafe pushed in tight, letting go of Quinn's hand to wrap his arms around Quinn's waist. Burying his face in the crook of Quinn's neck, he rocked them slightly, sighing when Quinn's arms came up to hold him. "*God*, magpie. I just couldn't let you see how far I fell. How much I fucked up."

"Well, that's stupid," Quinn murmured, stroking at Rafe's back. "You saw me when I was so broken I wanted to fall… wanted to die… and you didn't care. You were there for me. You left the road to be with me. Why would you think I'd turn away from you when you needed me the most?"

"'Cause I'm stupid? I was scared?" Rafe laughed, sniffing through his tears. "I couldn't lose you, Q. I was so fucking ashamed, and now I'm scared shitless I'm not good enough to stand up next to those guys and play… because they're that good, and I'm a fucking broken mess. And you'll see me fail there too. Then what?"

"I'm yours, Rafe. Through everything. I'll always be here." He held on tight, feeling Rafe's sob shudder through their entwined bodies. "They'd be stupid to not want you. You're Rafe fucking Andrade, rock god. Who is now leaking down my neck."

"I think that's snot," Rafe mumbled.

"Oh." Quinn chuckled. "That's okay, then. Just glycoproteins and water. Drool you've got to watch out for. Being a god and everything. Your saliva could turn out to be venomous."

"You are so damned weird, Q." Rafe's burst of laughter felt good against Quinn's skin. "And thank fucking God for it because I wouldn't have you any other way."

THERE WAS no mistaking death had come. It'd struck often in San Francisco, and Kane knew of at least three people in the city who'd gone pining for the fjords just that Sunday morning. The bloody, pulpy remains lying at Kane's feet brought the number to four.

Chinatown stretched out around them, a draconian maze of alleys and buildings layered thick with soot and desperation. It was too early for tourists, but the back streets were already bustling with deliveries and people who saw nothing, heard nothing, and who slipped away into the shadows like liquid when anyone who smelled of cop drew near.

Fog settled down deep into the cracks between the pressed-in buildings, pushing back the dank, ripe-green stench leeching out from the old cobblestone corridors. The cold mists ran thick, steeping the alleys in its own tongue-scraping shadowy tea, providing enough cover for a rattle of roaches to brave the heavy cop boots stomping back and forth. The insects slipped out from under a row of green dumpsters, their sides scraped and black with cast-off food, a skittering tide of chitin and antenna rolling in and out to sip at the body's leaking remains.

Restaurants dominated this end of the area, cramped little holes manned by generations of silent, angry people working off loan-shark debts incurred by their grandfathers. Smaller unmarked businesses pocked the alleys, slender thresholds with cracked wooden doors and no signage, but the rough murmur of angry Cantonese shook through the cracks, quieting when a uniform rapped on the door in his hunt for a witness. Near the victim, a crate of cabbage sat on its side, rotting blackened heads oozing out from between wooden slats, and Kane stepped carefully around it, spotting a bristle of whiskers poking out of the sticky mess.

"Should I push in, sir?"

The uniform, a scrub-faced blond kid who creased his pants nearly to a razor point, adjusted his cap and called out to Kane as he walked by. Even in the alley's milky dimness, Kane could see the green tint in the young cop's face and how his too-bright eyes slid away from the remains.

"Nah, leave it." He steered the young man to a pack of hunched-over elderly women at the far end of the alley, their fingers coated with a layer of flour. "Chances are they're prepping the kitchen and left the security door open. It gets hot as shit in the back, and they'd want the cold air. See if any of them saw something. Take Muñoz with you if you need help with translating."

Kane knew enough Cantonese to know it would be bad news all around if one of those doors opened up. He'd run with Vice for a few years before being tapped for Homicide, and he'd been quickly educated on how much violence lay behind Chinatown's thin wooden planks.

Cause of death was going to be muddied, despite the apparent battering. Crouching a few feet away from the victim, Horan from Medical and Forensics took pictures of teeth and bone splinters while instructing her assistant on how to angle a measuring T so she could capture a reference scale. The blonde medical examiner looked up when Kane stepped over, and he held out a hand to help her up as she began to rise.

"Thanks." She took his hand, using it to support herself. "Where's your partner? I thought he was back on the job."

"Yeah, he's all blessed and Pope-ified. Kel's doing a perimeter run around the block with the cadaver dogs." Kane stood steady as Horan got herself upright.

Perky and amiable, Horan was both a blessing and a curse on a crime scene. Blessing because Kane knew if there was something to be found, she'd be the one to dig it out, but a curse because the petite blonde was exacting, taking hours to process a scene before kicking information out for an investigating officer.

He was going to try anyway. "Got anything?"

"Really? We've been here for an hour, and you want something?" Her snort was a touch away from derisive, but Horan's smile lessened its sting. "Cause of death could be a beating or a gunshot. I won't know until I get him on the slab. I can tell you we found a wallet, but I can't confirm ID or even if it's the right guy until I match the body to prints."

"Lots of blood," Kane murmured, sniffing the air. "Can't tell if there's body decay or if that's the damned rotten food."

"I'd say he's fresh. Rigor and body temp are pretty consistent with death happening a few hours out. I'm even going to go out on a limb and say he was killed elsewhere and dumped here. Alessia! Do you have a moment to give to Detective Morgan here?"

The morgue doctor called out to a tall, willowy young woman in forensic scrubs digging carefully through an overturned trash can. The Italian woman picked her way carefully out of the area, avoiding the evidence lines the forensics team laid down.

"Alessia—Doctor De Gustibus—just joined our team. Alessia, this one's Kane. There's a few other Morgans you'll run into. If you're lucky, and it's a long night, this one will bring you coffee."

"My da would bring you coffee," Kane muttered. "I think."

"Morgan, if your father ever is called onto a scene I'm working, coffee's going to be the last thing on my mind." Horan snorted. "I heard about what happened over at your brother's place. Apparently one of the tech guys told Donal he didn't know when he'd get to working on the debris. Last I heard, the guy's working the road-kill unit on the Bay bridge."

"Good to meet you, sir." Smiling broadly at Kane, she brought up her notes on the tablet she'd been using.

"Oh no, sir's my da. Can't miss him. He's the one with captain bars. Kane's fine. Or Morgan. What do you have so far?"

"Victim appears to have been killed off-site—"

"Still say there's a lot of blood for an off-site kill here, Horan," Kane rumbled.

"She's getting to it. Patience, Morgan," the doctor shushed him. "Go on, Alessia. He's probably just grumpy because he hasn't had coffee yet."

"It's five in the morning, and I left Miki curled up in bed more than an hour ago. Coffee's been had. I'm about ready for my third cup," Kane grunted. "Sorry, go on."

"There's a bloodied tarp tucked under the edge of the dumpster. I'm going to go out on a limb and say the victim was killed on top of it, then rolled up and transported here." The technician tapped through her notes. "Splatter marks on the tarp are consistent with a blunt object hit, and when he stashed the tarp, he took it out of the elements, protecting the evidence. The kill was pretty recent. Some of the inside folds are still damp and sticky."

"Question we'd be asking is, did he shove the tarp there on purpose? Or was it convenient?" Kane mulled, turning to look at the scene. "There's bits and pieces of the victim strewn from that box there to the dumpster. Alleyway's tight. Our killer would have had to pull, then drag the victim over there, then back out to the street. I wouldn't trust getting anything wider than a speck of a car in here."

"Unless he backed in," the technician suggested.

"Either way, there's no getting around the dumpster unless you're on a motorcycle, and that wouldn't happen here. Too hard to handle and balance. Had to be a car." Kane took another look at the battered body. "It's a good forty feet from the street to here. If our doer parked on the street, there'd be more bits and pieces from the sidewalk over to the dumpster, and he'd have run the risk of being seen by the restaurant crews."

"Delivery truck wouldn't have fit," Horan agreed. "Those have wider wheelbases. Even some SUVs would be too wide to get in here. I can see where you're going with this, Morgan. I'll have my team check for fresh paint scrapes on the walls."

"Needle in the haystack shit, but it might help. Kel's going to see if there's cameras on the street. It'll be on this side. Hopefully we'll catch a break here." Kane tried to rub the tired out of his face. "What's the ID say? Sanchez and I can at least go hunt that down. If we knock on the door and find the guy in his bathrobe, we'll have to wait until the print run to verify ID."

"Kappelhoff. Simon Paul Kappelhoff. His address is—"

Kane didn't need to hear the rest of it. Instead he stepped in close and stared at the picture of the victim's ID. It'd been a few years since he'd seen Kappelhoff, but the man probably hadn't updated his license picture either. Kane's memory of Kappelhoff hadn't been a good one, especially since he'd been throwing books out onto the street as Kane drove up to the curb. It'd been an ugly breakup on Simon's part, a lot of shouting and accusations of emotional immaturity.

"Well, fucking hell," Kane muttered under his breath. "Professor Simon Kappelhoff."

"You know him, Morgan?" Horan asked gently.

"Yeah, kind of." Any chance of the day brightening was washed away by a flood of dread and gloom, and Kane sighed, "He's Quinn's ex-boyfriend."

CHAPTER SEVEN

Midnight, on the phone
Rafe: It was great eating lunch with you today, Q.
Quinn: You listened to me on the phone as I ate a ham sandwich in my office and talk about why I thought it was a shitty thing people never developed the ability to see other spectrums.
R: To be fair, it sounded like a really kickass ham sandwich.

SAN FRANCISCO flirted with Quinn from behind its veil of fog and drizzle. It stretched out in front of him, a lushly curved and redolent landscape of mounds and flats shimmering between thinning misty patches, a coy Rubenesque tease, casually seducing him with a peekaboo dance. He'd woken up too early to do anything other than make coffee, dress his cat in a sweater, and take her to the one spot he'd found he could breathe without the walls closing in on him— the warehouse's rooftop shanty-house tent overlooking San Francisco Bay.

Unfortunately, it was also where everyone was able to find him.

A thick faux mink blanket kept back most of the Sunday morning chill, and Harley settled her floppy body beneath the crimson cover with a contented sigh, her whippet-thin tail marking time in slow slashes over his toes. Along with the cat, he'd brought up a large, thick-walled thermos big enough to hold nearly a quart of coffee and a book he'd been meaning to finish for years, but as captivating as Kingsbury's world-building was, Quinn's thoughts wandered away from the maran-Kaiel of Geta and back to the profane destruction of his peaceful life.

The truck didn't make sense. The fire didn't make sense. Someone fucking up his car and house was insane, but as often as Quinn turned the events over in his mind, he couldn't find a connection to an event or person to the craziness he'd found himself in. And if the police didn't find one soon, he'd go crazy living in his older brother's back pocket.

"Or I'll kill all of them." He spoke to Harley's serpentine tail, nudging at his cat's belly with his bare toes. She lazily grabbed at them, a molasses-fluid movement beneath the plush cover, and her teeth gently gnawed at his anklebone, a halfhearted attack she lost interest in nearly as soon as she launched it. A few licks at the barely fanged skin, and she went slack again, her soft, even snorfling tickling the bottom of Quinn's foot.

It was a comfortable three-sided tent, and Miki'd built a nest out of papasan frames and about a thousand soft pillows on the large riser Kane'd built to keep the area out of any standing water. The Miki-nest was set to the side, away from a circle of chairs and tables where they normally gathered on clear nights, a slice of an Irish pub set above the busy streets below.

In the rain-drenched mornings, however, the nest was all Quinn's.

He dreaded the sound of the rooftop door opening, its telltale creak nearly as ominous as any below-board thump written by Poe, but he knew it would come. Hardly an hour went by without *someone* seeking him out and hunting him down, as if he'd become a fragile glass ornament being tossed around in a game of hot potato.

"It's because Mum raised them. She always has to poke. And she's passed that on to them. Each and every single one of them. Double dose for Con," Quinn muttered at his oblivious and uncaring cat. Nudging Harley again got him a tiny mewl, its sweet rasp almost drowned out by the squeak of the access door opening. "Fuck, it's like clockwork. Kane just won't leave—"

The man stepping through the swirling fog definitely wasn't his older brother. Kane never in his life possessed the liquid grace and feral prowl of the sienna-haired man walking across the warehouse rooftop. No, the slender pour of muscle and sinew coming toward him was Kane's lover, Miki, a sure sign Quinn's older brother was stooping to playing dirty to roust him out of his solitude.

But the oddly conflicted expression on Miki's face turned Quinn's snarling protest to be left alone to dust in his throat.

Quinn moved over without thinking, opening up a space for Miki. He was ill-dressed for the brisk weather, a thin T-shirt and jeans holier than Quinn's grandmother, the ex-nun. He lifted up the edge of the blanket and waited for Miki to get settled under in its toasty warmth.

Miki was having none of it.

"You've got to be fucking kidding me. Do I look like I'm going to crawl under there—"

"It's freezing, and your lips are turning blue. I have a blanket, hot coffee, and the pillows," Quinn pointed out. "It's stupid to stand there to talk to me when you could be warm. And why wouldn't you want to be warm?"

Miki's hazel eyes churned gold and flat, but he shucked his shoes off, then climbed in under the blanket. Grumbling under his breath, he shivered against Quinn. "Like some fucking slumber party or something. You guys are so damned weird."

"Weird but warm." Quinn felt Harley slither over his ankles, more than likely trying to get away from the shot of cold air he'd let in.

A moment passed, then two, and just when Quinn was about to ask what was wrong, Miki spat out, "Your fucking cousin's an asshole."

"Sionn." It wasn't a question. More an affirmation and one Quinn generally agreed with. "What's he done now?"

"I feel like I need to have this conversation someplace I can rage." Miki shifted under the blanket, sitting up against the pillows. "Fucking lying here is...

what the *hell*? Is that your cat?" He peeked under the cover. "She's got a damned sweater on. Your butt-naked, ugly cat is wearing a damned sweater, Quinn. There's something wrong there."

"Harley's not naked. She has fur. It's just very short. And the sweater keeps her warm." Quinn sighed. He liked Miki. He liked Miki for Kane. Mostly because the mercurial singer kept Quinn's older brother jumping, and despite his deep affection for Kane, there was something satisfying about watching the guy who bossed him when they were kids get his comeuppance. "Again, what's Sionn done now?"

"Fucker brought Rafe up. Sionn wants Damie—wants us—to let him audition. They're downstairs going at it." Miki stiffened when Harley crawled off Quinn's legs and went searching for a new place to perch. Quinn guessed she'd found one somewhere on Miki's body. "Swear to God, that thing bites me and I'm going to turn it into a wineskin."

"You don't even drink wine, Sinjun." Miki's bluster was more bristle than fang, and Quinn knew it. He thought on the Rafe he'd once known and compared him to the broken-spirited man he'd seen at Forest's coffee shop. When they'd been younger, Rafe'd always thrown himself into the troubles he'd caused but never dragged anyone in with him. He'd also never asked anyone for help getting out of them. "Did Rafe ask Sionn to do that? Ask Damie?"

"He says nope." Miki tensed again as Harley undulated over them, a feline basking shark moving through her warmed lair. "D got all—"

Damien hit the rooftop running. He cleared the access door's threshold before it'd begun to swing back and was nearly halfway across the long stretch of roof when it clicked shut behind him. If Quinn thought Miki'd gone stiff when Harley touched him, he was practically stone as Damien approached the tucked-away pillow mound.

"Where the fuck did you go?" Damien snarled, his feet pounding away the distance between them. "You don't fucking walk away from me when there's shit going down."

"Fuck you back, dude. That shit downstairs wasn't even about me. That was between you and your guy." Miki was gone from under the blanket, sliding out before Quinn could protest the cold. Harley mewled her displeasure, and he flipped the cover back over them, trapping what little warm air was left. "So yeah, I walked. Because it was none of my fucking business."

"It was about the band. So yeah, it involves you, asshat," Damie bit back.

The fog was rolling in thicker, refusing to let the sun in, and Quinn wondered if he and Harley could slide past the other two and back downstairs without them noticing. When Damien's angry gaze spilled over him, he tightened, aware he'd been caught in a trap he couldn't chew out of.

"Instead you're up here bitching about me to Quinn? When you should have been down there backing me up?"

"I'm really not a part of this," Quinn volunteered. It was uncomfortable being caught between the rough sandpaper of a relationship—especially one he didn't understand at times. Damien and Sinjun were... volatile, sipping fire from a hose volatile, and they were passionate about everything—music, their friendship, their loves, and now, as Quinn was recently made aware, their fighting.

"The band right now is *you*, D," Miki tossed back at his friend. "And yeah, I came up here to bitch with Quinn 'cause sometimes he's the only sane one in the house."

"You're the reason I want a damned band. We're—"

"Really. I came up here because I wanted to read. And it was six in the morning. None of you are supposed to be awake this early." Reaching down under the blanket, Quinn tried to fish a reluctant Harley out so he could beat a hasty retreat. "And... I don't know if there's an and. There's probably a but, because there always seems to be a but. But maybe not. And yes, there it is. The but."

The cat was definitely not cooperating, and Quinn sat up to peer under the blanket at her smug, wrinkled apricot face.

"You are *not* helping. Come here," he hissed at her. Harley ignored him, lifting her leg up to chew on her toes as she did every morning when Quinn got up for coffee. It was their routine—and a lost one at that.

He hated *not* having a routine. Or at least knowing where and when he could be without someone else *being* there next to him.

It was one of the things his family never seemed to understand. Just *being* made noise. On some subdermal level, he *heard* them under his skin, itching away and scratching his nerves. It wasn't as bad with Miki and Damie. Neither one of them felt the need to poke at him until he bled out of his mind—until now.

"Quinn, you know Rafe." Damie cut Quinn's wheedling short. "Tell me one good reason why I should let a fucking drug addict into my band."

"Oh, up here it's your band, but when you're screaming at Sionn it's our band?" Miki scoffed. "Make up your damned mind."

"You wanna make those calls, Sinjun?" D turned, his chin up. They were nearly the same height, but Damien's British was out, a strong slap to the face of Miki's streetwise sneer.

"You want a band so badly, just like the last time. Whatever you want, I'll be right there fucking beside you, but don't push me in front of you when Sionn pisses you off."

Miki didn't seem that impressed. Not from what Quinn could see. Especially when he stepped into Damie's space until they stood toe-to-toe.

"I'm good with you steering the whole band thing, but this whole Rafe mess—"

"Do you think it's easy with this? Andrade's a decent player. Good, even. Collins loved the fuck out of him, and look what happened to him... to them?" Damie's voice dropped soft, pleading with his best friend. "I can't have that happen to you. I can't risk you. Not again. Not like I did before."

"Fucker," Miki grumbled, grabbing at Damie to pull him into a hug. "So we don't audition Rafe."

Quinn threw his gaze up to the sky, wishing he could keep his mouth shut and let the two men deal with the ripple of Andrade hitting them as hard as it hit Quinn every time he saw Rafe. But for the remains of Sinner's Gin, Rafe loomed above them as a specter of death and destruction, not the man Quinn'd seen grow from an angry, confused boy.

"He tries, you know," Quinn said softly as he extracted himself from under the blanket, then stood up. It was better to speak softly. It drew the ear to follow the sound, forced the listener to pay attention. If he was going to trespass where angels feared to tread, Quinn knew he had to go in carefully. When both men turned to look at him, he continued, "Rafe, I mean. He tries to be better. Well, still is trying. It can't be easy to live down to everyone's expectations, even when they believe the worst of you."

"Q, Rafe's been with you guys since you were little kids, but shit happens—people change." Damie pulled himself loose of Miki's hug, but Quinn noticed Damie slid his best friend behind him, an unconscious protection he probably didn't even realize he was doing. "He seems like a nice guy. I just can't risk it. Not the band. Not Miki."

It made Quinn smile, then hurt because he couldn't remember ever having someone *not* named Morgan love him enough to stand between him and danger. There was a part of him crying at the emptiness inside him, and once again, Quinn reminded himself of the cracks in his sidewalk no one wanted to fall into. He had friends—people he knew like Graham and… sadly, his brothers and cousin—but none as fiercely loyal as Damie was with Miki. And his brothers didn't count. They were more smothering than protective.

Now there seemed to also be a Rafe when he didn't remember putting one there. Rafe stood in front of him—had before. Had since then. It was definitely time for Quinn to do some standing as well.

"Rafe gave a guy some shit that killed him," Damien said softly. "And he doesn't remember a damned thing about it. That's not the guy I want with me up on stage, and it sure as hell isn't the one I want in a tour bus with me and the guys. If he even shows up. If we do this band—when we do this band—it's got to be all in. Everyone needs to be solid."

"It's been years since that, Damien," Quinn reminded them both. "A lot's happened to all of you. You came back from the dead, and Miki fell in love. You did too. You worked hard to get here—to the coast—because you knew someone was here waiting for you, worrying for you. Rafe had a different struggle, a harder journey. You went looking for Miki. He had to go looking for himself."

"Dude, you have no idea what shit he's done. You knew him here. Not out there. Not on the road. And sure as shit not in his band," Sionn's lover pointed out.

"Everything you know is what was fed to you… sold to you," Quinn remarked. "You don't really know him. Not then when he was dying inside and not now when he's trying to live."

"He's a good bassist. Or was," Miki interrupted Damien before he could speak. Waving off his friend's withering look, Miki sneered right back. "Look, sure I liked him, and yeah, he wrote a lot of Rising Black's bass lines. Either we give him a chance or we don't. But shit, Damien, we've heard or talked to about twenty-five guys already."

"Just guys?" Quinn frowned. The cold was beginning to creep into his body, leeching away the warmth he'd built up inside of him.

"Figure of speech. About seven were chicks." Damien scowled back at Quinn. "Women, girls, not male. Shit, one was a girl becoming a guy. I don't care what bits someone's got, they've just got to fit in with us."

"And be dedicated to working through difficult times." Quinn cocked his head, watching the two musicians exchange a look and a shrug. "Kind of like having to go through a bunch of shit, rehab, and then only now coming back to join the living?

"Why do you think you're only now seeing Rafe, Damien?" Quinn asked. "He's Sionn's best friend. As close to Sionn as Miki is to you in a lot of ways, but he's not really crossed your path, right?"

"Kinda weird," Miki agreed. "They go out a lot, running or something. Right?"

"Yeah, every morning. Almost. And the gym." Damien nodded. "I saw him a couple of times down at Finnegan's before I got my marbles back into the bag, but we never did face time. He'd have known who I was, probably, if we had. Would have made the whole who-the-fuck-am-I shit go a lot faster."

"Rafe licks his wounds. He always has." Quinn rubbed at his arms, jealous of his cat's burrow under the blanket behind him. "He's avoided the family since he got released from rehab. Sionn's been making his excuses, and Mum's done with that. She's about ready to go kick down his door and drag him out by his hair. If he talked to Sionn about wanting to audition, it's because he thinks he's good enough—strong enough to do it. Rafe wouldn't waste your time if he thought he couldn't be what you needed.

"Music's all he had for the longest time. And even that was kind of yanked away from him." A flare of unexpected anger kindled inside of Quinn, anger at the friend Jack Collins should have been to his bassist. "Did he crash and burn? Yeah, but we failed him too. All of us. The family, Sionn, and hell, even his friend Jack should have helped him climb back up, but Rafe wouldn't let us. Well, I don't know about Jack, but the family? Rafe knows we'd never turn our backs on him."

Damien eyed Quinn, his stare dosed heavily with skepticism and doubt. "So I'm supposed to just ignore all the shit that's happened?"

"No, but you can give him a chance. The audition might not work out. But if it does, you should be honest with him. Set lines. Set boundaries. Be a better friend than Jack was to him on the road," Quinn replied. "Don't be his babysitter, but be a friend to your lover's, Miki. Just like he'd be a friend to you because of Sionn. If anything, he'd have more to lose than himself if he fucks up again. He'd be risking our family—his family—and that's not something Rafe *ever* wants to lose."

"I so don't want to do huge tours," Miki grumbled. "Dude, I just got to breathing again. I'm not sitting in a goddamn tour bus for four months at a time. Albums. I'm there. Some shows. Right there again. Longass roadwork? Not happening, and that's where the drugs and shit happen."

"No. Agreed." Damien nodded. "The three of us don't do anything but booze. He won't get any shit from us. But now we're counting fucking chickens before we've raided the hen house. We don't even know how Rafe's playing is. He could have gone to crap. Hell, we might give him a listen and say no. Then what?"

"Then it's a no." Quinn shrugged. "Look, did Sionn cross the line when he asked you about Rafe? Yes. But you'd do the same for Miki. If you knew Miki wanted something so bad he hurt inside, you'd do everything you could to make it happen for him."

"Only reason Kane's still around and not being chewed on by crabs down in the Bay." Damien stumbled forward a step when Miki pushed him. "Being honest. Kane does things for you... to that pain you've got inside of you and makes it a little bit better. I'm good with that. Hell, I'm happy for that, but it's hard sometimes, Sinjun. And don't tell me it doesn't go both ways."

"Nah, it does. I'm just not the asshole who says it out loud," Miki rumbled. "Look, you didn't like any of the last squillion we heard. Why not give Rafe a try? What's the worst that can happen? We have to go looking again? That's pretty much where we are right now anyway."

Quinn saw the minute shift of something dark and terrified in Damien's expressive features, a quivering fear he stilled nearly as quickly as it rose up. Something lurked behind the guitarist's arrogant amicability, something Quinn wanted to scrape at and expose to the surface to heal.

"Damie, you asked me what I thought about Rafe? I don't think Rafe's the issue here. Either he'll be good for the band or he won't." He paused, catching Damien's frown. "I think the question you need answered is if you really even *want* to form a band. Maybe the reason you don't want to hear Rafe isn't because you're scared of what he might do, but because if you actually do choose a bassist, you're starting something new. Something without the other two. Without Johnny and Dave. A bassist—actually choosing one—will be the final nail in Sinner's Gin's coffin, and maybe, just maybe, neither one of you are ready for that yet.

"Hell, you might never be ready for that," Quinn continued gently. "But that's something you have to figure out for yourself."

They were silent as Quinn gathered up his reluctant cat, his blanket, and the thermos he'd brought up with him. He smiled at the friends, ducking around them as he made his way back downstairs. "Now if you'll excuse me. I'm going to go see if my brother's found out who is trying to kill or scare me, feed my cat her breakfast, and then get ready to go to my parents' house so they can flay the skin off my back with their prying into my life. I'll see you both when you get there."

Quinn got to the door and had his hand on the knob before Damien finally said something. Oddly enough, it wasn't the tongue-lashing he'd been anticipating.

"Okay, is it me, Sinjun?" Damien's words chased Quinn inside. "Or is that cat wearing a sweater?"

CHAPTER EIGHT

Splash of wine, sip of gin
Twisted metal 'round my heart
And nobody wins
Fire coming down hard
Coming hard from above
Skin torched clean off my bones
And my soul's done scarred.
—Fire and Bones

RAFE CAUGHT himself checking his hair in his rearview mirror, fluffing back a few blond strands from his face. Showing up a few hours early would help him settle his nerves, and if he was lucky, he could get Donal to talk him off the ledge he felt he was on. He'd already spent half an hour trying on clothes, wondering if he should dress up or dress down. What he personally knew about Damie and Miki could have fit between his fingers. Sinner's Gin had been a fortress of personalities and friendships, impossible to break into but with glimpses of golden promise other musicians envied.

Or at least *he'd* envied them.

Back then, Rafe thought he had what Damie and Miki had. He and Jack, plus or minus the sex, they'd been tight. Next to Sionn, Rafe would have bet his life Jack would have stood by him no matter what.

"Shit, you've got no one to blame but yourself, Andrade," Rafe reminded himself as he turned onto the street. "You're the one who set everything on fire. Jack would have been a fucking idiot to tie himself to a loser headed to hell. Now you've got to convince these guys to give you a chance. Good fucking luck."

The Morgans' house looked the same, a gut-punching, heart-twisting same. Rafe caught one glimpse of flowers and yellow paint on a rambling Victorian perched on a hilly corner, and he knew he was home again. Brigid's green thumb was in full force, although Rafe was halfway convinced she merely stood on the front lawn and shouted at the landscaping to produce what she wanted. His back still ached from weekends of pulling weeds for extra money. Then his eyes stung when he thought of all the halfhearted arguments he'd fought with Brigid or Donal about the extra cash they'd shoved into his hand.

His world then had been made up of Morgan hand-me-downs and leftovers in plastic containers for him to take back to the tiny one-room apartment his mom found above a dry cleaner's. There'd been times when his heart hurt at his mom's grateful expression when he'd come home with a new pair of sneakers and clothes Brigid bought but said didn't quite fit any of the boys, and the guilt he'd felt when Donal convinced his mother Rafe wouldn't be a bother on their trips to Disneyland or even the three times he'd gone with them to Ireland.

He'd grown tanned from afternoons in their pool and learned how to drink from stolen whiskey bottles right before he'd perfected the fine art of throwing up in the toilet bowl. He'd been caught smoking cigarettes with Kane behind the garage, and neither one of them expected to see twelve when Donal'd found them coughing their lungs up. Rafe'd stupidly eaten his cigarette, burning his tongue, then threw up on Donal's shoes immediately afterward.

Actually, Rafe grinned to himself as he maneuvered around Con's black Hummer parked at the curb for a quick getaway, he seemed to spend a hell of a lot of time throwing up at the Morgans'. Eating, fighting, and tossing his cookies defined his childhood and teens, with not much changing when he'd become an adult.

It'd been Donal who'd given Rafe his first *good* bass, a 1970 cherry-red Gibson EB-0 he still preferred over anything else he owned. At the time he'd been speechless at the gift and the faith Donal had in him. Later, alone and mourning his life, it'd been the Gibson he'd turned to, hearing his surrogate father's voice in its deep, rolling tones.

In many ways the yellow house on the corner was home, a home that meant fighting for parking space, but still—*home*.

And a home, Rafe found out when he opened the front door and stepped in, that definitely was weathering a ferocious storm.

A loud, testosterone-fueled, Gaelic-accented storm.

"He's dead, Quinn. If that doesn't get it into your thick skull that someone's after you, then what the… don't you walk away from me. Quinn!" Rafe recognized Kane's as the first crackle of thunder rolling out of the house. "Fecking hell. Da! Talk some sense into him."

The storm hit Rafe hard when Donal's third son stalked into the front vestibule to snag a leather jacket from a coat rack in the corner. Passion and a Morgan temper lit an emerald fire in Quinn's gentle eyes, and the golden specks hidden in their depths were drowning in his blown-out pupils. His black mane was a bit wild and fell in soft waves nearly down to his broad shoulders.

An inch or so shorter than Rafe, Quinn was all Morgan, a long-boned Celtic simmer of fallen-from-grace angelic looks and wickeder-than-sin body. He came up short when he spotted Rafe standing in front of the door, his full mouth parted slightly and his chest heaving beneath a white shirt thin enough to look as if it'd been poured over Quinn's torso. Quinn's chin tilted up, a Morgan challenge if Rafe'd ever seen one, and the fire Rafe caught earlier turned molten when Quinn's thickly accented growl broke the silence between them.

"You here to box me in too, Andrade?" Quinn snarled. "Because I am not going to be *handled*."

If Rafe hadn't already wanted Connor's little brother naked and spread out on a bed underneath him, the Quinn standing in front of him right at the moment would have done him in.

"Hey, Q, I don't even know what's going on." Rafe held his hands up in mock surrender. "I just got here."

"Breac." Donal came into the foyer, nodding a hello at Rafe, then turning his attention back to his son. "Ye've got to think this out. Kane's only thinking about—"

"You know what Kane's thinking of, Da?" Quinn stepped around to face his father, the poet folded into the warrior Donal and Brigid bred into all their children. "He's thinking I'm nothing more than a scatter-brained, broken-headed little boy who can't take care of himself. That's what he's thinking, Da. That's what they all think. And most of the time, I don't give a fucking rat's ass what they think because it's no skin off my nose, but this time... I'm done, Da. No more of this."

The foyer grew crowded fast, especially when Connor and Kane shoved their way in. The brothers dissolved into shouting, flinging heavy Gaelic about so fast and furious Rafe with his meager understanding of the language was mostly lost. He was able to pick out a lot of the profanities—he'd learned those first and well—but the rest of it was a battle of temper and spit.

Donal stood quiet for a second, meeting Rafe's uplifted eyebrows with a resigned shrug. The three brothers were a gradation in size and fury; the smaller the Morgan, the hotter the anger, and for once Rafe seriously contemplated stepping outside before the foyer erupted in a fistfight where even an innocent by-stander would take a punch to the face.

Connor and Kane had Quinn cornered, never a good sign in the Morgan household. If they'd been smart, they'd have given Quinn room. If there was one thing Rafe knew about Quinn, it was that he was the most vicious when his back was up against the wall and he had nowhere to go but forward. He'd been witness to the final moments of Quinn's temper snapping when they'd been younger. Rafe'd been too far down the hall when a pair of seniors decided a pubescent Quinn Morgan would make a good target. One shove too many and the soft-spoken, too-young Morgan turned deadly, pulling out every trick he'd learned growing up in a brawling, loud Irish family.

Rafe'd only stopped laughing long enough to pick up one of the guy's teeth and hand it back to him.

Clearing his throat, Rafe shouted in between a break in the Irish, "Can someone please tell me what's going on? 'Cause if I'm going to get punched out here, I'd like to know why."

"No one's punching anyone." Donal shut his sons down before they could begin again. "Quinn, walking away doesn't solve anything. Ye know that. Come back inside, and we'll be talking this out."

"There's nothing to talk out, Da," Quinn argued, but he shoved past his brothers to put his jacket up. "Kane's got the crazies."

"Simon's dead, Quinn. That's not the crazies," Kane retorted. "I'd ask Rafe here to talk some sense into you, but that'll be like…."

"Hey, now, standing right in front of you," Rafe protested as he followed them into the large main room beyond. "And who's Simon?"

"His ex." Connor's voice dropped deep, a granite whisper rolling through the grass. "Don't know how much of an ex he could be if they never had sex. Two years. No sex. Who does that?"

"Wait, Quinn has an ex?" His voice carried through the space, and Quinn frowned. "Not that you can't have an ex, Q. It's just... dude. Guess in my mind, you're still that kid tagging along behind us."

"I haven't been a kid in a long time, Rafe. I'm skipping past thirty. Thought we'd had that discussion, you and I." Quinn slapped Kane's arm when his brother rolled his eyes. "You laugh like you're so old there, K. But need I remind you, there's only two years between us."

"It's 'cause you're wee," Kane shot back.

"Compared to the lot of you, maybe," Quinn countered. "In the real world, I do just fine."

"You do fine here too," Rafe muttered to himself, and Donal shot him a look from under thick black lashes. "Can someone back this up a bit and tell me the whole story? Or do I just fill in the blanks on my own?"

RAFE SAT on one of the long couches and listened, stroking at the son of an old marmalade alley cat he'd found and brought to Brigid years ago. As the cat purred, Rafe's heart stopped and started, then stalled as Kane laid out Quinn's narrow escape from a rampaging truck, then a slashed-apart tire. Connor's pacing picked up when an explosion was mentioned, connecting the road rage to the assault on Quinn's life. Simon Kappelhoff's death was the final straw for Kane, and he'd spent the last half hour trying to convince Quinn to hole up somewhere until Kane and the other badge-wearing Morgans figured things out.

It was like Kane didn't even *know* his younger brother.

"Okay, now keep in mind, I'm not the cop here," Rafe started to say.

"Probably the exact opposite," Connor muttered. "But sure, you go on there, Andrade."

"Thanks for your vote of confidence there, Connie."

He ignored Con's middle finger, knowing Donal would take care of it for him. A second later, Connor was shrugging and mumbling out an apology that sounded more forced than a man complimenting an ugly baby.

"How did we get from the fire thing at Quinn's house to it being someone killed Quinn's ex? What connected them?"

"I'm connecting them," Kane snapped. "Southern's the cop house that pulled the truck, but they've done jack shit about it. I want to pull it all into my house. I've got more faith in that cat you've got in your lap there, Rafe, than I've got in the desk jockeys running Q's case."

"Probably should have some more protection on him," Connor suggested. "Truck and fire's one thing. Dead is escalating things fast."

"Can we stop for a second?" Quinn cut them all off. "That's not the point of it. Simon's dead. I had a couple of incidents, but none of that means I'm going to take a leave of absence and go hide away someplace. Not going to happen. I have classes. I have a fucking job—"

"One you can put on pause, can't you?" Kane moved in, edging into his brother.

Rafe did not see the confrontation ending well for Kane. He silently wished his friend luck and kept his mouth shut, hoping beyond hope none of Kane's blood splattered on him once Quinn struck.

"What? Because I'm not a cop? Because I don't carry a badge and gun?" Instead of backing up, Quinn stepped in, lowering his voice until the eerie calm of it rolled softly over Kane's anger. "If it were you, brother mine, would you tuck your tail between your legs and run off? I didn't see you packing up Miki like he was a china doll and shipping him off somewhere safe—"

Connor snorted. "Oh, I'd pay to see that."

"Money's on Miki boy," Donal agreed. "Quinn, back off your brother and take a breath. Kane only wants what's right by you. He's scared. Can't blame a man for being frightened for his brother."

"No, but I can blame him for trying to unman me because of it," Quinn replied. "I'm sorry Simon's dead, but we don't know for certain he died because of me. It's been two years since we've even spoken to one another. Hell, we work on the same campus, and I haven't seen him since we—"

"You kicked him to the curb. That's what you did," Connor finished. Donal huffed at his son, but Con shrugged it off. "Sorry, Da, but the man wanted our Quinn to sit in the closet with him and play Ken doll. No balls, no sex, and no life. Can't say I'd be wanting that for my son, least of all my brother."

"While I'm thankful everyone's so invested in my love life, get the fuck out of my business. I'm saying you're being reactionary, Kane." Sliding onto the couch, Quinn stroked at the orange tabby's fur, ruffling it slightly when he began to purr. "Nothing's happened to *me* in weeks."

"I'd feel better if you were someplace safe. I'm at work, and Sionn's off learning how to brew IPAs." Kane sat down on a leather ottoman in front of his younger brother. "Damie and Miki are going to be in the studio a lot. I just don't like knowing you'll be there alone so much. I'd rather you be someplace safer."

"I don't like knowing I'm there, period." Quinn widened his eyes, mocking Kane's surprised huff. "Please, I love you all, but I hate being there. It's like I'm a pinball in a porn arcade. Every time I turn around, someone's beeping or banging, and I'm scurrying off to find someplace safe. I like living alone. Or at least quieter."

"Shit, I've got a suggestion." Rafe's mouth appeared to be having a private conversation with his dick, and his brain began to scramble to keep up. Before he could stop himself, lips and cock evaded capture and containment, and the most horrendously bad idea tumbled out of his mouth. "Just move Quinn in with me. Until all this shit's done."

THE APARTMENT behind the Morgan garage was cold, and Miki wondered what he'd done to piss off God enough to give him Damien as a best friend. It was bad enough he'd started his day with Kane gone, and his not-quite-awake brain muttered something about a phone call, a murder, and Kane's loving kiss on his mouth before sliding away into the dark of an early Sunday morning.

God. Sunday.

Sundays were torture, a long anticipation of food, haranguing, and loud, messy Morgans. Maybe the murder would mean Kane couldn't make it to the family trough, and Miki half wondered if he could skip out on that technicality alone.

"No, she'll just come get me if I went home. Fecking witch," he grumbled at his snoring dog. "Haven't been in few weeks. Gotta go punch the son-in-law card once in a while or I'll get docked. It's not fair, Dude. Not like I can drag *him* somewhere—"

Miki didn't bother finishing his sentence. Kane would go anywhere he needed Kane to be, even a few places he didn't, and not for the first time, Miki felt irritated at his cop's willingness to jump into everything Miki was into.

The smell of cocoa-brushed coffee brewing was tempting Miki to crawl out of his nest. He lay on his back, debating the pros and cons of searching out a cup when Dude solved the dilemma for him.

Dude and the sneaky realization someone'd given the terrier a lima bean from last night's dinner, because the green cloud wafting out from under Miki's duvet was thick and foul enough to fell a T. Rex.

It was a clotted stench so strong it drove Miki from his place on the bed and into the bathroom to brush his teeth. Anything to remove the taste of dog-processed lima bean from his tongue before he had to face the fray he suspected was brewing in the main house.

He'd already walked into one maelstrom of biting politeness and sneering rejoinders that morning when Sionn and Damien circled one another around the one empty space. The brittleness in the air was sharp enough for Miki to seriously contemplate killing both of them, but instead he'd fought past them and been caught up in their argument.

Now midafternoon, Miki finally realized he'd never actually gotten his cup of coffee.

"Fuckers." Waving away any lingering remnants of Dude's lima-bean incursion, he was about to head out and brave the elements when the apartment door swung open and his brother and sometimes best friend came in, skillfully maneuvering into the room while holding a pair of steaming mugs.

"Here, take one so I can shut the door," Damien ordered.

To be fair, Miki supposed, Damien was always ordering. Or pushing. Sometimes even bullying if he were allowed. Miki took great pleasure in being the pin to prick his best friend's arrogance, so he stood there, waiting. Damien sighed and gave a tight smile.

"Please, you asshole. Can you please take one so I can shut the goddamned door?"

"Better." As a concession he took both cups, sipping at the creamier one as Damien nearly gagged on the smell of Dude's stealthy emissions. "Hey, reap it. Pretty sure Sionn slipped him a bean last night."

"Why the fuck would Sionn do that?" Damien scraped his tongue against his teeth, then retrieved his coffee from Miki's warmed fingers.

"Because Kane told him not to. You and I, we know better. Those two, they're assholes about shit like that." Sitting as cross-legged as he could on the bed, Miki cocked his head at his friend. "Unless it was Quinn. He's sneaky sometimes, but don't think he'd do it."

"Nah, he's too… righteous. Wrong word. Something or other. Not someone who'd fuck with a dog's ass." Damien joined his friend on the bed, waiting until Miki was settled in before easing against the wall. "We going to audition Rafe?"

"You asking me or telling me?" Miki sipped at his cup. "'Cause I thought we'd already decided it was at least worth a chance."

"We've got to be sure, Sinjun." Damien made a face when Miki snorted at him. "Okay, I've got to be certain. There's a lot at stake."

"How's it different than before?" he asked softly. "When we were going through all of the shit before Sinner's broke open, we had to dig through some guys to find out what worked... who worked. Not like we found Johnny and Dave on the first go. Remember that Brenton guy?"

"Shit, I forgot about him. Him and his banana fetish." They shared a laugh, the experience of finding their drummer with a banana peel wrapped around his dick and jacking off to the soundtrack from *Xanadu* much funnier years later. "Can't even look at a banana without wondering if it's a virgin anymore. That kind of ruins it for me, you know?"

"What about Cherry Phil? Took us three weeks to find out he was peeing in that juice container and leaving it in the fridge in case of an animal attack." Miki shuddered at the memory. "That was disgusting."

"Dude, I almost *drank* from that apple juice bottle. How do you think *I* felt?" Damien sighed, reaching out to stroke Miki's knee. "Just don't want you to be... I just want you to be safe. Shit, I want Forest to be safe. I've got to *trust* this guy with everything. That's a lot, you know?"

"Yeah, I know," Miki agreed softly. "But D, it's always going to be like this. At some point in our lives, we're going to be falling off the edge and just hoping we land okay. You're talking about touring... about albums... like we're starting over. So if we're going to start over, we've got to be willing to do that. Banana-peel fuckers and all."

"Scary, you know that, Sinjun? This whole beginning thing," Damien admitted. "I keep trying not to think about the pressure to be better than we were... because no matter what we do, there's Sinner's standing behind us, looming. Suppose I fuck that up? Suppose everyone comes out and says shit like 'they should have let the band rest in that grave'? I don't want that for you and Forest. Hell, I don't want that for me."

"What does it matter what people say, D?" Miki set his cup down on a low table next to the bed, then scooted over until he was against the wall, sitting shoulder to shoulder with Damien. "We started this shit without giving a crap about what everyone said before. Why should we give a shit now? So we make music. So people might hate it. What does it matter if *we* like it? What the fuck does it matter if no one else does?"

"Because it does." He shrugged, nudging Miki aside a bit. "I'm a shit. I know it. You... you're different. You don't need to have people tell you you're alive—"

"Well, that's 'cause people keep declaring you dead." Miki's sharp laugh woke Dude up enough for the dog to look up, then roll back over.

"Hear me out, asshole," Damien muttered. "Doing the music's enough for you. Shit, you don't care if no one ever hears what you make, but me, I've got to. I need that, Sinjun. I need people to hear it and see me and fucking want to come back to it. And yeah, that's a shit-ton of ego, but I'm going to own that shit. I want a stage. I don't care if there's five or five thousand, but

I *need* there to be someone in that black beyond the lights listening to my shit and thinking, yeah, my life's better because I heard this guy play."

"And you think Rafe's not going to bring that?" Miki ventured. "Or are you scared he is?"

"Don't know. Maybe both. Suppose we're the ones who are fucked-up and can't get up there anymore?" Damien slid a glance over his best friend. "Screw that. You—you're still there. You've still got it. I've heard you sing. Still can make a fucking stone cry. Forest—he's just here for the ride. He wants to play and doesn't give a shit so long as he can make music. If I suck now, he's not going to care, but Rafe—"

"Rafe's going to care." Miki rested his head on Damien's shoulder, contemplating where they were going to go. "Because you think he wants back up there. Like you do."

"Shit, you saw his face when we started talking about this shit at the Amp. He was itching harder than a crack fiend. He's that addicted to the stage, then I've got to ask if he's that hooked onto the shit he put into his veins. Can't have two masters and one puppet. One's got to give." Damien sighed, hooking his arm around Miki's shoulders. "Then Quinn goes and lays things out for us, and now I'm asking myself, suppose he gives in to the one I'm chasing… our own fucking dragon, and I'm the one who stumbles. What then?"

"Your band. You stumble and—"

"And I bring him down with me." Damien sighed. "So for all the crap I'm spouting about him falling off the wagon and taking us down, I could be doing the exact same damned thing to him. And then there'd be no going back for him. Not from that."

"Risk he's going to have to take," Miki pointed out. "And I think you're still pissed off about Sionn bringing it up. Because he got in your face. Because you were an asshole and spit in his. Quinn's right about that. He did for Rafe what you'd do for me. Pisses you off, but it's true."

"Sionn fucked up. It's not his business what we do in the band." He yelped when Miki's fingers found and pinched his nipple. "Shit, what?"

"You ever think maybe he didn't just bring it up for Rafe's sake but because he gives a shit about you?" Something snapped into place, and Miki grinned to himself, seeing a pattern connecting Rafe and Damien. "You want up on stage so fucking badly you can taste it. Sionn knows that, and who is the one bassist he knows? The one guy who could take what we give him on stage and throw it back to us? Rafe Andrade. Sionn isn't just trying to help Rafe. He's trying to get you back to where you want to be—where you need to be. And you're just too much of a stubborn asshole to see it."

"Think so?" Damien sighed, nudging the dog with his toe. "Fucking hell. He is. He was. Fucking shit."

"Well, Sionn knows you almost as well as I do."

Miki poked D in the ribs, making him wince.

"Go talk to Rafe about coming in. He's good. We know he's good, and we can use him."

"Neither one of them replaces Johnny and Dave. You know that, right?"

"Any more than anyone could replace you, ass-wipe." Miki sighed. "It's a new thing. A new band. Remember? Back from the gutter. Or maybe never leaving it. So long as we play. Don't forget that part,

D. It doesn't matter where we go so long as we're there."

"Can I be a little bit of a dick? You know, just on principle." Damien chuckled at Miki's sneer. "Don't want him to know we want him. We're going to have to make him work for it."

"Dude, he came here on a Sunday and braved the whole gauntlet of horror. Probably figuring out when's the best time to talk to you. Before the she-demon descends with her flying monkeys, or after they've all been fed so everyone's in a food coma and she's rattling about the turrets looking for new victims."

"Sinjun, not everyone's scared to shit of Brigid. He grew up here. With them." He grabbed Miki's cup and handed it to him. "She loves him like a son. Just like she loves you."

"Yeah, I love her too," Miki said through a mouthful of coffee. "I'm just not going to tell her. 'Cause I'm thinking that's how she levels up, and I don't fucking want to know what bonus power she'd get then."

CHAPTER NINE

Warehouse kitchen
*Kane: Your coffee's kind of sweet today,
    Mick. Too much sugar?*
*Miki: I didn't put any sugar in it. I just
    poured it into the cup.*
*K: Must be sweet because I kissed you
    before I took a sip.*
*M: Shit like that makes me throw up in
    my mouth, dude. Really.*
*K: Isn't there a single romantic bone in
    your body?*
M: Only when you put it in me.

"WOW, SO they shot you down?" Sionn handed
Rafe an ice-cold beer, then settled into pillows strewn
about the Morgans' covered widow's walk. "Just like
that?"

"Yeah, didn't even entertain the idea." Shoving his hair away from his face, Rafe sighed. "Sure, kind of out of left field, but it had some merit. Really, is there anything *that* wrong with me? How much more fucking penance am I supposed to do before people don't think I'm shit?"

"I'm pretty sure they don't think you're shite there, Andrade," his friend countered. "Probably just a bad time for it."

"Dude, Donal couldn't say no fast enough." Rafe saluted Sionn with his bottle. "I was just offering Quinn a place to stay, not knock him up and leave him at a train station with a one-way ticket to a nunnery. It got even uglier after that."

The widow's walk was a long-standing male Morgan tradition, a hideaway Brigid and the girls rarely intruded on. Built more for aesthetics than a longing to watch the ocean for a returning sailor, the broad platform provided a safe harbor during the family's storms.

And from the tempest brewing beneath them, Rafe wasn't sure the widow's walk would survive if any of the thundering Morgans took it into their heads to follow him.

The view still took his breath away. Even after all the years he'd climbed up three stories and flung open the door to the walk, seeing San Francisco tumble to his feet in front of him humbled Rafe. The sun began to steal under the foggy horizon, pearling the sea as it sank down beneath the water. Oddly, he could see more from his penthouse on Nob Hill, but he *felt* much more while under the Morgans' eaves.

"Probably best for you he said no—" Sionn yelped as the door to the walk opened and struck him in the elbow. "Fucking hell! D, you're supposed to knock first. Walk rules."

"Yeah, rules. You all need to post them on the wall or something. Who the hell would think about knocking when they leave the house?" Damien ducked his head under the eave overhang and took the bottle out of his lover's hand. "Get lost, Murphy. Rafe and I have a few things to talk about."

"Love you too, asshole," Sionn grumbled as he stood. He caught Damien's chin in his hand, turning his lover's face, then sliding in close for a kiss. His mouth was brutal on Damie's, a fierce, possessive assault that softened into a tender caress when Damien curved into Sionn's body. They pulled apart, Damien breathing hard while Sionn wore a smug smile. "That's something to keep for later, D. Oh, and I didn't tell him I talked to you yet. So I'm leaving that for you to deal with too."

"Fucker," Damien muttered at Sionn's back as his lover went inside. He pinched at the inseam of his jeans, adjusting the wrap of denim around his zipper, then looked over his shoulder, snarling at Rafe's amused smirk. "Don't get cocky there, dick. I'm not up here because I want to fuck you."

"Then why *are* you here?" He couldn't look at Damien, not when apprehension and dread hooked into his throat and pulled it closed. The last thing he wanted was Sionn talking to his lover. Coming back to the music had to be on his own terms—not by standing on someone else's back. Certainly not Sionn's back. He'd ruined nearly every relationship he had. Rafe *couldn't* lose Sionn too.

"We've got business. And not because Sionn asked me to give you a chance." Damien's cold-washed Brit tones were a hard blue compared to the rolling green heat in Sionn's voice, made harder by an edge of steel pissiness rolling off of Damie's tongue.

"I told him not to—"

"Yeah, he keeps saying that too. Pisses me off that I believe him." Damien stalked the length of the walk only to come back to where he started. Looking down at Rafe, he growled, "Stand up. 'Cause I'm not going to talk about this sitting down in a bunch of pillows."

"Too much like sex?" Rafe grinned, putting his beer down.

"No, not sex but close. Too intimate. Too much like we're friends or brothers sharing this space—like they all do. Like Miki does. You want this spot, you fucking stand up for it and deal with me eye to eye."

Rafe's blood itched, crawling toward a want he'd shoved down time and time again. There were too many things fighting for space in his head: the hurt he'd felt downstairs, Sionn's heartfelt, skewed support, and now Damien's anger. He'd hoped, damn it. Fucking hoped the Sinner's boys would take a chance on him, if only because he was damned good at the one thing he knew he could do—play a bass until it wept with release. And there was that little whisper of a promise to make it all go away, if only he dipped his toe back into the quicksand he'd pulled himself out of.

"Sounds like you've already made up your mind." He stood anyway, jutting his chin out as if daring Damien to pop him one. "So why the fuck should I bother?"

"See, it's shit like *that* that makes me want to say fuck you," Damien spat.

"So again, then why the fuck are you here?"

"Because Quinn said something to me when— well, it doesn't matter when—just that he said it." The guitarist punched his fists into his jeans. "Fucker asked me why I couldn't give you a chance to come back from the dead when I'd done it too. Can't argue with that kind of shit. Much as I'd like to. So yeah, here I am. Dealing with you wanting a chance with us."

"I wish Sionn hadn't told you that. It would have been better coming from me." Rafe grabbed his beer bottle, then walked to the railing, leaned his elbows on the thick plank, and looked out onto the Morgans' backyard. Damien followed him, shoulders stiff with resentment as he took a sip of his purloined bottle. "Seriously, I should have been the one to—"

"Better this way. Because I would have told you fucking hell no to your face and walked away," Damien admitted. "Instead I got to climb all over Sionn, spit at Sinjun when he walked away, then got my ass handed to me by Quinn when I went up to the roof to pick a fight with Sinjun."

"Yeah, that's going to make you love me." Turning, Rafe faced the guitarist, studying him. The years had layered a polish on Damien Mitchell.

His age shone in the crisp, wintery blue of his eyes, and the self-assured swagger of his walk no longer seemed to need a dash of bravado and challenge in it. Instead, he carried himself more like a man who'd seen it all, done it all, and come back stronger for it. His death, while greatly exaggerated, had been a good one, and the world clamored to find out what Damien had up his sleeve to herald his resurrection.

It surprised Rafe on how badly he wanted to be one of those to help roll back the stone.

"I fucked up. No two ways about it." Rafe watched Miki's dog tear around the yard below, chasing a bouncing purple tennis ball. "There's a lot of shit I can't take back. I know that. But I can't let it bury me. Do you know what it's like to *need* to play, and there's nothing there but yourself?"

The look Damien shot him was all the response Rafe needed.

"I'm not asking for anything you wouldn't give anyone else—"

"You're asking for a fuck ton more than anyone else." Damie rounded on him. "You're asking me to *risk* Sinjun, because I'm dragging him back into the studio… back on stage, and I'd be trusting you to not screw it up. You're putting Sionn on the fucking line, because if you fuck me up, you mess me and him up. You think about that? So yeah, Andrade, you're asking me to fuck up everything I have with the two people I love more than goddamn music, and you think you're not asking me to give you anything?"

Damien's hand clenched on the beer bottle, and for a brief moment Rafe feared the glass would crack in his hand.

"I'm good," he ventured. Rafe heard the thread of begging in his voice. Hell, it was more tapestry than thread, but he didn't care. If ever there was a time to beg, it was now. "I'm better than any other damned bassist out there. You know that. Or you wouldn't be up here. Even if Sionn asked you."

"And what about that other shit?" Damien's lip curled. "I'm not having you smear me like you smeared Collins. Yeah, so you're good. Maybe as good as Johnny was, but that's not enough, Andrade. You've got to fit. You've got to be willing to haul your own shit, set up your own gear. We're not going to be doing this in stadiums. It's been too long… we've been gone too long. We're starting from the bottom again."

"You don't need to—"

"Yeah, we do."

Rafe chuffed out a breath. "You ever going to let me finish a fucking sentence?"

"Maybe." Damien briefly lifted his shoulders in a half-assed apology. "Probably not. We're going into this just like we did the last time. We need to. Forest needs to be a part of this band's beginning. We're going to book clubs and play the shit out of our crap until our fingers bleed. We might never fucking play stadiums. And we could crash and burn because the world's sick of our shit. You've got to bring your damned best and know it might not be good enough, Andrade."

"And that's if I even get in?" Rafe set his bottle down on the walk's floor.

"Yeah, *if* you get in." Damien drained his beer, then wiped his mouth with the back of his hand. "We've got a practice session down at the Sound tomorrow around nine. Bring your shit and let's see what you can do. After that I'll talk it over with Miki. You've got to fit, Andrade. Rub someone the wrong way and there's no going forward."

"St. John's not the easiest guy to get along with," Rafe pointed out. "Kind of like a wet, blind cat caught in a burlap bag kind of not easy."

"Dude, that's your problem. I get along with Sinjun fine," the guitarist grunted. "You want in. Make him like you. Fuck, make him love you, because Forest, that's easy. He likes everyone."

"And what about you?" Rafe ventured.

"Me? I'm a fucking breeze to get along with. Do what I say. Listen to how I want things, and we'll be fine." Damien opened the door leading to the house. "Just so we're clear. All of this works and you get in, that's good for you. Fuck me over like you fucked over Collins? I get one damned hint that you're dosing up, and you'd better be the dead guy on the floor this time around, because by the time I get done with you, you'll wish you were."

"TALK TO me, Kane." It wasn't his father who barked at him from across the study. No, not the man who'd cheered him on at baseball games, hugged him tight after pinning Kane's first badge to his tightly creased dress blues, and held him up when the hospital doctors patched Miki up. No, the steel-eyed, stone-jawed man standing by a wall covered with photos of his family was pure cop, a captain of the force, and a hardass demanding answers from a detective with little to give him. "Talk to me about how all of this is connected to Quinn, and what the fuck are you all doing about it?"

There'd be no asking for a shot of Irish whiskey, not now, but Kane poured one anyway, sighing when his father shook his head as Kane held up the bottle. Sipping at the burning amber, he leaned against his father's desk and gathered his words carefully.

"Kappelhoff is—"

"The end of it. The recent of it. Ye start at where ye think is the beginning, and then we'll go from there," Donal interrupted. "We've got two incidents for certain—the truck ramming into the boy and then the thing at his house. You tell me how you think this and Kappelhoff's death are connected here."

"Sir, Kappelhoff's murder just… it sticks something in me, and Sanchez agrees he was killed because of his connection to Quinn." Kane shifted under his father's glare. "And yeah, we were looking into Southern's case without their approval. But shit, the brass down there wasn't moving on it. They're calling it road rage, but you and I know something's up. I want the whole thing wrapped up into one case, and I want that case on *my* desk."

"I don't know that for sure. Ye've got nothing here but threads and mirrors. Maretti's the captain down over at Southern. He's not going to let go of something easy." Donal chewed on his upper lip in thought, pacing a few feet of carpet. "If ye had more than a few maybes, he'd go for it, but right now, Kane, ye've got nothing."

"Just a gut feeling. And a few nibbles," Kane admitted. "Kappelhoff's death wasn't pretty, Da. And I'll be the first one to tell you I stared down into what was left of him and saw my baby brother. I don't want that to be real. I don't ever want to find Quinn like that. I never want Quinn to become one of mine."

His odd brother, Quinn.

Of all Kane's siblings, Quinn was the one he and Connor were closest to. As much as he loved to get a rise out of Kiki and Riley or put the younger ones' backs up with a well-placed verbal jab, Quinn was the one brother he felt as if he'd had a hand in raising. Through all the tears and stuttered thoughts, Quinn'd kept pushing through his childhood, racing toward an adulthood where his body matched the brain too tightly packed into his skull.

Despite the years, Quinn's deep green eyes still held a wide-eyed wonder as bright and shiny as the day he'd opened them for the first time, and a two-year-old Kane declared the wrinkly pink larva his best little brother.

"Gut feelings don't convince captains to give up cases." Donal finally settled down at the cabinet, where he poured himself a shot of amber whiskey. "If I could, I'd be shipping him off to Ireland. That'll take our *breac* out of anyone's reach."

"He wouldn't go," Kane murmured, resting his hip on his da's desk. "For as smart as he is, he's plenty stupid where it counts."

"That's the truth of it," his father agreed. "Like yer mother in that."

"The only thing of Mum he's got 'sides his eyes." He sighed, wondering if he could trust Miki to drive them home if he got sick-drunk with his father. "The problem is I don't have anything connected, but it's there, Da. It's right there. I can feel it. If I felt like I had the time, I know I can connect Kappelhoff and everything else. There's just too many small things to chase down, and Quinn's itching to run loose in the fields."

"Yer brother's never run loose in any fields." Donal chuckled. "He'd sooner sit and collect bugs. Ye need to find me something solid I can bring to the table, son. Or there'd be no arguing it. Why'd this one move up to murder? What happened?"

"Unless things have been happening, and Quinn's not said shite about it." Kane stiffened at a knock on the door, relaxing only when Connor slid in, then shut the door behind him.

"Are we talking about Q-bert? He's right pissed at the moment. Mum's got him cornered in the kitchen. I figured it was safe to find the two of you while she's got him in circles." Con nodded to his father's glass. "It's bad enough to get hammered at four in the afternoon? And can I get in on it?"

"Just seemed like it would lubricate the conversation," Kane replied, handing his brother the bottle and a glass. "Considering I'm trying to convince the captain here to throw his weight behind my craziness. Da's just brought up a good point—fast escalation between blowing up cars to killing Kappelhoff. I think Quinn's either been hiding stuff from us—"

"Or he's as oblivious as he's always been." Connor put the bottle up, then sidled in next to his younger brother on the edge of the desk. "Quinn's intelligence doesn't extend out to simple things like walking around a bad neighborhood and hiding his wallet, but maybe one of us can pry something out of him? He might have dismissed something before, but now—this asshole got his car. That's enough to piss a man off."

"He likes cars," Donal spoke up. "Notice that, did ye? Cars and fire, but with Kappelhoff, he went a different route. Uglier. More personal."

"Just now." Kane nodded. "Sure, Kappelhoff is an escalation, but for what? If I knew what Quinn did to get this guy's notice, I could chase that down and find him."

"Now, Simon there. Lot of rage there from what ye said was left of him. A man does a killing like that, it's personal to a deep level. If Quinn's done something, then why lash out at Kappelhoff and not our Quinn?" their father asked softly, his accent thickening nearly to the pea soup of his childhood. "Someone wants Quinn's attention. Summat bad."

"The guy warned Quinn off or is leading him to something," Con pointed out. "Maybe killing Kappelhoff is his way of pushing Quinn somewhere? But why would that be important? Why is Quinn this guy's target?"

"Has to be someone Quinn knows. Someone who's known Q for a long time, because it's been years since he's been with Simon. Hasn't given him the time of day since." Kane shook his head, more confused than resigned. "Guess I better go shake baby brother's tree and see what falls out. He might know more than he realizes. I just know I start poking, and he's going to push back."

"It's because he doesn't think it's serious." Connor drained his glass, hissing at the bite of whiskey in his throat. "We'll have to corner him in without him knowing. Can't let him wander too far without some backup. Too much of a risk."

"Kane, if ye find out anything, ye tell me," Donal rumbled. "I'll see about getting Southern to let you have the truck, but ye've got to stitch this all together, Kane."

"Trust me, Da," Kane reassured his father. "I'll do the stitching. I just need the rest of you to help me wrangle in Quinn."

CHAPTER TEN

Time's come for me, momma
Time's come to take me away
Leave a coin on my eye for the toll
'Cause the river man needs his pay
Don't cry 'bout the way I've gone
Or the mud I've got on my soul
I've lived the way I needed to live
No way was I going out whole
—Toll for the River

"SO THEY think someone is trying to kill you?" Graham sniffed—as he always sniffed whenever he poured himself a fresh cup of tea. He spun a spoon of honey into the dark steep, stirring it hard enough to splash a few drops onto Quinn's desk. Patting at the spill, he sighed. "And you *still* came to work? Is that wise, Quinn?"

"I couldn't just stay home. It's not even *my* home." Quinn refilled his electric kettle with bottled water and set it to boil. There was enough room on the low bookcase beneath the window to set up a make-shift hot beverage station, and he'd grown accustomed to Graham dropping by for a cup of tea before they did their afternoon office hours. Dumping two packets of Vinacafe into his mug, he listened for the burble of the kettle. The boil came quickly, and he filled his mug, then sat down with a sigh. "And then there's... Simon. God, I didn't even *think* about him in months, and now he's...."

Quinn couldn't say it. Not out loud. He hadn't wanted to admit the man he'd tried to fall in love with... a man he'd hoped he would find happiness with... was dead. And he'd been more wrapped up in his anger at his family for boxing him in than mourning Simon's death.

Guilt couldn't begin to describe how shitty he felt about it, but Quinn felt even guiltier when he realized he couldn't quite recall Simon's favorite foods, the sound of his voice, or even why they'd continued their relationship when Simon realized he really didn't want to go any further than a hand job in Quinn's office.

They'd fought small skirmishes of double-meaning words and knifelike snips where Quinn was outmatched and outgunned. It'd gotten to the point where he'd decided he didn't really want to be around Simon anymore, and the whole thing blew up in Quinn's face when he'd tried to talk about it.

Quinn'd been so confused and then so angry he hadn't even cared when Simon left. He'd just wanted Simon *gone*.

Just not… *dead* gone.

A week since Simon's death, and Quinn'd exhausted his memory and patience with Kane and his partner, going over details of his life until he'd been about to commit murder himself. The only soothing part of living in the warehouse were the times in the middle of the night when Rafe called, seemingly looking for company, but Quinn wondered if there was more to it than that.

God, Quinn couldn't let himself hope for more than being company. Even when his chest tightened when his phone chirruped a hello and Rafe's number flashed on the screen, or the sticky mess he made of himself after hanging up, his body thrumming and satiated as he stroked himself off in the dark afterward, he buried his longing for Rafe. It was safer that way. At least that's what he told himself.

"You're going to break it if you continue to do that."

Graham's voice shocked Quinn out of his thoughts of Rafe, sticky sheets, and warm mouths, and he patted Quinn's thigh.

"What?" Quinn stopped rattling his spoon about his mug and looked down at his dick, its length curled up in its nest of denim and cotton. Slightly hard from his lingering thoughts of Rafe, it seemed fine.

"Stop stirring. You're going to break the cup." Graham leaned over the desk and took the spoon from Quinn's fingers. "Honestly, you're hard on the crockery, Dr. Morgan.

"Did you… still have feelings for Simon? Are you sure you should be here? I'm sure everyone would understand if you went home."

"God, I *have* no home, Graham. I'm still at Kane's, lodged up like an old spinster aunt under the rafters." Grumbling felt good, especially when Graham nodded and let him ramble about, looking for a thread of something in his own brain.

His friend made clucking sounds, tiny pricks of ticks meant to soothe. "And you hate it there?"

"No—yes. But not because I don't like them... don't love them. I just can't—God, I'm never alone. There is *always* someone there." Quinn rubbed at his eyes. "And can I be honest with you?"

"Of course. Anything you tell me goes no further than me. You know that, Quinn," Graham promised.

"I feel like a fucking shit for not... I haven't even *thought* about Simon in forever. Sure, right after he—" The last time he'd been with Simon had been an ugly, confusing experience, and he'd gone out of his way to avoid Simon ever since. "He *hated* the shit out of me, Graham—"

"No.... Quinn, that's not possible—"

"Oh yeah, trust me. You didn't hear the things he said to me. What he thought of me." Everything Quinn'd feared he truly was, Simon found in his bilious pour of words, each dripping with acid and shot through with razors. "He dug into me. Threw back everything I'd shared with him. Every single goddamn fear I had inside of me, sharpened it and stabbed me with it. He stood there screaming at me, and I couldn't... just couldn't breathe. And now he's dead. And it's my fault. It's my *damned* fault."

"Do they know who killed him? Your ex?"

Graham's fingers butterfly-skipped again over Quinn's knee, a flicker of sensation he barely felt beneath his jeans.

"*Any* idea?"

"Not a damned one," he confessed.

"Then you don't know it's your fault. The rest of it could be someone's idea of a sick joke, and Simon—well, that might have been anything from a robbery to maybe someone else he hurt. You can't blame yourself for his death, Quinn," Graham said softly, rubbing at Quinn's knee. "If he treated *you* as badly as that, I can't imagine he treated anyone well. You'll be back home soon. We're all more comfortable in our own surroundings. That's normal. Human nature."

"I feel like I'm five all over again," Quinn muttered. He liked Graham, counted on him, but the feel of the man's fingers on him rattled what little calm he had left. Shifting in his chair, Quinn moved his leg, breaking their contact. "Can't stay overnight at my friend's house because I'm homesick, and the bathroom's on the wrong side of the hallway. Everything's off… off pattern, off routine. Off everything."

"Once again. Normal. Especially for you. You need some steadiness in your life. We both do. We've talked about that."

Graham crooked his head, angling his beak-like nose into Quinn's face until their chins almost touched, and Quinn chuckled, pulling back.

"See, normal as ever, Doctor Morgan."

"I hate when you call me that." Quinn blew on his coffee.

"You hate it when anyone calls you that," his colleague pointed out. "Even the students. Really, Quinn. You've earned that—"

A knock on Quinn's office door stalled Graham's tirade, and he stuttered, a tight-lipped Fokker Dr.I stalling out before he could crest into a full lecture on protocol and honorifics. A very familiar young woman popped her head in before Quinn could answer the knock, and she beamed when she spotted him behind his desk. Blonde and endowed with curves broad enough to bend light, her face was a study in cat-eye makeup and glittery powder.

"Hi! Can I borrow you for a minute?" She bounced in, her body packed tightly into a pair of yoga pants and an eye-bleeding neon-pink tank barely strong enough to hold her chest in. "I wanted to talk to you about my paper."

She looked familiar, and Quinn frowned, knowing he'd seen her somewhere. Something about her wiggle and flashing white teeth triggered a spark in his memory. "Oh, 'Industrial Revolution and its Artistic Influences.'" His brain crackled, chasing down the threads connecting her to his class and then her assignment. "You didn't turn your paper in. It's... a week late, I think."

"Yeah, that's what I wanted to talk to you about." She moved aside to let Graham pass by, pressing herself up against Quinn's desk.

"I'll see you later, Dr. Morgan." Graham's mouth was a thread of flesh in his gaunt face. "You're coming to the readings tonight, right?"

"Oh yeah. Um, I'm bringing a friend of mine. Rafe. He said it sounded like fun." The word *fun* was stretching the truth, but Rafe'd been enthusiastic. Quinn shrugged at Graham's raised eyebrows. "Okay, so he said interesting, but he wanted to go."

"You've got a boyfriend?"

LeAnne—her name popped into Quinn's brain, slamming into the space behind his forehead. Her wiggling against his desk stopped.

"Wow, you so don't even—I mean, I didn't—"

"I'll see you there, then, Quinn. Try not to work too late." Graham's eyes washed cold over LeAnne as he left. "And I'll leave the door open unless you want it closed."

"No, open's fine. Thanks." Quinn waved LeAnne over to the chair Graham'd been sitting in. "Okay, tell me, what do you think there's left to talk about?"

BY MIDAFTERNOON Quinn'd gone through a lot of coffee and most of his patience. After LeAnne, there'd been a river of students with elaborate claims of alien abduction, paper-hungry dogs, and in one case, a vomiting baby and a ruined laptop. The last one he gave a pass on, especially when she'd brought the baby in a tie-dyed sling and it proceeded to provide a repeat performance of its assignment-ruining act over Quinn's desk and, more importantly, in his coffee cup.

Shoving aside deadlines meant more papers shored up onto one end of his schedule, and Quinn cursed his calendar, inputting the last realignment for the day. Muttering as he cross-checked the regurgitation victim's name against his student list, Quinn caught a glimpse of his clock and nearly panicked.

"Shit, the bridge is going to be a mess getting across."

His office was relatively small, a tiny oasis of chaotic calm in the middle of a busy hall of other professors. Somehow he'd gotten a corner square—possibly an ex-broom closet—but he hadn't cared. It was an office, his own space, and more importantly, came with two wide sash windows overlooking the greensward beyond. His desk was an old one he'd dragged from his parents' house and refurbished after a *tsk* from his father about the band stickers his youngest sister stuck to its sides.

He'd lost some wall space placing it against the wall next to the door, but the tree-line view was more important than storage at the time, and he had no regrets since. There was enough storage on the bookcases lining what wall space was left, with enough space for an old leather wing chair and an iron chandelier lamp, two other refugees from the Morgan furniture stash.

It was homey, a warm space with buttery cream-painted walls, a beaten but still serviceable Persian rug his mum bartered off a man at a garage sale when he'd been ten, and a mounted wooden sign from the Whistling Penguin pub he'd helped Kane steal during a visit to Dublin in their teens.

The office was as much his home as the house he'd torn apart and rebuilt, and Quinn *needed* to be in a space of his own—especially since he was still living in Miki's warehouse without a vacate date in sight.

"Shite, I'm tired." The Gaelic came easier to him sometimes. Better than English when his tongue was too curled up in his mouth to speak.

It was tempting to close the door. His office hours were done for the day, and the siren of a final cup of coffee called to him. Well, murmured, at least. Quinn regarded his much abused and now clean coffee mug. The watery porridge sluice did help him clean his space, and he'd quickly discovered there wasn't a lot on his desk he couldn't live without. He had a minor debate on whether the tiny cactus needed yet another rinse but didn't think the prickly ball could take much more dousing.

"Steady on, Spike. You'll be okay." Quinn hit the power button on his laptop and sniffed at his shirt, sure he'd somehow gotten splashed in the onslaught. "Let's go back to the insane asylum and shower."

One thing about having a family of cops—besides running amok over their siblings' privacy—was the fear of death they could put into a university administration about where Quinn should park his car. He hadn't permission to use the closest structure. Only tenure, some odd ranking of politics, and possibly a mythical ritual performed with eggs from a virgin platypus could provide that, but somehow Kane'd wrangled him a spot.

A few hundred feet of grass and sidewalk lay between him and the second Audi he'd begged from the dealer. Digging his keys out of his coat, Quinn muttered at the fob, still confused by the plethora of buttons needed to open and start a single sedan.

The cold was brutal on his face, scraping at his cheeks and nose, and Quinn sniffed at the air, wondering if a hard rain wouldn't be too far behind the thick fog rolling up into the hills. His sniff reminded him of Graham, with his prim, martial walk and tilted-up nose.

"Like a stork," he chuckled, staring down at the fob. The path to the structure was clear, a brisk five-minute walk, and then he'd be tucked inside a car with a suspension as thick and unwieldy as a truck. "Five more weeks, Q, and you'll get your baby back. They promised."

Something lingered on the wind, a sharp sting in the chill. Quinn glanced around, letting his eyes drift over swells of faded landscape dotted with sparse-leafed trees and beds of dormant ice plant, a slumbering wealth of green and purple waiting for the first burst of spring. The hall loomed behind him, unimpressive compared to the colleges' other buildings but renowned for the nearly mazelike confusion it cast on unsuspecting freshmen.

He'd grown up in the hall, Quinn mused, turning his back on the building. Stumbling up its concrete steps and through its plain doors, he'd gotten his first whiff of old papers, dead languages, and centuries of layered culture and fallen in love. Next to his parents' home, the hall was the closest thing to home—probably even above his own house—and Quinn briefly debated if he could somehow sneak a futon into his office and camp out there until the nonsense moving against him was over.

Pleasant thought—he smiled, finally deciphering the spray of rubbed-off buttons on the fob—but impractical. If only for the lack of a shower and the clomping of feet in the outside hall as soon as the front doors were thrown open for the day.

"Oh, but it would be awesome." He wrinkled his nose. "Okay, maybe not for Harley and her litter-box excavations."

He was five feet from the short wall cordoning off the structure when Quinn caught the scent again, slightly pungent and abrasive. It grew stronger, fouler as he turned the corner to use the pass-through into the structure, when the rankness hit him full in the face.

The Audi had been white. Not a color he wanted in a car, but beggars couldn't be choosers, especially when he'd pretty much gotten the last one blown up. A fire he could handle. This time Quinn wasn't sure he had it in him to stay conscious, much less do anything productive—like dial for help.

His fingers were cold, numb from the shock slowly shutting his body down, and he had a hard time finding his phone despite his messenger bag being nearly empty. He finally found it hidden behind his tablet, but it swam away from him, avoiding his grasp. Another glance at the car changed nothing. Did *nothing* but etch the horror of what he'd seen further into his brain.

Profane.

Quinn'd never truly contemplated the concept before—not until he stood cold from shock and horror in the middle of a campus parking structure and took in the remains of a young woman spread across the hood of his borrowed car.

He'd spoken to her only a few hours before. Listened to her tell a long, convoluted story about how she couldn't write five thousand words on probably the easiest topic the British Industrial Revolution had to offer. They'd danced about the topic until he'd pushed her into a corner and half walked her through the steps of researching cosplay and steampunk. Short of writing the paper for her, Quinn'd sighed and let LeAnne Walker head on her merry little bouncy way.

Not knowing she'd end up dead and spread out on his car like a biology experiment gone wrong.

The blood was everywhere. Her blood, Quinn corrected himself. A part of him wanted to check to see if she were okay, as if she'd somehow survived someone slashing her open and peeling the skin back from her torso. LeAnne's head rested on the windshield, her eyes open and emptily staring at him as if she knew he'd come across her, too late to do anything but choke down his own cries. She was clothed, barely. Her killer'd pulled up her shirt to expose her belly and sliced her open at least once. Quinn couldn't be sure. Her pants appeared to be up but were soaked through in blood, her exposed skin pale against the drying umber wash.

Quinn couldn't stop staring at her belly, or what her killer'd left of it. The carve was deep and vicious, slicing her apart in a jagged half-moon stretching under both sides of her ribs. Gravity or her murderer pulled her insides out, her intestines a loose spill of mass, pouring out of the crater carved out of her belly to dangle down between her spread legs. The punctured loops dripped copiously, nearly weeping fluid, seeping down the Audi's front bumper and onto the parking garage floor.

It was the sickening rotten green of her torn guts he'd smelled on the wind and the taint of her blood chasing its foul stench with a metallic thread. Her blood was sticky wet, a drying crimson pool on the Audi's white paint, and Quinn backpedaled when something dark slithered out of the cut above her mons and nearly slid free of her body. It caught itself, pulled back on a stringy mess of greenish-beige ligaments, bouncing back up in a yo-yo spiral against her ribs.

"Coronary ligament." He hated the machine-gun fire of information his brain was offering up to him. Quinn didn't need to know he was staring at LeAnne's hepatobiliary tree or the left lobe of her liver. Neither did he care about intestinal contents being isotonic or anything else the fucked-up part of his mind decided to dish up to him.

There was enough sense left in him to stumble back out of the parking structure. He had to be sick, but it couldn't be too close to the scene. There was evidence, probably footprints in the damp grass and mud he'd walked through. Quinn needed to get farther away, distance himself from contaminating the area, but he'd gone only a few feet when he lost control of his stomach, and the coffee he'd drank all afternoon burned up his throat and into his mouth.

Bent over, staring at the grass now covered in his vomit, Quinn found he had the taste of LeAnne's death on his tongue and the stink of her slaughter on his conscience.

This time it was easy to find his phone. Blindly dialing, Quinn wasn't even sure who he called until he heard a rough light bit of Irish brogue answer and his own last name barked back at him.

"Kane? This is Quinn." He shivered, wondering if he'd ever be warm again. "I need you to come here. There's been a murder."

CHAPTER ELEVEN

Rooftop at sunset

*Damie: How much coffee do you drink,
        Sinjun? Give it a guess.*

Miki: Not as much as I'd like. Why?

*D: Think about how much more calm
    your stomach would be if you cut it
    in half.*

*M: I think about cutting you in half be-
    cause I'd be calmer, but then com-
    mon sense kicks in. So I don't.*

*D: And you'd miss me. Admit it. You'd
    miss me.*

M: Not as much as I'd miss coffee.

YEARS OF nuns, rulers, and long walks down to
the principal's office should have inured Rafe to hard,
cold stares and off-the-cuff judgment. He'd had bottles thrown at him while playing and more than once

been booed off stage by a crowd and stared down by truckers at two in the morning in a roadside diner skanky enough to star in its own horror flick.

But nothing prepared him for the stone-cold hard stares of Damien, Miki, and Forest when he walked into the Sound's rear studio carrying his bass and a cup of Starbucks.

"Okay, first rule—you drink coffee, you get it from next door," Forest grumbled loud enough to be heard over the hiss of the air-conditioner vent pumping mildly cold air into the room. "We've got people to feed, and if you're going to fork over four bucks for a latte, give it to them."

"Got it."

He saluted Forest with his cup and got a grin in return. There was a bit of Frank in Forest's demeanor, an easygoing nature where very little ruffled his feathers. The coffee shop thing was pure Frank. It'd been a rule of sorts at the Sound, one he'd forgotten in his rush to get out the door that morning. Support the musicians, support the coffee-shop crew, and he'd blown it.

"Sorry. I knew that. I just was—"

"Brain dead?" Miki's honeyed chuckle should have brought Rafe's back up, but the singer was already on the move, heading to a guitar leaning against the studio's long wall, and his tone had been more of a tease than a cut. "Shit, I can't even remember my name without a shot in the morning."

Miki's limp caught Rafe by surprise. He'd not noticed it at the Morgans' or even at the coffee shop, but in the stark, unforgiving studio lights, the singer's slight hitch was apparent. He took a step, nearly offering Miki a hand with the equipment, but common sense and Damien's warning glare brought him up short.

"Plug it in, Andrade. Show us what you've got," Damien ordered. "See if you can keep up."

RAFE WAS flying. Hands down. Balls out. Flying.

An hour into the set, something deep inside all of them seemed to shift and click into place. After that moment—that wonderful, sweet pop of a bubble—the four of them simply became something else, something larger, and it was a feeling Rafe'd never quite had before, even during Rising Black's heyday.

This, he thought, was pure playing. Flat-out strings against his fingers, sliding into the groove of the music as Damien and Miki shifted them from blues to hard rock and over into a bit of funk. It was easy to find his place amid the rhythm, guiding the lower tones along and shoring up Damien when he meandered off into the upper ranges.

Miki growled, threatened, and crooned his way around the melody, dropping down into registers Rafe didn't even know he had, and played a tight rhythm guitar, flirting with Damien and Rafe as they bracketed his singing. Forest thundered along behind him, pushing Rafe into harder streams, forcing them both to catch up with Damien in spots and reining him back in others.

He bled and sweated on his bass, the back of his hand caught by a snapped string and tearing the edge of a nail on his middle finger, but Rafe kept going. A towel and his jeans were enough to keep himself dry enough to play, and by the end of the third hour, he was hoarse from providing backup, but Damien pressed on.

Wrung dry, Rafe caught a second wind, drawing
Miki out with a telltale thumping line from the Sinners' first album. There was a hitch, something dark
fluttering into Miki's face. Then it was gone, burned
away by Damien's screaming lick, and Miki joined
in, purring his way into a song about a blind man and
shadowy rivers.

For Rafe, it was like coming home.

Damien came up for air about the time Rafe's
fingers were buzzing, numb from the vibrating steel
strings. Catching a bottle of water Forest flung at him,
Rafe heaved a sigh of relief when a shot of cold air
blasted down at him from an overhead vent. Forest'd
shed his T-shirt at some point during their drift into
SRV, and Miki somehow came up with a few hand
towels, offering Rafe one to wipe his face down with
as they took time to breathe.

"Pretty decent," Damien shouted from the mixing
room as he extracted juices from a mini-fridge. Coming back into the studio, he handed one to Miki. "We
should—"

Rafe's phone sang at him from its spot in his
open case, Quinn's number flashing across the screen
along with a photo he'd taken of him at the coffee
shop when Q hadn't been looking. The picture of the
dreamy-eyed, angelic-faced Morgan made him smile.
The panic in Quinn's voice when Rafe answered
wiped that smile clean off.

"Hey, hey. Hold on, Q. Slow down. What's going
on?" Damien was forgotten. So were Miki and Forest. The studio faded away around him, white walls
and instruments becoming nothing but visual noise
as he tuned in to Quinn's heavy breathing and tightly

wound nerves. "Babe, come on. Breathe, then talk. What's going on?"

"I need you here."

Quinn's whisper was hot, needy, and scared. Rafe's heart clenched in fear as Quinn continued.

"Something's happened. One of my students… she's dead, Rafe. Someone killed her. And—fuck—he left her on the car… my car."

"Okay, did you call the cops?" A towel seemed to be clogging up his other hand, and Rafe tossed it aside so he could sling his bass off his neck. "Where are you?"

"I called Kane and then 911." Quinn cursed in Gaelic. "I shouldn't have called you. You're playing still? Shit. *Shit.*"

"Q, you're a fuck more important than anything else, okay? Stop that. Tell me where you are." Rafe sighed when Quinn rattled off the college hall he was standing outside of. "Okay, I know where that is. I'll be there as soon as I can. Are you going to be okay until then?"

"Yeah, one of the security guards is here. Nice guy. Got me some water. Kane's on his way, and the cops got here a bit ago. They want to talk to me." Quinn's voice broke. "Suppose they think I killed her? Do you think they'll think that?"

"Honey, anyone who knows you can vouch you'd never do that. Hang tight. I'm probably closer to the bridge than Kane is. Might beat him over. Hang tight, okay?" Rafe reassured Quinn. "And just breathe."

"Thanks. For coming. For… everything."

Quinn sighed, and Rafe could almost hear him card his fingers through his black mane.

"I just… need you. Is that okay?"

"More than okay, Q. Stay someplace safe and wait for me. I'll be right there." He turned and found the band staring at him.

It was an uncomfortable stare and one Rafe couldn't read, but Quinn's fear reverberated through him, and he tucked his phone into his back pocket.

"What's up?" Miki perched himself on a low stool. "What's with Kane?"

"Nothing. I don't know the full story yet. Look, I've got to go. Sorry." Rafe spared Damien a glance, long enough to catch the flat look in his eyes. Turning his back on the band, he said, "Quinn needs me."

Walking out the door… that door… at that time probably meant losing his chance with the guys. He was literally turning his back on the band, for what? Quinn Morgan. But nothing in his gut, soul, or heart screamed at him to do anything other than pack up his bass and head over to the university where a green-eyed Irishman needed him.

In that moment Rafe realized he needed Quinn a hell of a lot more than he needed Damien, Miki, and Forest.

"Call me when you're done, and tell Kane to call Sinjun, or he's going to go insane about it."

Damien's words stopped Rafe in mid-cable-pull, and his stomach jumped up into his throat in shock.

"We can do this again at Miki's place. The sound's better over there, and the studio's cooler."

Forest's protest came in hot and fast. "Hey, fuck you. The sound here's fine."

"Air-conditioning sucks." Miki stood to grab another bottle of water. "Gotta admit that."

"Yeah, well, the maintenance guy said he had to replace a compressor or something, but not like we're cooking in here," the drummer scoffed.

"Dude, I'm drenched down my back," Damien grumbled. "If you can't do tomorrow, Rafe, we can do the day after."

Fortune always favored the bold, or so Sister Terese Mary'd always told him, so Rafe asked as calmly as he could, hoping to keep the jitters out of his voice when he spoke. "So what's this mean? I'm in?"

Damien was quick to answer, "No, we've got to—"

"Yeah, you're in." Miki shoved his best friend back a step, nudging his shoulder with the flat of his hand. "We've got to play more. Play live. But yeah, don't let this asshole fuck with you. It fits. You fit. Everything else? That's got to shake out."

"Fucker." Damien shoved back lightly, barely rocking Miki's slender torso. "I'm supposed to say—"

"Don't be an asshole, D. Okay, don't be *more* of an asshole," Miki muttered, crowding his brother in until Damien took a step back. "You know he works. Let him go. He needs to go."

"Yeah, you work. Go head out."

Damien agreed, and Forest murmured a good luck as he took the cables out of Rafe's hands.

"We'll clean up. Call. Let us know what's going on, okay?"

"Okay. Thanks." Rafe stumbled, nearly tripping on the strap on his bass. Packing it into its case, he tried to shove away all the emotions bombarding him—worry, gratitude, and under it all, a severe need to wrap his arms around the man who'd called Rafe to his side. "Fuck, thank you. I'll talk to you later.

Promise. Right now, Quinn. He's all that matters, but... fucking thanks."

"HERE YOU go, Doctor Morgan." The security guard handed Quinn a cup of hot chocolate. His thick red hair was blown back from his craggy round face as if he'd been caught in a wind tunnel, and he reached up to smooth it down, fighting to get the unruly strands to cover his high forehead. "Cocoa always makes you feel better. I even got Sally to get you some of those tiny marshmallows. Never go wrong with marshmallows."

"Thanks, Sam." Quinn took the cup gratefully. His fingers were as cold as his belly, although his chest burned with worry and stress. "And no, you can never go wrong with marshmallows."

Sam's broad smile was an uneven stairstep of teeth and gums, and he patted Quinn's shoulder awkwardly, then trundled off to chase away curious students lingering a few feet away.

The man lived with his sister, or at least in a converted garage behind his sister's house somewhere in Mission, and his nephew'd just gotten a turtle, naming it Donatello despite the fact it was a girl, but his name was easy enough to remember, mostly because the first time Quinn saw the security guard, the resemblance to the Warner Brothers' sheepdog was uncanny. Jowly and pale with a belly built on cafeteria burritos and Hostess cupcakes, Sam had been a fixture since Quinn entered graduate school, a steady barrel-chested figure in cadet blue and gray cotton who often stopped by when Quinn was working late to check on him.

He didn't want to wait at the parking garage, so he'd found a nearby bench and sat down to wait for the cops to arrive. And arrive they had. From the sheer glut of squad cars, unmarked sedans, and a pair of ambulances, it looked like a cop-mad three-year-old had emptied her entire toy box onto the lawn to reenact Jake and Elwood Blues playing in a ballroom. Kane's thick-bodied SUV perched on a curb near the parking structure's entrance, and his Irish-washed voice could definitely be heard over the low murmuring din behind the cement wall blocking Quinn's view of the Audi and LeAnne's remains.

The structure's shadowy entrance disgorged a gangly limbed man, his brown suit a bit too short for his long arms and legs, a pair of navy blue socks playing peekaboo over his dark sienna loafers with every step he took. A gold badge hung from the man's maroon belt, a choice he'd obviously made to match the tie he wore with his beige shirt. The color combination tickled an annoying spot in Quinn's brain, and he forced himself to look up from the mismatched suit, socks, and shoes before he went mad from the irritation.

Taking a good look at the man's scowling, pockmarked face, Quinn decided the shoes were a much better thing to stare at than the nuclear-hot glare he was getting from the detective. When the shoes appeared nearly beneath his nose, Quinn clutched his cocoa a little bit tighter and looked up at the man standing in front of him.

"Doctor Morgan?"

The detective made a slight show of flashing his credentials, and Quinn nodded absently, having seen more than enough badges in his lifetime.

"I'm Detective Ziortza. I want to talk to you about what happened here."

"I gave my statement to... that other detective... um, Kelley. And to the responding officers." His fingers were still cold, and Quinn debated plunging them straight into the cocoa to warm them up.

"I want to clarify a few things."

Ziortza removed a small notebook from his jacket's inner pocket, then clicked open a pen. Running over the pertinent details, Ziortza made little scratches on the paper as Quinn reaffirmed the answers he'd already given three or four times before.

"Now, care to tell me why you called Detective Morgan prior to dialing 911?"

"He's my *brother*?" Quinn frowned, matching Ziortza's darkening expression.

"How long did you wait between calling your brother and dialing for emergency services?"

"Not that long. I think as soon as I hung up. I don't know. I can check the logs." Quinn fumbled for his phone, then realized he'd given it to Kane. "Um, my brother has my phone. I think he was going to check on something—probably times. I don't know. He said something about... timing."

"Great." Ziortza sounded less than happy about Quinn's answer. "Make any calls besides your brother and 911?"

"Yes, um.... Rafe Andrade. I called him to...." Quinn couldn't remember why he'd called Rafe other than needing him to be there beside him. At the time it'd seemed like a perfectly reasonable thing to do, and in the cold of Ziortza's shadow, asking for Rafe to stop what he was doing to hold Quinn's hand seemed a bit silly—still necessary but silly. "He's a... friend."

"A friend," Ziortza repeated flatly.

There was something edgy in his voice, a familiar cant beaten in around the edges, and Quinn chased down the accent, turning it over in his head.

"This friend—"

"Ziortza. You're Basque. Second generation here?" Quinn cocked his head, studying the detective's flat-planed face and hooked nose. "You've still got the edges of it in your words. Just a little bit. Do you speak it?"

The detective reared his head up, his shoulders thrown back, then replied, "We're not here about me, Morgan. I'm here because I need to verify your alibi for the time of LeAnne Walker's murder—"

"You think I killed her?" Quinn didn't realize he'd stood until he found himself eye to eye with the tall detective. "You think *I* did *that*? Why? Who the *hell* would—"

"Detective Morgan's pointed out a recent string of unfortunate events happening around you, and I've got to wonder if he's clouded his judgment because you're his brother," Ziortza replied hotly. "Lots of chaos seems to be following you, Morgan, and no one's bringing up your less than stable mental state—"

"*Fuck you.*" Quinn stepped up into Ziortza's face, snarling as he spoke. "I will *not* be stigmatized because some fucking mouth breather of a cop's got some issues. There's nothing wrong with me. I might be wired a little bit different, but I'm not *wrong*, Detective, so you can take that badge you're wearing and shove it up your ass—"

"Hey, Q, rein it in." Kane hooked his arm around Quinn's waist to pull him back. "Ziortza, step off. You're over the line."

"Let me tell you what's over the line, Detective," Ziortza spat. "I'm looking at a dead young girl cut apart like she was a piece of meat, and I'm seeing your brother over here with a history of mental shit. You're telling me I'm stupid for looking at him for this?"

"Yeah, I'm telling you you're stupid." Kane's words were icy drops on Ziortza's heat. "Quinn's alibi is solid. Which you'd know if you hadn't walked the fuck away."

"Shaky. Liver temps are iffy, so don't give me this shit about TOD. I know we've got cut security feeds, and your boy here is already tangled up in one investigation where his brother's the primary." The detective ticked his points off on his fingers. "I did some sniffing before I got on scene, and wouldn't you know, the college pushed hard back on me when I started to poke around a certain leave of absence Morgan took when he had issues with another teacher here, a Professor Kappelhoff.

"Tie that in with the mental issues some birdie dropped into my ear about your brother and the fact Kappelhoff was carved up a few days ago. I'm perfectly within my rights to be looking at Doctor Morgan, *Detective*. Or are you primary on the Kappelhoff case just so no one *will* look at your brother?"

"I went to Ireland." Quinn spoke up. "If you'd asked, you'd have found out I'd been planning to go to Ireland *with* Simon. I wanted him to meet my gran and the rest of the family. He didn't want to go. Hell, he didn't even want people to know he was dating me or that I was gay. It's why I broke it off with him. We didn't want the same things."

"It was a loud and ugly breakup. Cops were called." Ziortza's sneer stretched over his face, a parody of a clown's grin over a scarecrow's face. "And there was your brother, Kane. Already picking up the pieces. I skimmed the report. The incident at your house could have been staged so when you did Kappelhoff, it would look like you're at the center of a shitstorm."

"And I somehow murdered LeAnne in the twenty minutes I had between seeing my last student and calling the cops?" Quinn held his hands out, showing the detective his fingers. "No way I could have done that and stayed this clean. Unless I changed my clothes and scrubbed down? It takes me five minutes to brush my *teeth*. God, I can't believe this is happening."

"Sounds like you spent more time digging crap up on my brother than you did the victim or Quinn's schedule," Kane muttered, shifting his feet apart. "Your partner's talking to the students he saw before he walked down here. The two students manning the hall's info desk said he passed by them and said hello about ten minutes before he hit 911 up. Figure in the minute or two he used to call *me* because he was rattled. That would have given him eight minutes to walk down here—a pretty long stretch even at a full jog—kill Ms. Walker, arrange her on the car, and then clean up after himself."

"He's smart—"

"Smart doesn't equal speedy. And yeah, I love my brother, but having shared a fucking bathroom with him growing up, I can tell you Quinn does *not* do speedy in a shower—especially since the closest one to the structure is on the second floor of the hall behind us." Kane ground his teeth. A deep, rumbling engine drew Kane's head up, and his eyes followed the progress of a vintage Chevelle cruising up to the edge of the police barricade. "What the fuck? What's he doing here?"

"I called him." Quinn shook off Kane's hand. "Are we done here? Because I can't—I need to get some space from this."

"Don't decide to take any trips out of the country just yet, Morgan," Ziortza ordered, stabbing a finger at Quinn's chest. "I'm not done with you yet. Either of you."

"Morgan!" Sanchez called out over the short wall. "Kane! Not you, Quinn. ME wants to talk to you. Bring Ziortza if he can break himself away from his witch hunt over there."

"Fucking unprofessional assholes." Ziortza shot Quinn one last warning look, then ambled up the slight rise to the parking structures.

"Go someplace and wait for me, or tell Rafe to be useful and take you back to my place." Kane pressed Quinn's phone into his hand. "I'll call you when it's time to leave. They're going to impound the car for Evidence. College is probably going to want you to take a leave of absence, whether you want one or not. There's going to have to be some damage control."

"I didn't kill her, Kane." Quinn grasped his older brother's arm, squeezing gently. "I *didn't*."

"I know that. They do too. It's just how things are, Q-bert," Kane reassured him. "Just don't worry about it. I'll take care of you."

"But I don't want you to take care of me," Quinn grumbled loudly as his brother walked away.

In the waning hours of the afternoon, Rafe Andrade looked like a god coming through the fading sun to find him. A very disreputable god with dirty-blond hair pulled back from a strong, handsome face and wearing a pair of torn and stained jeans barely on the side of wearable, but a god just the same. Earthy and sensual, he moved quickly through the blockade of people, murmuring something good enough to get him through Sam the security guard's tightly held perimeter. Kane's frown pushed his eyebrows into a thick storm over his blue eyes, and Quinn spat at him, a hard Gaelic reproach.

"*Damnú ort*, Kane. Don't be a dick. I don't need anyone—"

"Hope that doesn't include me, babe, because I'm pretty sure I broke a few laws of physics to get here." Rafe smiled as he jogged up to Quinn's side. "How are you doing, Q?"

"You—you're different. Kane can go to hell, for all I care right now." Quinn let himself be folded into Rafe's arms, reveling in the heat he'd been longing for. Rafe smelled of sweat, sugar, and weariness, but Quinn held on tight, wishing he could fall into Rafe's body and stay there until all the shadows lapping at his feet went away. "Gods, it's good to see you."

"Hey, I got you. Tell me what's going on," Rafe muttered into Quinn's hair, slowly letting him go. He didn't go far, about an arm's length away with his hands resting on Quinn's hips. "What happened?"

The more he told Rafe, the harder Quinn had to fight to keep his stomach where it belonged. Halfway through, his knees gave out, and Rafe caught him, easing them both down to the bench. He got to the anger he felt when Ziortza accused him of murder when Rafe pulled Quinn back into a tight hug.

"Fucker. What a fucking asshole."

Rafe's hug tightened, and Quinn nearly squeaked from his lungs being squeezed out of his throat. Loosening his embrace, Rafe muttered an apology.

"I'm glad you called me. Fuck this."

"I don't want to deal with Kane. Call me a chicken-shit, but I just… can't," Quinn confessed. "No way the dealer's going to give me another car after this, so I'll be stuck in that damned brick box until I get a rental. And I am fixated on that instead of blowing my mind apart about LeAnne. What is wrong with me? Might as well put me in a straitjacket."

"Okay, what have you got over at Miki and Kane's place?" Rafe asked.

"Clothes, books, and, well, Harley."

"The cat, right?"

"Yeah, she's a cat. Mostly," Quinn amended. "Why?"

"Think the Chevelle can hold all of it?" Rafe let Quinn go to eye his car. "Trunk's huge. The amp's up against the firewall, so that's not an issue. Couple of boxes, maybe? Suitcases?"

"And a kennel. Harley's cat litter box." Quinn cocked his head. "Again, why?"

"Because you, magpie of mine, are going to come live with me for a bit." Rafe stood, tugging Quinn to his feet. "I'm your only hope."

Quinn's already abused stomach lurched, and his tongue swelled, sticking to the roof of his mouth. "Um, the cat… and Kane… shit, are you sure?"

"Yeah, I'll take care of Kane." Rafe nodded to the parking lot, where a large black Hummer rumbled past the police cars. "Better decide fast, 'cause I think once Connor and your dad get here, chances of them letting you do anything other than breathe hysterically into a paper bag are slim to none. You up for it?"

Connor swung out of the Hummer, and Quinn nearly bit through his tongue when he saw his father get out of the car's passenger-side door. The light struck Donal's badge, winking at Quinn as Donal authoritatively strode through the packs of uniforms clustered at the parking structure's main entrance. Quinn gave himself three minutes at most before he was bundled up like a stray and tossed into the back of Connor's Hummer, where the family could keep an eye on him.

He was tired of his family's swaddling. As much as he loved them, Quinn was sick of their coddling, nudging, and eggshell walking whenever something ruffled him. It was a mutual game of do not wake the baby whenever he was near, and the murders only kicked their protectiveness into overdrive. He needed space—to think, to breathe—and if Kane and the others got their way, he wouldn't be able turn around without banging his elbow on someone he was related to.

Enough was enough, and Rafe was waiting for him to say something—anything—to the offer he'd made to give Quinn what he needed the most.

"Yeah, sure." Quinn nodded curtly. "Just let me go pack up my cat, and I'm all yours."

CHAPTER TWELVE

Gator sausage, dirty rice
Johnny Lee begging not to go
Cheap-ass whiskey sours
Getting ready for the show
Can't think of you right now, baby
Can't remember the taste of your lips
Made you a few promises
Shook those off when she rattled her hips
Hope you don't go thinkin'
I'm the man for you
Not worth your time or money
'Cause I'm looking for something new
—Bad Dog Blues

RAFE'S PENTHOUSE looked nothing like him.

The guitars on the walls, definitely Rafe. Their orderly march down toward the back of the penthouse, not so much. A yards-long view out through a wall of crystalline windows was fabulous, and Quinn caught a glimpse of the marble-and-steel patio outside, perfect for an elegant al fresco dinner or hot coffee and croissants during a clear-sky sunrise. The penthouse's warm colors were mostly Rafe, and the furniture looked comfortable, but as Quinn took in the sleek cabinets and pristine floors, he was amazed at how little the place looked like its owner.

Sterile, Quinn thought. That's the word. And if there was one thing Rafe Andrade was *not*, it was sterile.

There should have been more clutter, more vibrancy, more… everything in the space. Instead it was a pristine picture-perfect magazine spread with little to do with the hot-blooded, passionate man standing behind him.

Quinn was almost afraid to take his jacket off and toss it on an ottoman and ruin the layout.

Rafe had no problem. He shimmied out of his leather jacket, draping it over the back of a couch when he got his arms free. Harley howled her displeasure from the safety of her kennel, a chittering yodel sharp enough to send shivers up Quinn's spine. Rafe merely laughed and patted the plastic cage as he went by.

"Let her out. Where do you want me to set up her litter boxes? Bathroom? Laundry room? Middle of the kitchen?" he called out from the foyer as he dragged the rest of Quinn's things in.

"She's not picky. Anyplace she can find them." Quinn fumbled with the catch, murmuring at his cat. "Don't eat him. He's nice. We like him. He is not food."

Harley slunk herself out of the kennel, her long legs stretched out behind her. Sniffing imperiously in Quinn's general direction, she shook her head lightly, getting her ears situated as she looked about the living room.

"I put one in the laundry room, and there's a guest bathroom off the hall we can—holy shit, what the fuck is that?" Rafe stopped dead in his tracks, bobbling a half-full container of litter. "Seriously, dude. What happened to your cat? She looks like she's from Chernobyl or something."

"She's a Cornish Rex. That's how their fur is. Just a little bit of it, really."

He was quick to jump to Harley's defense, standing up to face Rafe. Bending down, Rafe wiggled his fingers at the cat.

"Don't be offended if she takes a little bit to warm up—"

Damned if Harley didn't make Quinn a liar and trot up to Rafe for loving. Delicately standing up on her hind legs, she pressed her front paws on the top of his knee, purring up a storm as she rubbed her face against Rafe's chin.

"Hey, kinda like velvet." Rafe picked Harley up, and the cat buried her head in his hair, rumbling deep in her chest. "She's cool. I like the spots. Great name—Harley. Very badass."

"My coworker Graham suggested it." Quinn unsnapped the latches of the kennel to break it down. "I was kind of surprised because he's not the motorcycle type, but it suited her. She sounds like a Harley once she starts purring."

"This Graham guy, when he suggested her name, did he say something like 'You should call her Harley,

Quinn'?" Rafe scritched the cat's serpentine body as she wiggled in his arms.

"Yeah," he replied, packing the crate down.

"He was probably telling you to call her Harlequin, like those Italian clowns." Rafe laughed, probably at the astonished expression on Quinn's face. "'Cause she's spotted."

"Well, shit." He felt a flush creep across his face. "Graham didn't even say anything when I told him I called her Harley like he suggested. God, what an idiot."

"I love you, but man, sometimes for all your smarts, you're a git—as your mom says."

Rafe jerked his head down the hall, obviously not hearing the heavy pounding of Quinn's heart.

"I'll show you the guest suite. You won't believe the bathtub in there. I think the designer thought I was going to have water orgies or something. I think it fits five people."

Rafe was right about the tub. The room was incredible, overlooking the Bay, but the bathroom was built for lounging and possibly water sex. It was the only reason Quinn could come up with for a marble tub that size. He put his toiletries bag on the counter, then began to unpack his things. Rafe came in behind him and set Harley down on the counter. She mewled her discontent, wheedling to be picked up again, but Rafe ignored her and palmed one of Quinn's medicine bottles.

"What's this?" He turned it around, finding the directions.

"It's to help me… focus. Sort of," Quinn mumbled, reaching to extract the bottle from Rafe's fingers. Or at least he tried to, but Rafe closed his hand before Quinn could grab it. "Give it. I don't like—it helps me be… *normal*. Focused. Kind of."

"Nothing not normal about you, Q. It's your normal, and if this shit helps you, then great, but I've got to ask you one thing." Rafe shook the bottle. "This stuff. Do I have to be worried about it?"

"Worried how?"

"If this stuff's addictive… I can't have it in the house, Q."

Rafe's face was cold, a mask of indifference Quinn knew he was hiding behind. Despite the chill in Rafe's expression, Quinn could see the pain and fear in Rafe's soft brown eyes.

"I just… can't, babe. I can't trust… me."

"I didn't think about that. Shit. I thought you were talking… never mind what I thought." Quinn tapped the bottle's top. The marble was cold through his clothes where Quinn leaned against the bathroom counter, but all he felt was the hot length of Rafe's body pressed up to his side. "It's not addictive. Not controlled in any way."

"And it helps you how?"

Quinn dug down into everything he knew about reading faces and the lessons he'd learned fucking it up, but nothing in Rafe's face held any judgment. He was curious, concerned a bit, but for the most part—wondering more about the how of the pills and not the why.

It'd been so fucking long since the *why* of the pills wasn't important to someone, and *that* person'd been Miki St. John, not exactly a poster child of stability himself.

"The dosage I take's just enough to help me edge off the… spiders in my head. Like coffee, but better."

"You're the only person I know who drinks coffee to calm them down, Q," Rafe murmured, brushing Quinn's hair back from his forehead. "How does it make you feel? Taking it. Not what it does to your body but... you? Are you okay with it? I don't think I'd be."

"It's usually okay. It just gets... old," Quinn confessed. There he was, standing in a bathroom about the size of his father's study, digging his soul and heart out about the one thing he never spoke about, then handing it all over to Rafe, of all people. Oddly, the whispering secrets, the heat of Rafe's hand, and the gentle push of his voice brushed away the sharp edges prickling Quinn's thoughts.

"Talk to me, Q." Rafe's smirk was gentle and teasing. "Just you and me here."

Quinn's fingers seemed to find Rafe's waistband of their own accord, and he hooked two into a belt loop, tugging on Rafe's jeans as he spoke. "Truth? It's fucking shitty because it makes you... makes *me* feel like I can't be normal unless I take something. And then I get used to it until one day I get mad again. Then I don't want to take it. So, most of the time it's okay, and then it's not.

"I guess sometimes I hate it. I hate it because the family's always saying shit like 'Did you take your meds?' Especially if I'm grumpy or pissed off about shit they do. Because I can't be mad or pissy. Like it's a magical little gumdrop I just forgot about, and if I take one, it's all better, and I won't cause any problems." He tugged again, staring at the denim loop, unwilling to look up into Rafe's face, afraid of what he'd see there. "And I love them, but they're always there, always in my face, and sometimes I just want to be normal so they don't handle me like they do. They treat me differently, and I hate it. All because I need ten milligrams of a fucking drug to help me even things out a bit."

"It was worse before, right?" Rafe stepped in closer until their hips brushed. His breath was hot on Quinn's cheek, a warm kiss of wind in the bathroom's slightly cold air. "I remember…. Q, it wasn't a good time for you before. Does this shit help with that?"

"Some. Mostly better now that I'm out of puberty. *That* shit didn't help. Some behavior modifications worked. Tools to focus on things I forget." He made a face, mostly at Rafe's chest. "There's no instructions, you know? I have to stop and remember what to say to people or try to fix their names to their faces, and I can't recall their faces.

"It's worse if they talk to me first because I answer automatically, but then the follow-through—like asking how they're doing—that doesn't always follow. It's worse when I'm tired because I forget. And if I don't control everything—every damned little thing—something falls through the cracks. I panic, and it swings so high or low, cutting into me, and I can't stop that feeling." He shrugged, trying to ease away the rising helplessness inside of him. "So there's the *why* for the pills. To keep everything from swinging too far. To keep *me* from going SuperBall in my brain."

"People joke about better living through chemicals." The heel of Rafe's hand ghosted under Quinn's chin, forcing him to look up. "For me, not so good. For you, maybe okay."

"Mostly okay," he whispered softly, trembling under Rafe's touch. "I just have to remind myself sometimes that it's worse if I don't take them. But oh, I *hate* having to need to."

"*That* I understand, magpie," he laughed. "Come on. Bet that clan of yours is about to light the torches because you've gone AWOL."

"I left Kane a note." It was a stretch of the truth, a piece of hastily scribbled-on paper tacked onto the kitchen fridge. "Sort of. I left Da a voicemail. Let him deal with their shit. He made them. He can deal with Kane and Con."

"I'm game if you are. How about some dinner? Feel like some food?"

Rafe's fingers were back in Quinn's hair, and he resisted the urge to move his cheek into Rafe's palm. Not daring to speak, Quinn nodded.

"Good," Rafe said. "One thing, though, why's your cat splashing around in the toilet? 'Cause I sure as shit don't know where a mop is in this place."

QUINN WAS choking on blood. No matter how much he tried swallowing, it bubbled back in, a steady river pushing past his teeth to flood his throat and sinuses. He tried screaming, tried doing anything other than drowning in the thick metallic mass pouring over him, but nothing came out—nothing *happened*—and when Quinn's eyelids won their fight against the rushing tide of blood, he opened them to find only darkness.

LeAnne came out at him from the shadows, her mouth stretched wide in a vulgar mockery of the gaping wound carved into her belly. Her lips were slung down low, pushed nearly to her chin from the weight of her intestines spilling over her broken teeth and undulating tongue.

He fought to be free of the shadows wrapping around him, but they clung too firmly, a stygian strait-jacket Quinn couldn't work loose. If anything, the pressure on his body tightened, cutting off his airway and pushing his ribs in, the bones turning knifelike to slice through his flesh. Horrifyingly, a jut of steel bone burst through his belly before curving a half-moon cut into his skin.

"Come on, baby. Come back to me here."

Rafe's purring rasp broke through the gurgle of blood pouring from Quinn's mouth, and he blinked, losing his battle to the gush once again.

"Hey. Hey, I'm right here, Q. Just pull up, babe. For me. Come on."

Rafe shouldn't have been there. Not in the middle of the gore and foul-smelling ichors. The darkness lightened, peeling away in ashen sheets. Then Quinn gasped, finally able to breathe despite the sour metallic wash in his throat and lungs.

"There you go. Come back to me, magpie. I've got you."

A warmth encompassed Quinn, burning away the last remaining cold tendrils wrapping around his chest.

"Open those gorgeous eyes of yours. That's it. Hey, there you are."

The dream wisped away into smoke, flecks of gray lingering in Quinn's mind as he surfaced out of his nightmare's drowning pool. He blinked, and Le-Anne was gone. He'd sat up at some point, or Rafe'd pulled him up, because he found himself nearly sprawled over Rafe's lap, his arms wrapped around Quinn's waist.

Then LeAnne came to him, her empty eyes fogged with confusion and pain, and Quinn felt the panic ride him again as he tasted blood in his mouth and the sting on his tongue where he'd nearly bitten through its flesh.

"Oh God, the girl," Quinn gasped, thankful for the rush of cold air burning when he took a breath. "Her eyes, Rafe. God, her eyes. She kept staring at me. Just looking at me—"

"I know, babe. Come on," Rafe murmured, rocking Quinn in a slow curve. "Hey, Q. I'm right here. It's just a dream."

"She's *dead*, Rafe. And I killed her." The image of LeAnne's shocked slack face blurred, swaddled by emotions and other memories. "God, she looked at me… like when I had to put Tommy to sleep, the cat you brought home to us. Remember him? He was so sick… and so old… and when the vet said we couldn't do any more for him, I wanted to be the one who held him then, you know?"

"Yeah, I know, babe. But this… she's not on you."

"She is. And she had the same look in her eyes that he did."

He had to get free of Rafe's arms, if only to shake the feeling back into his hands. Rafe refused to let go, shifting to keep hold of his waist, and Quinn gulped in more air.

"It was like she was saying 'Why are you making me go away?' Like he did. God, I didn't want to let him go, even though I knew there wasn't anything I could do, all I could think was he's asking me why I am sending him away. She was dead, and I could hear her screaming at me—"

"You didn't kill her, Q." Rafe shifted, rocking Quinn back. "You didn't kill Tommy either. Don't—"

"She had the same look in her eyes—like he did, Rafe." Everything hurt. His heart lost control of itself and threatened to beat its way free of its prison, and no amount of breathing seemed to calm it down. "I held him, and he looked at me that way. And I didn't want to let him go. Because he was all I had left of you. That's how LeAnne looked. It's crazy because she's… a person, and he was… but she looked so confused. Like he did. He was so confused and—"

"Baby, I need you to focus on me." Rafe turned, settling Quinn against the headboard. Straddling Quinn's lap, he rested his weight on his knees and took Quinn's face into his hands, forcing Quinn to stare straight ahead. "Listen to me, okay?"

"Okay." He knew he was crying. It was childish and stupid, a nova of emotions he couldn't quite seem to tamp down, and Rafe's voice promised so much.

"LeAnne… was a dream. You didn't have anything to do with her dying. Someone else did that. Some sick fucking asshole took her from her family, and *that* person fucked up her life. Not you." Rafe leaned in, his hair curtaining around their faces. "Can you see that? Tell me you see that."

It sounded so simple, so logical, but the stain of LeAnne's death ran deep. "I led him to her. She wouldn't have died if—that *tuilí*—he shouldn't have seen her. He wouldn't have even known she was alive if I'd—"

"We don't even know for certain *you're* the one this guy is after."

Rafe stroked his thumb over Quinn's chin. It was a silly caress, almost as if Quinn had smeared ice cream on his face, but something in Quinn's belly turned over and begged for more with each pass of Rafe's finger.

"And if he is, I'm not going to let him get even five miles near you. I've got you now. Here. Okay? It'll be okay."

"Tommy was my fault," Quinn confessed. "I just didn't want to... I argued with Mum about letting him go. Because he was so sick. I kept hoping he'd get better. I kept hoping, you know? And when I knew I couldn't let him suffer anymore, I still couldn't... I kept thinking I wasn't doing enough for him."

"For the record, Tommy was fucking ancient. And I'm not sure how one has to do with the other, but in that too-smart Moebius-strip brain of yours, they do. And I'm going to tell you flat out, he was kind of old and beat up before he ever went to live with you guys. He was horny, mean, and somehow got your mom's cat knocked up in the *one* hour he was in the house before he headed to the vet to get snipped."

Rafe brushed his lips over the tip of Quinn's nose, and Quinn shivered under the contact.

"That cat loved you. No two ways about it. Fighting, fucking, and Quinn. That's what that cat lived for. And you've got to know, Q, you didn't lose any of me when Tommy went on. You've *always* got me, okay?"

Despite Rafe's soothing hands, the dark lingered around the edges of the room, shoved back only slightly by a slender twisted-metal lamp on the nightstand. Quinn tugged at his waist, finding he was still wearing the jeans and T-shirt he'd changed into so the medical examiner could take his work clothes off to the lab. The denim was sticky and heavy, dragging along his thighs where the fabric twisted around as he'd slept.

It had to be late, much later than he'd imagined, because Rafe was half-naked in a pair of long shorts and bare chested, his dirty-blond hair rumpled from sleep. Quinn halfway remembered wanting to lie down for an hour before he ate something. He'd been so tired, and the last thing he'd heard from Rafe was something about a pizza.

"Talk to me, Q." Rafe patted his cheeks, a devilish smirk lurking on the pout of his mouth. "Do you need a pill? One of those magic ones?"

"Is that a joke?" He cut Rafe a look, but the smile tugged him higher out of the black. "Fucker. You know I hate that."

"I know." He could feel Rafe's laugh echo through his hands. "It's why I said it."

"Dick." Quinn sighed, feeling the butterfly sharp of his panic settling down, its serrated flutter slowing as his breathing got easier. There was more than the panic in him, something softer and sweeter—something whiskey-hot and golden—Rafe. He could actually *feel* Rafe's affection touching the coldest and dampest parts of his soul, a spray of *bokeh* to fill the emptiness he had inside of him. "Oh God, I can feel you."

"I'm almost sitting on top of you." Rafe chuckled. "I hope you can feel me."

"No," he whispered, shaking his head as much as he could, clasped in Rafe's palms. "I mean... inside of me. Do you know how hard it is to *feel* anything? I can *feel* you. I mean, I usually have to guess... hope... that what I feel for other people is how they feel about me. I hear Mum say she loves me, but—"

"Q, if you think your mom doesn't love you, you've got more than just that one loose screw. She'd fucking *kill* for you."

"I know she would, but a lot of times, I can't… it's hard to explain. It's like my heart doesn't… I can feel *out*, but I can't feel *in*. I have to trust in what people tell me. Da, I can feel him… I can *hear* him inside of me. He's like this bass drum, rumbling away behind my soul. Kane I get tingles from all the time… and Con. But—" Quinn stopped short, aware of Rafe's piercing stare and how close he'd come to spilling out the secret he'd held inside him for longer than he could remember. Feebly he tried to recover, hoping to gather up what little shreds of his dignity he had left. "Never mind. I'm rambling because I'm tired and—"

"Yeah, I feel you too, magpie," Rafe whispered, and Quinn's darkness exploded in a rush of stars.

It was a perfect kiss, the taste of Rafe on his tongue bursting with maleness and heat. Quinn was aware of every inch of Rafe's body, of his hands as they held his face and the flat of Rafe's bare chest where Quinn placed his palm to steady himself as the room spun around them.

It was unlike any other kiss he'd had before. There was no wondering when it would end or listening to their teeth clinking. Instead Quinn fell into Rafe's mouth, needing more—begging for more—and when Rafe pushed him back into the headboard, Quinn's dick responded, growing hard and wanting beneath the tightness of his dream-sweaty jeans.

Their mouths broke apart, and Quinn heard himself mewl, a needy sound he'd dragged up from his balls to lay out before Rafe in the hopes for more. Rafe leaned forward, resting his forehead on Quinn's temple so his breath washed warm over Quinn's flushed face. His shorts bagged down, the heft of his cock pressing into Quinn's hip, and Rafe ran one hand down Quinn's side, stroking at him through the fabric.

Quinn didn't know what to say or how to say it. Too many doubts crowded in—whispering smoky trails of reasons Rafe Andrade would plunder his mouth or push him hard against the heavy wood. He was there, his mind vomited back. Rafe was being nice because Quinn had a bad dream. Or even the deeply buried fear of Rafe Andrade teasing out a kiss just because he could.

"Rafe—" He needed to find some way to let Rafe go, anything he could find so Rafe could slide off the bed and leave Quinn's borrowed room without having any guilt or obligation. But for the life of him, Quinn found nothing but the fading stars Rafe left inside him and the bruised promise of Rafe's lips on his own.

Then Rafe sighed sweetly, and the emptiness inside Quinn trembled, threatening to shatter into a million black specks, too tiny and impotent to gather up again.

"Fucking hell, Quinn," Rafe whispered, skimming his mouth over Quinn's, his tongue teasing the plumped flesh of Quinn's lower lip. "You have no idea how long I've wanted to do that. Or how good you fucking taste."

CHAPTER THIRTEEN

Tearing down the road, Devil on my tail
Told you not to love me, Told you I'd bail
Kittens and daisies, Picnics and wine
Till the day I walk, and you're no longer mine
—Devil on My Tail

"DON'T... DO this. Don't play with me, Rafe." Quinn's anguished whisper tore through Rafe, shredding the pleasurable glow their kiss left in him. "I can't—"

Rafe didn't know what was funnier—the shock of Quinn believing he'd lead him on, or his own arrogance in thinking Quinn would be all in solely because Rafe'd kissed him. The pain in Quinn's eyes was real, the anguish in his voice a tear across Rafe's soul.

"Hey, no, no, no." Rafe brushed a kiss across Quinn's cheek, then shifted his weight back onto his haunches, careful not to rest on Quinn's legs. "Q, you've got to know, I'm not—babe, today when you called me, I was in the middle of playing with the Sinners' guys, but I heard your voice, and all I could think about was getting the fuck out of there to be with you."

"You should have stayed with them. You should have...." Quinn's teeth worried at his lower lip, dimpling the swell Rafe'd just tasted. "You *want* that so badly—"

It was rough hearing his dreams spill from Quinn's mouth. Harder still to understand that the passion he'd felt in his blood that morning in the studio was like the flaring rush of a drug in his veins instead of the simmering burn of Quinn's body against his own. The burn stayed, Rafe realized, no matter where he was. The want for Quinn was there, and a part of him sighed with relief whenever Quinn was around.

"Yeah, I did want it. I do. But Q, right there at that moment when I heard you, I found out I could walk out that door—and never come back—if I was walking towards you," he whispered, cupping Quinn's cheekbones until their foreheads touched and all Rafe could see was Quinn's face. "And it scares the shit out of me, Q. I'm not going to lie to you. *You* scare the shit out of me.

"You are everything to me, Quinn. Today I figured that out, and I'm sorry it took me so fucking long about it, but... when it's all said and done, you're kind of who I've been running from my entire damned life, because not having you—not loving you—made me hurt so much inside. All this time I've been trying to fill this hole inside of me, fucking around, drugs and shit, when what I should have done was just come home—and find you," Rafe whispered into the tight space between their faces, the slice of air and shared breath that'd become their world. "I'm shit. I know that. I'm fucking nothing… especially compared to you. I kissed you because I *need* you. Because I finally fucking figured out—today of all shitty days for you—that I need you, and I don't want to let you go."

Quinn's lashes flew up, fluttering black sweeps over his glittering green eyes. His breathing was shallow, held tight in his chest as he studied Rafe, his lips parted and glistening. When he finally spoke, the mists of an Irish forest followed, his thickening accent blurring the edges of his words. "You are *not* nothing, Rafe Andrade. Don't you be saying that to me—to yourself, even—not to anyone. You've—"

"I was handed a fucking gift of a life, Q, and I screwed it up," Rafe whispered over Quinn's melodic rumbling. "Not good at school, hated the world, and the one thing I could do, I fucked it sideways and threw it away."

"You have a chance again. With Damie and Miki—"

"I'd rather have a chance with you," Rafe murmured, chuckling at Quinn's sharp intake of breath. "Sure, I'd love to be a part of whatever the fuck Damie's putting together, but if I've got to choose between you and them—even if you aren't a sure thing and you want to walk away from me—I'm going to choose you. Just like I did today. Because apparently that's what's got to happen. I just need you to know that. I want you to understand the *last* thing in the world I'd do is hurt you—tease you or lead you on."

"You never looked at me before," Quinn whispered back, a soft reproach riddled with doubt. "Why now?"

"Jesus, Quinn. You think I didn't look? I couldn't help but look." Rafe grimaced ruefully, recalling the sharp glances he'd gotten from Connor and Kane. "You were a kid. I wasn't much more of one and a selfish asshole. Don't look at me like that. It's the truth. And let's face it, your brothers would have kicked my fucking ass if I touched you when we were younger. You forget you were *sixteen* when I went on the road the first time? Looking was my best bet. Then leaving was the only thing I could do to keep sane."

"Don't think it worked," Quinn teased, and Rafe smiled, seeing a lightness touching the edges of the dark lingering in Quinn's mood.

"Today I was driving to get you, and it felt like I was choking down razor blades. I was *that* balls-out scared." Rafe shifted on the bed, evening his weight out on his knees. His thighs ached a bit, muscles stretched out while he straddled Quinn's thighs, but for the first time in his life, Rafe had Quinn Morgan where he wanted him, under him—mostly. "Not because I didn't think you weren't strong enough to handle what was going on. It was because I didn't want you to be alone… and I wanted to be the one who was there for you. Like I should have been before."

"We wouldn't have worked before," Quinn replied, his lips ghosting a kiss on Rafe's thumb as it moved across his chin. "You needed to get lost, and I needed to get found. But now…."

"Now's different, babe." Rafe cocked his head. "I wandered off way too far before. I had to come back to you to find myself. Man enough to admit it. Man enough to know I'm shit without you. All of the noise and screaming inside of me just goes away when you're near me. I *forget* about the crap that doesn't really matter."

He could have said more. Hell, Rafe knew he could have strung words together like a pearl necklace, but they wouldn't matter much to Quinn. His magpie would be more interested in the glisten or a single drop slightly off color than the rest. He'd pick it apart to examine the knots, then laugh when it scattered, broken into a confetti splash of noise and sheen. The whole never mattered. Not to Quinn. Not to the man who saw into Rafe's soul and knew who was there.

"No one else understands how much I need to play," Rafe whispered. "Do you know that?"

"Pretty sure Miki and Damie do." Quinn's hands were light, gentle touches on Rafe's bare chest, curving over the planes of his stomach with a delicate, feathery skim.

"They don't matter." Rafe chuckled at Quinn's snort. "They don't. Trust me, Q. They're not who I want to do this to."

This kiss was deeper, hotter, and Quinn moaned against Rafe's mouth when Rafe pulled him away from the headboard and down onto the bed. Stretching out over Quinn's lanky body, Rafe fisted Quinn's black mane, then held him still as he plundered his mouth. Their teeth brushed, humming a pearly chime, and Rafe chuckled, feeling the sound reverberate across their tongues.

Then Quinn's passion flared, deepening their kiss, and Rafe lost all thought of pearls and chimes.

Licks of fire spread under Rafe's skin, and he fought to get free of his clothes. Quinn's tongue flicked over the roof of his mouth, sending a sparkling trail of desire careening down Rafe's belly and straight to his cock, hardening his shaft until Rafe was sure it would burst from his anticipation. He needed to breathe, his lungs tightening under his ribs, but Rafe couldn't bring himself to break away, not with Quinn's hands moving over his hips to push his shorts down.

"I don't know what to do with you," Quinn panted. He squirmed beneath Rafe, the button on his jeans scraping across Rafe's bare stomach. "I mean.... Rafe, I'm not good at this."

Quinn's fingers pressed dimples into Rafe's ass, spreading his partially nude cheeks out. A lick of air touched Rafe's balls, and its slight chill slapped a bit of sense into the primal growl in Rafe's brain. He needed to slow down, take his time exploring Quinn's body and letting him do the same back. Forcing himself to focus, Rafe panted into the crook of Quinn's neck.

"Babe, you get any better at this, you're going to kill me," Rafe groused playfully. "Just do what feels good. If I do anything you don't like, tell me, because, Q, I want you to feel *good*."

"I already feel good." Quinn squeezed again. Then his hands drifted down under Rafe's waistband, and he ran his fingertips through the soft hair on Rafe's thighs. "I just want you to show me what to do. I've never done—*that*. All of it."

"*That* isn't all there is, you know," Rafe hissed through clenched teeth when the elastic on his shorts was pushed all the way down past the rise of his ass. "You tell me. You want what? What do you want me to do? Flat out. Just say it."

Quinn looked up at him, his long fingers working their way out of Rafe's shorts and up along the groove

of Rafe's spine. His quizzical expression was so familiar it brought a twinge of joy to Rafe's heart, and
he laughed, then bit Quinn on his shoulder.

"Stop thinking so hard, magpie. Just spit it out. I
can take it." Rafe pulled up, smirking playfully. "Or
put it in. Whatever you say goes."

"I've never... fucked anyone." Amid the heat
of their bodies, Quinn's whisper was a tiny breath
of chilling doubt. "Last guy I was with... I didn't....
It's different with you. I want *this* with you." Quinn's
voice broke, ragged with need and emotion. "I want to
be inside you. At least... once. And, well, you in me."

"Been a long time for me, Q. Not going to lie, but
we're sure as hell going to do it more than once." Rafe
cupped Quinn's chin, giving him a fierce kiss. "Stay
right here. We're going to need some things."

RAFE ANDRADE'S mouth was on his cock.

It'd been other places on Quinn's body as well,
but at that moment, in that pristine, perfect, crystalline
moment, the lips he'd wanted to kiss for as long as he
could remember were wrapped around his dick.

And he could barely stop himself from shooting
long threads of come down Rafe's tight throat just
from the sight of it.

Stripped naked, Quinn felt embarrassed, nearly
shy. Every sexual encounter he'd been involved with
had been in the dark. With Rafe, the lights were a
golden glow spreading across the room and onto the
bed, casting the bassist's hard, toned body into a stark
relief of flat planes and strong curves. Rafe's long
limbs and broad chest rippled as he moved, his shoulder muscles bulging with every dive and dip of his
head as he sucked down Quinn's shaft.

Rafe's hair, gilded from running in the sparse San Francisco sun, poured over his face, mingling with the trail of soft black hair feathering down from Quinn's belly button. It tickled. Not as much as Rafe's fingers as they explored Quinn's balls, but enough to make him tense at the teasing sensations along his hip.

"Going to lose myself, Rafe." He hated he didn't have a nickname for Rafe, the smooth offshoot of affection easily spun out by others. His mind wandered down that path, threatening to dislodge him from his pleasure. Then Rafe's lips nearly brushed the root of his dick, and his head slid into the tightness beyond Rafe's tongue, and Quinn gasped, his thoughts scattering beneath the desire Rafe called up from him. "Oh… God."

He was pretty sure he'd lapsed into Gaelic. Or at least the bastardized version his family was known for. What came out of his mouth was a combination of curses and pleas amid the muttering of sordid English phrases uttered in a dark, guttural moan, and from the smug, satisfied look on Rafe's face as he pulled his lips free of Quinn's cock, the throat swallow had been done solely to keep Quinn from meandering away in his own mind.

"I like that you know me," Quinn whispered, stroking Rafe's face. There was a bit of a scruff, a rough velvet along Rafe's jaw. He'd felt the burn of it on his thighs and neck where Rafe'd brushed up against him, rubbing into Quinn's skin like a cat marking its territory. "I don't have to… explain with you."

"Never—or hardly ever," Rafe murmured, crawling up the length of Quinn's torso to reach his face for a kiss. It was oddly salty, spiced with the lemony mint of Rafe's mouth and a tingle of something muskier beyond. With that kiss Quinn was lost, fallen hard for the soul he'd known for years. "Now, your turn. You and I, we're going to make some music of our own."

Quinn bungled it. As graceful as a three-legged flamingo, he swore when he lost the bottle of lube someplace in the sheets, then nearly gave up when he tore the wrapper off the condom Rafe'd given him only to somehow puncture the sheath with his index finger.

"Found it," Rafe declared, holding up the recalcitrant bottle. His burst of laughter at Quinn's dejection was bright, a splash of color on the dim of the flaccid latex. "It's okay, Q. There's about ten more. We'll go for testing. Then… we won't have to deal with those—"

"Past tonight?" The thought punched a hole in Quinn's chest. He was already shaken to the core at the idea of sliding his body into Rafe's. Suddenly there were breakfasts and movie nights with long battles over which way the toilet paper went on the spool and arguments about cat horf in shoes. The butterflies in his stomach grew teeth—no, fangs—and they savaged Quinn's nerves, tearing him apart. "Shit, I can't—I'm not. You can't want me for that. I'm not—"

"Breathe, baby," Rafe murmured softly, holding Quinn's face.

They shared a kiss made only of their breath, and Quinn tasted himself on Rafe's exhale, marveling in the surety in Rafe's golden-brown eyes.

"This isn't a one-time thing, Q. Not us. Not ever. I told you. I'm in this. If you want me. Don't let that hay-and-needles brain of yours skew things sideways, and don't go borrowing trouble. You and me… we work, don't we? In our odd, weird way?"

There were confessions to be made, gentle admissions of truth Quinn held in the folds of his heart. They came pouring out, a rush of words and flailing fears, stinging his throat as they coursed out from his belly. Nothing made sense... not until the final dense chunk of words he choked out, its hard edges nearly bleeding him dry as he flung them at Rafe in a hurried panic.

"I think I'm in love with you," he burbled, pulling away from Rafe's hands. "God, is this what that feels like? This sucks. I feel sick and scared and.... Jesus fucking Christ, Rafe—"

"You said you feel me, Q. That you've always felt me. Now hear me. I'm not going to go anywhere. Not unless you tell me you want me to get lost." Rafe caught him up again, pulling Quinn's attention back. "I'm getting a second chance here—with a band that kicks ass and most of all, with you. Best of all, with you. And if I lose everything all over again, I am going to fight like fucking hell to *never* lose you.

"I see you looking at me—all warm and sweet— and all I think about is how I don't deserve you. Don't deserve that affection, but see, I'm an asshole, Quinn. Because I'm going to take it—and hold on tight." Rafe pressed a sweet kiss to Quinn's lips, chuckling at their mingled sighs. "I love you, Quinn. Hell, I fucking *like* you. But most of all, I love you, magpie."

"Are you sure?" Quinn heard himself whisper. "Because I have to make sure you're *sure*."

"Oh yeah, Q. I'm sure." Rafe dug the lube bottle out of the sheets again. "And right now, I want you. So fucking much I'm hurting in places I never even knew my dick had."

Rafe was playful. Quinn'd never *played* before, and the *laughter* was extraordinarily sexy. He fumbled again with the condom, his fingers going cold and numb from nerves until he could no longer stand it and handed Rafe the wrapper.

He could only gasp when Rafe took Quinn's cock in hand, then slid the latex sheath snugly down its length.

"Can't wait for you," Rafe whispered, nibbling Quinn's ear. "Cannot fucking wait."

The lube was a slick mess on their fingers, running into a puddle on Quinn's palm. Stretched out on his back, Rafe watched Quinn with hooded eyes as he knelt down between Rafe's bended, spread knees, murmuring encouragement when Quinn touched the rim of his hole. Rafe's fingers clenched and pulled at the sheets as Quinn explored the crinkled edges of Rafe's entrance. Then his body stiffened when Quinn slid two fingers into Rafe's heat.

It was like nothing Quinn ever felt before, yet the pulse of Rafe's flesh around him was as familiar to him as his own heartbeat.

He dove in, carefully exploring the curve of Rafe's inner core, watching the reactions he could wring from his lover, spread out before him on the bed. Rafe's cock jutted up from its curled golden nest, spearing the musky night air with its rigid, flushed form. A bit of liquid welled up along its velvety head, a daub of pearl in its silken divot. Sliding his fingers in as far as they could go, Quinn pushed up against the ring of Rafe's ass, then bent over, licking at the sweet bitterness of Rafe's seed.

"God, Q... shit," Rafe groaned, reaching down to clamp his fingers around the base of his cock. "Need you in me before... *please.*"

A part of Quinn longed to plunge in... straight in with no looking back. He was holding his breath. He realized that when the world went sparkly around the edges and his chest hurt. Taking in sharp pulls of air, Quinn steadied himself and looked down at Rafe's waiting body.

He was beautiful. Quinn had no other word for Rafe but beautiful. Earthy and angelic, he was everything a mother would warn their sons and daughters about, and yet no one made Quinn feel as cherished... protected... as *loved* as Rafe. The tangle of his gold hair and the sly, teasing cant of his mouth was as familiar to Quinn as his own face—perhaps more so since Quinn'd spent more time staring at Rafe than he had himself—yet Quinn was still fascinated with Rafe's beauty and delighted at the *normal* they shared.

"God, you make me feel normal," Quinn whispered. "Like I'm just... like there's nothing wrong with me."

"There's *nothing* wrong with you, babe," Rafe replied, stroking Quinn's cheek with his thumb. "You're who you are. You're *Quinn.*"

If Rafe's whispers freed him, Rafe's touch gave Quinn wings. Guiding himself into Rafe, Quinn met his lover's eyes, holding Rafe's gaze as he sank in deeper until he strained against the push of Rafe's legs against his shoulders. Wrapped tight in Rafe's body, Quinn let go, flinging himself into the beyond of their joined bodies.

And discovered he could fly.

There was nothing else around him. Some part of his mind *knew* the noises and disturbances of objects and colors were there, lurking at the periphery of his awareness, but none of it mattered anymore. He couldn't feel the harsh tickles of light on his mind or have to fight against the pull of something moving around him. All he had in his thoughts—at his fingertips—was Rafe. Rafe and the pleasure sliding into his body, setting his nerves on fire as lightning tendrils broke through the thick membrane of his thoughts and drowned him in their white flares.

Rafe quieted his world—became his world—and Quinn reveled in its blessed, sweet silence.

He thrust hard, riding some thoughtless urge to plunge deep into Rafe's body—into Rafe himself— until their skin slapped wet and hard where their bodies met. He'd never felt so alive, so *physical*, with only the thought of pulling Rafe's pleasure out of him.

At some point Quinn was distantly aware of the burn in his thighs and the gouge of Rafe's fingers into his ass. Rafe's voice, broken and buttery, urged him on, nearly pleading Quinn to tear him apart so they could heal within each other. There was wet on Quinn's face, a spill of tears nearly as scorching hot as Rafe's clench around his cock. Then he felt Rafe stiffen, shouting hoarsely while Quinn continued on.

There was an angle Quinn twisted into, a certain spot he could find in Rafe's body, and when he glided over it, Rafe shook with desire. As Rafe's hands clenched and roamed over Quinn's chest, twisting at his tight nubs, Quinn found that spot again, and Rafe seized, shoving himself as far down Quinn's cock as he could, unable to do anything but take what Quinn gave him.

"Come for me, Rafe," Quinn whispered, hunkered over Rafe's belly with his head down. His hands were fitted under Rafe's ass, pulling him up so Quinn could find the sweet spot in Rafe's core. "I want to see you. Want to watch you. I want to see what I do to you."

There were no more words Quinn could find on his tongue. Something molten built up in the churn of his balls, and it licked up his cock, arching up in a rush to find release. Trembling, Quinn thrust again, rocking his hips over and over into Rafe's ass, barely aware of the sting of Rafe's nails scoring his arms.

"Shit, going to lose it, Q." Rafe reached for himself, tightening his fingers over his own cock. He twisted and pulled, working his length in time to Quinn's pounding. Something broke in Rafe, and he cried out, clenching down on Quinn hard enough to pull at Quinn's soul.

The hot gush hit Quinn's face, and he gasped, surprised at the pungent thickness of Rafe's spill. A dab of his tongue swiped through the fluid on his lip, and Rafe's essence bloomed in Quinn's throat, drowning out everything beyond.

Rafe's taste in his mouth was enough to send Quinn over, and he shook with the force of his release, unable to hold himself any longer as his cock felt like it was splitting apart. He came, hard and fast, until Quinn wondered numbly if he would ever stop. The wave struck him hard, and Quinn went under, drowning in the release. A moment later he collapsed onto Rafe's stomach, gasping at the shivers rippling through him.

He was sad to feel himself slide free. Physics be damned, he wanted to stay inside Rafe for as long as he could—forever, if possible. One way or another,

Quinn knew he needed Rafe—with him, around him, and even in him.

Especially in him.

Rafe sighed, a heartfelt, nearly mournful noise, when Quinn slid over onto the bed next to him. Reaching out, he found Quinn's hand and carded their fingers together. They lay there, naked and covered in sweat and spend, bodies stretched to the limit. Catching a hitch in his chest, Quinn matched Rafe's sigh with one of his own.

"You okay there, magpie?" Rafe squeezed Quinn's hand. "'Cause I've gotta admit, you've fucked *my* brains out."

"Better than okay, babe." Quinn tested out the word, rolling it over his tongue. "So much better than okay, and I can't wait to do it again."

CHAPTER FOURTEEN

Living room session
Damie: Sinjun, ordering some Chinese.
    You want moo shu pork?
Miki: What the fuck is that?
D: Pork, like bits of pork with some egg.
    You eat it with little pancakes... sort
    of pancakes. They're... flat.
M: So it's kind of like a Chinese break-
    fast taco?
D: No... yes. Shit. Dude, do you want
    some or not?
M: Sure, why not. I like tacos.
D: Do you want tacos?
M: Yeah, but you wanted Chinese. This
    way, we both get what we want.
    Compromise, D. It's what brother-
    hood's all about.

THE MORNING came with a scatter of cloudy nightmares, soft whispers of images and sounds Quinn easily fought back into their own darkness. They were familiar anxieties, time-worn, aged playthings his mind threw back up at him when he wasn't looking. He woke to the sound of his own breathing, forced out of his tangled thoughts by a single push of consciousness. It'd been a long time since he'd had to shed sleep to shake off the demons he had inside him.

Or at least he'd once thought they were demons. Now he wasn't so sure.

Rafe. He'd woken up with Rafe wrapped around him, cuddled up behind his shoulders and breathing into his hair. Quinn still had the taste of Rafe in his mouth, around his cock if he was going to be honest with himself. That honesty was hard to accept... hard to imagine, especially since he'd been imagining it for years. Long, cold, and lonely years.

"You're thinking too hard there, magpie," Rafe rasped. "Go back to sleep. It's got to be, like, four in the morning."

"It's...." Quinn leaned forward to check the digital clock ticking time off on a credenza next to the bed. "Ten. It's ten in the morning."

"Gotta be four someplace. Go back to bed, baby." Rafe's voice grew muddled, drawn back down into sleep. "Or at least let me go back to bed."

"That I can do." Quinn waited until he heard Rafe's breathing even off, then allowed himself another minute of the man's embrace. He *liked* the power in Rafe's arms, enjoyed the strength in his hands when they'd roamed over, pressed into him, and delved deep into Quinn's heat.

The sex had been... extraordinary, a windswept blur of emotions and sensations Quinn couldn't absorb all at once. He'd been left boneless and weary after he'd come, sheathed in Rafe's ass, but his lover'd been playful afterward, teasing Quinn into a semihardened state with a few licks of his tongue and an oiled finger toying at Quinn's rim. They'd tangled again, hands and mouths learning each other's bodies until they'd peaked, pouring into one another's throats and nearly choking with laughter.

It'd been *never* since he'd laughed like that. Effortless... sweet... and most of all, unguarded.

He could just... be around Rafe. No modifying behavior, no stopping and asking himself if he said the right thing or missed the meaning of something. He had a freedom with Rafe he'd never had with anyone before.

The idea of it made Quinn nearly giddy.

The press of his bladder, however, told him he had to pee.

It was hard to slide out of the bed. Rafe's arms were loose around his waist, and Harley was easily moved out of the way, but Quinn just didn't want to go. Another deep breath and his body threatened him with release, so he reluctantly pulled himself loose from the covers, dressed quickly, then headed to the bathroom.

The cold marble shocked him awake, and as he stared at the line of bite marks down his throat, Quinn resigned himself to being awake. Exploring the chain of tiny purpling bruises on his skin with his fingertips, he hissed when one throbbed beneath his touch, a thickened swell warming the area.

"Okay, next time Rafe gets dinner before we go to bed." He stopped putting toothpaste on his brush, and the enormity of where he was… what he'd done and whom he'd done it with, struck him anew, leaving Quinn breathless. "Hell, Rafe Andrade—and he bites."

It was both surreal and comforting to make coffee in Rafe's kitchen. The fridge was nearly empty, boasting mostly a variety of nondairy creamers, bags of ground coffee, and condiments. A limp carrot danced a solo on the top shelf next to a half-used stick of butter. He grabbed both the crème brûlée creamer and the carrot, disposing of the sad, wilted root in the trash before fixing his coffee. Harley padded into the long kitchen, mewling her displeasure at her empty belly, and Quinn grimaced.

"Aye, I didn't feed you last night. God, I'm…." A quick peek at the cat dishes in the kitchen corner bore evidence of wet food scraps and a brimming pile of dry kibble with a dent on one side where it'd been nibbled on. "Huh. You're lying to me, baggage. Rafe took care of you just fine."

He gave her a small pouch of wet food anyway, leaving the crinkled cat behind to munch away at her fishy breakfast.

At some point a spring storm bullied its way into the city, and it tore apart the sky in a fierce display of thunder and rain. Spikes of light forked across the belly of a cloud bank not far from the penthouse, their sporadic flashes bright enough to leave dots on Quinn's vision. Taking his coffee over to the living room, Quinn set his sights on the soft, comfortable couch running lengthwise across the room. Facing the sliding glass doors to the patio, it looked to be the best place to sit, drink coffee, and read while the storm snarled over them.

He got as far as putting his mug down on a side table when a pounding on the door froze Quinn in his tracks.

His first thought was of Rafe and how the muted noise would wake him. His second was of LeAnne and Simon, wondering if trouble had somehow found him at Rafe's door. A quick look at the monitor next to the door had Quinn sighing in disgust.

"Kane," he muttered, scanning the intercom buttons below the monitor's screen. "Come on, Rafe. You paid for a penthouse, and this thing's got more buttons than the Mach V. Shouldn't there be a sleeping gas function for the foyer?"

Resigned, Quinn opened the door.

"I brought over the cat's food." Hefting a flat of cat food in his arms, Kane took a step over the threshold, then stopped short when Quinn didn't move out of the way. "*Breac*, this shit's not heavy, but you know, I'd like to dump it someplace. Move."

"Where's Tanngrisnir, Tanngnjóstr? Did someone catch him and suck the marrow from his bones?" Quinn grumbled as his brother pushed past him. He followed Kane into the kitchen, then leaned against the counter as Kane opened the box to put the cat food cans away. "If you're going to use the cat as an excuse to come over, at least buy the brand she eats."

Quinn saw the moment his brother spotted the bites on his skin. Kane stiffened, one hand clenched hard on a can of tuna-and-egg flaked cat food Quinn knew Harley would like. She was a finicky cat, but anything with tuna, egg, or cheese would set her to purring. More to save the can than himself, Quinn closed the distance between them and took the can out of his brother's grasp.

"You were about to pop that open." There was a bit of delight in seeing his brother's nostrils flare slightly when Quinn opened a cabinet door, then placed the can among the others he'd brought with him. "And as Rafe and I found out last night, he doesn't own a mop."

"Rafe." His lover's name came out strangled, a guttural slither from Kane's gritted teeth. "Really, Q-ber—"

"I'm going to say this once, Kane. Once." Quinn stepped into his brother's space, standing nearly nose-to-nose with a face he knew nearly as well as his own. "That is the *last* time you call me Q-bert and sure as fucking hell the last time you have anything to say about what goes on between me and Rafe."

He turned to leave the kitchen, but Harley spoiled his smooth exit, sliding between his legs to wind about his ankles. Quinn did a fast quickstep around the cat, his hand slapping at the counter as he flailed to keep his balance, but he recovered enough to stride into the living room where he'd left his coffee.

As usual, Kane followed. Not as usual, his older brother remained silent until Quinn had his first sip of his now lukewarm coffee. Kane paced—a common enough thing for Kane to do. They all had their quirks, things they did when they needed to think. Connor brooded, his eyebrows beetled together until they looked like some odd avian mating dance across his forehead. Their mother, Brigid, picked at her nails, and Donal moved his mouth to one side, as if caught in midswish while using mouthwash. Quinn knew he bit his lower lip, but he wasn't going to give Kane the satisfaction of seeing him worry.

Instead he drank his coffee and waited.

He didn't have to wait long.

Quinn gave Kane credit. He used every single comforting, approachable trick they'd taught him, from sitting down diagonally from Quinn to turning his body inward, minimizing his bulk and making him appear receptive. Quinn knew better. This was, after all, the man who'd once stapled a brad through a towel and into Quinn's shoulder when they'd wanted to play superheroes.

"So... Rafe." Kane stumbled over his friend's name. Giving up any pretense of calm, Kane scrubbed at his face, then sighed. "What the fuck, Quinn?"

"Not your place, K," Quinn reminded his brother. "And... he brings color, you know?"

"Not a fucking clue," Kane admitted softly. "I came over here because I was worried about you."

"I'm not a fragile, delicate flower." He cut Kane off before his brother could object. "Not anymore. Not for a long time. It's just that you all refuse to see it, and I don't know what to do with that."

"Doesn't mean I can't worry. People you knew *died*, Q. Died. Murdered. And we don't have a fucking clue who's doing it. Hell, I can't even convince Berkeley PD that it's all connected. So I let you go—"

"You don't *let* me do anything, Kane," Quinn asserted, laying down as much steel in his voice as he could. His brother's eyes met his, and they had a brief battle of wills, a silent, deadly skirmish Quinn knew in his guts he'd have to win. "And I swear to God in heaven, if you don't get that by now, I'm going to punch your face in. You might have some weight on me, but right now, here while you're in Rafe's house, you've got nothing to say on this, understand?"

A moment passed and another. Then Kane shifted in his chair, giving way. Nodding, his brother said, "Fair enough. All right, then. You left with Rafe, and that was the last we heard from you."

"I left a note. And there were texts," he replied softly. "Then I turned off my phone. Because, brother mine, I don't want family intruding on me. Or Rafe. I told you I was fine. He told you I was fine. What more did you need? What more did you want?"

"Rafe's...." Kane stalled, sputtering to a stop before forcing his way through again. "God, Quinn.... *Rafe*. Rafe. Rafe *Andrade*."

"Yeah, I've met him," Quinn drawled. "Little bit taller than me, blond, and one of your best friends. One of mine too. Hell, one of my few friends. Someone I can count on to make me laugh and forget I'm a bit fucked-up in the head."

"Ain't nothing wrong with that head of yours, Q. I like how it works just fine. Hey, K. Not that I mind you dropping by, but how the fuck did you get in? Security didn't buzz through." Rafe strolled out of the hall, his hips rolling in a cocky swagger. He stopped long enough give Quinn a fierce kiss, stole a gulp of coffee, then jerked his head toward the kitchen. "Any more of that?"

"Most of the pot's left. Kane didn't want any." Quinn's head swam from Rafe's tongue sliding over his lips, and no amount of breathing seemed to calm the flutters in his crotch. "Wait a second. How *did* you get in, K?"

"Flashed my badge and told them I was doing an emergency cat-food run for my friend's visitor," Kane tossed back. "I was okay with it until I got up to the door. Then I was pissed off about it."

"Yeah, I'm kinda pissed off about it." Rafe's frown competed with the twinkle in his eye. "Security and I are going to have a discussion—"

The door buzzer startled all of them, and Rafe's scowl deepened to the point where his humor fled.

"Now who the fuck? Seriously, they've got one fucking job to do, and that's keep people down there until I clear them."

"Rafe." Kane shook his head, hunkering over his hands. "God, Quinn… just…. *Rafe*."

"He's never been just Rafe to me, Kane," he replied softly. "You know that. And now he does too."

"Shit." The man in question paled as he stared at the screen. "I've really got to ream out security."

"Who is it?" Kane craned his neck to see over the back of the couch. "Con?"

"Worse," Rafe muttered darkly. "Your mother. Before I let her in, you wanna go get a beer?"

"It's ten in the morning," Kane objected, and Quinn panicked, shaking his head no at his brother.

"Do you really want a piece of this?" Rafe opened the front door, smiling broadly at Brigid. "Come on in. How'd you get up here? Don't tell me you flashed a badge too?"

"A badge?" She frilled, a red-haired dilophosaurus coming in for the kill. "I don't be needing any stinking badges. Now where's Quinn—ah, there ye be."

She was short, shorter than most women, but standing firm in the middle of Rafe's living room, Quinn felt himself cower beneath her height. She'd donned heels and dressed for battle in jeans and a

UCB sweatshirt, yet unlike Kane, Brigid Morgan came armed with nothing but her Irish temper and a concerned maternal look on her face that could wither up any objections her children might make against her pushing into their lives.

Kane took one look at his younger brother, then nodded at Rafe. Standing, he patted Quinn on the shoulder, then slid past him. "Beer sounds like a great idea, Rafe. Let's go."

"Coward," Quinn slandered Kane before he got out of earshot.

"Yep," Kane agreed cheerfully, giving his brother another pat. "He's all yours, Mum. All yours."

HIS BROTHER and lover were faithless cowards. Sniveling, soft-boned assholes who'd sooner crawl off into the safety of a well-poured Guinness than help him stave off his mother's coddling. Even Harley'd abandoned him, fleeing as soon as she heard the *tick-tick* of Brigid's heels across the penthouse's wooden floor. Once more Quinn couldn't help but sympathize with Miki. His mother was a menace, and there wasn't a damned thing anyone could do about it.

Then she sat down next to him and burst into tears, sending Quinn down into a spiral of thick guilt and sticky remorse.

She was so frail in his arms, a bird of a woman made large by personality and a whirlwind determination, but Quinn panicked when he felt his mother's heart skip and stutter in her chest as he held her tightly. They sat together, unmoving while being serenaded by the storm outside. A crack of lightning bleached the sky. Then a rumble of thunder shook the windowpanes, rattling the glass under its shocking boom.

Brigid's penny-bright hair tickled Quinn's nose, and he patted down the errant curls, hoping to give himself a bit of breathing room. There was so much to say to his mother, but he didn't know where to start. Going through everything weighing on his soul, he chose the most important slice of his life to bare himself with.

She cried herself out, leaning back so she could dig in her pockets. After coming up with a handkerchief, she wiped at her eyes, laughing when she showed Quinn the smeared eyeliner left on the fabric. "Can't even keep my face on. How am I going to keep *you* safe?"

"I don't need keeping, Mum," Quinn objected.

"Of course ye do, love. Ye all do." Brigid patted his leg, then picked up his cold coffee, sniffing at it. "How are ye doing? And here? Not at Kane's, then? I got yer message, but there was no understanding the why of it."

"Mum, I need to talk to you about…." His Gaelic scrambled his brains, floating toward words like *lover*, *mate*, and *a piece of his whole*, but nothing *right* seemed to come to mind. He didn't know how to tell her how he felt or the fears he had of Rafe coming to his senses and walking away. "God, this is shitty hard."

The tears in her eyes—his eyes—were gone, replaced by a sharpness Quinn'd felt pare bare him to the bone in the past. Her gaze flitted across his throat, then back to his face, digging into him until Quinn shifted uncomfortably on the couch. He reached for his cup for something to do, then remembered it was in his mother's hands, so he abandoned it, waiting for her reaction.

"I worry for ye, my Quinn." She answered in the same rolling tongue of her homeland, a misty, poignant burr under a sweet honey. "With everything going on with ye right now, I worry. And ye're here, Quinnigan. With Rafe."

It'd been forever and a day since she'd called him that, the teasing bastardization of Quinn and her maiden name. Quinn'd been a compromise of sorts. Donal hadn't wanted a son named Finn Morgan dogging his bloodline. There'd already been one, and he'd gone off to be a bloodthirsty pirate when trim frigates sailed the seas. If there was one thing longer than an elephant's memory, it was one belonging to an Irish clan.

First time he'd heard the story, Quinn wished his father had relented. It would have given him something to connect him to the perplexing fey creature who'd given birth to him.

"Ye've always been yer father's boy." Her gaze drifted from him to the storm churning black across the Bay. "I've understood that. And no matter what I've done or said, I know we've never been…. Ye've always been the one furthest from me, and I regret that above all other things. All other."

"I've never felt—" Quinn paused when his mother held up her hand to stop him.

"Ye step carefully. Around me. Around everyone. Ye're honest with yer father. I watched ye grow and mourned that I could never reach you. Aloof, yer grandmother once called ye, and I about scratched her eyes out for it. I didn't know—none of us knew—the differences ye had." Brigid took a deep breath, her body quivering with held-in emotion. "I'm asking ye to be honest with me, my Quinn. To toss aside the

masks ye wear and the words ye queue up to smooth
out my ego and just *be* honest about how ye are."

Brigid was a storm unto herself. It was easy to see
her in his brothers and sisters, intensity layered in with
their father's pragmatism. He had very little of her in
him, save her eyes, and he'd spent his childhood shoring himself up against her sallies of affection. She'd
been too much, too loud—too Brigid—for his fragile,
miswired brain to handle, and he hid himself from her,
cloaking himself behind behaviors and calm words.

"Answer me this, Quinn. Why Rafe? Why now?
After everything... with what is happening now... ye
turn to Rafe instead of...."

She almost said *me*. Quinn was sure of it, but she
stopped, shifting her words as he always did.

"Ye and I might have a valley between us at times,
but ye'll always be my son. *Always.*"

"You want me to be honest?"

She nodded, but Quinn only saw the motion out
of the corner of his eye. He couldn't look at her—his
mother—couldn't force himself to see the glimmer
of pain on her face and the tears falling uncontrolled
from her drenched lashes. Sighing, he tried to find the
words he didn't have to explain *why Rafe*.

"I've spent my whole life living in a world where
I don't speak the language everyone does." It was difficult, digging into wounds he'd let heal over, hoping
they wouldn't fester into poison beneath the surface
of his heart. "I understand what you're saying, but everyone moves and acts so oddly. Like I'm living in a
world made up out of broken mirrors, and every time
I try to reach for one of you, I cut myself on the edge
of the glass.

"And this world, Mum." He sighed as she took his hand, squeezing back when Brigid laid her head on his shoulder. "This world… it's all grayish. Monotones of muted hues where sometimes I can't tell the difference between a door and a window, but everything's sharp and everyone hurts. And there's so much noise. Everything chattering and demanding, pushing into me."

"We love ye. Ye know that, right?"

It was a mother's anguish roughening her voice, so Quinn bent his head and kissed her temple.

"I know I've ground some of that pain into ye, and I'm sorry for that."

"You're… loud. See, some people are like splashes of color against the gray. Sometimes it's too bright, and my eyes bleed from it… from them. That's when I have to pull back. I have to fold in on myself."

"And Rafe, he brings ye… color?"

"Mum, Rafe's a fucking spectral smear." Quinn chuckled. "He doesn't just bring color to my world. He peels back the gray and *shows* me the world as it is. Rafe takes the silver off of the backs of the mirrors and lets me see through the glass. He wraps the edges so it doesn't cut me, but he doesn't try to bind me as well. I'm not breathing in pain when I'm with Rafe. I understand how he works, and I don't have to worry about saying the wrong thing or not doing the right thing when I'm with him.

"He knows I don't like my food to touch and that I want to eat things one at a time. Rafe doesn't mind me getting excited over the smell of old books." He caught a breath, recalling Rafe's mouth on his heated skin and purring with pleasure when Rafe murmured Keats in his ear. "He listens to me when I unhinge and my thoughts bubble out… not only listens but enjoys it… enjoys me."

Brigid's murmuring dissent slithered free from her parted lips, and Quinn braced himself for what he knew was coming.

"He's one of the reasons ye tried to kill yerself, *breac*. Have ye forgotten that?"

"I was the reason I tried to kill myself, Mum. Because I was living in a minefield I'd laid down for myself, and no matter where I stepped, I ended up bleeding a little bit inside. I couldn't take being different… having to *think* about everything I did and said." He choked, forcing himself to stay at her side. Every nerve in his body told him to run, to hide from himself, but his mother asked him to be honest. And Quinn was tired of running. "I was *tired* and fifteen, with no end in sight for the misery I was steeped in. I'd spent my every waking moment trying to be *normal*. I hated taking medication to make me appear human. I still hate it, but I understand it now. But then? Back then? I broke, Mum. I broke *myself*. Putting my blood on Rafe? You might as well put it on the sun because it burned too bright for me to see."

"Where will he be in this, then? Our Rafe?" Brigid whispered, her hands warm in his. "Will he be here by yer side?"

"Yeah, he will. Because I think he loves me—he told me he loves me. And damn it, I *feel* him love me. I *feel* me loving him." He finally broke, caught on the swell rising from his heart. "And best of all, Mum, he likes my cat."

CHAPTER FIFTEEN

Three a.m. on the phone
Rafe: You 'wake, magpie?
Quinn, bleary-eyed: No. Yes. And I have
    school tomorrow. Didn't we say
    good night two hours ago?
R: Yeah, but I missed you. Lying here in
    the dark, I thought: you know, I miss
    my magpie.
Q: Why do you call me that? My da calls
    me that. It's kind of weird.
R: Because you like things that are bright
    and shiny. Aren't I bright and shiny?
Q: Shiny, yes. But calling a teacher who's
    got a 7 a.m. class in a few hours be-
    fore he's got to get up? Not so bright.

THE BAR was a no-name hole-in-the-wall tucked
into a shadow. If Rafe hadn't led Kane down an alley,

past a wrought-iron staircase, and through a partially open red door, he never would have found it. A long old bar stretched across one wall, neon signs reflected back at them in a clouded, browning mirror behind rows of half-filled liquor bottles. A rotund older man stood behind the bar, a faded red T-shirt celebrating the Year of the Dragon stretched over the breadth of his gut. He looked up from his pour, nodding at Rafe once. His bald pate shone, nearly as ruddy teak as the bar, glistening under the pink tinge of a flickering old advert for a vintage rum.

Despite the early morning, the bar was already a quarter full, mostly men in various stages of alcoholism, while a pair of hard-lived older women were running a quick low banter over a game of pool on the bar's lone table.

Rafe flashed the bartender a peace sign, then pointed to a table in the corner. Kane looked around, chuckling under his breath as he followed Rafe through the murky belly of the bar. Rafe glanced back over his shoulder, curious for a moment. Then he caught the hunched-over, do-not-see-me body language of the men sitting along the bar's expanse.

"Well, you do fucking scream *cop*," Rafe muttered, sitting down on one of the table's cracked red vinyl and wood chairs. "Hell, Miki probably screams *cop* when you guys are having sex 'cause you stink that much."

"Any reason I've never punched you in that pretty face of yours and broken it?" Kane growled, his eyes roaming over the room. "'Cause it's not too late, you know."

"Hey, I'd let you do it just so I could watch Quinn take you apart." He laughed, leaning out of the bartender's way when the man ambled in close to drop off a pair of enormous coffee mugs. Plopping down tubs of creamer and a handful of sugar packets, he grunted a hello as Rafe handed him a ten. "Thanks."

Kane waited until the man was halfway across the bar floor before he scooted his chair forward. "You really think Q-b—Quinn could take me down?"

"Yeah, I think Q's got a lot more incentive and inner rage than you give him credit for. Don't think you're his favorite person right now." The coffee was strong, nearly acrid enough to burn his nostril hairs, but Rafe sipped it anyway, hoping the pitch-black brew could chase away some of the anxiety bubbling in his belly. He didn't know what he liked less, the idea of leaving Quinn at Brigid's mercy or that he'd fled the scene with Kane. "You come over to ream Quinn a new asshole over leaving the crime scene? Or just leaving with me?"

Kane blushed. It was an odd thing, watching the slow rise of red pink his friend's face, and Rafe didn't bother to contain his smile. The sheepish expression on Kane's face slid into a light scowl, and Rafe yelped when Kane's foot struck his shin.

Rubbing at the spot, Rafe muttered, "Dick."

"Asshole," Kane grumbled softly. The teasing slipped away, growing somber as he added sugar to his coffee. "Kind of some of both. Can't help but... worry about him, Rafe. He carries a lot of shit inside of him. From being wired weird to, well... *then*. You expect me *not* to worry when he hooks up with the likes of you?"

"What do you think's going to happen? Because he's hooking up with me?"

"Not *if*, then. But *because*?" Kane's seat groaned, his shoulders straining the chair back when he pressed against it. "I don't know if... shit, Rafe. Not that I don't love you, man, but Q's... well, he's Q. You know how he is... how he was. There's a lot of baggage there. You ready to be taking that on?"

Rafe nearly choked on his tongue, patting at his own chest as the coffee seared his throat. "You think *Quinn's* got baggage? What the fuck you think I've got? A carry-on? I fucking *killed* a guy, screwed—"

"You didn't kill that guy." Kane stabbed at the air, nearly poking the end of Rafe's nose. "He died. Yeah, it's shitty, but you didn't kill him. You've got to get over carrying that, Andrade, or you're going to fall right back into that fucking pill bottle you were living in. And then what use are you going to be to Quinn?"

The coffee turned sour in Rafe's mouth, but he swallowed it anyway. Around them the bar continued to hum its own brew of a song, the clack of pool balls mingled with the glasses' clinking as they were moved around on the bar.

Despite the years-old smoking ban, the place still smelled of old cigarettes and burned tar, a stink probably seeped into the bar's wooden floors and the yellowed grout holding together its boiler-room brick walls. A glance at the men oozing over their barstool seats, and Rafe paused, seeing himself in their bloated, careless bodies. They stank of desperation and longing, eyes fixed on a space in front of them, more than likely ruminating over past regrets and stolen moments they kept alive in some fogged-over corner of their brains.

It was a far cry from where he sat now, his body run hot with pleasurable pain from Quinn's sharp teeth. He'd woken to an empty bed and, for a second, panicked with the fear he'd somehow dreamed up his long-legged, black-haired Irish. Then came the sinking feeling, the slight tremble in his lower gut. Quinn'd gone the way of the blond man lying limp and dead against a vomit-drenched hotel carpet.

No, not the life he wanted to lead—not by a long shot—and sure as fuck not one he wanted inflicted on his lover.

"I'm doing my fucking damnedest not to fall back into any bottle, K." There was no excusing it away. He *needed* drugs. At some point in his past, some critical pinpoint second, he'd turned a corner and found himself drowning in quicksand. He'd never *stop* drowning now. "I can't say I won't. That's the worst part about this shit inside of me now."

"Of all the people... seriously, Rafe... *you* becoming some junkie? Never would have laid money on that." There were stacks of creamer cups next to Kane's cup, and he played with one of the empties, smearing a drop on the table. "But what I would lay money on is that you'll stay clean. If only for Quinn. You won't do jack shit for yourself, but for Q, I think you'll stay straight... 'cause you'd sooner die than break him."

"I love him, Kane." The pounding of his thoughts dulled down enough for Rafe to face his childhood friend head on. "I don't know if you believe that. Shit, I don't know if *Quinn* believes that, but it's true. Last couple of days? I'm kind of scared for him because of all the shit that's gone down this week around him."

"Not just you, Andrade." Kane turned the heavy mug around in his hands. "I'm scared he's going to fall back down that black hole he's got inside of him—straight down into the still waters where he'll drown."

"He's not that kid anymore, K." Rafe shook his head. "That was a fifteen-year-old kid who was lost in his own head. Think about it, dude. There was so much damned shit going for him... and Christ, look at the brain God decided to stuff into that kid's head."

"You were a part of all of that, you know? Not that him standing on the edge of that building was on you, but he was tangled hard around you leaving." His friend stared into his coffee, as if the oily brew could reveal the answers to the universe. "Didn't really take it seriously, but now here I am sitting across of you talking about you and Quinn being a thing."

"Don't know how much I was a part of Quinn's... shit, I don't even know what to call it. Doesn't matter." Rafe exhaled the memory of Quinn's young, icy-white face and bloodless responses. Looking back, that moment—that brief, soul-frightening moment—was when Rafe realized how deep Quinn'd reached down into his soul and became a part of him.

A part Rafe'd run away from.

And he definitely was done with running.

"I think he missed me. Was he in love with me? Maybe not really. Maybe not then. Me hitting the road was just a small ripple in his world. He was a boy, going to fucking college, and you *know* people spit on that kid, or he worked himself into a spin trying to figure the world out so it would fit into his head. Quinn *thinks* differently than you and me."

"So fucking different," Kane agreed.

"You ever think that for him, it's *his* normal? We're all the fucked-up ones. He's making concessions for us. And he doesn't get the clues." Rafe made a face. "What's worse is our chaos isn't his chaos. And if there's one thing Quinn Morgan hates, it's when he figures something out, then it goes and changes.

"Think about it, K. He was drowning in change, and he's not good about change. Hell, he's still not good at it. People are dying around him, and he doesn't want to see it. Q likes routine. Even as much as he veers off in his own little chaos, it makes sense to him. It's routine for him."

"Like a fucking Escher painting, maybe," Kane snorted.

"Yeah, he's a bit Goblin King-ish," he conceded. "But it's *his* chaos. And he understands it. But with Q, the shit we get all hung up on, it's like adding two and two for him. Because that's how his brain works. Cuts right through the noise and shit we have to wade through and gets right to where he needs to be."

"This thing with his student… big fucking change. How's he doing with that?" Kane took a sip of his coffee, making a face at its bitterness, but he kept drinking it. "Simon, I figured he'd be shaken but okay, but the girl? That one… I worry Q's going to lose himself over it."

"Okay," Rafe murmured. "He had a nightmare. That's a problem for him, you know? His mind picks things up and replays it all for him, over and over. I think it's less now than before. Shit, he used to beat himself up over things he thought he'd fucked up. Doesn't seem to go over things until it twists him around, but yeah, she—her murder—gutted him."

"Blames himself?" Kane paused as the bartender came back over with a pot of fresh coffee. He waited until his cup was refilled, then packed the greasy sludge with sugar. The dollop of cream he followed up with barely tinged the black, eaten up by the pitchy liquid. "Yeah, Q would. He will. Probably until the day he dies."

"I just don't want him to relive this shit. And *that's* what I'm thinking about. How the hell do I help him with that? Because I'm all in here, Kane. Fucking all in. You might not believe me—"

"I believe you, Andrade." Shaking his head, Kane continued, "I know you. First time in your life... our lives... I've seen you this focused. Even with the music, you were always reaching... wandering about. But right now, Quinn's got you wrapped up tight and moving forward. Not just... around."

"Him and that Simon guy? Tight? Close? What happened there, really?" he pressed. "Quinn gave me some song and dance about how they drifted apart a bit. Hell, he wasn't even sure they were ever even together."

"Kappelhoff... Simon... never fucking liked him." More cream followed the first dribble, but Kane's coffee refused to give up its stygian ways. "Guy never took Quinn home to meet his family. Not fucking once."

"Did he get to any of the dinners?"

"A couple of times. I think the longest he stayed was about an hour."

Kane grimaced, and Rafe figured his sour expression was less about the shitty coffee and more about Kappelhoff.

"He dropped Q off a couple of times. Picked him up once by driving up and honking the horn."

Rafe jerked his head up, and Kane nodded knowingly.

"Thought Da was going to lose his shit. He didn't say anything, but you know how he feels about that. You come to the house, you get out of the car and ring the bell. No matter what. Last time Simon came by the house. I think Quinn was…. Pretty sure that was Quinn's last straw."

"I'm sorry he'd dead, but shit, Quinn deserves better than that." Rafe sighed. "I'd want that no matter what. Any leads on who killed the guy? Anything?"

"Not a damned thing." Kane tapped the edge of his mug, scanning the bar's occupants again as if he could find Simon's murderer among them. "Same with Quinn's student. Everything on them was wiped down. Hell, Q's rental's being gone over with a fine-toothed comb just in case, but it's too clean. We pulled nothing up from the hood. Hoping we can find something on the campuses' cameras. The parking structure's ones were taken out with something heavy, bashed in like a raw egg. So whoever's doing this, guy's strong."

"But why Quinn? See, that's what doesn't make sense. Unless there's something you're not talking about. Threatening notes? All of that shit."

Kane barked a short laugh. "God, I wish. *That* would at least be helpful. Quinn's got nothing. Not a damned clue. No past student threats. No one on staff he argued with. Doesn't make one damned bit of sense."

"What if someone has said something to him, and he's just not got it?" Rafe asked. "He doesn't read people well. Worst part about his wiring. He can't sync up what people mean and say."

"I thought about that too, but short of shadowing him 24-7, it's like trying to catch the wind. I've got to go by what he's told me. No one's approached him—good or bad. I'm looking into everyone he comes into contact with at the college. A couple of them tip my bells." Kane frowned. "I just don't want him to think it's because of something he did. Or could have prevented. Guess a part of me is still scared he's going to find a tall building and throw himself off the edge."

"He won't. He's better now. More assured. Or at least, knows himself more," Rafe said. "Your problem—the family's problem—is that you guys don't see that. For you, he's that skinny kid with his hair in his face and big feet he's always falling over. But look at him now—really look at him, Kane—because he's learned to walk. Hell, he's learned to run. Screams right past us, but you're still looking for that stumbling, gangly kid."

"Do you like that kid, Rafe?" Kane asked. "Can you live with that kid?"

"K, I liked that kid," Rafe murmured, taking another slurp of bitter black coffee. "But I fucking *love* that man."

THE CITY street overflowed with tourists and locals, a curious blend of cameras, bare knees, white socks, and sandals with an ambling dodge of slackers and hustlers. Kane broke stride long enough to let a gaggle of elderly women pass by him, a group of silver-haired, chattering ducklings riding a wave of delighted confusion.

"Gotta head out. Miki's got a therapy appointment I want to make sure he gets to." Kane puffed out his cheeks in an exasperated exhale.

"For his leg?"

"Nah, for that crazy grumpy kitten he's got living in his head," Kane replied. "Love him, but shit, some days, it's like he's wearing a bodysuit made out of razor blades."

"But you love him," he teased. "A fuck of a lot."

"Yeah." His expression softened, a smile touching the edges of his mouth. "I just want *him* to be okay. Inside and out, you know?"

"Where'd you park?" Rafe jogged around a man with a stroller stacked high with a baby and its paraphernalia.

"Underneath. Best part of the badge? Lets me park anywhere." Kane laughed at Rafe's derisive glance. "Hey, you've got, like, six fucking spaces under there. I'm only using one."

"So long as you don't fucking scratch the Chevelle." Rafe stopped, nearly slamming into Kane's back. "Dude, what the fuck?"

Kane turned, grazing Rafe in the stomach with his elbow. Rafe backpedaled, trying to give himself room to move, but Kane caught him quickly, wrapping Rafe into a hug. Surprised, Rafe inhaled sharply, breathing in a whiff of his friend's warmth, scented sharp with Old Spice and coffee. Kane squeezed, a brief wrap of arms and comfort. The embrace stretched back to a time when they were losing teeth and their bones ached from growing too fast. It caught up with long discussions on a rooftop, hidden from the stars by a stretched-out overhang as they struggled to find themselves, and past the moment Rafe said goodbye to follow his dreams. They fell into the now, a brotherhood tightened by trouble and love for the same man.

"Love you, Andrade," Kane muttered into his ear, nearly pushing the air out of Rafe's lungs. "Don't forget that, man. Okay?"

Rafe tightened his hold on Kane, rocking his friend slightly. The moment stretched, and then Rafe whispered, "Is this where you say you're going to kick my fucking ass if I hurt your little brother?"

"Nah." Kane let go, leaving Rafe with one final squeeze of his hands on Rafe's forearms. "This is when I tell you I'll be here for you when my brother drives you crazy or breaks your heart."

Rafe pushed Kane off, sending him into the depths of the building's lower-level parking with a brief wave. It was a quick jog to get to the entrance, and he fought the wind coursing up from the Bay's cold water. Rafe rubbed at his arms, wishing he'd grabbed a jacket before they'd run from his apartment, but beating a strategic retreat was a hell of a lot more important at the time. Turning the corner cut the wind back, the building's stretch blocking the chilly breeze.

There was a bit of hope in his heart that Brigid was gone, but the luck of the Portuguese apparently didn't run the same for the Irish. Rafe recognized the wide-bodied black town car idling in the valet's pass-through, mostly from the Finnegan's Pub and SFPD vinyl window stickers tucked discreetly along the back glass. If there was any doubt left in Rafe's mind, it was shooed away by Brigid's appearance at the building's entrance, her melodic Irish brogue thanking the doorman for letting her through.

She was a sharp explosion of red hair and personality, but Rafe's gaze drifted to the handsome dark-haired man following her. Brigid's hand fluttered as she talked, patting her son's arm or side, navigating down the walk to her car with clear, sure strides. Quinn took the touching gracefully, head cocked to one side as his mother chattered away. She was carrying a weighted-down brown bag, its jute handles clutched tight in her hand, and it swayed back and forth with each step Brigid took, knocking Quinn in the shin.

It was good to see them laugh. Especially when Brigid realized she was beating her son up with whatever she was carrying. Rafe heard her hearty burst of Gaelic, something teasing and tender he couldn't understand. Maybe never understand, really. Even at their most difficult of tense times, Brigid and Quinn loved one another—a mother and son relationship he'd never achieve with his own.

Yet when Brigid caught sight of him at the edge of the sidewalk and smiled as wide as a sunrise breaking through a San Francisco morning fog, Rafe knew he didn't have to look any farther than Quinn's flame-haired tornado of a mother if he needed any love.

"Hey, come into my house and clean me out?" Rafe teased, crossing the few feet between them. Nudging the bag, he sniffed down at Brigid. "Thieving baggage, isn't that what you guys say?"

"It's cat food," Quinn offered. "Harley's a food snob. She won't touch most of what Kane brought over."

"Whereas my worthless fleabags would eat the flesh off yer bones before ye've drawn yer last breath." Brigid slapped away Rafe's hand as he reached to carry it for her. "I've got this—"

The bag gave way under the weight of the cans, its bottom splitting at the seams. Brigid moved forward as Rafe bent down, grabbing at the rolling tins before they could launch off of the sidewalk and down the hill. They hit hard, smacks of metal on cobblestone and cement, but Rafe heard something else, a cracking sharp slap of sound he couldn't figure out, no matter how hard his mind turned it around. He blinked and looked, his attention snared by Brigid's alarmed gasp, wondering what she'd seen or heard.

Then all Rafe saw was the blood.

CHAPTER SIXTEEN

Reaper came for all of us
Jerked us up from the brine
Slipped out from his bony fingers
Landed on our feet just fine
Took four steps to Freedom
Took four souls to the line
Spat at the Devil at the Crossroads
Drank our sins with sweet, sweet wine
—Death, Devil and Sin

QUINN WAS covered in his mother's blood. He'd entered into the world covered in her blood, and now he feared she would leave while he stood in a cruel mockery of his own birth.

He didn't remember the drive to the hospital. Something primal in him snapped into place, and he'd thrown both his lover and his mother into her idling black sedan, ordering Rafe to press his hands to the wound on Brigid's chest. There probably were red lights along the way. He didn't remember those either. Nor was he surprised when he pulled up into the hospital's ER intake bay and found a phalanx of cop cars screaming up behind him, their lights and sirens set to full blast. Quinn hadn't cared about the wave of dark uniforms coming toward him. He was only focused on one thing—getting Brigid inside the cold cement box of a building before she drew her last breath.

"There's so much blood." The sheer amount of it staining his clothes and hands staggered Quinn. "She's so tiny. How can she have so much blood? God, suppose that's all she had?"

A second later panic hit, and he paced away from the wall he'd been near, almost bumping into a drawn-faced woman. His brain kicked into gear, slapping Quinn with her name—Kiki, his sister. Hell, he couldn't even remember his own sister.

"This is your fucking fault, Quinn." Ian rounded on him, cutting across Kiki's path. His younger brother—youngest, really—brought himself up to his full height, towering over their sister. Ian's expression was hard and sour, his not-quite-formed echo of Connor's strong features startling to see in another face. Quinn took a step back, but Ian followed, nearly shoving his chest into Quinn's. A quick finger stab into Quinn's collarbone, and Ian was off on a tear. "You're the reason she's in there. Fucking dying. You're the—"

"*Stop it.*" Donal didn't rise from his seat in the waiting area. He didn't have to. The shock wave of his low, cutting voice stilled his children, bringing them all to a poised apprehension. "Sit down or walk away, Ian. I'll not be having to hear ugliness while I'm waiting for yer mother to come back to me."

As hotheaded as Ian was, he sat, quelled by their father's biting reproach.

It was humbling standing near his father. Donal, the strongest of them all, sat quiet and small, his body tense and firm. A soft murmur came from his lips, a Gaelic spill of prayer and promises, words Quinn heard spoken over him when he'd been waylaid by a childhood bout of pneumonia fierce enough to put him in the hospital. The others were moving, talking around one another, but every eye was on the double doors leading to a surgical ward, where their lives lay blown open and struggling to survive.

"*Breac*, come here." There would be no arguing with Donal. Not now. Probably not ever. It was startling to see his serene, handsome face turned ashen and fraught. Dread pulled his skin down, a waxy pour of grief and worry over his strong bones.

"Da—"

"*Now*, boy."

Quinn took one step, then another until he was at his father's side, and Donal reached for his hand, clasping it tightly, then letting go.

"I can see what yer thinking. It's all on yer face. This is not on ye, *breac*. Yer not the one who put her there. But mark me words, we'll be finding the one who did, understand me then?"

"Aye." It was lip service. He'd just paid lip service to his father, and if there was any time God would strike Quinn down, it would be then. The guilt was still there, just cowering under Donal's cold steel gaze.

"Kane's looking for ye. Ye'll be wanting to change. No good to yer mum if she sees ye wearing her blood." Donal nodded at Quinn's shirt. "Don't want the first thing out of her mouth to be a scold on me because yer walking around like an extra on that zombie show she watches."

The door opened, and the Morgans strained toward it, hungry chicks anxious to be fed a scrap of news. Nothing. An orderly pushing a supply cart with creaking wheels ambled through, working to avoid the gathering crowd. Quinn turned away, unable to watch the sea of blue and stars clustered around his family.

It was too much like a funeral, creased uniforms and worried faces, all catching on his face when he passed by. Rafe'd gone to get him coffee, he remembered as he scanned the waiting area, unsure on when Rafe left. He was about to ask if someone'd seen Rafe when Kane parted the uniforms to thrust a T-shirt and a plastic bag into Quinn's hands.

"Go change, Q." His older brother brushed his knuckles against Quinn's cheek. "You'll feel better for it."

"She might—" He wanted to object, but the smell of blood was getting to him, and his stomach roiled at the idea of wearing his mother's life against his skin.

"I'll come get you if there's news. Put your shirt into the bag in case Evidence wants it. Don't think they will, but you never know," Kane said, pushing Quinn toward the bathroom. "Go wash up. I'll be right here. Looking for Miki but right here. Go on. Mum'll be okay. It'll take more than a bullet to stop her."

The bathroom was cold. Cold enough for Quinn to swear there were ice crystals forming on the urinals' drains. Arctic air blasted through the vents as Quinn stripped quickly, shivering in the chilly tiled room. The water from the sink wasn't much warmer, but he made do. Slightly damp from the lukewarm water, Quinn shoved his arms through the T-shirt's sleeves when he heard a retching noise come from the bathroom's single stall.

Curious, he tossed the plastic bag with his bloodied shirt onto the counter, then padded over to the stall. A push on the door swung it open, and Quinn sighed, saddened by the sight of the man he found hunkered over the toilet.

He'd found Kane's Miki—emptying his guts out into the blue-tinged water of a hospital's toilet bowl.

It broke his heart to find Miki—tough, growling Miki—curled up into a ball from the pain inside him. Quinn knew that pain. It lingered in him now, biting and snapping at his sanity. He came up beside his brother's lover, brushing his fingers through Miki's chestnut mane.

And wasn't surprised when Miki recoiled instantly.

Mimosa pudica had nothing on Miki St. John.

"Get the fuck out."

As a snarl, it was a watery attempt. Certainly not one of Miki's best. Quinn crouched, his hand sliding down Miki's lean back.

"Seriously, just—"

"It'll be okay," Quinn murmured into Miki's hair, his lips brushing the soft, long strands. "She'll be okay."

Then he held his brother's lover as Miki cried.

The cold was still there, on his ass and legs where the denim did little to protect his skin from the icy tile, but Quinn felt very little of it seeping through. His face ran hot with tears, his lashes sticky with salt as he rocked Miki back and forth, rooted together at the base of the toilet's porcelain sides. Miki's tears seared Quinn's neck, burning rivers of grief pouring from his anguish-filled eyes. At one point Quinn heard the door open, then close quietly soon after, the stilted peace of the bathroom settling down on them again.

"She can't fucking die." Miki's whisper feathered over Quinn's neck.

"She's not going to." It felt like a lie, one he would tell a child after seeing their dog get hit by a car, but Quinn had to believe it. *Had* to. To think otherwise would change his world too much... too soon... too hard.

"She just fucking can't," Miki spat out, hot and furious. Then he broke, catching a sob up in his throat. "I haven't told her I love her."

The walls pressed in on them, a flat pewter cage drenching them in shadows. Everything sharpened as Quinn's mind shook off what little control he had remaining, and the world rushed in all at once. Miki's shirt rasped over his skin, prickling the hair on Quinn's arms, and something metal—probably the rivet from a jeans pocket—ticked on the tile floor. Quinn cringed under an assault of smells, everything from the lemon hint of soap on Miki's skin to the astringent stink of hospital antiseptic burning his nose. He was thankful for the dullness of the stall. Color was the last thing Quinn needed. His eyes would bleed with the loud of it if there was something other than beige and muddy gray. As it was, Miki was an explosion of textures and prickles, a vivid swatch of noise violating all Quinn's senses.

Now was *not* the time for him to lose his shit. It took Quinn one shuddering breath and then another to shove back at the world before it cracked his skin. The two-dimensional flatness receded slowly, reluctant to snap back into reality.

Quinn shifted—or at least he thought he did—his knee made contact with the bowl, and the smack sent pain tingles up into the base of his skull. The pain shot him back, telescoping the stall back to nearly normal, but he resisted the urge to strike himself again.

It was an addicting pain. One he knew well. He still wore a few scars on his arms from a time when he needed pain to feel real... to feel alive. The pain was a siren, seductive and sweet, promising to leave him in a numb reality when he was done.

Thing was, Quinn knew he'd never be done. Not if he fell into that hole again. He'd come too far from its edge. Quinn'd be damned if he danced along its lip once more.

Miki felt small in his arms, shivering as much from shock as the cold. Quinn hiccupped, unable to swallow down the bitter guilt gurgling up from his belly. His brother Ian'd been right. If their mother died, it would be on him. Just like Simon and LeAnne. And he had no way of stopping the killing.

He must have said something under his breath, a murmuring of guilt... something to draw Miki up stiff, because damned if Miki didn't slide back away from Quinn's arms, then shove at Quinn's chest in disgust.

"You didn't do a fucking thing. Shit, why do you do that to yourself?" The fire was back in Miki's eyes, gold fallow leaves rich with flames against forest greens and bark. "How many times do you got to hear that, huh? Why doesn't that shit stick in your head?"

It wasn't the best place to have *that* particular conversation. Hell, curled up into one another on the floor of a hospital bathroom stall probably wasn't the best place to have *any* conversation, but Miki didn't seem like he was willing to budge.

Miki was also using the anger to burn off the desolation lurking in his heart. Quinn understood that. He needed some anger of his own.

He just couldn't find anything but fear.

"Can I borrow a cup of anger?"

The shift on Miki's expressive face was priceless, and Quinn laughed despite himself... despite the cold. They were sitting wrapped around one another in the ugliest of times, and Miki's confused head jerk still made Quinn chuckle.

"I think I need to get angry."

"Yeah, well, shit. I've got a lot to spare," Miki muttered.

He made no move to get away, a sullen, sulky hedgehog reluctant to admit he liked being stroked. They both disliked contact, Miki probably even more so than Quinn, so it felt odd to sit there—just being together—while their mother lay in shattered pieces on a table somewhere close by.

Their mother. Brigid's heart was large, all-encompassing, and sometimes overwhelming. Often overwhelming, Quinn corrected himself, and two of her worst damaged sat huddled around each other hoping beyond hope she'd pull through to harass them a bit more.

"She loves you, you know." He moved a bit, keeping Miki in his arms but sliding his legs around so they faced one another. It was cramped, and his knees banged against things... the wall, the toilet, a paper holder, but Quinn didn't want to move. Not yet. Not even away from the cold. In a lot of ways, Miki was the brother he never had. He had a shit-ton of brothers, but none so *like* him. Or at least in the ways it counted. "I'm glad Kane brought you home."

"Thank Dude for that. Fucking dog wouldn't leave him alone. Me? I was ready to toss him into the Bay." It was a soft grumble, opening the way to other things. "Fucking Morgans. Damn it. I didn't want this. Didn't want you. Didn't want *her*."

"Mum's kind of hard to get around," Quinn drawled. His face ached from the tears he'd shed, but Miki's righteous fury lightened his heart. "But she does love you."

"She loves everyone," Miki disputed. "We're all just rabbits named George to her. But yeah, I know she loves me. Loves you too, asshole. You two just don't fit sometimes, but she's there. Just like she's there for me. Hovering. With jazz hands. And those tick-tock heels she's always wearing."

"I love you too, you know. I think we all do." Once he'd said it, Quinn had no regrets. Admitting his fondness for Miki surprised him... surprised Miki even, and they sat in the discomfort of Quinn's stark honesty for a long, weighty moment. "I'm serious. I do love you. It's nice to have someone confuse Mum like I do. You're a good brother, Sinjun. And I like you for Kane."

The stall blurred, swimming in Quinn's vision, and he gulped, wondering how he could possibly cry anymore.

"She'll be okay." This time Miki was the one reassuring Quinn, a tit for tat in response to the tears stinging Quinn's eyes. "She's too *fierce* to die. Probably spat the bullet up and hit the doctor. That's probably who they're operating on."

Quinn was saved from responding by the slam of the bathroom door against a wall. Someone called out to them, Irish and hard, startling Miki into a scramble.

He fumbled, his knee refusing to unbend, and Quinn caught Miki in his arms before he bashed his head into the toilet. A vicious bout of swearing parted Miki's lips, and the stall door pushed open, Braeden filling the wide space between the stall's posts.

"Doctor's back. Came to get you both. Da's heading in. Mum's out of surgery. She'll be in ICU for a bit. Then they're moving her to a room." Brae bent down, hooking his hands under Miki's arms. "Up you go, Prickles. Kane's going to be looking for you."

"Pat me on the head or ass and prepare to pull back a fucking stump. You got that, Brae?"

Miki shook him off, baring his teeth at Braeden. Miki's limp to the door was painful to watch, but the look on his face made the Morgan brothers step back.

Relief turned Quinn's legs gummy, and he buckled, grabbing at the slick wall to stay upright. Breathing hard, he stared at the floor, a grid of white squares held firm by cocoa-colored grout. Brigid would be okay. She had to be okay. Did Braeden say anything about how she was going to be okay?

"Never know with that one. Kane's Miki is an odd one." Brae helped Quinn up. "Come on. Da said to bring you along. She'll be wanting to see you when she wakes."

"I can't, Brae. I—"

Quinn's protests didn't seem to matter because Braeden shoved him toward the door.

"Is she going to be all right?"

"She's fine. Blood loss. Punctured lung. So she'll be screaming at our heads less until she gets better there. Imagine that'll take about a day, because volume's the best she's got when dealing with our lot. And you'll go in because Da said so, and Mum wants you." His brother snatched the plastic bag off the counter, peering at the bloodied shirt inside. "She'll need to know you're fine too. She won't rest until she knows."

"Mum shouldn't—"

Braeden was big, nearly Connor and Kane big, but a loving tenderness shone out of his face as he cupped Quinn's cheeks. "You go see her because you'll both need to sniff butts and see you're alive. Swear to God, *breac*, sometimes talking to you is just like talking to Mum. All stubborn and none of the giving way. Both of you would pick up a sword or climb on a cross if we'd let you. So for once, brother mine, listen to the black sheep of the family and go see Mum first. You've earned it. For good or bad."

"Wait, how are *you* the black sheep? I'm a *teacher*." Quinn sniffed, his eyes threatening to spill again. He was parched, too drawn out to think clearly.

"I'm a *fireman*, Q," Brae reminded him. "And you're a *professor*. Something for the family to be proud of. Any of us can hold a badge or a hose. You, *breac*, you're the one who molds minds. Now, watch your step. Looks like someone vomited all over the floor there."

THE ONLY thing worse than hospital coffee was cold hospital coffee. There were two cups on the table at Rafe's side. Finger-bent, battered cups filled with murky skinned coffee more bitter than a religious hawker set up on Pier 39 and just as palatable. He'd panicked when he couldn't find Quinn following his cafeteria run, and his heart only just started back up again. Rafe didn't know what he'd thought, only that his green-eyed magpie was nowhere to be found, and the place was filled with all manner of cop, all dead eyed and tense.

It was like he was a seven-tailed cat in a rocking-chair factory.

"Mum's fine," Quinn said for the fifth time since Braeden shoved him out of a nearby bathroom and into Rafe's arms. Rafe caught him up, wrapping his arms around Quinn from behind, crossing them over his chest. "She's going to be fine."

"Yeah, baby, she is." It was better to let him say it, something his family sometimes didn't understand. The circular groove embedded Quinn's words into his crinkled thoughts, driving down into his mind until they reached the skeptical core. Quinn needed the ritual—needed a routine—even as he tumbled headlong into his own chaos. There were rules. As odd as they might have seemed, there were rules.

"I'm tired." Another repeat, this time laden with thick emotions. Quinn's heart fluttered and skipped under Rafe's touch, a frantic canary lost in the dark of his thoughts. "She's going to be *fine*."

"That's what they said, baby." Rafe tried to look through the uniformed throng around him but couldn't see much more of the door than he had before. Stepping back, he pulled them back until his shoulder blades were up against the wall and Quinn was safe from the cops tripping over their feet. "Kane finally made you a cop, huh?"

"What?" Rafe's question jerked Quinn out of his mental pacing, his eyes widening with confusion. Then he glanced down at his shirt when Rafe tapped his torso, tracing over the SFPD logo emblazoned over Quinn's chest. "Oh. Yeah. Closest I'll get, really.

Should have gotten an SFFD one from Brae. Black sheep have to stick together."

"You and Brae are so much the black sheep of this family." Rafe laughed. "Maybe you guys will be lucky, and Ryan'll become a public defender or something."

"Bite your fecking tongue, Andrade," Kane rumbled as he approached.

Horror flickered over the youngest Morgan's face at Rafe's words, and she pointedly flipped him off from her post a few feet away.

"The day a Morgan becomes a public defender is the day Da wears a thistle on his jacket."

Rafe took a moment, turning Kane's words over in his mind, then said, "I have no fucking idea what that means."

"You'll learn soon enough." Kane nodded to the door they could barely see through the hustle of people around them. A nurse lingered at the threshold, impatience mottling her face. "Go on with her, Q. Mum's awake and asking after you. Da said for you to go on in, but keep it short. She's in and out right now."

Quinn nearly tugged free of Rafe's arms, but he held his lover close, turning Quinn around. Rafe teased out a kiss from Quinn's pressed-in lips, coaxing a soft sigh from him. The stiffness in Quinn's spine eased, and he leaned into Rafe, their hands clenched together as their kiss deepened.

"Sheesh, get a fucking room," Ryan grumbled. "Bad enough I catch Mum and Da doing that in the kitchen, I've got to see it here too?"

"She's just jealous because I love you," Rafe re-assured Quinn. "'Cause you know, I'm a rock star. Probably had my poster all over her walls."

"Hah!" She tossed back her red curls, a nearly ex-act mimicry of her mother's wicked sneer. "Miki and Damie, *they're* my rock stars. You? You're just Rafe."

"Oh, the serpent we cradle to our breasts." Rafe winked at Ryan, then let Quinn go. "Take your time, Q. I'll be here."

Rafe gave Kane credit. The keen-eyed cop wait-ed until his brother was through the doors and then another four beats of time before he turned to Rafe and pinned him against the wall with a sharp glare. Throwing his hands up, Rafe threw out the one thing he knew would save him, a trump card he could al-ways use when one of the Morgan boys set their sights on him.

"Hit me, and Brigid will come down on your ass so hard you'll have four buttcheeks."

It apparently wasn't going to work this time be-cause Kane shoved him lightly toward the hall.

"Dude, what?"

"I want to talk to you. Without the others hearing us. So keep your voice down."

Kane turned slightly, blocking them from view. Rafe looked over Kane's shoulder, satisfied he could still see the ward's doors.

"I want to talk to you about what happened today."

"Can't tell you much more than what I told Brownie. And didn't they yank the case from you?" Rafe cocked his head. "You're too close to all of this, Kane. I'm not a cop, and I can see that. First Quinn and now your mom?"

"Yeah, Riley's off it too, but Brownie said he's going to see if he can pull a few strings. Captain said for us to step back and let it go."

"Like that's going to happen." There was more activity at the door but nothing remotely Morgan related, and Rafe tuned Kane back in. "Going to back-door it, then? Get your two cents in when no one's looking?"

"Stick around a bit. Brownie's going to swing back over here so we can go over a few things. He wants you there. Not going to lie about that one, An-drade." Kane raked his hands through his short black hair. "I talked to Quinn. Something he said made me think. He said you were standing next to the curb, right in front of Mum, before the shot hit."

"Yeah, she, um… there was a bag of shitty cat food she had on her." Rafe ignored Kane's disgusted snort. "Look, like Quinn told you. If you're going to come over with an excuse, at least make sure it's shit the cat would eat. She's as picky as Quinn."

"They were coming out of the front door and heading to Mum's car. You met them at the curb. Mum was walking in front of Q and holding a bag of cat food. What happened then?"

"Um, the bag tore," Rafe replied. "It was paper. 'Cause, you know, we're not to be trusted with plastic anymore. I bent down to pick up the cans, and that's when the shot went off."

"Mum was between you and Quinn, then?" Kane angled closer toward Rafe.

"Yeah, I guess. Why?" Rafe frowned. "You think the asshole was trying to shoot Quinn and Brigid got in the way?"

"No, Andrade," Kane replied. "I think he was trying to kill you, and if that bag hadn't broken, you'd
have gotten it right in your heart. This asshole? He's
not trying to fuck with Quinn. I think he's got a thing
for Quinn, and he's getting rid of anyone he thinks is
in his way. And unfortunately, Rafe, *you* are at the top
of that list."

CHAPTER SEVENTEEN

At the hospital chapel
*Donal: Never thought you'd be the one
    I'd catch praying.*
*Miki: I'm not praying. I'm threatening.
    Figured none of them out there has
    the balls to do it since they've been
    talking to Him since they were kids.
    Me, I'm new. Figured He'd hear me
    through all of their fucking noise.*

"SHE CAN hear ye, son." Donal eased a chair under Quinn before his knees gave out. "She's coming in and out of things, but the doctors say she's here with us. Probably going to be for a while yet."

Brigid was so tiny. So very tiny. A wee sprite, his father once called her. Once in Quinn's memory. Right after that, she lobbed a bedroom slipper at Donal's head.

There was an oxygen feed under his mother's nose and tiny burns from tape over Brigid's cheeks, but from what Quinn could see, other than the monstrous gauze patch peeking out from under her hospital gown's neck opening, Brigid appeared to be fine. An orchestra of machines sang a merry, discordant tune along the smoked glass partition behind the bed, their noise masking most of the ambient sound drifting through the care unit.

"Shouldn't she have—" Quinn mimicked squid legs with his fingers in front of his nose and mouth. "—stuff coming out of her face? To help her breathe?"

"Yer mum was fighting the tube. Doc said she's doing fine, but they'll watch for fluids," Donal explained.

The tired in his voice concerned Quinn, and he glanced up at his father, rising slightly to get out of the chair only to be stopped by a firm hand on his shoulder.

"Sit. I'm going to be finding her doctor and see when she's going to her own room. Ye know how she is. She'll be wanting the lot of ye around her while she's cooed over. We'll be needing room for that."

The flecks of gray at his father's temples were nearly white, stained by the fluorescent panels above them. Their stark light pooled shadows into the lines radiating from Donal's bright blue eyes and deepened the bruised-looking circles beneath his lower lashes. Strain turned Donal's skin waxy, and he rubbed at his face, Brigid's tiny wedding set sparkling on his little finger. The gold bands were marred with scratches, worn in from decades of marriage. Donal's ring matched hers, nearly scrape for scrape, and Quinn realized he'd never seen those rings off his parents' hands—not until Donal sat vigil over his injured wife.

"I'm sorry, Da. For bringing this to your door." The words were out before Quinn could check himself. "God in heaven, I am so—"

"I thought we already had this talk, *breac*." Donal bent over Quinn's back and embraced him from behind, a hard crush of strength Quinn hoped his father would never lose.

"I know. Hell, Miki and Brae beat it into me too. It's just that... I'm... it hurts to see her here. Like this," Quinn confessed. "It just... hurts."

"It does, aye." Donal's granite-whiskey rumble poured gold on the darkness stretched over them. "But ye know yer mum. She's going to be pampered for a few days, and then we'll have to be fighting her to get her to rest. So don't feel so sorry for her. Ye just be holding yer sympathy for the likes of me once I get her home and she starts chewing on us because she can't sit still. *That's* when ye should be coming around with yer sorries."

Donal laid a kiss on Quinn's temple, then headed out to the corridor, his firm strides taking him off to do battle with the hospital's unsuspecting medical personnel.

It wasn't as if Quinn'd never been *in* a hospital before. Growing up with seven Irish-tempered siblings meant frequent trips to the emergency room and a few bedside visits when one or another Morgan did something beyond foolish. Hell, there'd been a long stretch of hours, darkness, and tears back when he was a teenager and the world had gotten a bit too close for his liking, but Quinn'd never stared down at his own mother—still and pale—on sheets so white they hurt his eyes.

They also smelled of bleach. Acrid, nostril-burning bleach.

"Couldn't they have used the lemon-scented kind?" The cotton was stiff beneath his fingers, an unyielding, stark prison. Tugging at the corners, Quinn pulled the top sheet free, flapping it slightly to loosen its tight fold. Satisfied, he patted down the blanket and was about to do the other side when he noticed his mother watching him, her hooded and dazed deep emerald eyes—his eyes—catching his every movement.

"My Donal said... ye and Rafe were fine." She sounded raw, like she'd swallowed glass, but every inch his hard-scrabble, take-no-prisoners mother. The Gaelic was welcome, a comforting catch and song so familiar to his ears. "Then... yer arm?"

"What?" He twisted about, looking first right, then left. The turn did him in, ripping the fabric from his torn skin, and then there was blood. A lot of it, gushing from his now open wound, and he scrambled to grab tissues from the table next to his mother's bed. She must have seen the dried trickle of blood on his arm, something he'd missed entirely. "Shite, I'm bleeding."

"Call... doctor." Brigid motioned toward the call button, straining to reach the module dangling from her bed's side rails. "Need... stitches. How?"

Quinn pulled up the sleeve of Kane's dark blue shirt, grimacing when he realized how crusted the fabric was. He'd leaned against Rafe, probably smearing blood all over him as well. Or maybe not. He frowned. It was a deep scratch—a groove, really—burned into his upper arm. "Probably sealed into the shirt when I put it on in the bathroom. I thought all the blood was yours. Well, hell."

"Turn 'round. Let me... see," Brigid commanded. Her wan face was nearly as bleached out as the sheets she lay on, and someone'd pulled her mane up into a queue, its wild curls spilling an auburn sunset over her pillow. Her eyes and hair were all the color she had, a frail Irish fey ghost lying too still for Quinn's liking. "Ach, he shot *ye*. He'll die—"

"Don't worry about me, Mum. Probably would have been worse if I hadn't bent down for the can next to me. I'll have them look at it after I get kicked out."

It was a sincere promise, but Brigid gave him a practiced side eye. If he hadn't the reputation of avoiding any and all medical procedures, Quinn would have protested her damning and silent accusation, but Brigid had more than just cause.

Crossing his finger over his heart, he asserted, "I promise, Mum. On Harley's head."

"That's... good. Promising on a... naked-ass cat," Brigid rasped. She coughed, paling further, and Quinn nearly reached for the call button. "Stop that, ye wee naff... throat hurts."

"Da said you could have ice chips. Do you want some, then?" He reached for a cup filled with icy slivers, then scooped a few out with his fingers. His mother took them, birdlike nibbles from his hand. She'd always seemed larger—much larger—and Quinn trembled, wondering how his tiny mother had the strength to survive being shot.

"Don't look like that," she scolded. "Always the guilty one. Should... have been a priest."

"I've discovered I like sex too much," Quinn confessed, mostly to see a smile on his mother's face.

Brigid laughed, gasping in pain after a second. He grabbed her hand, wincing when she dug her fingernails into his forearm. "Sorry, I just... didn't mean to hurt you."

"Laughing's good. Alive then, I am." Her lids drooped, and she fought them back. "Promise me... ye'll stay inside... stay safe until... catch him. And Rafe... be good to him. Kick his ass if he's a wanker."

"I will." Her hands were cold when Quinn touched them. Tsking, he folded his mother's arms under her blankets, tucking them around her shoulders.

"Not the feet," she admonished, her words burbling to sandy mumbles at the end.

"I know, Mum." He left a kiss on her temple, thankful for the strong thump of her heartbeat beneath his lips. "Your feet get hot."

"M'feet get hot." Brigid sniffed, snuggling down into the bed. "Ye know...."

A shadow fell across Brigid's bed, and Quinn turned, expecting his father.

It was Ian.

So not their father.

There were traces of Donal in Ian. Physically, he ran to the same mold used for most of the Morgan brothers, thickly muscled, tall, and a thatch of black hair that, using Donal as a guess, would be flecked with silver in their fifties. Emotionally, Ian was all Finnegan.

Ian stood uneasily at the end of Brigid's bed, his fists punched into the pockets of his jeans and his head bowed down low enough for his chin to almost brush his chest. Smaller than Quinn—something that often surprised him—Ian still held the promise of heft to his frame, unlike Quinn's more lean body. They were nearly ten years apart, each with different childhoods, with different sets of siblings, really, something Quinn'd never truly understood until he looked into his baby brother's barely-out-of-teens face and saw the fear and confusion in his eyes.

"I saw Da outside." Ian shuffled his feet a bit, dragging his sneakers over the tile. "Thought I'd come see her, you know? Just... they won't let us all in, but... I needed to see her."

"Yeah, I know. Come in quick," Quinn replied. Hooking his hand in the crook of Ian's arm, he dragged his brother over to the chair. A quick, fierce one-armed hug, then Quinn pushed Ian down into the seat, smoothing the hair from his face. "We look enough alike. Nurse'll think you're still me. Just don't cover her feet—"

"They get hot." Ian nodded. He looked lost, more like the little boy Quinn remembered standing on the front porch waving goodbye when they all headed off to school... then to college... then to their own lives.

"She'll wake up in a bit. It'll be good for her to see you." Quinn grinned at Ian's wrinkled nose. "What? You're her favorite."

"You're off in the head," he snorted back. "We all know that's *you*."

"You're the one most like her—well, of the boys." The correction came quickly once he figured Kiki into the equation.

"Yeah, but you're the one she sighs over," Ian refuted. Inching the chair closer to the bed, he rested his elbows on the mattress. "Can I ask you something?"

"Sure." Quinn rested his hip against the bed's metal bars.

"Did they—Da and Mum—were they mad when you told them you weren't going to be a cop?"

"I never wanted to be one." He crouched next to Ian, bringing himself in close. "I don't think we ever even talked about it." Cocking his head, Quinn caught the flicker of something unsure in Ian's expression. "Ian, let me tell you something, then. If you don't want to wear the badge, you don't have to. Brae doesn't. I sure as hell don't. Ryan's probably going to go off and buy world domination, so she'll not be wearing the blues. If you don't think that it's for you, then you shouldn't do it."

"Not like I can go to school. Not after you—" Ian stumbled over his words. "I know. Not a competition, but there's so fecking many of you ahead of me. I get lost, you know? I wonder if Mum even remembers my name half the time."

"It doesn't matter who you are. I grew up thinking my name was Con-Ka-Quinn." He squeezed his brother's arm, rubbing at the spot before sighing. "Just be you."

"Easier said than done," Ian grumbled. "I don't know who *me* is."

"I'll tell you a truth, brother mine—no one ever really knows who their *me* is." Quinn took one last look at his mother, then stood, the tear on his arm wrenched apart when his shirt rode over the muscle. "Mum made me promise to see a doctor. So I'd better be going before she tears my face off."

"Hey, Quinn," Ian called out to Quinn just as he reached the break in the glass partitions separating Brigid from the rest of the ICU ward. He turned, and Ian gave him a wry smile. "I'm sorry I was an asshole to you. Back there. I just get… scared and angry. I mean it, though. I am sorry. I just don't think."

"Then you lash out." It was a common trait among them, especially when they were younger. "It's just a bit of Mum stuck in our teeth."

"Hah." Ian grinned. "Not Da?"

"Nope," Quinn shot back, winking at his younger brother. "The bit of Da is when you apologize because you mean it."

"How long is he going to be in there? Quinn, I mean." Inspector Browne nodded toward the double doors Quinn'd disappeared through. "Because now's the time to do any talking we need to be doing, and I don't want to get him involved in this if we don't have to."

Brownie was a throwback to Rafe's childhood, possessing a semi-uncle status among the Morgans and their satellites—namely Sionn and Rafe—and now Riley's senior partner. He was slimmer than Rafe remembered, his lackluster gray suit hanging on his shoulders as if he were a little boy playing dress-up in his father's clothes. A bout of appendicitis was to credit for his weight loss, that and a hard-nosed wife who'd laid down the law about sweets. The man'd reminded Rafe of a basset hound before he'd trimmed up. If anything, the loss of twenty pounds only added to his jowls, making Browne look like he was one step away from starring in a movie with a Scottie named Jock.

Kane'd pulled Rafe into a conversation that'd obviously been started way before the doctor descended from the mount to tell them Brigid was going to be okay. An alcove served as a de facto war room, a cluster of folding chairs appropriated from the waiting area giving them a place to sit as they plotted. Riley sat in one, his long feet tapping out a rhythm so off beat, Rafe was a second away from bashing his head in when a look from his partner stopped him. Kel Sanchez joined them a second later, handing out cups of bad coffee turned milky by watered-down creamer, much like the cups Rafe'd tossed before he'd been dragged over.

"Con and Sionn going to keep the Sinners boys busy?" Browne grunted at Kane's nod. "Nosy pieces of shit. Don't want them in this."

"Hey, I'm one of those boys now," Rafe protested, sniffing at the coffee. It smelled as bad the second time as it had the first. "'Course I just stuck my nose in this shit."

"*You* don't count. You're scared of me. Those other two—the Addams Family twins—those two would be in our shit just because they think they should be." Browne pointed at one of the chairs. "Sit. All of you. Riley, you take notes."

"Quit your bitching," Kane cut Riley off before he uttered a word from his opened mouth. "You're the junior here."

"And apparently I don't count." Rafe shrugged off Riley's middle finger when it pointed his way. "Shit, they let just anyone into the SFPD now."

"Settle down. Rafe, you're here because I need to have you keep an eye on some things, and sadly, you're my best bet in this mess." Browne took one of the coffees, slurping at its rim like it didn't taste like cat piss colored with a handful of powdered shit. "As of right now, the two of you—Morgans—are answering to me. Captain Book's just agreed to let you ride shotgun on this. Kane, Sanchez is going to take lead on anything you're assigned. As far as any of your reports go, he's primary. If there's any reason you feel the need to do something, you're to run it by Sanchez first. He's to make the call."

"At least on paper," Sanchez interjected. "Brownie and Lieutenant Casey don't think you two are going to go all Wallace on someone, but let's face it, some asshole just shot your mother. Department's probably a hair away from asking you guys to step back and take a breather."

"Not something I want to do," Kane growled at his partner. Riley nodded, his face stern and set in a frown.

It was interesting seeing Kane pull on his full cop face. It was all business with the second Morgan son, and the fourth as well. Riley's build ran more to Quinn's, slightly leaner than his beefy oldest brothers, but Donal'd left his stamp. Both men sat forward on their seats, focused intently on the other men sitting at the table, and it was clear to all they had one thing on their minds—taking out whomever put their mother under a knife.

And who probably wasn't done fucking with Quinn's life.

"One question, why am I here? Yeah, keeping my eye on things... what things?" Rafe raised his hand, pulling the older inspector's attention away from the case files he'd begin laying out on a triangular table someone'd pulled over for them to use. "Not a cop. And I don't know enough about who Quinn's got in his life now to say shit about who to trust."

"That's *why* I want you here. Kane said you don't know anyone in Quinn's circle but Quinn, and apparently...." Rafe couldn't read the look Browne exchanged with Kane, but they'd definitely come to some sort of agreement between them. "Well, since Quinn's... with you, I want you to watch out for anyone who approaches him."

"And don't let him outside." Riley tapped Rafe's knee with his pen. "Ever."

"I'll try." Rafe held up his hands at the cops' rumbling threats. "What do you expect me to do? Tie him to the bed? I can talk 'til I'm blue in the face, but once he gets something in his head, not a lot can be done to get him to change his mind."

"That's the fucking Morgan family motto. Never listen to reason." The older inspector nodded at the two brothers sitting across of him. "Just do your best. And if you have to, call in reinforcements. I think we need to keep Quinn in lockdown until we can flush this asshole out."

"'Cause you think someone's after him?" Rafe processed what Kane'd told him before. "And that puts a target on me?"

"Or just trying to get his attention. Shitty way to ask for a date, but classic stalker slash controlling partner. Eliminate everyone close to the victim so they turn towards the abuser." Kane's chair ground on the hospital floor as he inched it closer to the table. "Problem is, how long before this guy turns on Quinn? Hell, today might have been that day, and it was just bad fucking luck Mum got hit instead."

"Bad luck for him," Browne commented. "No one wearing a badge is going to let this die. You don't shoot a cop's wife and get away with it. Might as well have shot your dad through the heart when that asshole pulled the trigger. Hell's going to look like a vacation spot when he gets taken down. Right now, let's take a look at what we've got so we can plug any holes."

"So far we've got two murders and a shooting. Simon K., killed off-site and dumped. We haven't found the kill site yet. LeAnne W., killed on-site and displayed, arranged, even." Sanchez ticked a count off his fingers.

"Two different MOs." The younger Morgan stopped his scribbling. "Or are we counting it as escalation?"

"I'm going with escalation because the dump site got too busy for him. Uniforms canvassed the area, but no one saw anything. I want to go back there and see if any of the early-morning kitchen workers will respond to a memory jog," Kane suggested. "Long way from Chinatown to the college. Alleyway suggests the dump site was convenient. I'm not convinced he's local to that area."

"Yeah, anyone who lives in Chinatown knows that place is hopping at three or so in the morning." Sanchez found an overhead map of the area and circled the spot again for reference. "Not really accessible on both ends. One badly timed garbage truck, and he'd have been stuck."

"Could be he's just gotten a taste of killing with Simon. Then when he got to LeAnne, it became fun," Browne added. "There's the truck incident, which might or might not be connected—"

"I'm going to say yes." Kane shrugged off the skeptical looks he got from his partner and Brownie. "Look, I think it was the first big hey-look-at-me this guy did."

"Then he followed up with the house. Big display there. So yeah, he wants performance but didn't get it with Simon," Riley added. "Question I've got there is, why didn't he move in on Quinn then? After the house? Q said no one approached him."

"What do you mean?" Rafe frowned, watching the circle of cops nod in agreement to Riley's speculation.

"Because that's when someone'd move in close and offer Quinn protection. A place to stay." Kane grinned at Rafe, his eyes merry with mischief. "Kind of like you did at the house that Sunday."

"So I'm not a suspect?" He matched Kane's smirk with one of his own. "Fuck you, Morgan."

"You're not smart enough to be a suspect, Andrade," Kane replied. "'Sides, you're as Catholic as I am. You'd slit your wrists from guilt if you'd shot Mum. And, well, you *did* go hide behind Da when Quinn was on the warpath."

"Dude, he was going to pop your heads off of your necks and suck out the marrow from your bones," Rafe protested. "I'm kind of fond of you and Con. I mean, yeah, Donal lets you guys battle it all out until you get your shit together, but right then and there, you were marked for fucking death, and Quinn was going to be the one swinging the axe."

"Should have let him kill them. I'd move up in rank quicker." Riley popped his head up. "At home too."

"Like Kiki couldn't take you down," Kane shot back. "But yeah, the truck and the house—so a part of this."

"Let's take apart Quinn's life. You guys have talked to him, what... twice about who's around him?" Browne scanned a list, and from what Rafe could see, the paper didn't have many names on it. "Kid's got students… associates. We're going to have to expand the circle to include people he sees on a day-to-day basis. Start poking around into backgrounds. Find out where he goes often, that kind of thing."

"He's got a coffee shop he likes. Whyborne's. It's about a block down from my place," Rafe suggested. "They know him there. Like, making his drink as soon as he comes in the door kind of know."

"Something to look at. You go there with him?" Sanchez agreed, and Riley jotted it down. Rafe nodded, and Kel cocked his head. "Anyone stand out?"

"Not really. Kind of flourish, not pretentious, more like… elegant grunge. Didn't look like the kind of crowd who'd shoot a woman across the street from them." He shuffled through the impressions he'd gotten from the coffee shop's staff. "More like they'd slip you ground-up flour in your chai latte if you pissed them off and were gluten free."

"No one's off the list until we've got alibis." Browne did more page flipping, frowning as he skimmed his notes. "Kane, you and Sanchez start on this list of knowns. Riley and I'll take the outer circles, hit up the college staff to see if anyone's got something going for your brother. One thing Kane's right about. Whoever this asshole is, he's going to get pissed off that Quinn's not noticing him. His next hit *might* be Quinn."

"If we call the shot today for Rafe, that kind of confirms our suspect's targeting people Quinn's been involved with or has some sexual history with," Sanchez echoed what Kane'd said in the hall. "We don't have the luxury of hoping the shooter won't try again."

"Wait, back that up," Riley grumbled. "Simon… yeah. But Walker? LeAnne? That doesn't make sense."

"The Walker girl was known for being friendly," Sanchez supplied. "Problem was for her, Q doesn't swing that way. Hell, he didn't even notice. She made a play for him, and it bounced… bounced hard."

"Who told you that? Who noticed Walker being friendly?" the older inspector asked, shuffling through his papers.

"Graham." Kane scratched at his chin. "Graham Merris. He's a teacher at the college. Don't think he's in Quinn's department, but they share similar interests. Da said he saw Quinn and Graham at some thing. Shit, there was a flat tire. Da found Quinn changing it one night—the same night he and Merris were out."

"Merris have any record handling guns?" Browne pinned Kane down with a look hard enough it made Rafe shiver.

"Don't know. Wasn't looking at him." The older Morgan made a disgusted sound in his throat. "Fucking should have looked at him. He just didn't seem… hefty enough to do the damage."

"Never underestimate crazy. I have a couple of ex-girlfriends that looked all petite and delicate, then hulked out when you didn't compliment their shoes," Sanchez reminded them. "Okay. Kane, how about you and I go pay Professor Merris a visit. Rafe, if you know what's good for you… keep Quinn off the streets. We've already had one Morgan too many taking a bullet this week."

CHAPTER EIGHTEEN

Garage studio, Miki's warehouse
Damie: You ever think about what it would have been like if we'd started Sinners with Forest and Rafe?
Miki: Nope.
D: Not even a little bit?
M, shaking his head: The world happens because it happens. I miss Johnny and Dave, but after them came Kane... and then you again. Just like if something happens to me, I'd expect you to keep going... keep playing music.
D: Without you, Sinjun... there is no music.

RAFE WOKE to the sounds of splashing. He blinked, trying to adjust to the dark, but the blackout curtains across his bedroom's windowed walls were too good at their job, and he couldn't see a damned thing. The length of a warm body next to him was familiar, intimately familiar and welcome.

The splashing sounds grew furious, and Rafe was about to slide out of the bed when he remembered Quinn'd come with a dash of demonic fur.

Harley.

Rafe hit the ground running. He didn't know what he'd imagined the cat'd gotten into, but whatever his stress-frazzled brain sparked off against his skull, Rafe wasn't quite prepared to find Quinn's fuzz-assed cat sitting tail down in the bidet, playing with the spritz of water coming up from the bottom of the bowl.

Shit, *he* wasn't even too sure how to work the damned thing, but there was Quinn's cat, a smile on her triangular gargoyle face and playing patty-cake with a tiny geyser.

There wasn't enough of a stream to get the floor wet, and when Rafe stuck his fingers into the water, it ran cold against his skin. Harley eyed him suspiciously, her paws paddling furiously. Shrugging, Rafe headed back to bed, leaving the light on so the cat could see what she was doing.

"What's the matter?" Quinn mumbled when Rafe snuggled up against his back.

"Your cat's in there playing with the bidet." Quinn smelled good, vanilla soap and male skin, and Rafe nuzzled his face into Quinn's hair, breathing him in. "Took me like five days to figure out how it worked, and the cat seems to have aced it on her first try. Gotta admit, the two of you really make me look stupid."

"Shoulda chased her out."

The Irish was high in Quinn's sleep-velvety voice, and Rafe's cock thickened when Quinn shimmied up against him, closing the space between their bodies.

"You'll get cat hair… up there."

"Dude, she might as well have some fun. I don't use it. I'm not sticking my ass over a water fountain. Paper's good enough for me." He nuzzled again, getting a low purr out of Quinn. His briefs were getting too tight, pulled up by his dick, and Rafe tugged at the elastic, hoping to give himself some room. "How are you doing? Okay?"

"I'm good. Tight. Skin's tight, but that's… worry. Still. Why?"

Quinn ground into him again, and Rafe hissed, this time certain Q knew what he was doing to him.

"What time is it? I should call—"

"It's four in the morning, Q." It was hard hearing the break in Quinn's voice. Rafe feathered his fingers over Quinn's stomach, stroking softly. "Your mom's probably asleep, and Donal's snoring in a chair next to her bed."

"Mum's the one that snores. Little poodle whimpers. Da makes fun of her for it." The tenseness along Quinn's spine receded, and he sighed, uncoiling slowly under Rafe's touch. "You keep doing that, I won't be able to go back to sleep."

"Sleep isn't really what I had in mind for you. Well, not for an hour or two." Rafe bit Quinn's earlobe, teasing it slowly between his teeth. "It's early, still dark outside, and your cat's busy playing in her own bubbling fountain. I say we take advantage of—"

"Do you know I almost called her Mangalica? It's a type of furry pig."

Quinn's breath hitched again, but Rafe knew the slight gasp was less about anxiety and more about Rafe's fingers sliding into Quinn's boxers and finding his balls.

"God... shite and hell."

"I love hearing filth come out of that pretty mouth of yours, magpie," Rafe growled, gently squeezing Quinn's sac. He got a response he liked. Quinn's ass clenched along the length of Rafe's crotch, snagging Rafe's cock in its cleft. Pulling Quinn onto his back, Rafe bit at the soft spot under Quinn's jaw. Hunger coursed through him, making it nearly impossible for his hips to stay still. Muttering, he trailed kisses up to Quinn's ear, licking the ridge he found there. "God, I want to fuck you so bad."

"Should we be doing this? Mum's in the hospital—" Quinn began to object, but Rafe's mouth shut him down.

Their tongues clashed and teased, long enough to be called a skirmish but not wet enough for a battle. After sucking out all of Quinn's breath, Rafe pulled back, leaving him gasping. Rafe slid his finger between Quinn's parted lips, then used the damp tip to trace around Quinn's mouth.

"That's exactly why we should be doing this. Celebration of life, Q. It's what we do as a species. We laugh...." Rafe punctuated his words with nibbling kisses, working his way down to Quinn's nipples. "Cry. Fear. And best of all, fuck. Because as much as I love your mother, and you *know* I love Brigid, I am so damned glad you were okay today. If anything'd happened to you...."

Rafe swore his heart stopped. Literally stopped. The darkness being held at bay by the bathroom light descended upon him, drowning his senses and choking his lungs. Sliding over onto Quinn's body, Rafe lay down on his lover, draping his thighs on either side of Quinn's hips, then capturing Quinn's face in his hands. He needed to breathe. Wanted to, even, but the simple act of getting his muscles to respond seemed beyond him.

"I know it's not been long... the two of us, I mean—" Rafe started.

"It's been forever. You used to take the puddings from my lunches." Quinn covered Rafe's hands with his. "You've known me since forever. It just took you a bit to... look."

"Oh, I looked. I just made sure no one noticed. I wanted to keep my nose where I had it." He sobered, seeing his affection reflected back at him in Quinn's face. "Love you, Quinn. Today... I was so fucking scared. In the car. At the hospital. You scare me more than anyone else in my entire life, Q. And I can't imagine it being any other way."

"Not exactly the most romantic thing there." He squished his cheeks together with his own hands, making fishy kisses at Rafe. Letting go when Rafe laughed, Quinn said quietly. "I love you too."

This time was different. Their second time. Gone were Quinn's nerves, and instead of shivering from the unknown, they trembled with anticipation. Clothes were obstacles to overcome, and Rafe had a gut feeling Quinn's boxers would be useless for anything other than buffing wax off of the Chevelle after he felt them rip in his hands.

He took his time with Quinn, finding all the secret places on his lover's body. Rafe marveled at the sleek skin along Quinn's ribs, then the velvet-rough texture of his balls, their rich, musky scent a perfect complement to the sweet-smelling soap. Soft, delicate hair ghosted over Quinn's thighs, sparse and fine, a contrast to the thick silken trail around and under his navel.

Rafe found Quinn was ticklish, mostly on the bottoms of his feet, his big toes stiffening, then curling under when Rafe playfully raked his teeth over the meat above his arch. Quinn made some noises about the spot being connected to the chest or heart in reflexology, and Rafe dove back into his explorations, not giving Quinn any more space in his brain to think.

There was a single, simple moment when Rafe knew Quinn'd gone over the edge of his mind and sank down into the animal hidden deep inside him.

It was a sigh, a murmuring, mouthwatering sigh, and Rafe *knew* Quinn's focus snapped in on him. Nothing outside of their joining bodies would intrude, and Rafe could savor every moment he had with his quixotic lover.

He couldn't imagine his life without having a green-eyed, curious Morgan poking at the edges of the universe, unraveling things like the twist of thread or why some people thought cilantro tasted like soap. He'd never been bothered by the hummingbird scramble of Quinn's mind. It fascinated Rafe—intrigued him beyond all measure—because he simply couldn't imagine having that much of everything pouring down on him at the same time. Being Quinn meant bailing out the flooded rowboat of his brain with little more than a thimble. Rafe knew that feeling—knew it well.

After all, he'd had his own bailing to do.

With a kiss, Rafe dampened the torrential gush of sensations, leaving Quinn to experience the pleasure their bodies could give. One touch at a time.

His mouth found every inch of Quinn's body, laving and teasing with teeth, tongue, and fingers. Quinn's nipples were pink, roughened to a peak, and he clutched at the sheets when Rafe's mouth closed over the head of his cock.

Quinn, master of languages and ponderer of the vast universe, dissolved into the filthiest string of Gaelic Rafe'd ever had the problem of parsing out.

He understood *fuck* and possibly *dick*, although Rafe wasn't quite sure. He sank the barest of bites into the ridge of Quinn's cockhead, and he got another smattering of hot Irish. Yes, he thought, licking at the spot. That definitely was *dick*, *arse*, and *now* in the dirty stew Quinn spat out.

"See, I'm not understanding you exactly, babe. I'm definitely going to have to become fluent in that tongue of yours, Q." Rafe got to his knees, parting Quinn's thighs on either side of him with a nudge of his hands. "The one in your mouth too."

"*Is fearr Gaeilge briste, na Bearla cliste,*" Quinn growled, grinding his ass against Rafe's hands as he was lifted up.

Their joining came hard. Quinn demanded it. Fiery and insistent, his hands clutched at Rafe's shoulders, then his hips. When Rafe put one oil-slick finger to Quinn's hole, he was met with a round of begging, cloaked verdant and steamy.

"Please, Rafe." Quinn strained to pull more of Rafe's touch inside him. He twisted his fingers, drawing them out of Quinn in a leisurely pull, catching the rim ever so slightly. "God in heaven, Rafe… *please.*"

"Anything you want, magpie." Rafe slid more lube over his sheathed cock, then pressed its head up against Quinn's hole. Bending forward, he captured Quinn's mouth in a fierce kiss, whispering through Quinn's slightly swollen lips as he slowly pushed in. "We'll take this slow, Q. I want this to be good for you. So fucking good."

He eased in, holding back despite Quinn's impatient urging. It was the right thing to do, especially when Rafe felt Quinn's body resisting him at first. Stroking Quinn's sides, he calmed his lover down, reminding him to breathe.

"Relax, baby. Let me in. Take your time. We've got forever," Rafe reminded him. Quinn inhaled sharply, and their eyes met, a kindling of evergreen and cognac. Then Rafe slid in, seated up to the root of his cock with a simple push of Quinn's hips.

It was like heaven folding over them.

Rafe didn't want to move. No, he'd planned to remain engulfed in Quinn's hot clench for as long as possible—maybe even forever if he could figure out a way to get the cat to call for takeout—but Quinn moved, a small shiver of a rocking motion, and Rafe lost his mind.

They ran hot and fierce, coaxing out every last bit of strength they had in their bodies to ride the pleasure of being in one another... around each other... touching belly to belly, hands tangled together and thrusting. The bed squeaked and rocked, its headboard slamming against the solid wall in booming ripples of sound deep enough to rattle Rafe's teeth.

It was all Rafe could do to hold on. And he held, wrapping Quinn up in his arms, and rocked, pistoning his hips forward in sharp snaps, thrusting in time to Quinn's mewling, primal cries.

His shoulders stung, bruised from Quinn's punishing grip on them, but Rafe continued, throwing his head back when Quinn bit down on his neck. There was a taint of copper in the air and his throat grew hot, its skin painfully raked as Quinn bit again to get a better purchase. Rafe rode the pain, letting it shock him from the edge. With Quinn's hard cock trapped between them, he rolled his hips, rubbing his belly against Quinn's shaft.

"Come for me, baby," he rasped, torn between reaching down to stroke Quinn off and holding Quinn's hips up so he could hit the spots of pleasure he'd found in his lover's clench. Quinn ended the debate with a gasping shudder, his body stiffening as his eyes rolled back in his head.

Rafe felt the splash of hot seed hit his chest, and he was done for. He poured himself into Quinn, wishing he could fill every bit of emptiness inside him, washing away the awkward disjointedness Quinn felt whenever he opened his eyes. He longed to cradle Quinn, holding him in synch with the people and things around him.

But if he did, Rafe's heart whispered, Quinn would no longer be Quinn. No longer the magpie caught up in the flashy silver of his next thought. There'd be no more journeys into mystical places of unexplored dreams and certainly no babbling streams of Irish-brewed imaginings, laden heavy with rainbows and the most secretive of stars.

Quinn *made* Rafe's world explode with experiences—from the notice of a dew-jeweled spiderweb while walking for coffee to the wonderment of the city's bedazzling cloak of lights, a garment she could only truly don once all the penthouse's lamps were doused. He'd learned the magic of a melting tiny marshmallow on his tongue right before it slagged into a mug of butterscotch-schnapps-dosed hot chocolate from Quinn.

Just as he'd caught a glimpse of heaven buried in Quinn's body and splatted by Quinn's come.

His body folded in on itself, pouring out every bit of Rafe in its gush to fill Quinn. Rafe panted, resting his weight on Quinn's heaving chest as he was wrung dry by Quinn's asscheeks squeezing around him. It took a few seconds for the drunken, drowned feeling to subside, leaving only the sticky salt of their sweat and come. Rafe tried to catch his breath, giving in when he realized how silly he sounded trying to control his heaving intakes. Quinn sighed, grunting slightly when Rafe slid off him so Quinn wouldn't be crushed by his weight.

When Rafe felt himself pull free of Quinn's rim, he mourned their parting, his cock bright with sensations. He needed to get the condom off. It only seemed important because the latex slithered around his cockhead, its blood-flushed skin too prickly to be handled with anything other than the gentlest touches. Still, Rafe tugged the sheath off, then slid it onto the remains of Quinn's boxers on the floor.

Sliding his arms around Quinn, Rafe felt his bones droop, liquefied in the soft afterglow of sex. His neck ached, probably torn open by Quinn's teeth, and he wasn't totally certain his shoulders weren't black-and-blue from Quinn's powerful hands, but Rafe didn't care. He'd take the pain. The pleasure of having Quinn in his life... in his heart... was well worth it.

Clearing his throat, Rafe tried out the one Gaelic phrase he'd worked hard to learn, hammered into him by Kane as they waited for Quinn to return from seeing Brigid. Pushing Quinn's damp hair from his strong features, Rafe whispered, "*Tá tú iontachá lainn.*"

He must have come close, because Quinn's lips parted in surprise and his eyes misted, folding a hazy lace over the green. "Ach, Rafe. Oh... *tá mo chroí istigh ionat*. Truly."

"Sorry, Q, but that's the only sentence I know," Rafe replied ruefully. "You're going to have to teach me what you just said. 'Cause other than telling you that you're beautiful, the only other Irish I know has to do with fucking and asses."

Quinn's bark of laughter was loud enough to scare the cat out of the bathroom, and Harley tore through the room, launching herself off a corner of the bed to trebuchet herself through the open door and out into the hallway.

"Not to worry, *a ghra*." Quinn teased Rafe's mouth with a simmering kiss. "Those are words I can work with."

"YOU UP for this? 'Cause, you know, Brownie and I can handle this." Sanchez put their police-issued unmarked into Park and stared at his partner. "You had it rough last night, man. Nothing stopping us from turning the car around and taking you back home."

"Kel." Kane shot his friend a disgusted look. "It's six in the morning, and I'm sitting outside of some teacher's house, holding a cup of coffee Miki made— which could go from soup to oil—and hoping the guy inside of said house doesn't have a hard-on for my baby brother and is killing people out from under

Quinn. What part of this face says 'Sure, let's turn around and go have pancakes at IHOP instead'?"

"Just saying." Sanchez sighed in return. "Something tells me we're either going to need riot gear going in or get laughed out of the force coming down on a guy with petunias in his front yard."

An access alleyway was going to be as good as they got for a parking space, especially in the tight streets of Merris's old-tree neighborhood. The houses were on single lots, long rectangles taken up mostly by old wooden structures built with a longing for a frillier time. Kane counted five turrets among the three houses near Merris and about as many bay windows as there were cars. It was a few blocks of nostalgia, dew-kissed streets where children chased after ice cream trucks in the afternoon and people sat out on Adirondack loungers to drink iced tea in the early evening.

He'd grown up in a neighborhood much like the one Graham Merris called home, and while Kane couldn't imagine the earth-tone shingled walls concealed a murderer, he knew better. His gut told him ugly lived just under the skin of most people, and sometimes all it took was one ill-timed word to let go of the killing beast seething beneath the surface.

Although—taking another sip of Miki's dinosaur-remains coffee—it wasn't that far of a leap to go from placid to rage if he drank much more of the sludge he'd tried to offset with sugar and cream.

"Can't anybody in my damned family make coffee right?" Kane got out of the sedan, glancing at the blooms lining the short cement walk up to a pristine, prissy bungalow draped with enough gingerbread to attract packs of out-of-work Christmas elves. "And those are impatiens, Sanchez."

"Gotta admire a man who knows his flowers," Kel muttered at Kane's back. "Want to put on a couple of vests, or do you think we're going to be safe from the mad professor?"

"Shit. Go in vested, he'll know we've popped him." He chewed on the inside of his cheek, thinking. The alley gave them a bit of cover, as did a high, thick hedge wrapping around the property next to Merris's. They'd thrown their gear into the unmarked's trunk, mostly as a precaution, but Kel'd called out a good point. They just didn't have enough on Merris to know how he'd react to a pair of cops coming down on him. "But I don't want to go in stupid. We got any info on guns for him?"

"Nothing that says stone-cold killer." Kel tapped his phone's screen, scrolling through his transcribed notes. "Just what you've got on him and the twelve hundred activist groups he belongs to."

"Yeah, he's big into saving the show-tune sing-ing naked mole whales covered in gluten, but nothing with a gun." More chewing, and Kane forced himself to stop before he drew blood. "Vests on. Jackets over. Let's not be stupid."

It took them a few minutes—minutes Kane felt were worth the time—and other than a little old wom-an wearing a pink floral housecoat toddling out to get her morning paper, they saw no one else on the street. The eye fuck he got from the purple-haired woman was enough to bring a smile to Kane's lips, and he winked at her before she headed back into the house.

"Quit flirting with the natives," Sanchez growled.

"Hey, she started it." He adjusted his harness, then slid on his leather jacket, checking his radio clip. "You ready?"

"Yeah, let's do this." Kel peered down the alley. "Want to do a walk-around? There's a pass-through back there. We can check to see if his car's in the back garage."

"Sounds good. Didn't see what he's got registered to him out front." Kane scanned the street again for Merris's import. "Let's go knocking on Merris's door."

They didn't go in hot. Nothing in Merris's background said he'd come out to introduce the cops to his little friends. Instead, Kel kept watch as Kane checked out the single-car wood-slat garage behind Merris's tidy little house. He had a sense of déjà vu skulking around the structure. It'd been almost a year ago he'd come around Vega's broken-down house with its rattle-boarded shed in the back to find Miki lying on the ground, hands bloody and teeth bared.

Kel cleared his throat. "Kind of weird. Garage kind of looks like—"

"Yeah, that crossed my mind too." Thankfully, they ran into nothing more menacing than a beady-eyed crow perched on a weathered wrought-iron chair. Peering through a small diamond-shaped window built into the end wall, Kane spotted a squat silver import inside. "License plate matches to Merris. So unless someone grabbed him for a pancake buffet, he should be inside."

"You've got pancake buffets in your neighborhood?" Sanchez added something in petulant Spanish. "Seriously, it's like you guys have hot and cold running maple syrup in your toilets up on that hill."

"Sanchez, I'm four blocks from Chinatown and living with a boyfriend that on his good days can be called feral." Kane gave his partner a nudge in the ribs with his elbow. "All we've got in that house are packets of shoyu and sriracha."

"Still, hot boyfriend."

"Yeah, best thing about the whole deal." Kane grinned, knowing he probably looked foolish. "Stupid crazy about him. Enough to give up maple syrup."

"That's just crazy talk, Morgan. Fucking crazy talk." Sanchez stopped in his tracks, carefully sidestepping a concrete squirrel perched on a herringbone-tile patio spanning the back of the house. "Hey, check out the back door."

Kane spanned his fingers over the hilt of his gun, easing carefully around an urn of strawberry plants, their tiny white buds just beginning to push through. The back door was open a crack, a filmy curtain hem fluttering through the space. He cocked his head, drawing close enough to listen through the slightly open door. Kane held his breath, concentrating on any noises coming from inside the house.

The crow shot out a caw, startling Sanchez. Kane fought back a chuckle, then nodded to the door. "Cover me. Let's go in live and see if Merris just forgot to close up the place after tossing the bird there his morning liver."

"Damned thing looks like it eats livers too," Kel groused. He drew his weapon, keeping its muzzle down. "Let's go in, Morgan."

The back door swung open with the barest of touches, a testament to Merris's attention to detail. Kane waited until Sanchez seated his feet into place, poised to go in on Kane's lead, then called out, hoping to draw Merris out. "Professor Merris! This is the police. Your back door is open. We are going to come in. For your safety, please position yourself in the middle of a room with your hands up."

The house echoed with Kane's forceful voice, but no one answered. The crow bitched its displeasure, rattling off a long caw before taking wing. Somewhere in the neighborhood, a pair of dogs began to exchange a flurry of barks, trailing off after an old man's weedy voice told someone to come in.

Kane craned his neck slightly, keeping an eye on the door as he reached for his call button. Clicking on the mouthpiece, he cleared a channel. "Dispatch, Morgan and Sanchez, 10-35. 910 at current address. Request possible assistance."

He rattled off their unit codes, listening through the traffic as Dispatch gave them clearance to go in. A nearby unit caught the call, responding to their request for backup, and Dispatch rattled back an acknowledgment. "Clear to go in, 5A17. Responding unit inbound to location. ETA two minutes."

"Acknowledged, Dispatch." Nodding once at Kel, Kane jerked his head toward the door "Let's go, Sanchez."

Merris's house was cool, drenched in shadows and chill from the morning air and shrouded sun. The back door opened up into a mudroom, a matching pair of old Whirlpools dominating one long wall. A black metal shelving unit held cleaning supplies as well as several pairs of bright yellow Wellingtons, their rubber sides and soles scrubbed clean of dirt.

"Kind of a neat freak," Sanchez noted softly. "Not the kind of guy who'd leave his back door open. Let's push it in."

The mudroom became a square kitchen, an avocado, black-and-white throwback from the 1950s. The appliances were vintage, gleaming a soft buttery green despite the lack of direct light. The air tasted of lemon, wax, and air freshener. There was no sign of a dog or cat, no bags of kibble or a stray hair caught up on the metal-and-Formica table set into a breakfast nook off the kitchen.

They got five feet in when Kane spotted a glistening trail of blood speckling a tied-rag rug near an arch leading to the main part of the house. The rug bunched up against a shoe, a white sneaker with a coin-sized crimson dot soaked into its canvas top.

"Fucking hell." Sanchez took a step back, requesting Dispatch for a lockdown on the street. His gun stayed pointed down, his shoulders stiff and ready should someone or something burst out from the front of the house. "Dispatch, acknowledging response."

The rest of the house was empty, lacking even the shoe's twin. Merris's clothes were there, no obvious spaces in his closet or dresser. The living room bore signs of a struggle, a turned-over magazine rack, its accordion sides shattered into pieces and tossed about the opening foyer. The morning's paper littered the few feet of hallway connecting the front door to the living room, its pages crumpled. A few more drops of blood soaked through the Sports section, mottling an article about a badminton league in Russian Hill.

"Blood looks pretty new. Not quite brown in the middle," Kane noted, lifting his voice loud enough for Sanchez to hear. "Merris definitely isn't here, but he was. And just about an hour ago."

"I've got some blues coming in. We'll start canvassing the area. Someone had to have seen something." Kel exhaled hard, an irritated scowl etched into his forehead. "God damn it, Morgan. We were so fucking close."

"We've got even bigger problems than Merris missing." Throaty engine sounds shook the front windows, thick-bodied cop cars pulling up to the curb. "Without Merris, we're back to fricking square one—and I sure as shit don't want to be telling my baby brother he might have lost one of his friends."

CHAPTER NINETEEN

Sliding around in my dreams
Your inky black kiss
Staining my life
With something I'll never miss
You pushed yourself into me
Down deep into my soul
Wish I could dig you out
Burn you till I'm whole
—Ink Black Kiss

RAFE WOKE to an empty bed. Empty except for a wrinkled, barely furred cat sprawled out on Quinn's pillow like a runny pancake. Harley sniffed once at his face, then began to nibble on Rafe's eyelashes, huffing heavily when he jerked his head out of the way.

"Okay, time to get up when the cat starts chewing on you." A quick piss and toothpaste across his teeth, and Rafe was ready to start the day. Or at least the midmorning, he confirmed with a glance at the over-sized clock in the hallway. Tossing on a pair of sweats, shirt, and Vans, he winked at Harley as she watched him from her perch on the pillows. Dressed, he gave the cat a scritch across her pink belly and intended to go looking for his lover.

Lover.

It was hard to wrap his head around. Quinn snuck up on him. One second he was there, in the background where Rafe'd needed him to be. Then the next, Quinn was in his face… in Rafe's heart… and had no intention of fading back to the nebulous shelf he'd been put on back when they were barely men.

Rafe's knees gave out from under him, folding him onto the edge of the bed. Harley slithered around on her adopted perch, angling herself beneath his fingers, and Rafe absently rubbed a spot he knew would make her drool with pleasure.

"I'm fucking stupid in love with your daddy. You know that, Harley?" If the cat knew her name, she made no sign of acknowledging its use. To be fair to the cat, she appeared more interested in getting the velvet on her stomach ruffled than actual conversation, but Rafe didn't care. In some ways, talking to Harley was a hell of a lot easier than having a discussion with practically everyone else he knew.

Except Quinn.

"You know a lot of people say your dad's off his head, gargoyle." The drool started, a slow well of saliva on the edge of her curled-up lip. "He's not, you know. Just kind of looks at the world through a stained-glass brain. And see, cat, he *shares* that shit with me. Me. Some fuckup who had the damned fucking good luck of hooking up with some badass Irish kid named Connor who didn't give a shit I was going to school with too-short pants and worn-out shoes."

Harley mewled her displeasure as Rafe patted her stomach, butting his arm for him to continue.

"Sure, hard life you've got here, cat." He gave Harley a quick ruffle, running his nails over her body, and she stretched, working her toes out. "You're just like him, you know? Kinda odd at first, but then you slid right under my skin. Okay, Harley, time for some food and maybe talking your dad into doing nasty things on the living room couch."

There was a hint of coffee in the air, acrid and bitter as if brewed too strong and too long ago. Curious, he headed first to the kitchen, cutting off at the V in the hall and found… no Quinn and a definitely scorched coffee maker.

Its death was glorious. From the carnage of its corpse, Rafe figured it'd given its life up valiantly for the service of their mugs, or perhaps, feeling overworked now that Quinn was around, decided to burst into flames in one final protest.

Either way, the brewer's body was a melted slag of plastic and parts. The carafe appeared unharmed and sat smugly by the sink, its glass scrubbed to a sparkle.

But no Quinn.

Rafe's stomach curdled into a ball, spiked and sharp with worry. Hurrying to the living room, he found it empty. Again—no Quinn.

"Shit, no. Did we not talk about not leaving the house?" Rafe hurried from the balcony off the living room and then to a room the designer called a study, where Quinn'd made cooing noises over the comfortable sling chairs and good lighting. He churned back around the kitchen corner, hoping he could find Quinn in one of the spare rooms, when he noticed writing on the chalkboard wall next to the fridge.

Killed coffeemaker. Be back soon. I'll bring some home. Left at 10 a.m. Don't feed the cat.

As notes went, it was succinct. A to-the-point missive about where Quinn'd gone and, more importantly, how long ago he'd broken loose of his restraints and was out wandering the city, open for a crazy's attack.

"Son of a fucking bitch." Rafe had other words, harder words, but they would have to wait. Putting his keys on a table next to the front door so he could find them later, Rafe stopped himself and took a breath. "Phone. Try the phone first. Text him. See where he is. Use your brain, Andrade."

A few short keystrokes, a couple of panicked words Rafe backspaced over, and the text was sent.

Seconds later, he was still standing in the foyer looking at his damned phone with no answering text.

"God damn it, Quinn. What part of stay the fuck inside didn't you understand? I can't... fuck, don't end up like Brigid. Please." Pacing across the foyer, he debated the wisdom of hunting Quinn down.

He flashed to Brigid's lifeless body sliding across her sedan's back seat, Rafe helplessly trying to press down on the gaping hole in her chest as Quinn drove like a madman through red lights and around slowing cars. They'd picked up a cop car, sirens blaring, then two, loudspeakers ordering them to pull over and get out of the car, and all the while Quinn sat stern-faced and pale, a cold block of stone putting the car through the ringer to get to the hospital.

The smell of Brigid's blood was still in his nose, and he'd scrubbed his nails until they were raw, needing to get them clean. Quinn'd finally pulled him out of the shower, muttering something about Macbeth and damned spots.

"Couldn't have gone far." Rafe's hand closed on the door handle, and he jerked his shoulders up, Quinn's note sinking in further. "Home. He called here *home*. Well, shit yeah."

His mind must have been on Quinn... all his mind, because Rafe didn't see the shadow looming in the hall outside his door. Not until it was too late. A second after stepping out to take the elevator down, the shadow struck, and Rafe toppled forward onto the hall floor, the penthouse's locked front door closing behind him.

WHYBORNE'S WAS only a few blocks away. At the most it should have taken Quinn about half an hour to go to the shop and back with two cups of coffee. Maybe add in another three or four minutes for a scone or three, but just a hair over half an hour.

Plenty of time to get back to Rafe. Probably before he even woke up.

And considering Quinn'd done everything he could to make sure Rafe was still sound asleep when he snuck out of the penthouse to get a moment of freedom, coming back before Rafe woke up was optimal.

What he hadn't planned for was a pregnant woman in a minidress who'd been five steps ahead of him when her water broke as she tottered down Nob Hill.

And Quinn would have thought it was funny that there didn't seem to be a cop car within five hundred miles of a pregnant woman huffing and puffing in the vestibule of an Italian restaurant with a Peruvian cook screaming at him from the kitchen about needing more ice.

What the fuck ice had to do with helping a woman get a baby out of her womb, Quinn didn't know, but the Peruvian was insistent they needed more.

Luckily for his nerves, the ambulance arrived before the infant, the now relieved Peruvian cook was packing up a travel jug of coffee for Quinn, and he'd gone to the restaurant's employee bathroom to wash up.

Where he found the ice, lurking in wait for the moment Quinn turned on the faucet and stuck his face into the stream.

By the time he got the feeling back in his cheeks, the cook had the coffee ready to go and threw in a few biscotti for good measure. It was only then Quinn checked his phone and saw Rafe's text.

"*Mierda!*" He must have cursed in Spanish, because the cook looked alarmed at the outburst. He'd been speaking it for nearly an hour since he'd first begged the cook for help through the restaurant's front door, but then after the panic of water, blood, and screaming woman, Quinn didn't blame the man for being a little bit jumpy. "Lo siento. No era mi intención asustarte."

"You're welcome," the cook replied slowly. "Now, you go. Got to clean the front of the house. Owner's not going to like this shit."

The coffee was a little hard to handle, a thick-bodied cardboard-and-plastic construct built like a square milk jug, but Quinn was glad for it. Even if the cook brewed up the crappiest coffee in existence, he was running late—way too late to expect Rafe to still be asleep.

"A blow job. That would have done it." Oddly enough he got a strange look from a passing woman, and Quinn smiled broadly as he edged around her. "No, really. A blow job. That would have made him sleepy. It always makes me sleepy."

Quinn got another five steps when his phone sang out at him. He set the coffee down on a café table outside of a boba shop and dug his cell out of his jeans.

"Oh, for Christ's sake, I'm only a block away. Promise—" A tingle in his brain told Quinn to shut up. The ringtone wasn't the one he'd chosen for Rafe. No, there was no rolling hips slither song about drips this time. The music he'd heard was the telltale jingle he'd assigned to Kane, not the person he'd ever want to tell he'd fled the penthouse in search of coffee. "Hey, Kane. What's up?"

"Where are you?" his brother snapped. His Irish was up, slapping Quinn in the face.

He was going to lie. Quinn fully intended to lie, but the lack of emergency vehicles in the area became a thing of the past as a pair of fire trucks screamed down the hill past him. Quinn waited a second for the ringing in his ear to stop, then another few moments for Kane to stop yelling at him through the phone.

"Are you done?" Quinn moved out of the way of a jogger, tucking himself in closer to the wall. The coffee sloshed about in its container, and he briefly gave a thought as to how hot it would still be by the time he got home.

"No! I am not fucking…. Kel, bus. The bus!" Kane swore again, this time at his partner. "What the fuck am I thinking, letting you drive?"

"Hanging up now," Quinn threatened. "Look, I went out for coffee. I kind of cooked the machine Rafe has at home."

"Get inside. I'll have a unit come pick you up," Kane ordered. "They can be there in ten minutes."

"Bullshit. They still haven't shown up yet for the pregnant lady." To be fair, Quinn reasoned out, any cops coming in probably veered and went off to do other things since the ambulance showed up. "I'm close to the building. I'll go through the garage to use that elevator. You need a pass code to get under there, and there's a security guard at the gate. I'll be fine."

"Fucking Rafe should have done his job and kept you inside." It was a faint mutter but one Quinn caught anyway. "Q, listen—"

"Did you just say Rafe was supposed to keep me inside? Like I'm some fucking dog to be kenneled when everyone leaves?" The coffee wouldn't get a chance to be cold. His anger would be enough to boil it back to molten once he picked it up. "Look, I get that Mum was hurt. And yeah, I understand it's not safe to be out in the open, but I spent a damned good amount of time keeping my ass covered—"

"We lost Graham Merris, Quinn." Kane cut through Quinn's rant. "I just left Merris's house, where there's blood on the floor and shit tossed to hell and back. So while I don't know if your friend's alive or dead—considering what this fuck bastard's done in the past, things aren't looking good. So, little brother mine, you get your fucking skinny ass someplace safe and let me call someone to pick you up."

Not Graham.

As exacting and sniffy as Graham could be, Quinn was fond of him, even loved him a bit, because no matter what oddness Quinn expressed, Graham let it roll off him. No teasing. No sarcastic remarks about his behavior. Instead, Graham Merris merely accepted Quinn at pure face value, enjoyed contemplating silly theories about books and events starring people long turned to dust.

For all his prim, tight ways, Graham Merris definitely counted Quinn as his friend, and Quinn'd always been thankful for it.

Then the thought of Rafe lying in a pool of his own blood, his life smashed out of him, chilled Quinn so deep his balls pulled up in fear.

The building's security had been tightened, but Quinn knew better. There were always cracks, always places someone determined to get in could do just that, work themselves through a gap by any means necessary and no one would be the wiser—not until it was too late, and by then Rafe would be dead.

Quinn didn't think he could survive another loss… not like Rafe. Fear tightened the spit in his mouth, and a heavy pressure formed over his breastbone, punching down into his lungs and spreading over his ribs.

He wasn't going to *not* wake up next to the man he'd had in his heart since they'd shared a stolen pudding cup under their school's bleachers as a thunderstorm tore the skies apart. His mouth still tingled from their first kiss, his body holding in the hum of Rafe's touch invading him. He wasn't going to lose the sunsets they'd watched over the phone nor the sparse few they'd had on the penthouse balcony.

And Quinn sure as hell wasn't going to lose the man who'd given his bidet over to a cat with less sense than a damp loaf of bread.

Not Graham. *Not Rafe.*

His heart couldn't take the emptiness, and his soul ached at the thought of a life without Rafe's callused fingers stroking his lower lip or the insides of his thighs, Rafe's playful, oh-so-skilled mouth teasing out one last kiss before they wrapped around one another and slept.

Fear, Quinn discovered, tasted as wickedly rotten as bile and as cloying as drying blood.

"Find Graham, Kane." Quinn left the coffee jug, hurrying down the hill. He'd cut through an alley, knowing it would lead him right back to the building's underground garage where he'd come from. "Don't let him be dead, Kane. Please."

"Q, just stay—you're not staying, are you?" Kane sighed, more resigned than surprised.

"Just find Graham. Save him, Kane," Quinn replied, turning down the alley. "I'm going to Rafe and make sure he's safe."

HIS HEAD hurt. Hell, his eyelashes hurt, especially when Rafe blinked to filter out the bright light shining down on him. The white glow flickered, stuttering between a light and dark that had nothing to do with his lashes, lids, or any other part of his eyes he had any control over. Someone was whimpering nearby, and Rafe hoped it wasn't him.

Feeling around in his bloodied mouth with the tip of his tongue, he deduced it couldn't be him whimpering, because his jaw felt too swollen to move.

"God damn it. Shit," a man swore. Nearby, a thump on the floor sent shock waves through Rafe's aching head. "I hit him too hard. Who the hell is going to believe this pussy could hit this guy like that? *Damn it!*"

The sniveling grew louder, then another thump, the sound of bone hitting flesh, and whimpering faded to small hiccups. Rafe bit the inside of his cheek to prevent himself from groaning, then risked peeking out from under his lashes. He couldn't see a damned thing but the hall's marbled floor and a single black boot.

Pain ratcheted up his spine when Rafe tried to move his hips, a slight roll and hopefully not enough to alert the boot's owner. He needn't have worried. Apparently Boots was off in his own little world, ranting on about how he had everything planned but now things were ruined—he was ruined—because he'd hit Rafe too hard.

Rafe definitely didn't see the need to argue that particular point.

Not since it felt like Boots'd dislocated every single bone in Rafe's body.

The thumping continued, stomping off a few feet away, and Rafe risked opening his eyes another half inch, hoping to get a good idea of what was going on. What he saw did nothing to calm his nerves.

As front halls went, it was a fairly simple design, a rectangle of marble, wood, and a couple of waxy-leafed plants Rafe'd assumed were fake until he'd come across someone from maintenance watering them one day. One of the rectangle's long sides was taken up by the two elevators keyed to reach the penthouse, with his front door on the other wall. Much longer than wide, the hall served its purpose for the most part, giving visitors someplace to stand until Rafe could open the door or providing a floor for him to dump his grocery bags on while he tried to find his keys.

And sadly without a hidden machine-gun turret. Once he got his shit together and Boots taken care of, he'd talk to the building about its lack of foresight in case of a hostage situation.

How long before he'd stop being a hostage and move on to being a murder victim, Rafe couldn't say, but judging by how the skinny '50s crooner looked as he lay slumped against one of the plasticky plants, things were going to escalate quickly.

It took Rafe a second to recognize Graham Merris, Quinn's colleague from the photo he'd seen of them on Quinn's phone. The name'd escaped him for a second but Rafe never forgot a nose, especially not one that looked as if it should have sat square in the middle of a Dark Arts instructor.

Engrossed in studying the gaunt-featured man, Rafe failed to see Boots coming back over until his vision filled with a layer of thick leather and sole. Slamming his eyes shut was out of the question, especially when Boots's shadow stretched over him, cutting off any light he got from the hall's sconces and skylight.

Rafe flipped over onto his back, trying not to let the aching creaks in his shoulder and neck distract him. Boots's meaty hands grabbed at Rafe's shirt, scrambling to get a hold before Rafe could wiggle away. Kicking up, Rafe connected with the man's round, acne-pocked face, rippling his jowly cheek with a blow of his foot. Boots's head snapped back, but instead of falling away, Rafe caught the sight of a blood rage forming in the man's rheumy blue eyes, and his stomach sank, catching sight of the gun holstered to the man's thick utility belt.

Rafe pushed up, his sweaty hands sliding about the marble floor, but his shoes caught on the slick tiles, squealing up a desperate storm when Rafe fought to get to his feet. He was halfway up when Boots struck, kicking Rafe in the stomach with a hard-soled leather toe. The blow churned Rafe's innards, and he gagged, choking on the bile rushing up from his empty stomach and pouring over his tongue.

Spitting a mouthful of viscous green saliva into the man's face, Rafe gritted his teeth and backed up into the wall, using its flat surface to leverage himself up. He was dizzy, a bit groggy, and the world seemed to be brighter around the edges, a starship lens flare across his right-hand side. Rafe's stomach argued with the movement, gurgling ominously, but for the first time since he'd been coshed across the head, Rafe got a good look at his assailant.

Boots wore a security-guard uniform, much like the ones the building's own staff wore with one key exception—a patch embroidered with Quinn's university logo affixed to his right sleeve. Nearly cavefish white, puberty hadn't been a friendly time for Boots's face, if it had ever left. Deep scars gouged his cheeks, and a spotty, pale ginger fringe sprouted nearly straight out from his thin upper lip.

Oddly, Boots appeared to be pretty pissed off about Rafe standing up, despite his previous worry about hitting Rafe too hard. The scowl on the man's face clicked things together for Rafe. He knew that scowl. It'd been used on him before, same amount of venom, but this time the poisonous stare made sense, especially if Boots was the killer hot on Quinn's ass. If anything, the heat in the security guard's eyes melted off any humanity left in his face, and Rafe slammed into the wall, trying to take a step away from the man now reaching for his weapon.

"Oh fucking shit, you're Sam," Rafe blurted out.

"My name is not Sam! Quinn can never get it right!" Furious, Boots brought up the blackjack instead of his gun, swinging wildly at Rafe's head as he screamed, "My name is *William*."

CHAPTER TWENTY

Moonshine and ice
Bathtub swill and broken dreams
Climbing up on a stairway
Made of nightmares and pain
A slip of my hand
Wet blood on a rung
Hitting the stone down beneath me
Made me think 'bout what I've done
Thought about how I've hurt you
How deep and how long
Can't ask to forgive me
Since I've done you so wrong
—Moonshine and Ice

THE SAP hit Rafe hard, slamming into his forearm when he tried to block the hit. Sam—William—
wrenched the blackjack back, ready to bring it back
down on Rafe again, when years of dealing with bar

fights and jealousy-enraged ex-lovers fired up Rafe's survival instincts.

Hit fast. Hit hard.

Uniforms were thick, usually a cotton meant to withstand a lot of abuse. Grabbing one meant skinned-up knuckles and sore fingers, but knees, those worked the best.

Slamming his leg up, Rafe clocked the guard straight in his nuts. William went down, his fleshy body hitting the tile in a wet-sounding smack. The strike threw Rafe off-balance, and he toppled, the throb in his forehead ramping up to a full scream. Or it could have been William's moaning hitting new heights when Rafe tried to stop himself from falling and brought his foot down hard on William's nose.

The fall still happened. Thrown off by the wavering slosh of his brain against his skull, Rafe stumbled over William's writhing torso, tumbled off the man's thick belly and onto the floor. A movement to the left of Rafe caught his eye, and he saw Merris scuttling on his hands and knees to the elevator. Rafe made a desperate attempt to get up, but the hall burst into a sea of stars and pain, something solid and fast striking the back of his head hard enough to slam his face into the floor.

Rafe tasted blood, and the edges of the room grew dark, fragmented shadows closing in until all he could see was a wavering pinprick of light. Graham's screams grew louder, and Rafe spat out the fluid pouring down his throat, wishing he could risk shaking his head to clear his sight.

Then Graham went silent, and the hall was filled only with the sounds of their frantic breathing.

"You weren't supposed to come out."

William sounded mournful, but Rafe wasn't buying any of his remorse.

"I was going to knock on the door and tell you I had something for Doctor Morgan, something from the college so you'd open up. I wasn't ready for you. I don't know what Merris was thinking. I locked the elevators off of this floor. You don't even need a special key for the building. They pretty much all use the same one."

Rafe pulled himself up, instinctively throwing his arm up when he found William looming over him. The pinprick of light expanded, easing back the shadows until Rafe could make out the guard's face. He'd have to guess at William's expression. His vision wasn't quite ready to give him that much clarity, but it was enough for him to go by.

He spat again, not liking the taste of his own blood filling his mouth. Rafe poked around with his tongue, finding he'd bit not only his cheek but the inside of his lip. More blood was coming from his sinuses, probably because he'd popped his nose on the floor. It felt tender, not as bad as his head, but probably not broken. Breathing seemed okay.

Graham didn't look good. Slumped down against the elevator wall, his breathing seemed shallow, and blood speckled his fair skin, his cheeks nearly deathly pale and his thin lips white at the edges. He seemed smaller than he should have been, and for a frightened moment Rafe wondered if William had killed him, but a flare of Graham's nostrils reassured him the man was alive.

For now.

It amazed him the insane man could have gotten not only into the building with a reluctant Graham but also to the penthouse floor. Every thought in Rafe's mind whispered for him to keep the guard busy, engaged at least long enough for someone—anyone—to come. Quinn would be heading back soon—a thought that sent Rafe's heart into a panicked stutter—but when he found the elevators wouldn't go all the way up, Rafe had faith Quinn would call for help.

God, let Quinn get back and call for help, he prayed.

"Why Quinn?" he stuttered, tripping over his thickening tongue. Sitting up, Rafe scooted a few inches back, grateful again for the wall to hold him up. His vision was spotty, speckled with dark flashes. "Why did you try to kill him with the truck? You don't like gay men? He didn't share his ice cream cone with you? He turned you down for a date? What the fuck was going through your head there, Sam?"

Taunting was probably stupid, but it was all Rafe had. His keys were still on the table, locked behind the front door, and the elevator was blocked off. The only one with weapons was a porcine-faced madman who seemed to have forgotten he had a gun, preferring to use the leather-wrapped sap he swung back and forth as he stalked toward Rafe.

Rafe prodded again. "Come on, Sam. Give me the rant about how stupid we all are. Not like I can go anywhere, right? You think someone like Quinn would give you the fucking time of day? Not like you're smart enough to—"

The guard was quick. Rafe had to give him that. He didn't even see William's hand until it connected with the side of his face and left behind a ringing sensation in his ears.

"Do not talk about Doctor Morgan like that." William clenched his teeth, shaking a finger in Rafe's face. "You don't get to talk about him like he's one of those other assholes who don't even see me when I say hello. Doctor Morgan *always* stops and talks to me. *Always*."

William crouched in front of him, leaning forward so his hot breath washed over Rafe's face. The guard's leather belt squeaked, and the button on his pants strained against the pressure of his bulk, his shirt gaping slightly at his waist. Ironically enough, William smelled of sugar, a sweet confection of a breeze coming from a man who'd killed at least two people and seemed intent on doubling down on that number in the next hour or so.

"You're not so pretty now, are you?" William hunkered down, resting on the balls of his feet. His boots were worn across the toes, a crease in the leather deep enough to assure Rafe the guard spent a lot of time crouched down, waiting. The man rubbed at his face, sweat dappling his cheeks and forehead. "The truck? I didn't mean to hurt him. And his house…. God, that just went. That wasn't supposed to happen like that."

"You didn't think hitting him with a truck would be bad?" The hall was sliding about again, and Rafe had to blink furiously to keep it in place. "Did you see what was left of his car? You almost killed him."

"He wasn't supposed to drive like that." William's face flushed red, his emotions running to hot frustration. "Doctor Morgan is calm… gentle… he wasn't supposed to zip around like one of those insane kids on campus do. I was just going to bump his car and then pull over to help him. It all just... got away from me."

"Got away from you?" Stalling seemed to be working, or at least it kept William talking. The seconds were ticking by fast, and Rafe didn't know how long he could hold the guard there. His phone... he couldn't remember where his phone had gone to. "What got away from you? You kept bashing his car. And then blew up his house."

"Okay, the house... that wasn't my fault. I didn't know about the gas lines and stuff," the guard protested, a nearly childlike pitch to his voice.

"You almost killed his cat." Rafe sent a brief mental apology to Harley for using her to get under William's skin. "If you talked to Quinn at all, you'd know he loves that cat."

"God, I didn't think about the cat." His skin glistened now, a rivulet coursing down the side of his face and into the collar of his uniform. William shifted his feet, marking the floor with black rubber burns. "*That* would have made him come to me. He *loves* that cat. I should have killed the cat. But see, I kill you... well, make it look like Merris killed you, then he killed himself, and Doctor Morgan's got no one else to turn to but me. Just me."

"Wait, you did all this shit so Quinn would—what? Be so broken up about things he'd turn to you for... what exactly?" Rafe felt his tongue go sideways, and he slurred, dribbling out of the corner of his mouth. Fighting to stay focused, he rounded in on William again. "Dude, Quinn wouldn't give you the time of day. That why you had to go around killing people he knows? So he'd cry all over your shoulder?"

He caught William's punch across his cheek, and Rafe gagged on another rush of blood. The blow might have hurt, but the motion took William forward, throwing him off, and he had to slam his hand against the wall to keep from falling on top of Rafe.

Close enough for Rafe to grab William's gun.

He had it in his hand. Rafe felt the rough diamond pattern on the hilt, or whatever they called the spot someone held a gun by. It was hard, a bit cold but definitely heavy. Even as he tugged to get the gun free of William's holster, it felt so damned heavy.

"What the…?" The guard careened over, twisting to get away from Rafe's grasp.

They went over together, tangled in on each other in a macabre mockery of sex fueled by fear and violence.

It was a struggle. The gun wouldn't shake loose, no matter how hard Rafe tugged and jerked. William pounded on his back, jarring his spine and getting in shots at Rafe's kidneys. If he made it out of there alive, he'd be pissing blood for weeks, but Rafe was willing to take that chance.

Quinn was worth every single bit of blood he had in him.

William was big, nearly too big for Rafe to get around him. They rolled, slamming into the wall near the elevators, almost crushing Graham. The guard kicked, trying to get Rafe loose, but he held on, hooking his hand into William's belt for leverage. Neither could get to their feet, not with their limbs entwined and Rafe's hand clamped down over the gun. Twisting about, William tried to shake loose Rafe's hold, tearing at his wrist and fingers to get his weapon free.

Rafe refused to let him. Hanging on to the gun was his only hope. His last hope. Especially since the hall seemed to be darkening again and his stomach threatened to scale up his throat to escape the jerky roller-coaster ride he'd put himself on.

The gun went off, blowing out Rafe's eardrums. Then everything went still and black.

QUINN HEARD the gunshot, and his heart died. Fighting with the elevator and then yelling at someone from Dispatch to send over a car or five already sent him into a panic. Lightning rode his nerves, crackling terror under every inch of his skin, until Quinn was certain he'd burn up before he could get up the stair-well to reach Rafe.

The thundering echo of a gun shattering the stair-well's silence brought him that much closer to dying inside.

Quinn grabbed a fire extinguisher from the wall and went through the door—only to slide across the tile when he hit a pool of blood.

He saw Rafe lying on the floor, curled in on him-self, and Sam the security guard tottering to his feet, an unsteady monolith in sweat-soaked cotton. His meaty hand clutched a blackjack, its metal tip peek-ing out from between a space in its leather wrap. The guard's lip peeled back when he saw Quinn. Then his face changed, becoming docile and placid, his eyes sliding down to the weapon in his hand. They widened as if he was surprised to find himself holding the sap before drifting back up to Quinn's face.

"It's not what it... um, Doctor Morgan." The sap swung out of his hand, caught on a loop around Sam's wrist. "Professor Merris... he...."

Quinn edged closer to Rafe, keeping one eye on Sam. He couldn't put the extinguisher down, not when he wasn't sure who'd attacked whom. For all he knew, Graham'd been the one to beat Rafe's face, but the wounds were bruised welts, meaty explosions under Rafe's skin. They were growing too thick, too fast for someone of Graham's build to have done, especially since Graham was lying motionless against one of the elevator doors.

The fire extinguisher was heavy, but Quinn didn't want to let go of it. Somewhere there was a gun. He'd heard it go off, and Sam's holster was empty. One of the marble tiles was blackened and cracked, a large hole punched through the stone. The air smelled of powder and metal. Reaching Rafe's side, Quinn ran his hand over Rafe's chest, his gaze pinned to Sam's face. Rafe's breathing was steady, but his sweats were bloody. A tear through the fabric gave Quinn some small reassurance. Outside on the meat of his thigh, the wound seemed deep enough to bleed but not too worrisome.

The contusions on Rafe's face bothered him. As did Rafe's unfocused, wandering gaze when Quinn whispered his name.

"Oh, Sam," Quinn exhaled in a soft whisper as he felt Rafe's pulse beating strong in his throat. "What have you done? All of this? LeAnne? Simon? And now Graham and Rafe? Why?"

"My. Name. Is. William. I get it. Sam. Like you're Ralph. But you were supposed to be my Ralph. Not his. Never *his*." The innocence in Sam's—William's—face curdled into an ugly hatred. Gone was the gentle man who got Quinn hot chocolate or stopped on his rounds long enough to say hello if he was on Quinn's floor. "Why won't you remember that? Why don't you understand I've done this all for you? So you know how much I love you?"

Quinn stood, his fingers numb from gripping the extinguisher's handle. His palm was bloody, and he held it up for William to see. "*This* is not how you show someone you love them. Killing people is not love. How could you think that? How could you even think I would *want* that?"

"You were supposed to come to me… not turn to him." William glanced over his shoulder at Graham. "Or Professor Merris. You were supposed to—"

"I was supposed to what?" Quinn's anger raged up inside him. "What did you think I was going to do? Simon is dead. Simon, who was an asshole, but being an asshole isn't enough for someone to die. And Le-Anne is dead. She didn't *do* anything to you. She was just going to school, and you killed her why? *Why?*"

"She wanted you. Couldn't you see that?" he pled with Quinn, his lips quivering with emotion. "Every time I saw her with you, she touched you, stroked at you. How could you even let her touch you? Like that? Every year, I've watched students and some-times even other teachers come up to you, wanting to be near you, and you never see them, Doctor Morgan. You never ever let them in. Not until *him*. Pretty little rock-star druggie. Not until he came into your life, and then you let everyone around you in. Even Pro-fessor Merris."

"So this is about Rafe? Because he makes me hap-py?" Quinn struggled to understand William. "We're friends, Sam…. William. God, all of this is nuts. I'm not worth this. No one is worth what you've done. No one should be a reason to kill. It's stupid. And senseless. And—"

"Do not call me stupid!" William's spit flew across Quinn's face. "I killed the whore because she thought she was good enough for you. I killed Professor Kappelhoff because he treated you badly. Just like I need to get rid of *him*. Can't you see? He'll drag you down. I killed those people so you'd be free of them. So you could have a life without anyone who'd take advantage of you or—"

"You know what, Sam? *Fuck you*," Quinn grunted, swinging the heavy metal canister up with as much force as he could put behind it.

His hands were wet, damp from Rafe's blood, and the handle slipped slightly in his grasp. Clenching his fingers tighter, the pin blew out, forced free by Quinn's double grip, and the extinguisher shot out a blast of white spray, catching William in the face.

Quinn couldn't hold on to the canister, and it struck the floor, breaking one of the tiles, then rolling unevenly to a stop near Rafe's feet. The mist drifted, swirling on the light push of air coming from the building's air-conditioning vents, and Quinn held his breath, his lungs too tight on air to hold out for much more than a second. He caught the trailing edge of the spray, and his chest burned at the hit of chemicals on his inhale.

William staggered back, his temple split open and bleeding. His arm jerked back, the sap arcing behind him. Roaring, the guard rushed forward, swinging the blackjack up over his head. Quinn counted off the man's steps, watching for a hiccup of time when his right foot was up in the air. Then he struck, slamming his foot into William's left knee. He heard a crack, ominous and painful, and William went down.

Quinn scrambled to Rafe's side, hoping his lover was lying on the weapon. Shoving his hands under Rafe, he muttered a quick apology, then heaved Rafe over, flopping him onto his side. Rafe's eyes fluttered, opening when he landed with a pained grunt.

The gun wasn't there.

"Ouch, babe," Rafe grumbled. "God, this fucking hurts."

"Busy right now, Rafe." Quinn shoved his hands under Rafe's clothes, hunting for the weapon. He did a wild search of the area around them, peering into any shadows nearby in case the gun slid into a corner or ended up next to one of the plants.

"Now I'm going to have to kill you, Doctor Morgan," William groaned angrily. "I don't understand why you won't let me love you. But if I can't, then he's not going to either."

"Oh God, he's crazy." Quinn snuck a quick peek at the guard. William was reaching for the sap he'd let drop. His eyes were swollen nearly shut from the blast of foam he'd taken from the extinguisher, but the insane focus in them was fixed on Quinn. "Where is the damned gun?"

"Hey, babe," Rafe mumbled past his swollen lip. He wedged himself onto an elbow, then forced himself upright. "Do me a favor?"

"Not the time, Rafe," he argued. William was moving around behind him, and Quinn didn't think he could hold off the guard and get the other two men to safety.

"Now's the perfect time, magpie," Rafe replied, clasping Quinn's shoulder to force him out of the way.

He raised his other hand, quivering from the weight of the gun he held. "Time for William to go the fuck to hell."

The gun went off, a rippling boom sharp enough to prickle pain through Quinn's eardrums. He caught a face full of powder and the heat of the muzzle flash. The bullet caught William in the shoulder, spinning him back off his feet. His body jerked, riding the pain of the shot, then went still, his chest shuddering as he drew in uneven breaths.

"Hey, Q, you know what?" Rafe gasped as he let the weapon drop back to his side. "I *think* you are worth killing for."

"I don't think you killed him, Rafe." Quinn sighed, kissing Rafe on his bruised mouth. "He's still breathing. I think he fainted."

"Well, shit," he grumbled through the kiss. "Can't I do *anything* fucking right?"

EPILOGUE

Bled onto my hand,
Shoved his fist into mine
Stood tall against anyone
Who'd break through our line
No matter what they do
No matter what they say
Death's already tried to part us
And we've already made him pay
So lift a glass to the Sinners
Lift a glass of cheap ass gin
Put your lips on the Gates of Heaven
'Cause we're taking you to sin.
—Sinners' Calling

A Few Months Later....

DINO'S WAS exactly what Quinn expected. It was a dingy, worn-around-the-edges club with a stage barely large enough to hold a band and a rowdy crowd loud enough to make his teeth ache from the noise.

But the band waiting to go on stage was loving every minute of it.

The club was small as clubs went, a backdoor blues-and-rock bar tucked behind a San Francisco noodle shop old enough to have survived the Great Quake. Dino's smelled of beer and flour with a touch of oil and probably pot, Quinn decided after taking a sniff. Down an alley from a fire escape and more than a few years since two very young men met for the first time, Dino's was a comeback of sorts, a slip back into a time before the world got too big around them and their own lives became filled with Morgans and song.

There were rituals, odd little things Quinn couldn't help but be fascinated by. A few feet away, Forest slung his arms around Connor's waist, their foreheads touching, voices dropped to a murmuring low whisper. Seemingly unfazed by the bustle of the band's crew as they wove cables from amplifier towers set on either side of the stage, Connor and Forest were lost in one another, sharing a still, sweet moment untouched by the chaos.

Damien, on the other hand, bounced in place, shaking his arms out as his eagle-sharp gaze followed every speck of movement from the stage to the back. He muttered, then paced a foot, burning off or storing nervous energy. Quinn couldn't tell which. Sionn stood nearby, bemused and drinking a Finnegan Dark, one of the first to come out of his fledgling brewery. Damie stopped short in front of his lover, stealing first a kiss, then a sip of beer before starting up his pre-show pacing again.

"Leave off," Miki muttered behind Quinn. Pushing Kane's hand away from his face, Miki bared his teeth at Quinn's older brother. "I'm going to get all fucking sweaty anyway. It doesn't matter how I look."

"How the hell can you even see?" Kane grumbled as he attempted to get his fingers on a shock of Miki's chestnut hair, the thick strands falling over his forehead and across his nose.

"See good enough to kick your ass if you keep Brigiding me." Miki's teeth flashed white, and Kane jerked his hand back, fingers barely scraped by Miki's bite. "Seriously, leave me the fuck alone. A kiss is okay. Fucking with my face, not going to happen."

"Like loving a honey badger." Kane caught Miki up, yanking the lanky singer toward him. He risked a kiss—even Quinn could see it was a risk—and Kane pulled back, his lips slightly swollen by the passionate draw from Miki's full mouth. "Nervous?"

"Yeah," Miki admitted. "Scared, fucked-up, and nervous. But we're going to kick fucking ass. Just you watch. Dino's isn't going to know what fucking hit them."

"Hell yeah," Rafe said, slapping Miki's ass as he walked by.

"Hands off, Andrade."

There was a teasing lilt to Kane's warning, more a habit than a threat, and Rafe laughed, taking a step back to slap Kane's as well.

"There, so you don't feel neglected." Rafe nodded at Miki and then handed Quinn a bottle of iced tea. "Here you go, magpie. One cold dirt and leaves for you and one red cream soda for me."

"No beer?" He fought to get the cap off, then realized he was turning it the wrong direction. "Left to loose, right to tight. Unless it's a piercing... or a countersink."

Rafe waited a moment, and Quinn shot him a curious look. Grinning back, he said, "Just waiting to see if you kept going before I answered. And yeah, no beer. Not before a gig. We don't want to go all Good Ole Blues Brothers Boys on the tab."

Quinn searched his brain, then shrugged. "I don't know what that means. I don't think I've seen that one."

"Oh, babe," Rafe gasped, playfully clutching his chest. "Your brothers done did you wrong. I'll take care of that this week, then. Probably something we can all popcorn and beer at Miki and Kane's place."

"Kane. I was going to ask Kane about William. He said something about an evaluation—"

"William's never going to see the light of day, Q." Rafe made a face. "Let's leave him in the dark hole they tossed him in, okay?"

"Five minutes, guys!" A squirrelly, thin man shot through the band and their lovers, his headset sliding back on his sparse hair. "We're good to go in five!"

Damie began to bounce even more, and Miki rolled his eyes, detaching from Kane's arms. After giving Kane one last kiss, Miki shoved him to the front of the house. "Go find the family. Time for me to go be a rock star."

"Take care of my Miki, you hear?" Kane stabbed a finger in Damie's direction. The guitarist flipped him off, and Kane laughed. "Break a leg, Mick. I'll be in front. Screaming your name like some fourteen-year-old girl."

"Don't think you can get your voice that high." Sionn cut by Connor and Forest, tapping his cousin on the back as he went past. "I'll be happy to be kicking you in the nuts if you really want to be giving that a try."

"Thanks. No." Kane shook his head. "Con! Come on. Brae's holding tables for us."

"Do good, *a ghra*," Connor murmured through a kiss, then reluctantly let Forest go. "Have fun. Even if it's work. Have fun with it."

"It's not work, Morgan," Damie sneered. "This? This is as close to flying on your own wings that you're ever going to get. Gonna be more than fun. It's going to be awesome."

"I better get going. Da's probably trying to run herd on Mum right now. He'll need backup." Quinn squeezed Rafe's hands gently. "Take care of you out there. Look for me if you can."

"Can't ever see a fucking thing because of the lights." Rafe chuckled. "But I'll do my damned best."

"On in one! One, people!" The stage manager bustled back, nearly knocking Quinn over before righting himself.

Quinn stepped to the side, taking one last look at the man he'd fallen for so many years ago. Rafe stood shoulder to shoulder with his band, the three men he'd come to trust and love as much as he did the Morgans—maybe even as much as he loved Quinn.

Forest nudged Rafe in the elbow, their smiles more in comfort than anything else. They would be the new part of an old equation, pieces fitted in between a pair of brothers soldered together in both tragedy and joy. Rafe slung on his bass, adjusting it slightly while Damien hooked his guitar strap over his neck. Miki'd taken up Damien's bounce, a slower beat but still a roiling of his body on the balls of his feet.

Their fingers grazed, a brief touch between singer and guitarist and obviously a ritual performed before every gig.

The lights in the house flashed, and a deep, Italian-accented voice rumbled through the club's speakers, urging everyone to get up onto their feet to welcome the best fucking band to come out of Chinatown and Dino's.

Quinn was stepping off of the last step from backstage to the floor when the stage lights splashed up to full, and Dino's voice yelled over the tightly packed crowd's screaming.

"Make some noise for a band that's here for the first time—*again*—at Dino's Bar and Grill! Ladies and gentlemen, I give you—*Crossroads Gin*."

SEE HOW THE STORY CONTINUES IN

BOOK FIVE OF THE SINNERS SERIES

RHYS FORD

ABSINTHE OF MALICE

"From the get-go I was absolutely enthralled." — *Novel Approach*

Sequel to *Sloe Ride*
Sinners Series: Book Five

We're getting the band back together.

Those six words send a chill down Miki St. John's spine, especially when they're spoken with a nearly religious fervor by his brother-in-all-but-blood, Damien Mitchell. However, those words were nothing compared to what Damien says next.

And we're going on tour.

When Crossroads Gin hits the road, Damien hopes it will draw them closer together. There's something magical about being on tour, especially when traveling in a van with no roadies, managers, or lovers to act as a buffer. The band is already close, but Damien knows they can be more—brothers of sorts, bound not only by familial ties but by their intense love for music.

As they travel from gig to gig, the band is haunted by past mistakes and personal demons, but they forge on. For Miki, Damie, Forest, and Rafe, the stage is where they all truly come alive, and the music they play is as important to them as the air they breathe.

But those demons and troubles won't leave them alone, and with every mile under their belts, the band faces its greatest challenge—overcoming their deepest flaws and not killing one another along the way.

www.dreamspinnerpress.com

CHAPTER ONE

Devil by my side, devil that I know
Riding down the Crossroads, heading to
   the next show
Hearing my name on the crowd, never
   thought I'd be back
House lights going down, time to dance
   in the deep-silk black
—Breathing Again

THE ROAD wound around them, a blacktop snake with metal guardrail markings and a dashed yellow stripe down the middle of its back. It grew fat and thin as the lanes increased, then dwindled down to one, a single strip of ebony tar cutting into the Earth's flesh.

They were somewhere outside of New York. Or maybe it was Boston. Miki'd lost track of where exactly they were heading since they'd all stumbled out of a cheap motel that morning. It didn't matter where they'd been. It was where they would end up that mattered. That single shining spot somewhere at the snake's head, a pearl embedded between the kirin's horns to guide them where they would begin.

Where Crossroads Gin would begin.

The gig they played at Dino's was the first kiss of a months-long fuck the band had fallen into. No amount of prep, compromise, or cajoling would prepare them for the orgy to follow. Miki dreaded the road. He hated the haul from one place to the next, but he loved the feel of the boards under his boots and the squeal-sing of a mic when he wrapped his hand around it for the first time. He'd been giving oral to microphones for so long he'd almost forgotten what to do with an actual dick when one appeared in front of him.

That wasn't a problem now. No, now Miki's biggest worry was the echoing hollow inside of him, because Kane was nearly three thousand miles away, and he was stuck in an elongated metal box hurtling toward the unknown.

In the time and space between Sinner's and Crossroads, Miki'd discovered he really didn't like the unknown.

The road sang its own song under the van's heavy tires. A clip-clip shush punctuated every once in a while by a deeper thrum when they passed over a crease or snick in the asphalt. If Miki wasn't careful, he'd be lured into sleep, rocked by the gentle movement of the drive and the low humming Damien did in his throat as he worked out rhythms to the melodies Miki'd laid down for him a few weeks before.

Forest and Rafe were passed out across the two rows of seats behind them, propped up by pillows and thin, velvety blankets Brigid insisted on packing. Rafe snored, nothing delicate or gentle about the sounds barreling from his open mouth or the snorting gulps he took every few minutes. Their bassist was a loud thrum of bumps and noises, even in his sleep, and after a particularly long cha-cha-cha snuffle, Miki debated shoving a sock between Rafe's teeth.

A rare streetlight flashed yellow through the van's interior, sliding past the lightly tinted windows. The glow turned Rafe's hair wheaten and snagged just a little tuft of sunlight-shot gold peeking out from under an argyle-patterned blanket.

The lump of red, gray, and black fabric could have been a free-form sculpture for as much as Forest moved underneath it. A few hundred miles ago, their drummer pulled a blanket out from under the long seat and cocooned himself so tightly Miki wouldn't have been surprised if Forest emerged with bruise-hued wings. Only a little bit of his hair poked out of a fold, and one long, pale foot rested against the chair's arm, wedged in tight between the vinyl seat and a metal brace.

"Zoning out, Sinjun?" Damie's raspy growl tickled Miki's ear. "You're supposed to be keeping me company, remember?"

"Yeah, right. Like you don't love to hear the sound of your own voice. We going to pull over soon?" The clock on the dash said it was two in the morning, but he wasn't sure anymore about what time zone they were in. Across the horizon, a faint lightening of the sky showed between a copse of trees, but for all Miki knew, it was the sun coming to beat them into submission.

"Yeah, the motel's supposed to be another fifteen miles." The nearly pitch interior went pale and Cheshire, a curve of teeth lit up by the dashboard lights. "I'd ask if you wanted to drive—"

"Right, I can't back a goddamned car out of the garage, and you're going to put me behind the wheel of a Death Star." The van was huge, over twenty feet long, and just the thought of the driver's seat cushions hitting Miki's ass made him break out into a cold sweat. "I'll leave that shit to the three of you."

A yawn stretched itself up from his chest, wrapped around his uvula, and then clawed its way out of his lips. The roof of his mouth went thin, pulled in on itself, and Miki gagged on his own tongue. Wiping the spit off his chin with the back of his hand, he grumbled at the wet on his skin.

"Nothing worse than choking on yourself." Damien laughed at Miki's uplifted middle finger. "Not the way I'd want my obit to read."

"I read your obit. Made it sound like you were a cross between Hendrix and Jesus." The captain's chair was supposed to be comfortable, but Miki hadn't quite found the right slant to it. Adjusting it back another notch, he leaned into the curve, a knot unraveling from his lower back. "Edie had you walking on water and playing the national anthem in your sleep."

"Well, you know… it's me." The teasing was light, but the undercurrent between them darkened the already black shadows they'd gathered. Another mile marker flew by, a pale stone sentinel counting off the click while bringing them closer to Damien's crazy dream.

They'd been together for more than a decade, even if they took off the time Damien spent walled up in an institution after a semi tore through their limo, ending the lives of their band members and leaving Miki alone and broken. He'd folded in on himself, tangling his grief with barbed-wire words and songs sharp enough to cut his own heart out.

Damien—alive—had been a fucking godsend, a gift Miki never in a million years would have imagined he'd be given. Much like falling in love with a damned cop. A damned Irish cop named Kane Morgan.

"Talk to me, Miki," Damien urged gently. "Tell me what's going on in that busy head of yours. What's buzzing on in there?"

"Just…." He didn't know how to say what he felt.

Words only came to him on slips of music and strings. His world was pretty much black-and-white for so long, he didn't know what to do with the infusion of color. Of Kane's eyes, bright enough to mimic ice but so very warm when they raked over Miki's body, or the blush dew pink of his lover's mouth after kissing Miki senseless. He'd fallen for a man with the same coloring as his best friend, inky-black hair and blue eyes, but so very different in personality. The roll of Kane's slightly accented words, a strong Gaelic purr from long summers and holidays spent in his Irish parents' homeland.

He missed his cop. Missed waking up next to a thickly muscled man who teased him into smiling. And he missed his fucking dog. Miki huffed, frowning over the thought of Dude sprawled on the living room couch without him. The last thing he'd ever expected was that he'd miss the damned fucking *dog*.

"Every roll of the tires is taking me farther from… home, Damie." He scoffed, alarmed and shocked at the rawness welling up inside of his soul. "I mean before… it was okay. You're… family. And still are, but… it's like I'm leaving *home*. And I've never had a fucking home before. You… I mean I'm always… we're… shit, I don't know what the hell I'm saying."

"You miss Kane." Damie nodded. "I miss Sionn. Yeah, I have you, but that other piece of me? It's not here. He's not here. I get that. But it won't be for long. We can do this. We kind of have to do this. If we're going to be a band, we need to get tangled in with each other. Know each other. Think I'd drag you guys across country to play in shit-hole clubs if I didn't think it was important?"

"Yeah, because you're a dick," Miki shot back.

"Not that much of a dick," he snorted. "I'm leaving home behind too, so I know what you're feeling, Sinjun. But you know, they're fucking waiting for us to come home. That's the awesome part about this shit. You know home's *right* where you left it."

"You think this is going to work?" Miki kept his whisper low, hoping the road noise would mask his words. "Us. Them. All of this shit. The band. Think we can pull this together? Between us?"

"Yeah," Damie replied smoothly.

Too smoothly for Miki's tastes. One glance over the cab, and Miki saw the glint in Damie's blue gaze. Reaching over, Damie squeezed Miki's thigh lightly.

"Trust me, Sinjun. It'll be—"

The deer came out of nowhere. Or at least Miki thought it was a deer. It could have been fucking Bigfoot for all he knew, because the blacktop world with its backlit trees was suddenly full of eyes and fur and scrambling slender legs. The van skidded a bit when Damie tapped the brakes, and Miki grabbed at the dashboard, his heart pounding hard and fast. The flutter of beige and glowing eyes was gone in a blink, swallowed up by the darkness on either side of the road.

"You okay, Sin?"

The question was soft, prodding and poking at the panic gripping the small of Miki's skull. Damie slowed the van down, banking into a curve.

"Do you want me to pull over? You look like you're going to chuck up your Cheetos."

His lungs hurt from working to suck in as much air as they could, and Miki couldn't get his heart to stop running laps around his panic. The moment flashed by so quickly, a tear of steel and screams—his own screams—but no one in the van heard anything, felt anything. Their bassist kept snoring, and their drummer was still tightly wrapped up in his crazy shroud. The road was open, clear sailing until morning for all intents and purposes, but Miki's tongue refused to crawl back up out of his throat.

"No, I'm good. I'm fucking great," Miki snarled back. "Let's just get to the damned motel so we can get some sleep. I'm kind of tired of the world trying to kill me."

THE ROCKING Oyster Bar was a dive. There'd been a halfhearted attempt to bolster it up, mask its furniture-store beginnings by painting the windows black and power washing its brick exterior, but when it was all said and done, no amount of lipstick was going to do the pig any good.

It still was a pig, and an ugly one at that.

"What a fucking dump." Rafe kicked at a chunk of gray something near one of the van's tires. It exploded into a flurry of dusty feathers and bones. Shaking the remains of the dead pigeon off of his sneaker, Rafe cursed, spitting out a rapid-fire string of Portuguese.

"I don't know. It's kind of cool. Very eighties." Forest lifted one of his bass drums out of the back of the van to load up the flat foldable dolly Damien bought in San Francisco. "And our name's up. We've got that going for us."

"Yeah, that it is." Damie's grin was stupid, wide, and manic. "So fucking cool."

Miki gazed at the white message board with its mismatched letters. According to the red-and-black jumble, CROS5RO4DS GIN was headlining that night, right after a band called L'4NGE. The apostrophe was an upside-down comma, but the Rocking Oyster made it work as best they could.

They stood shoulder to shoulder, a patchwork cobble of a broken band resurrected by Damien's dream, a fallen bassist who'd lost everything and found himself again in his life's ashes, and a session drummer who'd never imagined he'd leave the safe confines of the recording studio he'd inherited from the old musician who'd taken him in. Miki stared at the ground, seeing their shadows cast from the sun behind them. The lineup was different, yes, and the vibe was oddly strange and comforting at the same time, but the whispers of the past remained, reminding him the shapes on the blacktop weren't the ones he was used to.

No, maybe not, he agreed with the self-doubt pawing at him, but they were going to fucking rock the place to the ground.

"Maybe they should buy some more *A*s," Miki commented. The band's name displayed in weather-beaten letters made everything so much more real, even with the sign's plastic sunglass-wearing oyster playing a pink Flying V above the board. "Looks like we're some tweaking hackers who play Rock Band on the weekend."

The air bit, scraping its cold fangs across his face. Miki'd stolen one of Kane's jackets for the trip, an ancient black leather biker piece Kane grew out of years ago. It'd been buried in Kane's closet, a cherished memento of younger days, but it still smelled of Miki's Irishman. It also fit Miki a hell of a lot better than anything Kane currently owned.

"You going to help unload or just stand there being a grammar Nazi?"

Damie shoved a guitar case at him. Miki snagged the handle, then held his hand out for another.

Damien stared at him for a second, then asked, "What?"

"Give me two. Or I'm going to be off-balance." His knee ached a bit from sitting in the van for hours, then trying to sleep on the rock-hard mattress at the motel. He'd gotten in three hours before someone began jackhammering a headboard against the wall they shared with the next room. It'd gone on for a good ten minutes. Then it was quiet long enough for him to breathe a sigh of relief.

Then it began again.

Damien had the worst poker face, and Miki could see the debate the guitarist was having with himself wash over his features in a tide of conflicting emotions.

"Just give me the fucking guitar, D." Miki waved his hand. "And make sure someone stays behind so we don't get our shit ripped off."

"You're such a bossy shit," Damien replied, but he handed Miki another case. "Don't drop them."

"You're fucking lucky I've got my hands full right now," Miki spat back. "Or I'd kick your ass for saying that."

Despite the creeping slither of pain digging up out of his kneecap, Miki's body fell into the rote pattern of setting up a stage. For all its humble beginnings, the Oyster was set up well. Whatever money they didn't spend on the outside was blown on the sound system and a dual band stage running along the short side of the rectangular building.

It stank. Most clubs did, but the familiar sour beer and sweat rankness was stronger than Miki'd remembered. A stale whiff of pot smoke lingered under the club's still air, probably carried through the air-conditioning vents from the back rooms. A few metal tables and chairs were scattered around the front half of the club, but half of the space was devoted to an open floor in front of a wide wooden stage. The risers were about four feet tall, and from what Miki could see, the sound-and-light system seemed decent enough. A strip of white tape bisected the stage lengthwise, marking where the curtain would fall so their equipment wouldn't be tangled up with the opening act's gear.

Behind him, Forest whistled a low, long sweeping note. Dragging the dolly behind him, he came to a stop, bumping into Miki when the weight of the dolly shoved him forward, but the look on their drummer's face was pure childlike wonder.

"What?" Miki turned his attention back to the stage, trying to see whatever it was that struck Forest dumb. "What are you looking at?"

"This place... the stage." Forest gave a throaty laugh. "Up until right fucking now, this wasn't... real. Now... I'm in a goddamned band."

"Dude, I fucking hope so, because I'd hate to think we've come all this way for the damned chicken wings," he replied. "Because I sure as hell ain't eating any seafood in this rathole. Not even the oysters."

"See, you're used to... this, Sinjun. All of this stuff. Me? This is... my first time. I kind of want to savor it. Studio shit and once in a while a gig just for backup, but... this? It's goddamned... amazing."

"Nah, you're never really used to it. Not if you're lucky."

It was the truth. No matter how many doors they went through, from backwater bar to arena, Miki'd never grown used to it. The nerves were still there. So was the pressure to put everything he had into shouting out lyrics at a faceless crowd. They'd gone from no one knowing the words to a mantra chant of thousands screaming his own thoughts back at him.

Catching a glimpse of the blond man coming through the door, Miki said, "The moment you get used to it, you end up like Rafe did."

"Thanks for that," Rafe grumbled at their backs, lugging in a rolling suitcase. "Asshole."

"No problem." Miki matched Rafe's rueful grin. "Dick."

"But yeah, kid, don't ever get bored." After leaving the suitcase in the middle of the open area, Rafe dusted off his hands. "You get bored, your brain starts to look for shit to do. To catch that high again. Then it all goes to crap, and you spend the next couple of years eating crow, if you don't end up dead from stupidity. So yeah, Fore, go ahead and fucking celebrate we're in a goddamned band. It doesn't get any better than this."

The frizzy-haired older woman who'd opened the door for them left the band alone to set up, returning to inventorying the alcohol behind one of the two bars. Her safety-orange caftan was subdued compared to the graffiti on the walls, enormous scrawls of robots, chickens, and the occasional *Alice in Wonderland* character, but it was the painting of the club's mascot that drew Miki in.

Nearly nine feet tall and a virulent purple, the oyster's partially open shell was lined in black-light friendly paint, and a pearl sat on its lewdly drawn tongue. Or at least Miki thought it was a tongue. It was hard to distinguish between its body and face, other than a pair of eyes and what looked like an ear.

"Do oysters have tongues?" He set the guitars down, moving aside when Damien edged into the backstage area set aside for them. "I mean, aren't they one giant tongue? Or… whatever?"

"I can't say I've spent a lot of time reflecting on an oyster, Sin." Damien nudged him in the ribs. "How about we get shit plugged in, work a quick sound check in, and then we can talk about oysters and their tongues?"

THE SOUND check was a disaster.

Rafe was a beat behind, and Forest skipped through a chorus, throwing them all off. A few songs in, Miki gritted his teeth when an amp blew, screeching its death in a wave of feedback. One of the strings on Damie's guitar snapped, catching Miki's arm and tearing him open. Slapping a hand on the oozing wound, Miki called time and stalked off stage.

Or tried to.

The stage ended before he thought it did, and he went over the edge, stepping off into nothing but air. He tumbled onto the painted, cracked cement floor. His relatively good knee hit something, probably a riser, but he wasn't sure. Either way, he landed badly, curling up over his legs with his elbow smarting and stinging as he lay on the floor.

Shoving out what little air he had left in his lungs, Miki swore, "*Fuck.*"

"Sinjun!" Damie was a step behind him, landing better but with a loud enough thump. His shoes squeaked on the floor. Dangling from his neck by an old strap, Damie's guitar swung wide and smacked Miki's chin as he pushed himself up from the floor.

Miki wasn't sure if the blood in his mouth was from his lip, chin, or where he'd bitten his tongue when the guitar struck him, but there was definitely blood. Shoving Damie's hand off his knee, he swallowed, trying to clear the spreading metallic taint from his tongue. It didn't help. If anything, swallowing only made things worse, and Damien was squeezing at his throbbing knee like it needed a defibrillator to survive.

"Get off of me," Miki growled. He must have sounded like he meant business, because Forest skidded to a stop a few feet away. "I need to get the fuck away from this right now. Just… give me some fucking space."

He didn't remember getting up off the floor, but Miki did feel the smack of the metal back door on his palm when he pushed past it. Hawking a mouthful of bloody spit, he touched lightly at his chin, feeling the welt forming there. His tongue swelled at the tip, a bubbling-up slit where his teeth had gouged into the meat. Sucking on the cut, he drew up blood again, then spat it out.

"Should have grabbed some water." A broken cinder block was enough to keep the heavy fire door wedged open, but Miki didn't relish shoving his way back in just to grab something to drink. Not after theatrically storming out like some damned diva. Rubbing at his face, he muttered, "Fuck, I'm going to have to spend like five minutes apologizing for that crap."

His jacket held half a pack of *kreteks*, so he shook one out then fished the lighter out of the same pocket. Cupping his hand over the end of the clove, Miki coaxed the end to a bright red burn and sucked in a mouthful of fragrant smoke, thankful for the sear in his chest.

"God, I'm so fucking stupid." He blew out a stream of smoke, letting it billow around him. "And you know what D's gonna say. 'So things don't fucking go right. Who cares? Keep your shit together, dude. Make it right. Don't fucking just walk out.' I should have just stayed in there and—breathe, you shit. Finish this one clove, head back inside, and kiss some ass."

Sundown was still a few hours away, but it was getting cold, and Boston's heavy cloud cover dribbled gray over the surrounding buildings and darkened the Oyster's back alley. A garbage truck trundled by, leaving its sour kiss in the air and kicking up debris as it passed. A few feet away, the alley jogged, and the truck strained to make the turn, blowing back a storm of dirt. Miki ducked his head to avoid the dust in the air, and when he straightened back up, a young man stood a few feet away, buffeted by the truck's wake.

He was young, dressed in near-rags Miki knew cost more than some of Damien's guitars. Skinny to the point of being in danger of sliding into a heating grate if he crossed the sidewalk wrong, the teen listed to one side from the weight of the black backpack he'd slung over his shoulder. Thick black glasses hid the color of his eyes but did nothing to mask his heavy eyebrows. Lank brown hair hung on either side of his narrow face, and he pursed his lips when he saw Miki.

"Hey, you're Miki St. John." The Boston was strong in his reedy voice, cracking when he hit Miki's name. "Was that you guys inside? Playing?"

"Yeah." Miki stubbed out the clove against the wall, making sure it was dead, then tossing it into the open, now empty Dumpster.

The kid didn't look too much like a threat, but the alley was a short one, and he didn't know if anyone else lurked around the corner. A quick flicking look reassured him the parking lot was a short sprint away, but he couldn't depend on his knee.

The cinder block remnant by his foot would have to be his first option if something funky happened. The kid took another step forward, and Miki raised his chin, straightening up to his full height. Up close, the teen was a pimpled, baby-faced kid with a patch of hair under his nose struggling to grow thick enough to be called a smudge.

"I got tickets for tonight," he said, taking another step closer.

Miki felt his belly coil up, and his fingers itched to grab the block. "We're on late. Maybe around eleven."

"Yeah, I probably won't go. 'Cause you guys sucked."

Smug derision spread over the kid's face. Miki cocked his head, and the kid's cheeks flushed pink.

"Probably going to see if they'll give me back my money."

He wasn't off. Not by a long shot. But Miki'd be damned if some kid with manicured fingers and a backpack with someone else's initials all over it was going to slag the guys he'd just driven cross-country with. Stepping into the kid's space, Miki pushed himself in close until he was nearly nose to nose with the teen. The young man's breath smelled of mint and tea, and he quivered when Miki smiled at him.

"You go do that, kid," Miki said softly, cutting in low so the kid had to strain to hear him. "You go and fucking do that if you want to. But just so you know, you do *that*, and you're going to miss the best fucking show of your goddamned short life."

RHYS FORD is an award-winning author with several long-running LGBT+ mystery, thriller, paranormal, and urban fantasy series and is a two-time LAMBDA finalist with her Murder and Mayhem novels. She is also a 2017 Gold and Silver Medal winner in the Florida Authors and Publishers President's Book Awards for her novels Ink and Shadows and Hanging the Stars. She is published by Dreamspinner Press and DSP Publications.

She shares the house with Harley, a gray tuxedo with a flower on her face, Badger, a disgruntled alley cat who isn't sure living inside is a step up the social ladder, as well as a ginger cairn terrorist named Gus. Rhys is also enslaved to the upkeep of a 1979 Pontiac Firebird and enjoys murdering make-believe people.

Rhys can be found at the following locations:

Blog: www.rhysford.com

Facebook: www.facebook.com/rhys.ford.author

Twitter: @Rhys_Ford

RHYS FORD

SIN AND TONIC

"The perfect ending to a spectacularly touching series that meshes mystery, romance, and family." — Mary Calmes

Sequel to *Absinthe of Malice*
Sinners Series: Book Six

Miki St. John believed happy endings only existed in fairy tales until his life took a few unexpected
turns… and now he's found his own.

His best friend, Damien, is back from the dead,
and their new band, Crossroads Gin, is soaring up the
charts. Miki's got a solid, loving partner named Kane
Morgan—an Inspector with SFPD whose enormous
Irish family has embraced him as one of their own—
and his dog, Dude, at his side.

It's a pity someone's trying to kill him.

Old loyalties and even older grudges emerge from
Chinatown's murky, mysterious past, and Miki strug-
gles to deal with his dead mother's abandonment, her
secrets, and her brutal murder while he's hunted by an
enigmatic killer who may have ties to her.

The case lands in Kane's lap, and he and Miki
are caught in a deadly game of cat-and-mouse. When
Miki is forced to face his personal demons and the
horrors of his childhood, only one thing is certain: the
rock star and his cop are determined to fight for their
future and survive the evils lurking in Miki's past.

www.dreamspinnerpress.com